Get Out and Get Under

A L S O   B Y *Max Wilk*

Get Out and Get Under

by Max Wilk

W · W · NORTON & COMPANY · *New York* · *London*

Published simultaneously in Canada by George J. McLeod Limited, Toronto.
Printed in the United States of America
All Rights Reserved
First Edition

Library of Congress Cataloging in Publication Data
Wilk, Max.
   Get out and get under.
   I. Title.
PS3545.I365G4   1981   813'.54   80–26051
ISBN 0–393–01425–8

W. W. Norton & Company, Inc. 500 Fifth Avenue, New York, N.Y. 10110
W. W. Norton & Company Ltd. 25 New Street Square, London EC4A 3NT

1 2 3 4 5 6 7 8 9 0

For David and Richard

... good drivers, and good listeners.

(... and with thanks to Herbie Baker.)

Event of the Year!
First Southwestern Classic and Vintage Car Auction

TULSA, OKLAHOMA
at the Arena

Rolls Royce (Phantom II)

Alvis

Lagonda

Consign them now!
Call/Write for space

MAY 18–19, 1979
Donaldson Bros.

(Your reliable auctioneers since 1927)

Part One

Often when he was looking on at auctions, Socrates would say, "How many things there are which I do not need!"

Diogenes Laertius (circa 200 A.D.)

Except the American woman, nothing interests the eye of American man more than the automobile, or seems so important to him as an object of esthetic appreciation.

A. H. Barr, Jr., 1963.

"He who hesitates is honked."

Abe Martin's Town Pump
Kin Hubbard—1931.

 *Hong Kong*

Strange are the workings of the mysterious East.

Who could have imagined, for example, that the origin of The First Southwestern Classic and Vintage Car Auction, in Tulsa, Oklahoma, held by Donaldson Bros. (YOUR RELIABLE AUCTIONEERS SINCE 1927) would be a sliver of pork sparerib, a bone approximately five-eighths of an inch in length, carelessly chopped by Wo Hang Lin, an underpaid Chinese subchef?

. . . Which same sliver was to lodge itself, that same night, in the throat of Mrs. Joyce Donaldson Wade, while she gorged herself at the Floating Golden Palace of a Thousand Delights, in Hong Kong harbor.

Mrs. Wade was in the early phases of an eleven-course Mandarin banquet, a feature of the tour that she and three other Tulsa ladies had taken. (*19-Day Mysterious East. Visit Nine Countries— Adequate Time for Sightseeing and Shopping!*)

In the midst of a sentence, as well as the offending sparerib (her mother had always tried to keep Joyce from speaking with her mouth full, but to no avail), Joyce suddenly began to gasp for breath.

Then, simultaneously, she choked and coughed.

A strange rattle was all that emerged from her mouth.

Their chopsticks in midair, stunned, the three other Tulsa ladies at the table stared at their stricken friend.

But at the next table, a lean, grey-haired man in a trimly tailored dark blue blazer, dining with a party of other men all of whom wore the same club patch on their chests, that of the CCACC—Crown Colony Antique Car Club—pushed back his chair, jumped up, and moved swiftly behind the stricken Mrs. Wade.

He grabbed her and pulled her erect, wrapped one arm around her ample waist, yanked her backwards, seized his forearm with his other hand, and then jerked his arms tightly against her diaphragm, once, twice! Three times.

With the fourth, Joyce gasped. Heaved. Coughed and spat.

11

. . . And mercifully, it was over.

The tiny but lethal sliver of Golden Honey Thrice Barbecued Tender Rib was out on the tablecloth, and she was breathing again, raspingly, yes, but breathing—through a cleared throat miraculously, blessedly free of that lethal obstruction.

The samaritan in the blue blazer, whose name was G. Dudley Lester, snatched up a glass of beer from his own table and brought it to the exhausted lady from Tulsa. "Drink this down, madame," he instructed.

She did as she was told, wincing as she swallowed.

". . . Good Lordy . . ." she rasped, when she had finally regained her powers of speech. ". . . You really saved ma la-if!"

"You could say that," he agreed, modestly, "but under the circumstances, anyone else would have done the same thing."

"Maybe they would, but it was *you* who did it," said Joyce, swilling down the rest of the beer.

". . . Why honey, it all happened so fa-ist!" apologized one of the three Tulsa matrons.

". . . I mean, we could hardly tell what was happening!" said a second.

"He could," said Joyce.

She turned to smile at the gentleman who had so recently saved her from expiring in such an ignominious fashion on very foreign waters, in this harbor thousands of miles from downtown Tulsa. ". . . I just thank the Lord you were sittin' behind me," she said, staring at G. Dudley Lester. The male good samaritan was most pleasing to her eye. ". . . You some sort of a doctor?"

"No," he told her. "Luckily, I've had a little experience in these matters. So glad I could have been of some help—"

But before he could return to his own companions, Joyce gasped. ". . . Oh, I do think I could use a little fresh ay-uh," she said, and mopped at her forehead with a large silken almost-perfect imitation Yves Saint Laurent kerchief she'd purchased that afternoon in a downtown stall. ". . . Would somebody mind pointin' me in the direction of the deck?" She rose, wobbling slightly on her feet.

1 2

". . . Why, sure, Joyce honey, I'll take you out," said one of her Tulsa companions.

". . . Forget it," said Joyce. "This kind gentlemun will certainly show me there, won't you, Mr. —"

". . . Lester," he told you. "G. Dudley."

". . . What an imposin' name," said Joyce, grabbing his arm. "Lessen, o'course, you're occupied, I'd appreciate your help . . ."

"Oh, my pleasure," said G. Dudley, unable to extricate his arm. As they passed his table, he excused himself from his own party of friends, most of them middle-aged car buffs deep in a discussion of the merits of the snub-nosed Bentley Open Tourer of the pre–World War II vintage.

The couple made their way out of the main dining room.

"We'll be back in a wha-il," Joyce called to her tourmates.

As they encountered the headwaiter, G. Dudley told him, "I'm going up on your deck with this lady so she can recover. Meanwhile, I suggest you get after your kitchen staff, friend. If this were the U.S., my friend here—"

"Miz Wade," said Joyce. "Of Tulsa, Oklahoma."

"—could sue the living hell out of you."

"A thousand apologies," said the headwaiter. "The help situation is appalling. All they want to do is to get to New York and open their own place. What can I tell you?"

The three Tulsa matrons, suffused with guilt, tried and found wanting in the recent crisis, remained silent through their next three courses. It was only during the fourth—Mandarin Duck Balls with Velvet Sauce—that one of them dared to remark, ". . . Those two have sure been out there gettin' night air for some time, wouldn't you agree?"

By that time, seated upstairs in a small banquette on the deck, enjoying another drink, Joyce and G. Dudley had become somewhat better acquainted.

The banquette she had chosen, so small that the two of them were extremely close, was certainly an ideal place for rest and recuperation.

Above them, the wide panorama of the skyline of Hong Kong,

with all its thousands of lights, sparkled in the distance, through the soft humid night. An occasional junk drifted past. In the black harbor waters below the darkness hid whatever assorted garbage and carrion that was drifting by.

Now that she had recovered her powers of speech, Joyce was hard to slow down. She offered information about herself, her two grown children, one married in Phoenix, the other a grad student at SMU. Her dear late huband, who'd departed two years ago, leaving her to carry on in the family business with her father, dear old "Old Ed" Donaldson, one of the shrewdest and most respected operators in the entire Southwestern auction game. The obligations of carrying on Donaldson Bros., which someday, she'd be obliged to operate all by her lonesome.

She also managed to extract a small amount of information about G. Dudley Lester.

He was retired. He had been in real estate in Europe. He had done well enough, and was now living on an island in the Bahamas. He traveled a good deal. He had certain "interests," and he was here in Hong Kong on business and for his hobby, which involved a meeting of those same chaps inside at the table.

Most satisfying to Joyce, who was a sharp listener, was the absence of any mention by Mr. Lester of an existing Mrs. Lester.

". . . I do really think we might be getting back," he suggested.

"I suppose so," said Joyce. "I mean, they might think we'd fallen into the water, or somethin' . . ."

He rose, and she rose with him, albeit reluctantly.

". . . Mr. Lestah," said Joyce, fervently, "I simply do not know how to thank you properly for savin' my life tonight . . ."

Which was not entirely so. A long time back, Joyce had memorized Lesson One: *You do not get what you want by being shy.*

. . . Now she had a definite plan which involved gratitude, a ploy which, if properly carried out, should end up by pleasuring both donor and donee.

". . . Why it was my pleas—" began G. Dudley, and stopped, conscious of a hand that was certainly not his own, one which was exploring his well-tailored nether regions. " —plea*sure,*" he said, as the hand continued to make its way upwards, moved inside his jacket (completed just this afternoon by a local tailor of the finest cashmere), moved inside the silk lining, and then played a delicate tattoo against his well-tailored groin.

Then the grateful Tulsa lady was moving even closer, he was being embraced by her other arm, and her mouth covered his, the tip of her tongue darted towards his own, and he was now totally surrounded, was inhaling her musky perfume (Lancôme, also purchased earlier this afternoon, in Hong Kong, for only slightly more than what it would have cost in Tulsa).

When she finally released him, she sighed, ". . . I sure hope you don't think I'm bein' aggressive . . ."

"Why, who could ever think such a thing?" asked G. Dudley, after he'd regained his breath.

"Oh, I am glad you feel that way," said Joyce. "I do believe in complete honesty between two adult people, don't you?"

"At all times," lied G. Dudley.

". . . Oh, good," said Joyce. "I'm stayin' at the Mandarin, and luckily, I don't have anybody sharin' the room with me. Why don't I leave the door to room 610 open for you, Mr. Lestah?"

Under other circumstances, it is quite likely that G. Dudley Lester might have let the entire matter stop right there.

After all, any single man in Hong Kong with a valid American Express card could hardly find it difficult to indulge his appetites. Females of all shapes, sizes, ages, and price are one of that great city's major industries, and for the man, or woman, who has more exotic tastes, Hong Kong, which by day is the world's largest department store, is by night a sexual supermarket.

Why then, on such a night, should a sophisticated gent find himself even vaguely interested in the favors of a fortyish Oklahoma matron? She was far from unattractive, her figure was adequate, but Mrs. Wade would certainly have never made it as a cheerleader for the Dallas Cowboys. She was obviously well-to-do, but at this moment, G. Dudley Lester was hardly a *matelot,* on the prowl for a rich widow.

. . . But an hour or so later, he was in a taxi, on his way to the Mandarin Hotel.

1 5

Chalk it up to curiosity. G. Dudley had long since passed the age when the mere act of physical sex was fulfilling. In his early years, it had been the thrill of the chase that had spurred him on; now, as he approached a more sedate middle age, he found he needed more.

Young girls were certainly appetizing and athletic, but their conversation before and/or afterwards was so . . . mindless. G. Dudley had always been a student of human responses; in his various "businesses," such research had served him well. Up to this evening, he had never made it with a well-to-do Middle Amurrican Oklahoma widow lady, and if he spent a few hours with her, he might find out what made such a lady tick.

If she ticked.

She appealed to his sense of curiosity, as well as his appreciation of whimsy. Considering that she was obviously so grateful, why not probe (assuming she had one) her mind, as well as the lady herself?

. . . whatever happened in room 610 at the Mandarin Hotel would have to be more interesting than any further discussion about snub-nosed Bentley Open Tourers, with those boring members of the Crown Colony Antique Car Club, right?

When the pale morning light filtered through the blinds of room 610 at the Mandarin, the day after "l'Affaire Sparerib," Mrs. Joyce Donaldson Wade had discovered a few more facts about the man who had saved her life the night before. He was suntanned, just a bit overweight, and he snored.

Having spent so many nights alone in the past few years, Joyce couldn't care less about the steady riffling sounds coming from the figure beside her in the bed. Quid pro quo—such a man was entitled to snore. Since 11 P.M. last night, he had performed, superbly, three times. It had been a long time since Joyce had participated in such sexual athletics, and she was suffused with gratitude. For any single lady in her forties, in these youth-oriented days, such a man was to be treasured.

. . . Her muscles were stiff in various areas, but it was a joyful relaxed sort of pain. Joyce smiled, stretched, and with remembered pleasure, reached across to the recumbent G. Dudley and ran her fingernails slowly cross his suntanned back.

It was almost 8, and in a matter of two brief hours, she and the rest of the ladies on her tour would be assembling downstairs in the lobby, their bags packed, to leave at noon from the airport for Tokyo. Now that she had gotten so lucky, what could Tokyo offer to match this newly discovered sexual jackpot who snored beside her? Gently, her hands reached over to fondle him, enjoying the warmth of his sleeping member. Never to have it again, after only one night in Hong Kong? . . . What a rotten deal!

G. Dudley groaned, sighed, and rolled over, moving closer to her. ". . . Time is it?" he muttered.

She embraced him and began to kiss his face, tiny greedy nips. ". . . Early, lover," she whispered, and soon she was opening herself wide, thrusting herself against him.

". . . Voracious," murmured G. Dudley.

". . . You know it," she replied, giggling.

". . . Too early," sighed G. Dudley. ". . . Tired."

". . . Never," she told him, moving against him urgently.

With his hand, he clasped the back of her head, then moved it away, downwards, guiding her mouth across his chest, then further until she came to his stomach, and the journey was ended.

". . . You want me to do *that?*" she whispered.

". . . Don't they do that in Oklahoma?" he inquired.

". . . Only for very special people," said Joyce.

". . . And I'm not?" he yawned.

". . . Oh, God, *yes!*" agreed Joyce.

". . . Then *go,* baby," said G. Dudley.

She bent to the job at hand. Years ago, she had performed such an act for her late husband, but only in extremis, after sufficient alcohol to free her of her inhibitions. Here and now, she performed with pleasure. Triumphantly she felt him become firm; it was her accomplishment, it was gratifying to discover that she was possessed of such talent.

She paused for a moment to catch her breath. . . . If she were this skillful, perhaps she could put her artifice to work. There is a

17

tide in the affairs of men, which, when taken just before the flood—

". . . Don't stop *now*," he scolded, above her.

". . . Dudley, darlin'," she said, softly, "I just have to know—"

". . . *What?*" he demanded, hoarsely.

". . . Are we ever goin' to see each other again?"

G. Dudley groaned. Reached down his arm to pat her shoulder.

". . . Why not?" he asked.

". . . Me in Tulsa, and you on some crazy old island," she said, sadly. "Just a pair of ships passin' in the na-it . . . you'll never call me again, I just know it . . ."

"Of course I will!" said G. Dudley, reassuringly.

". . . You're sayin' it, but that don't mean anythin'," wailed Joyce. "You're such a dominant person, and I'm so helpless . . . how do I know this isn't the end of it?"

". . . *Trust* me," said G. Dudley, urgently.

". . . You'll leave me your address?" she asked.

". . . Absolutely!" he promised, and moved her back to where she could complete the task he had assigned her.

". . . You'll come to Tulsa?" she said, a moment or so later.

". . . I'll come, I'll *come!*" he promised.

". . . And visit for a while?" she asked, several beats later.

"*Yes!*" he said. ". . . Now for God's sake, don't stop!"

"Deal," said Joyce, and returned to her labors.

A strange bargain, one that would certainly never hold up in a court of law, sealed by Mrs. Joyce Donaldson Wade and G. Dudley Lester sans witnesses, but what he agreed to—under a certain amount of pressure, true—was to become the keystone of their eventual relationship, commercial and otherwise.

One could call their agreement strictly word of mouth.

*   *   *

1933 PLYMOUTH FOUR DOOR SEDAN
Motor No. 1676–337–1
Body No. B.631680

Motor, six-cylinder L-head, monobloc,
bore 3¼ in. stroke 4⅜ in. Coil
ignition: three-speed synchromesh
transmission, floor shift, spiral bevel
final drive: wheelbase 113½ in.; tire
size 5.25/5.50 x 17.

This Plymouth is finished in black,
and is original throughout. It has
been kept in first-class condition
by its original owner, who drove it
regularly throughout the past forty-
four years.

To be sold by order of an estate.

 **Fairfield, Connecticut**

"The very rich are different from us."

—F. Scott Fitzgerald

"Yes, they have more money."

—Ernest Hemingway

". . . And I'll thank you not to try and tell me what to do with mine!"

—Laura Richards Fox

. . . who sat in the large paneled dining room of her home in Fairfield, Connecticut, eating, as she had for the past half century, her breakfast of one half grapefruit, one soft-boiled egg, one slice of protein-bread toast, and a pot of Earl Grey tea.

Mrs. Fox, a tall lady with sharp blue eyes and a patrician nose, her white hair severely coiffed, affected mannish suits of sturdy Donegal tweed. It was now 7:56 A.M. Since she had always operated her life, both personal and commercial, on a system of punctuality, within the next fifteen minutes she would have read through her *Wall Street Journal* and finished her egg. Midway through the second cup of tea, she would then press the buzzer to notify old Mr. Hyde, down at the garage behind her house, that he had precisely four minutes in which to start her car and bring it around to the front door.

By 8:10 A.M., in fair weather or foul, there it would be, at the doorway. Its four-cylinder engine nicely warmed up and chugging away, black paint polished, chrome gleaming, a 1933 Plymouth four-door sedan, certainly in as good condition as the day years back when the dealer, a Mr. Feeny in Bridgeport, had personally delivered it to Mrs. Fox.

Many times over the years it had been suggested to Mrs. Fox that she retire her Plymouth in favor of a larger limousine and a chauffeur. Such suggestions were turned away by her forthwith. "Cars are too large," she would say. "Nothing more than painted freight cars. And chauffeurs stand around all day long, doing nothing.''

In winter, Mrs. Fox would put on her sealskin coat. In summer she changed to linen. Then she would pick up her sturdy British attaché case, plus the small wicker Abercrombie & Fitch picnic basket in which her cook had packed a lunch, carry them out the front door to her Plymouth, and climb in.

Then she would drive herself down the winding asphalt driveway past the well-kept greens, through the wrought-iron gates below, and head for the main highway. Barring unforeseen incidents such as traffic tie-up, she could usually arrive at her factory on the outskirts of Bridgeport within twenty-five minutes. She would steer her Plymouth into the special parking space reserved for her, lock it, and go upstairs. As she had for the past half century, Mrs. Fox would then proceed to her office to begin another day's work at her desk, behind the brass plaque that read PRESIDENT.

Doctor Lawrence Mainwaring, to whom Mrs. Fox had reluctantly gone last month for her usual check-up, had put her through all the tests on the expensive array of machines in his office. When he had completed his probing and poking, he had asked her to come join him in his office for a chat.

''You are in very good shape for a woman your age,'' he'd said.

''I always was,'' she told him.

''—In fact, you're in better shape than most of the people I see—''

''Yourself included?'' she demanded.

''—but—'' continued Dr. Mainwaring, ''there are certain areas of your behavior I do believe you might consider. Certain of your habits, for instance—''

''I enjoy my habits,'' said Mrs. Fox. ''That's why I have them.''

Dr. Mainwaring smiled. ''I certainly can't give you orders, Laura,'' he conceded. ''I know better . . .''

''Getting some sense as you go along, eh?'' she said.

''. . . But I can make a suggestion or two. For one thing, it's long past the time you got yourself a driver.''

"Anything wrong with my reflexes?" she demanded. "My blood pressure? My nervous system?"

Dr. Mainwaring shook his head.

"My eyesight?" she persisted. "Or do I need to pay a specialist with whom you'll split the fee to find that out?"

"Your eyesight is fine," conceded the doctor. "Anybody who can catch an error in one of my bills doesn't need glasses. No, Laura, what I'm talking about is stress. You and I, both of us, we've long since come to the age when we should be trying to avoid it."

"Oh, speak for yourself," said Mrs. Fox.

"I suppose, in a way, I am," said her doctor. "Last month I sat down and figured out the number of stops I had to make during one day in my car. Would you believe—between here and the hospitals and such, twenty-seven in an average day? So I decided it was time for *me* to hire a driver . . ."

"And a new Mercedes, I'll bet," said Mrs. Fox. "Lord knows you doctors can afford anything you want, what with what you're raking in on Medicare and testifying in court cases and all the rest. If the rest of us are fools enough to go on paying taxes in order to support this creeping socialism—creeping, hell, it's galloping!— well, we deserve what we get!"

"You benefit from Medicare," said Dr. Mainwaring, gently.

"Under a tax structure that's killing private initiative," said Mrs. Fox. "There'll be a day of reckoning, wait and see. If you want to throw the taxpayers' money around like a drunken sailor, I certainly can't stop you." She rose. "Now I've got to get back to my plant and do some honest work."

"I'd like to see you again, in say, three months," said Dr. Mainwaring.

"For something specific, or do you expect me and Medicare to help pay for your new Mercedes?" she snapped.

"It's an *Olds,* and believe me, Laura, I can manage that expense without your help, but let's be candid," he urged. ". . . At your time of life—"

"I have done perfectly well up to here," said Mrs. Fox, "and I fully expect to continue in the same manner."

"Don't we all?" sighed the doctor.

"I come here for medical advice, not philosophy," she said. "You go ahead and enjoy your sybaritic habits, doctor, and I will continue to drive myself."

When she had left his office, Dr. Mainwaring picked up his pipe, stuffed it with the tobacco of which he had deprived himself while Mrs. Fox, an antismoker, was in his office, and lit it. "Stubborn old bitch!" he muttered, between puffs. ". . . Well, at least, I tried." He buzzed his nurse to send in the next patient. ". . . And it's damned well *not* sybaritic!" he said, to the empty chair she'd left.

It was now 8:12 A.M. and Mrs. Fox emerged from her house, bade her housekeeper goodbye, and carried her attaché case and picnic basket over to the waiting Plymouth. Climbed into the front seat, tested the foot brake, adjusted the rearview mirror, which had somehow become a bit askew, released the hand brake, and drove slowly down the drive.

Dr. Mainwaring was far from the first who'd tried, and failed, to instruct Mrs. Laura Richards Fox in what was good for her.

Years back, she'd been told by her parents that it was beholden on proper upper-class females that they spend their formative years in an exclusive private school for equally proper young upper-class females, such as Wykeham Rise, or Emma Willard, or Miss Porter's, in Farmington. Young Laura had persisted in attending the local public schools in Fairfield.

Later, when she approached marriageable age, and her parents suggested a proper coming-out party at the local Hunt Club, Laura had flatly refused. If they wished to spend so much money on a stupid ritual, designed primarily to find her an eligible husband from her peer group, she would be pleased to forgo the festivities and to accept the cash that they would save by her sacrifice. "I can find much better uses for that money, thank you," she told her father. "I can use it for tuition at a business school."

"You're going into business?" asked her father. "Whose?"

"Yours," Laura told him. "We're certainly going to keep it in the family, or do you have other plans?"

The Richards fortune, an increasingly ample one, was very definitely "old money." Its origins were a group of patents secured by Elihu Richards, a canny old Yankee machinist, who'd invented certain clever mechanical components that became integral to combustion engines during the early years of this century. The Richards Calibrated Valve, in all its various sizes and adaptations, become part of farm equipment, small engines, and the burgeoning automobile business, and the Richards C. V. Company grew and prospered. It was not a large firm, but its management knew how to keep costs down and quality up; then came World War I, and the firm expanded into military production, and the profits kept pace with the growing size.

It was during those years that young Laura, her business-school education completed, found herself a niche in the factory offices and proceeded to learn how her father and his associates functioned.

"It's not proper for a girl of her status to be mingling with all those . . . *hands*," complained Laura's mother, who came from a very good family in Virginia.

"She's a go-getter at what she does," said Mr. Richards.

Mrs. Richards was persistent. "A girl your age should be married and thinking of a family," she lectured her daughter. "Factories are so . . . dégagé." Mrs. Richards had been educated in Switzerland.

"Would you rather I took a job with some other firm?" asked young Laura. "That way I wouldn't shame you, Mother—"

"You'll stay right where you are!" said her father.

. . . And it was fortunate for the Richards Company that she did, indeed, because within three years her affable father had died in a train wreck, while traveling to a fishing holiday in Canada. Two days after his funeral, Laura was installed in his factory offices, seeing to all the ritual complexities needed to keep the business moving forward. Since none of the other immediate Richards relatives knew much nor cared less about the operation of the plant, Laura remained in the driver's seat, and so long as the dividend checks continued to arrive in the family mail, none of the relatives evinced any prejudice against a female managing director.

Throughout the Harding and Coolidge years, Richards Calibrated Valve flourished. In the mid-1920s, Laura found time to take her first trip to Europe, alone. It was not a vacation; she was exploring future connections with various British and European customers.

It was on the return trip, on the *Berengaria,* that she met a cheerful young lawyer named Daniel Fox. He had gone to Harvard Law and was now attached to a very good New York firm; he was darkly handsome, knew all the songs from the latest Broadway musicals, and could play them for her. He found Laura's company enjoyable and made no bones about it. The fact that she was running a large business was interesting, but their conversation did not run to matters of commerce.

When he came up to Connecticut to visit her at her home, old Mrs. Richards was most unimpressed. "He's not any of the Foxes *we* know," she insisted. ". . . I wouldn't be a bit surprised if he turned out to be Jewish."

"Oh, he is, indeed," said Laura.

". . . How do you know *that?*" demanded her mother, stunned.

"How do you think?" said Laura.

Mrs. Richards took to her bed, and had her meals sent up on a tray. When she emerged, she had summoned up sufficient strength to make one final attempt to warn off her daughter. "You certainly are entitled to make a mistake or two," she conceded, "but you oughtn't to marry your mistakes! He's out for your money!"

"Possibly," agreed Laura, "but he's very attractive, and I'm not, and he loves me anyway. Or do you want me to become a very successful old maid?"

". . . What will I tell my friends?" sighed her mother.

"Tell them you're not losing a daughter, you're gaining a lawyer," replied her daughter.

Mrs. Fox steered the Plymouth carefully out of the residential street and onto the main boulevard that led down to the Connecticut Turnpike. It was a bright, sunny morning, and she was pleased to see that the traffic was a bit lighter this morning than usual. With luck, she might arrive at the plant a few minutes early, which would give her time to go through the cost estimates waiting on her desk.

Then she would go to the executive committee meeting at 10:30, be finished by noon, and have lunch in her office. Some Japanese customers were due after lunch; they expected to be entertained this evening, but that she would leave to the sales manager . . .

She and Dan Fox were married in 1925, and in the ensuing years, Laura found time away from her business duties to bear a daugher, Jean, and a son, Daniel Junior. Old Mrs. Richards barely tolerated her son-in-law, but she doted on her two grandchildren. She became their surrogate mother, for their own mother was far too busy at the plant to cope with such mundane matters as formulas, feeding, and diapers. Mrs. Richards and a reliable British nanny took charge of domestic matters; Laura stayed with the business.

Where she was so occupied with its expansion that it was some time before she became aware of the fact that Dan Fox was also occupied, with affairs of his own . . . one of which involved an attractive young matron in Scarsdale, a client of his firm.

When she received the news, it came directly from Dan: one of his virtues as a man (and failings as a lawyer) was his inability to be devious. He arrived home late one night from a "conference," walked into the library where Laura was studying weekly production figures, poured them both a nightcap, and explained that he would very much like a divorce.

For such a long time Laura had been accustomed to taking the initiative; now he was presenting her with a fait accompli. Laura was not so much hurt and offended as she was resentful at being forced into a defensive position. Her reaction was that of a true merchant, i.e., where had she and/or her product failed

". . . She's not anywheres as efficient as you are, dear," said Dan. "She knows absolutely nothing about business, and as a matter of fact, she's almost helpless . . ."

". . . Then how the devil could she possibly attract you?" insisted Laura, bewildered.

". . . I'm afraid I've already told you," said her husband, ruefully.

Mercifully, before she could chant a triumphant "I told you so," old Mrs. Richards has passed on. A court granted Dan his freedom, and since he'd signed a prenuptial agreement that waived his right to Laura's stock, she was left to carry on the family business.

Which, until 1929, continued to thrive. Then, down on Wall Street, there was that precipitous October stock-market tumble that was to be known as The Crash. It was followed by widening shock waves of depression. For the next few years, even the shrewdest management would be caught in a struggle to survive.

Every day presented deeper despair. Laura had to lay off loyal men who'd been with the plant for their entire working lives. There were several grim weeks when she could barely meet the company payroll for the workers still left to fill what scarce orders she could find, usually by personally pleading with her old customers. Often, she was forced to dip into her personal funds to keep the plant open. Somehow, she kept Richards Calibrated Valve afloat, but barely so.

When FDR was elected in 1932, Laura, a staunch Republican, reluctantly went along with his new administration. What else was there to do? She put up the NRA banner and tried, but as time passed, she soon became disenchanted with all the various New Deal policies that proliferated out of Washington, each one of which seemed to impinge on her personal freedom. Social Security, SEC, National Labor Relations Board, PWA, the attempt to reform the Supreme Court—all of FDR's bold legislation annoyed her. That smiling Franklin in the White House and his ubiquitous Eleanor—both of them seemed determined to drag this country into some form of a socialist state. A certain amount of reform was certainly necessary; when he declared a Bank Holiday to preserve the banking system, she could understand that, but when FDR announced that henceforth the U.S. would go off the gold standard, and that it would now be illegal for private citizens to own or trade in that metal, Laura took that as a personal insult. "Nonsense!" she snapped, when he finished his Fireside Chat. "I'll do exactly what I please with mine, thank you!"

Things were to become substantially worse before they got better. Regulatory authorities in Washington grew in size and strength, hobbling industry in reels of red tape. Personal income taxes rose each year; corporate taxes removed the incentive to expand. If and when the workers in her factory decided to unionize—after all Laura

Richards Fox had done for them—their right to do so was clearly protected. Each year Big Government and Big Labor grew larger— and the small corporation, which by God, as everyone with a spoonful of brains knew, had been the backbone of American free enterprise, was left to struggle for life . . . or to be gobbled up by some larger outfit.

Through it all, right up to World War II, she managed to carry on, firmly at the helm of her own ship. Sell out? No thank you! No matter how often and how vociferously Mrs. Fox complained about the problems of the small businessman, she'd be damned if she'd give away the firm that had been family property for so many years.

Other women had gardens to tend, families to raise, clubs and hobbies and husbands to retire with. Mrs. Fox had only her business, and it sufficed.

As she turned her 1933 Plymouth onto the main highway this morning, Mrs. Fox paused to find an opening in the stream of traffic. Beside her, a battered Vokswagen pulled alongside. Her eye caught that of its driver, a cheerful young man in a turtleneck sweater. He studied her car and then stared at her. He smiled and waved, and called out, "Beautiful old lady!"

"Thank you," said Mrs. Fox. He waved and buzzed out boldly into the main road.

. . . And she was almost a mile down the highway before she suddenly thought—*did he mean me, or this car?*

Her children grown now, with families of their own, she lived on, alone in that large empty mansion, with a staff to wait on her and to tend to the furniture and the daily upkeep. Jean had moved to Colorado, where she ran some sort of a ski resort with her Swiss husband and her family of cheerful blonde types who spent their days wedeling and their nights dancing with the customers. Dan Junior? Well, he'd never really settled into anything substantial. From his earliest days at Yale, he'd become interested in the theater . . . the *theater,* for heaven's sake! He'd spent years in Manhattan, trying to establish himself as a producer, losing a good deal of money in the process, and accumulating a lot of dubious friends.

Now he was out in California, working at some managerial job in a public television station.

. . . Leaving Mrs. Laura Richards Fox still on the job, well past anyone else's retirement age, but since she made the rules about such things, nobody would be handing her a gold watch for faithful service. She was Chairman of the Board (*not* Chairperson, thank you!), and there was a cadre of younger men she'd assembled to take care of the daily donkey work around the plant. She was still looking for a woman who'd like to make a career in the business, but for all their bold talk about making a place for themselves in industry, damned few of those bold talkers seemed willing to put in the hours and the work that such a job called for, no, they'd all rather go into fashion or advertising, wouldn't they?

Quit? Spend the rest of her days basking in Palm Beach at an endless poolside canasta game? "Thank you, no," she would tell anyone who'd ask how she could still manage those dreadful Connecticut winters. "I'm not ready for God's Waiting Room down there. I need the change of seasons. Those people down in Florida, they're zombies!"

When the time came for her to bow out, everything would be arranged, as efficiently as her life had been, neatly and with precision. Her lawyers had seen to that. The house and its possessions would go to the Historical Society, the Plymouth would be taken care of, and her beloved Richards Calibrated Valve would continue operating without a hitch. Its cadre of hand-picked executives in charge, the firm would spin off the profits on which so many assorted Fox and Richards heirs and relatives existed. As they had, for so many years. Once, when someone had interviewed her for some business magazine, and wanted to know exactly what her offspring did, Mrs. Fox had smiled and replied, "My family? Oh, they're in the inheriting business."

It was time to turn off the main highway onto the side street which led to her factory. Mrs. Fox put out her hand to signal a turn and slowed down.

Beepbeepbeep! She became aware that a car was following close behind, its horn blaring. Beepbeepbeep*beep!* A car? No, a small pickup truck with two men in the front seat, moving much too close—

—And one of the men waving his fist, as if to force her out of the way. But the lane had narrowed here and there was no room for her to move to either side, it was an access road. Couldn't they see that? She had no intention of speeding up; sedately she purred along at the posted speed, no more no less—

Behind her she heard one of the men yelling, something that ended ". . . dumb old bitch!''

Old bitch, indeed—she was obeying the speed limit, wasn't she, driving carefully, abiding by the law, preserving order and the status quo, that was her credo as it had been for seventy-nine years, and what for? To be abused by these good-for-nothings? She would *not* move out of their way!

—She felt a heavy, rocking jolt, it was the front bumper of that truck behind her precious Plymouth, nudging against her bumper, and her front seat reeled, throwing her forward from the impact, almost smack into her windshield—

Enough! thought Mrs. Laura Richards Fox, the anger churning suddenly within her. She was close to losing her temper, a thing she hated to do, but now this was beyond rational behavior on her part. She would have to take some sort of positive action to stop these two brigands!

She put her hand out to signal a stop, took her foot off the gas, permitting the Plymouth to roll slowly to a stop, thus blocking the truck behind her from any forward motion, bringing both vehicles to a halt on the littered access road.

Beepbeepbeep*beep!* went the horn behind her, but the driver was effectively unable to move, and behind him the traffic also braked, stopped.

Trembling with rage, Mrs. Fox opened the door of her Plymouth, stepped out, and took a deep breath to quiet her pounding heart. She was a citizen, and she was about to fulfill her obligations as such, no matter how unpleasant it might be. Laws were written and enacted by men who were dedicated to a law-abiding society! The sign specifically read 25 MPH, did it not?

The driver had leaned out of the truck and was waving his fist at her, a wiry, unshaven little man in a wrinkled jacket, yelling now in a rasping voice, "—Damn crazy old bitch, you think you own the whole damn road?"

"A good part of it, my man," said Mrs. Fox, and aimed an accusatory finger. "You are under arrest, by me. This is a citizen's arrest. Follow me, please, we're going to the police station—I'm accusing you of reckless driving and—"

"Ah, go screw!" yelled her adversary. As he gunned his engine, the truck roared forward, its bumper shoving her Plymouth to move it out of his path. Driverless, the small black sedan rolled aimlessly towards the concrete embankment, her precious Plymouth—mistreated by this dreadful riffraff—

"I warned you to *stop!*" cried Mrs. Fox, enraged, reached out to grab at the door handle of the passing pickup truck——And felt a sudden stinging burst of red-hot pain behind her eyes, a clanging echo within her head, in her ears a strange roar   ohmyGod, she thought, not *here*   not on a public street   after seventynineyears   thisisnothowIplannedtodie   so   humiliating *undignified* inmyownbedperhaps   or   at   my   desk? somewhere surroundedby friendsfamily   butnothere

alone!   completelyalone . . .

Her last coherent thought, a second before she fell to the cement pavement in a crumpled heap *Damn Dr. Mainwaring for being right.*

The pickup truck disappeared in the distance.

Mrs. Laura Richards Fox remained behind, in extremis, a few feet away from her 1933 Plymouth, which sat quietly, driverless, the engine ticking away as it had for all these years, on the side of the access road. While up above, on the main highway, the trucks roared past.

A passing driver braked to a stop, jumped out of his car, and ran over to the prostrate body, which lay, face upward, the hand outstretched, finger still pointing.

"Je*sus,*" he said. "Just like that."

While a mile down the road, in the front seat of the pickup truck, Guillermo Sanchez, an illegal alien, living and working for the past two years in Connecticut as a landscape gardener with his partner Roberto Tobriz shook his head. "Loco people, you know?" he said, and spat out the window. "She would make us late for work, and then we would be in big trouble!"

"People like that, they don't care for *nobody,*" said Roberto Tobriz.

 ## Wayside Gardens

Despite the name, Wayside Country Gardens was not a nursery. It was, true, an establishment devoted to planting. Not blooms spreading up, but senior citizens on the way out, whose families had decided to install their parents and relatives in a tidy, clean, next-to-closing spot, out of sight and out of mind, courtesy of Medicare.

As nursing homes go, Wayside Gardens wasn't too dreadful. There are others tucked away from scrutiny in Connecticut that are undoubtedly worse. This old-age money-spinner was housed in a Federal mansion in a section of the town that was once proudly middle class. Now spot-zoning had hemmed in the building with a Dairy Queen and a plumbing-supply warehouse.

Inside, the rooms for the "guests" were clean enough, and some of the fortunate ones had windows that opened on what was left of the rear garden. The dining room was hardly four-star, but then, older people don't need Craig Claiborne to feed them, do they? In the summer, there were chairs in which to sit out back; in the winter there were extra blankets on the beds. The hallways were brightly lit with flourescent tubing, but there was nothing the management could do in the way of paint or carpeting that would dissipate the aura of quiet desperation that pervaded Wayside Gardens like some thin grey fog.

". . . You come into a place like this," old Gus Konecki was fond of saying, "and each morning you wake up you know one thing for sure—you got one less day to go."

He sat in his shabby armchair and scratched the stubble of his beard. Gus was a wiry little man with sharp blue eyes that glittered behind his thick lenses. "Didja bring me my Topstones?" he demanded.

Benita Lorenzo nodded and produced a five-pack of the dark Connecticut cigars that Gus fancied, and which she found time in her busy schedule to buy for him. "These are bad for you, Gus," she cautioned.

"What's left that's good?" he asked, ripping open the package. "Booze rots your guts, tobacco eats your lungs, and women steal your money."

"I don't steal your damn money!" Benita protested, and tossed him his change. Gus lit a fresh black cigar and began to exhale clouds of fragrant smoke.

"Not *you*," grinned Gus. "You're a terrific chicken, with a beautiful pair of knockers—just like a nice plump pullet—"

"Dirty mouth," said Benita, and began to make his rumpled bed. Such a job was not part of her duties as floor nursing attendant but she was fond of the old man, and if it made him comfortable to sleep in a fresh-made bed, then what the hell did it cost?

"—And you're gonna make some lucky guy a terrific wife," said Gus, winking. "All you Spic girls are great wives—"

"I'm not a Spic, I'm an American!" she told him. "I was born in the Bronx!"

"Before or after they burned it?" asked Gus. "No offense, *cara mia*, geez, I *like* Spics. I had one marry me once."

"Yeah? Where's she now?" asked Benita, deftly making hospital corners.

"Gone with the wind, toots," said Gus, eyeing with pleasure the vista of Benita's ample rear as she bent over his bed. "That was back when I was down in Central America. Right after the war, working in the oil fields. Struck it rich there, rolled in dough, spending pesetas as fast as I could—"

"You made a lot of money in oil?" asked Benita, interested. She enjoyed listening to Gus; she'd heard so many different stories from the old guy, a new one practically every day. He wasn't like most of the other residents, most of whose conversation began and ended with complaint. "What happened to all the money?"

"I enjoyed it," said Gus, beaming. "Then some big outfit moved in and stole the well away from us—that's how it goes, *muchacha,* the big fish eat up the little fish—"

"Was that before you said you were a baseball player, or after?" demanded Benita.

"I was a baseball player, dammit!" insisted Gus. "Fastest shortstop in the league, 1924. You could look it up!"

"Not today I couldn't," she said, straightening the blankets. "I thought your people loved baseball," accused Gus.

"We do when we're not running our asses off looking after people like you," she told him. She plumped up his pillows. "Why don't you lie down and take a nice nap?" she suggested.

"Not unless you shut the door and lie down there with me, *mia cara,*" said Gus. "I could teach you a few tricks. Stuff I picked up when I was a merchant seaman."

"That's a new one," said Benita.

"You mean I never told you about those broads in Cuba?" asked Gus. "Boy, they were crazy. You could go in a place, and put money on the table, and this broad would come over, pick up her dress and—"

"Ah, shut up, you dirty old man!" protested Benita.

"And proud of it, too," said Gus. "C'mon, Benita, you look like you could use a little nap—"

"Sure, sure, but I'd be too tired to do either of us any good," said Benita. Five nights a week she was in charge of the entire second floor, the evening shift, 4 P.M. to midnight, and there were endless evening chores to handle. Fifteen residents on the floor, all over sixty-five, someone always needing something, the weepers, the ones who got up and sleepwalked, the ones with bad dreams who occasionally cried out—it sure kept a girl, even one in her twenties who had all her strength, on the move.

"I'll keep a light burning in the window," said Gus. "Didja bring me my paper?"

"Right here," said Benita, pulling it out of her uniform pocket and handing it to him. "I'll look in on you later, Gus," she said, and prepared to go.

"Change your mind and want to sack in with me *after* midnight, just shake me," said Gus. "Semper paratus, that's me."

"Semper what?" she asked.

"Always ready!" he said, and opened the paper.

Before she got out the door, Gus suddenly gasped. "Holy shit!" he cried. *"Look at this. She finally kicked the old bucket!"*

". . . *Who* did?" asked Benita.

"Old lady Fox!" said Gus. "Christ, I thought for sure she was planning to live forever—but she fooled me!" Chortling with laughter, he peered through his glasses at the paper, his lips moving as he read. ". . . Right out there on the main highway, zingo . . . and still in that stinking little car . . . the two of 'em, both together . . . *Look!"*

Benita glanced at his newspaper. PROMINENT INDUSTRIALIST DIES, read the bold headline, and beneath it was a large photo of a stern-faced old lady. "Mrs. Laura Richards Fox" was the caption. Beside it was another photo, this one of a small, boxlike sedan. "Her Faithful Auto" read that caption.

"They sure make a helluva couple, don't they?" demanded Gus, cheerfully. "Her and that precious little Plymouth—she never let anybody put a hand on that car, believe me."

"You sound like you knew the woman," said Benita.

"Worked for her for a while," said Gus. "Nobody really *knew* that old bag."

"Ah, c'mon, when was *that?"* asked Benita.

"When she hired me, that's when," said Gus, still reading the newspaper. "I could tell you plenty about Mrs. Laura Richards Fox, believe you me. *Plenty."* He looked up at Benita, and beckoned. "C'mere, sit down."

. . . Outside came the sound of a bell, ringing insistently. As usual, someone needed her. "It'll have to be some other time, honey," she sighed. "Can it wait?"

"Sure, why not?" said Gus. He went back to his newspaper. "It's waited a long time, what's a little more matter?"

Benita hurried out, leaving Gus, wreathed in blue cigar smoke, shaking his head and chuckling at the evening's news.

She wouldn't see Gus again for a few days. It was Friday night and she had the weekend free. Weekends were her own private property, her brief oasis away from the elderly for whom she spent so many night hours caring. Tomorrow morning she would be free to sleep till noon. Her mother, home from her job as a part-time seamstress in one of the local garment sweatshops, would be bustling around their small apartment, tending to the household chores. Saturdays, her younger brother Pete was not allowed to bring any of his pals into the place and make a damn racket with their disco records; he would be off playing basketball at the high school, and the place would be quiet, free from bells that rang and rang.

Around noon, Benita would rise, take a bath, do her hair, have something to eat, and then close her bedroom door to do some studying.

". . . You could relax and have some fun," her mother would chide her, as she fed Benita. "You work too hard, baby. Pretty soon you end up an old maid with wrinkles—sleeping alone, like me. No good."

"I've got plenty of time to get married," Benita would say. "Right now I need to improve myself."

During the week, she would go to her class at nearby Sacred Heart University, where she had enrolled in a twelve-week course that should eventually lead to her securing her real-estate license. When all the red tape was cleared away, she could be a broker-salesman.

". . . What do you want to go into real estate for?" Mrs. Lorenzo had asked. "That's not for a nice girl."

"Oh, *ma,*" said Benita. "Look around. Every woman in this state who's got time on her hands and is able to spell her name is peddling houses and land and making big bucks, and why the hell shouldn't we finally get a few of them into our bank account?"

". . . That's not all those women are peddling," said Mrs. Lorenzo, darkly.

Benita ignored the remark.

She was determined; her course was set. Another nine weeks of the course, and then the professor's exam. If she passed that, she would apply to Hartford to take the official state exam; she'd already made an arrangement with middle-aged Tom Poulos, the younger brother of one of her patients at Wayside Gardens. Tom had his own agency and was looking for someone to come in to help him so he could spend more time in Florida, where he had plans to go into a development deal. "You could handle it," he'd told her. "Most of the job involves personality, and you got plenty of that. The rest of it is connections, and that's my department."

If she passed the state exam, she'd move them the hell out of this cramped apartment, pronto, buy some decent clothes, take a desk in Tom's office uptown, and then Benita Lorenzo could start prowling around, looking for the big bucks!

". . . A man could support you," accused her mother.

". . . The way yours did you?" asked Benita.

Tears welled instantly into her mother's eyes.

"Oh, Lord, I'm sorry, ma, that was a cheap shot," wailed Benita, remorsefully, putting her arm around the maternal heaving shoulders.

". . . He wasn't . . . a bad man," said her mother, after the ritual sniffing and nose-blowing. "He couldn't help it if he got mixed up with the wrong types, could he? Underneath, my Lew was *nice.*"

"Nice doesn't win the lottery," said Benita. "Everybody in that damn Wayside Gardens started out nice—look where they ended up. Ringing bells for me to come and wipe their leaks."

"That fella Poulos," said her mother, her lips curling. "He don't mean you any good. I know what *he* wants."

"What they all want, ma," said Benita, picking up her real-estate textbook.

"You gonna see Mr. Formosa any more?" persisted her mother. "He's a very clean young man."

"Yeah, great if you dig clean," said Benita, and went to her room.

. . . She hadn't seen Don Formosa lately. He was an aggressive character who ran his father's marine-supply business down by the water and who'd been after her all this past winter, ever since they'd met at some dance. They'd had a couple of dates, he'd taken her to the movies, or dinner at the Jai-Alai, and then he'd moved in to collect on the tab. On their last few evenings out they'd ended up in a wrestling match on the front seat of his car. He was attractive, sure, but there was nothing subtle about his approach. She hadn't agreed to go up to his apartment so he'd settled for a drive which ended on a street that overlooked the Sound. There she had responded to his urgent embraces, God knows she was normal enough and she wanted to, perhaps as much as he did, but she wasn't ready to become one of his easy lays.

After the second go-round in his car, the subject of marriage had surfaced. "What the hell, baby, I respect you," he'd promised, as they paused from their front-seat grapples, the two of them panting, her good dress practically around her neck, the two of them like a pair of high-school kids, for pete's sake, suppose somebody went by and looked in at them? ". . . Are you one of those dames who won't do it until she gets a ring?"

She shook her head.

". . . Then what is it, baby?" he wheedled, his arms coming on like an octopus. ". . . You and I aren't exactly teenagers, we know the score, don't we? Listen," he cooed, ". . . if you're worried about getting knocked up, trust me, I'll handle it . . ."

"Wow, that's the most romantic proposal any girl could want," she'd told him, pulling free.

"What do you *want,* Benita?" he asked. "If it'll make you feel better, I'll get a book of Rod McKuen's poems and read 'em to you . . . before, or after . . ."

". . . *Instead!*" she told him. Even he had to laugh at that, and because she felt sorry for the poor bastard, it ended up with her massaging him to the point where he'd gotten relief . . . almost exactly as she might have done for one of her patients at Wayside Gardens.

Except nobody there could use such a treatment . . . unless it was Gus.

Satisfying it wasn't, not for either of them. He'd left her at her building with a brief good-bye and driven off, and she'd come inside to this cluttered apartment, in this broken-down lower-income housing project where her mother had been lucky to land them, years back when she'd moved up from the Bronx. She hadn't seen him since, but chances were, if she called him, he'd come running. And if she played her cards right, went with him to his apartment or the Holiday Inn, she was certain she could maneuver Don Formosa into marriage.

Yet she hadn't called, and had no urge to.

What would marriage mean, anyway? Taking care of Don in the sack, wherever and whenever. A move into some nicer apartment where she'd do his cooking and cleaning, keep his house, all the while keeping an eye on her own mother and Pete, eventually there'd be kids, with all the hassles that went with them, he'd leave her trapped at home to handle it all while he went off whistling to do what he damn pleased. Mrs. Benita Formosa, nursemaid, cleaner-upper, wiper, bedmaker, so what was the difference between such a life with him, and the one she already had going for her at Wayside Gardens?

Where, at least, she got paid for it.

No, damnit, what she was looking for was a man who'd want something more. Not just for himself, either, but for *her*.

. . . And that kind of a guy the banks weren't giving away when you opened a savings account.

"Hey, muchacha!" Gus called, as she passed his open doorway the following Monday. "Looka this!" He waved his newspaper at her. "Crazy old lady—know how she left things in her will? She wants to be planted in a special building, a mausoleum—can you believe it?"

". . . What's so terrible about that?" asked Benita.

STRANGE WILL OF MRS. FOX read the headline.

"I'll tell you what's crazy," said Gus. "She wants her god-damn car planted in there *with* her!"

Leaves Instructions To Have
Car Entombed With Her Remains

said the subheading.

". . . Ah, rich people are crazy," said Benita, handing him back his paper.

"You don't know the half of it," he told her, coughing. "You know what they say—you can't take it with you? Well, she sure made a liar out of them! Read it, read it—"

"I'm *busy*," she said. "Later—"

"Okay, then I'll tell you," he said. "She left money to build the mausoleum, to put in air conditioning, and all kind of alarms—I'm surprised she didn't want a neon sign outside, flashing on and off like some restaurant!"

"Listen, it was her money, she could do what she wanted with it, right?" asked Benita. There was a bell ringing down the hall.

"—And *me*, she didn't leave one frigging dime," mourned Gus.

". . . Why should she leave you anything?" asked Benita.

"Plenty of reasons, believe you me," said Gus. "After all I did for her—that old bag owed me a bundle!"

"Of course she did," said Benita.

"You don't believe me, do you?" he asked.

"Every word you tell me, Gus," she said. And hurried off to see to Mrs. McCarthy, down the hall, who was probably having trouble with her hearing aid again.

Lord, sometimes as they got older, they got crazier by the hour!

 ## St. James, Bahamas

Minutes after G. Dudley Lester and Joyce Donaldson Wade had said their fond farewells in the Mandarin Hotel, and he had sworn to keep in touch, the Tulsa lady had vanished from his consciousness.

Her name and telephone number reposed in the pocket Wafer-Thin diary he carried, but the odds against his making a overseas call to her in Tulsa from his island home in the Caribbean were very high.

At that time.

They were, however, to change, due to events that would take place thousands of miles to the East of Tulsa, in a city called Te-heran.

G. Dudley flew home to St. James Island, to his small but expensive beach house, "Bellevue."

St. James is a slender spit of sand and palms in the Bahamas whose economy is based on the harvesting of cane sugar, the entertainment of a few carefully screened tourists, and the preservation of its population's capital.

Put more bluntly, St. James is a palm-tree shaded safe-deposit box, a tropical tax shelter. True, the island is never referred to as such by the occasional travel writer who might drop by to do a piece about native cooking, or about the small but idyllic beaches, the access to deep-sea fishing, and the somewhat Gilbert-and-Sullivanesque local government (a relic of its earlier days as a Crown colony).

But the simple truth is that St. James, with its random mix of plantations and old stone ruins (now remodeled), its one main street lined with two blocks of colonial buildings that house investment firms, off-shore banks, and financial syndicates from all over the world, was invented some years back by a far-sighted group of the very rich who fled to it and made it their own. If the Government House were to fly any banner beside its flag, such a silk might carry the motto "Noli Me Taxere."

Why should such a man as G. Dudley, still in his mid-forties, who had spent his early years in active commercial pursuits and who thrived on challenge, whose mind was capable of spinning out complex financial ventures designed to spin off gushers of black ink, continue to laze out so many of his days on sleepy, sun-drenched St. James, while only a few miles away, the mainland continued to offer so many opportunities?

Long ago, G. Dudley had decided that one of these days, very soon, the financial structure of the Western world could collapse. When and if that disaster took place, and the nations were thrown into the ensuing tumult, where better to sit out Armageddon than on St. James, in his comfortable plantation home by the beach, living out his days in a sunny bomb shelter assured of ample supplies of scotch, food, cheap servants, with comforting stocks of gold, silver, platinum, and other such tangibles stashed away in the various international banks that would endure in Zurich, Hong Kong, and right here on St. James?

A week after he returned to St. James, in far-off Iran, the Shah's government collapsed. But before it did, billions in foreign capital had been systematically withdrawn from that country, to be spirited away to other, safer harbors.

Once there had been a Mrs. Lester in residence at "Bellevue," a taffy-haired lithe German lady named Leni, whom he'd brought with him when he first migrated here. Leni had found island life pleasant enough at first, but beneath that constant sun, their marriage had slowly baked into ashes. Leni had taken to designing flashy bikinis that showed off her spectacular form. Eventually she began to sell those minuscule cloth strings in a local boutique, and when they caught on, they became the rope by which Leni could swing free, to flee this island prison.

Now she was back in Europe, designing clothes full time, and G. Dudley was left to forage for himself. Alone, or *à deux,* with whatever female he was currently entertaining, each day he would drive his immaculate '56 Jaguar downtown to visit at his banker's office, to check the price of gold, and to supervise his various investments. To perform a bit of shopping at the local markets, and then return home for a swim, a bite of lunch, and an afternoon nap. Then dinner, either at home or at one of his neighbors, a game of bridge or backgammon, all counterpointed by the discussion of the price of gold, the rate of world inflation, and the cost of scotch in the local shops. A good night's sleep, and then tomorrow, the same program.

Overseas Holdings, Ltd., in which G. Dudley had a good bit of his capital invested, had decided to close its Teheran offices. Prudently, the manager in charge, a trusted employee named Renaldo Conforti, had converted assets into cash, packed them into several large cases, and then made his way to the airport, to take a Rome-bound flight. All was safe . . .

Life on St. James, then, was a long-run production, with the same scenery, a permanent cast, and with the only variable being the size and age of the lady who might currently be sharing G. Dudley's master bed. Barring anything unforeseen, this successful show in the sun could run on indefinitely.

Whenever life became too boring, G. Dudley could travel. Since he had various high-yield "stashes" in cooperative financial institutions, much like W. C. Fields, who opened accounts wherever he went, G. Dudley could combine business with pleasure.

For some reason, however, London was never part of his international rounds. ". . . Oh, nothing against you British," he'd tell his dinner guests, ". . . but it's that miserable climate. Positively lethal for these tired old lungs, eh?"

There was another, more specific reason why G. Dudley so studiously avoided passing through Heathrow, or Gatwick, or setting his foot on British soil. One which had nothing to do with his lungs.

. . . And if certain authorities in Her Majesty's Home Office, in Lamb's Conduit Street, as well as certain other gentlemen in Scotland Yard, have long memories and well-kept records, then one of G. Dudley's mottos had always been "Let Sleeping Dogs Lie."

Renaldo Conforti's plane made it safely to Rome. His final destination was Milan, where the cash would be converted and reinvested in gold, and then transhipped to Mexico, where Overseas Holdings, Ltd., would recoup its capital, and reinvest it into other, safer projects, at equally high rates of interest.

Alas, Renaldo Conforti never made it to the Milan bank. In the morning, he returned to the Rome airport. On the way to Fiumicino, his limousine was abruptly run off the Autostrada by another car carrying three gunmen. Swiftly they pumped bullets into the driver and into poor Renaldo, and snatched the bags. In moments, they had vanished into the early morning traffic.

Taking with them a large chunk of Overseas Holdings, Ltd., capital, all of it in untraceable cash.

Within hours there ensued a small internal crisis in the home office of Overseas Holdings, Ltd., in Mexico City. Due to carelessness on the part of the firm's lawyers, the firm's insurance policies did not cover the loss of cash by acts of violence committed on an Autostrada in Italy by person or persons unknown.

When G. Dudley Lester, who had a large investment in the firm, arrived a day or so later for top-level conferences, he was met with his partners' expressions of dismay, shrugs of the shoulders, and glum stares. And when all the arguments and discussions, with and without bankers, lawyers and accountants were over, G. Dudley was faced with one immutable fact. For the moment, at least, a large-sized hunk of his Mexico City "stash" had gotten away from him. Despite all his careful planning, he needed to replenish his exchequer.

He would have to go into action again, to recoup his losses.

. . . Well, why not?

Nothing like a challenge to sharpen up the old wits, eh?

Sitting in his Mexico City hotel room, he sipped a marguerita and riffled through his address book, checking for "live ones."

At the end of the book, in her own handwriting (with exclamation points after her name and number) was Mrs. Wade, of Tulsa, Oklahoma.

Ah yes. The rich Oklahoma lady.

. . . Tulsa lay between Mexico City and St. James.

Convenient.

. . . He picked up the phone and placed the call.

When the call came through, and he inquired whether or not she would be free for a bit of socializing in the next day or so, Joyce cried out "Lovah, where've you *been?* For you, I'm available *inny ta-im!*"

"I'm on my way," he told her. "Lord, how I've missed you."

". . . Oh God, me too!" she said. *"Hurry!"*

*   *   *

When he arrived in Tulsa, he was met with a hero's welcome.

She picked him up at the airport in her Mercedes and drove him to her mansion in the suburbs, steering the car with one hand. The other was occupied with G. Dudley. Narrowly avoiding two collisions, they arrived home, where she escorted him upstairs to her master bedroom, switched on the telephone-answering machine and snapped on the stereo. Deftly she shrugged off her mink jacket, skinned out of her Calvin Klein jeans, and hurled herself enthusiastically at her houseguest, welcoming him to Oklahoma with open arms, thighs, and mouth . . .

". . . My bag," he protested, pinned to her bed, ". . . in . . . the car."

"Shoot," she told him, "you won't need clothes for a while."

. . . For the first two days, all he saw of Tulsa was the view from her bedroom window. When they needed food, she padded downstairs, cooked him prime filets and brought them up, along with fresh bottles of Moet & Chandon from her private stock.

". . . Is this the way you welcome all your out-of-town guests?" he asked, during one of their more peaceful moments.

"Hell, no," she said. "You're gettin' the AA treatment . . . oh, I wanta tell you, if my friends could see me now! Hm-*mmph!*"

". . . You're not planning to have them in, are you?" he asked.

"Hell no, I'm keepin' you strictly to myself!" she said.

". . . When are you going to show me your town?" he asked.

". . . We can socialize later," she said. ". . . now lissen, how about this time, you pour the wine on *me,* mm?"

Eventually he persuaded his voracious hostess to venture out into the open air. Temporarily sated, Joyce agreed to take him to visit the country club, where he borrowed clubs and had a therapeutic round of golf.

Later that evening, the happy couple were joined at a small intimate dinner by Joyce's father, the legendary patriarch of the business, Old Ed.

Old Ed, whose voice was hoarse from many years of chanting out numbers at auctions, gave G. Dudley a firm handshake. "Delighted to make your acquaintance," he rasped. "You're mighty welcome, after all, you did save my daughter's life."

". . . For which I've been amply repaid," smiled G. Dudley.

In the next few days, between return bouts in Joyce's bower, G. Dudley spent time surveying this new territory with the practiced eye of the entrepreneur. He smiled and made small talk with Joyce's various friends, but all the while, the tiny computer in his brain was storing away facts.

Fact: Donaldson Bros. (YOUR RELIABLE AUCTIONEERS SINCE 1927), which was housed in a nondescript jumble of old buildings downtown, was a thriving enterprise with a high profit margin. The turnover in regular weekly sales of furniture, bric-a-brac, and household items was steady, but unspectacular. What really brought in the revenue were the auctions of farm equipment on nearby farms, and the sales of thoroughbred horses and purebred cattle on outlying ranches.

Fact: Auctioneers need to carry no stock in trade. Their business is to sell the property of others, for which service they charge a healthy fee, a percentage of the gross. Thus, Donaldson Bros. had a very low overhead.

Fact: Since the seller had consigned the merchandise for sale, the auctioneer ran no risk whatsoever. If a buyer did not show up and bid above the seller's reserve price, then the property would be returned to its owner, but not before Donaldson Bros. could and did charge said owner a stated percentage of its value.

Fact: In such a transaction, perhaps a buyer could be in over his head, or a seller might end up being hurt, but no matter the outcome, Donaldson Bros. could not lose.

When, over a friendly game of gin rummy with Old Ed, he checked out all these facts, Joyce's father nodded and stared up from his cards. "Pretty smart figgerin', friend," he said. ". . . What've you got in mind?"

". . . Nothing specific," said G. Dudley. "Just getting a little education."

". . . It's a mighty solid business," said Old Ed. "We make it in good times, we make it in bad. Joyce is a bright lady, and she picked it up real fast."

". . . She *is* very adept," agreed G. Dudley.

". . . Someday, when my number is called in, Up Yonder," said Old Ed, "and I turn in my gavel, she's gonna end up ownin' the whole shebang. And I worry about my little gal, swimmin' all alone in a sea surrounded by sharks . . ."

"I wouldn't," said G. Dudley. "I'd worry about the sharks."

He went gin, catching Old Ed with a bundle of face cards.

G. Dudley stayed on a few more days. He dined and discoed with Joyce and accompanied her to small gatherings of her intimate friends, where she took pleasure in showing him off to her other, less fortunate, single and widowed female buddies. There he proved himself to be a most interesting guest, capable of holding his own in conversation, a good joketeller, and despite his reserve, almost a good old boy.

At such social soirees, most of the small talk concerned such aesthetic matters as commercial and residential real-estate values, the price of beef, oil and natural-gas plays, tax-shelter deals in beef-feed lots or farm equipment leasing, the value of local bank shares, inflationary pressures, and a variety of other subjects, all of them designed to make more Keepin' Money.

". . . You like my friends?" inquired Joyce.

"Lovely folks," said G. Dudley, and sighed. "Only thing is, it seems to me that you and all those millionaires keep getting younger and younger."

"We're not millionaires," she said. "Shucks, we're just well-fixed."

G. Dudley went on smiling, making polite small talk with all the various well-fixed Sun Belt folks, and all the while, he was running more information into his private data bank.

An idea was beginning to percolate in the depths of his mind, one that might eventually blossom into . . . who knew yet?

Well he knew that in this world beset by inflation, cash money steadily lost its worth, and that when cash erodes, the shrewd move into Things, i.e., items that increase in value—the land and houses and condos and furniture and paintings which Joyce and her well-fixed friends were rapidly gobbling up (with the willing assistance of financial institutions anxious to lend out money at very high rates).

Years ago, G. Dudley had figured out about cars; namely, that the Cadillac Eldorado you bought depreciated from the moment you drove it out of the dealer's garage. Not so G. Dudley's classic Jaguar XK-120, which appreciated in value each year.

Fact: One thriving market which had heretofore been overlooked by Donaldson Bros., here in affluent Tulsa, was the one involving vintage automobiles.

. . . Having over the years met many other vintage-car owners, G. Dudley knew another valuable secret about them, i.e., that they never, never have enough of a good thing.

That no matter where they are, crouched over the engine of that '32 Packard Twin-Six, or tinkering with the transmission of their Model A Ford roadster, or polishing the chrome of their air-cooled Franklin, old-car buffs are pigeons ready for the plucking. That they spend nights poring over owners' manuals and used-car ads, meet with each other to swap information and spare parts, and that when they hear the siren song of a rare old model Whatever that is up for sale, somewhere, anywhere, they will beg, borrow, or steal to get their hands on its steering wheel. That their Achilles' heel comes equipped with wheels.

What is it that turns a normal, pleasant sober citizen into such a single-minded, driven collector? What is his Need—the sparkplug and coil that turns on his fire?

No one diagnosis can serve to explain his behavior. There are easily as many motives for a collector's dementia as there are makes and models to collect.

Status? Of course. No one on the Golden State Freeway gives a mundane '79 Seville a second glance. But that Santa Barbara broker in his '39 Chrysler Airflow, doing a sedate forty-five as he wheels down to the beach on a bright Saturday afternoon—he's monarch of the road. No matter if he holds up traffic. All the cars tailing him are driven by other men who'd dump their Olds Cutlass Supremes on the spot, merely to trade places with that lucky bastard up ahead.

Ask another collector and he'll tell you he likes the old ones better than anything new because it's an act of loyalty to keep his lean, round-nosed LaSalle convertible up to snuff. She's a treasured relic of an earlier, saner time, when in the Detroit factories there was pride of craft and skill, there was engineering one could rely on, not this plastic crap they're foisting on us today. That he owns such a solid vehicle and drives it once or twice a month is to pay homage to his Amurrican past. When his headlights flash on and his tires are up to pressure, it's an act of affirmation, and when the oil circulates in

48

the engine and those eight cylinders tick over, brother, the ritual is far more binding than any pledge of Allegiance.

For another, there's the reassuring sense of contact with his vanished youth. The first car he ever drove was a 1947 Chevvy, and he loved it more than life itself. On that leather front seat he passed through his *rite de paysage*. He became a Man . . . during the day, and when he got lucky, at night. To have that Chevvy back today, ah! such security. Better than any blanket.

You vish to discuss ze sexual symbolism of ze motorcar? Often pure, rarely simple. That '40 Buick Roadmaster is as satisfying as any wife, an MG-TD sports car is more exciting than any mistress, and in the front seat of a '56 Lincoln Continental, you're safe in the arms of your dear old mama.

And finally, there are the shrewd ones, the ones who, like G. Dudley, have found the best of both worlds. That European businessman who's invested in an antique Rolls, or the electronics wizard whose financial adviser has steered him into an old Duesenberg. There sits his baby, locked away in a garage, or in a barn at the Hamptons, appreciating in value each calendar year. When you've found yourself a hobby that satisfies your aesthetic needs, gratifies your cupidity, supplies you with status, sets you off from the rest of the crowd, fills you with pride and gives you a slight sexual charge, and all the while makes your accountant a happier man . . . is this not the best of all possible worlds?

G. Dudley Lester knew about cars, but there were a few details about Tulsa he needed to check out, so he lingered in the town for a few days longer than he'd planned. There was nothing pressing calling him back to St. James, while here in Oklahoma, there were some interesting possibilities.

In the depths of his computer, he was putting pieces together, designing a deal. One that might result in a very substantial return for a small amount of effort, less time, and (this being the prime component) no investment of his own capital.

Since Joyce's voracious appetites had been somewhat sated, he was left with spare time while she attended to business at the office. In a rented car, G. Dudley prowled around Tulsa, acquiring information, and asking pertinent questions. Then, when he had it all assembled, the pieces falling nicely into place, he moved into the next phase. The Sell.

". . . Lover," said Joyce, as they relaxed in her Jacuzzi, that evening, "what is botherin' you?"

". . . Whatever makes you think I'm bothered?" he asked.

". . . Well, the last couple of times we did it, I got the definite feelin' you were a million miles away," pouted Joyce, ". . . and gettin' further each ta-im . . ."

"Oh, I am sorry," said G. Dudley, and leaned over to nibble on her ear. "I had no idea it was showing."

"What was?" she asked, staring at various areas of G. Dudley.

". . . The fact that I'm worried for you and your father," he said.

"Worried about *us?*" she exclaimed. *"Why?"*

". . . You two are such fine, upstanding hospitable folks," said G. Dudley. "Pillars of society, with a business that has a sterling reputation. But somehow or other, I hate to say this, you've fallen behind the times . . . and it bothers me to think of you people losing all that money."

"What money?" she demanded.

". . . The profits you could rake in if you ran a vintage car auction," he said.

Joyce stared blankly at him as he floated gently back and forth in the Jacuzzi. "Vintage what?" she asked, at last.

". . . Of course I'm just thinking out loud," he told her, "but as far as I've taken it, assuming I had a business as solid as yours, this is how it would go." And he proceeded to outline his proposal in detail, patiently, like a teacher explaining the day's lesson to a favorite pupil. A vintage car auction, to be held a couple of months from now, the merchandise consisting of antique and classic cars, all makes and models up to Circa 1953, perhaps, in the case of thunderbirds, even later years. Where? Well, how about the old Arena, uptown, it was booked for the Stockmens' Fair, sure, but they might find two or three free days in August. Now, if that place was rented, the rest of it was a breeze. The advertising and publicity and hoopla would be started right away, it would attract buyers and sellers from all over, not just the rich locals here in Oklahoma, but there were buyers and sellers all over the country, even in Europe, certainly West Germans and perhaps even Japanese, and Arabs . . .

"What do they buy?" asked Joyce.

"The old cars," he said, patiently.

". . . Who wants an old car?" she asked. "Ah trade mine in every year, always have."

He explained the intricacies of the market to her, and when he began to cite a few of the five- and six-figure prices that vintage cars had lately brought, here and abroad, her eyes began to sparkle greedily. "Hoo-*eeh!*" she sighed. "How long has this been goin' *on?*"

He laid out the rest of it. For staff, there would be Old Ed, one of the greatest, and the rest of his people, all dependable boys with golden throats, some of the fastest tongues in the Southwest. And how did it all work? Well, the sellers would consign their vehicles and deliver them to the Arena. Donaldson Bros. would then operate the sale, collect a percentage from the price that buyers paid, as well as from what the seller received. If the sale were to gross, say, a million overall, that would mean a nice fat six-figure take in profits for Donaldson Bros., for very little effort, and even less investment of their firm's capital.

". . . Just like that?" sighed Joyce, hypnotized with greed.

". . . I almost forgot," he mused on. "You'd also collect from the concessionaires for food and parking and drinks and you print up the auction catalog. That means you sell advertising space, and peddle the catalogs. Why, you could have money coming in from every direction . . ."

". . . When the hell do we get goin'?" demanded Joyce.

". . . Far be it from me to tell you nice people how to run your business," said G. Dudley, piously, "but it's only a matter of time before some other character figures out how lush the pickings around here are, and beats you to it."

"No he won't!" said Joyce. She splashed over, kissed him passionately, then climbed, dripping, from the Jacuzzi. Padded across the bright red bathroom carpeting and grabbed her yellow Princess telephone, to dial. "Daddy!" she said, *"lissen*—I've been havin' me a little business conference here with G. Dudley, and he's come up with somethin' that is so damn tasty, you just got to hear all about it before that other guy gets to it!"

When she finished outlining the scheme for the Vintage Car Auction, Old Ed demanded that she put G. Dudley on. Joyce handed the phone to her floating guest.

". . . Son," said Old Ed, "you just got yourself a deal."

". . . Me?" said G. Dudley. "Oh, no, I don't know anything about the auction business—"

". . . Hell you don't," said Old Ed. "A fox like you don't come down the pike so often, and we need you."

"Well, thanks," said G. Dudley. "But I've never really been comfortable working for other people, no matter how fine they are, and I'm really retired. So you take the idea and run with it—"

"Hold on," said Old Ed. "Who said you'd be workin' for us? What I'm talking about is you bein' in as a *partner.*"

". . . Why thanks, but I really haven't the time . . ." said G. Dudley, modestly. "And I'd be out of my league."

The fish was securely hooked, but he wasn't quite ready to haul in his catch.

There was a splash beside him, and he became conscious of Joyce's trim shape pressing against him.

She seized the phone. "He'll think it over, Daddy," she said. "Leave everythin' to me!"

The receiver sank beneath the water as Joyce moved in, applying herself to the task of changing G. Dudley's negative attitude.

G. Dudley had never acquired a formal degree in psychology, but in the arts of persuasion he was a practicing Ph.D. Years ago, he had stumbled on a basic truth . . . that it is the ultimate triumph of the manipulator's art to maneuver his manipulatee into a circumstance where said pigeon feels that he (or she) is running the ballgame, from a position of strength.

(In this particular case, sideways, under four feet of swirling warm water.)

". . . Oh well, all right," he sighed, some time later, having enjoyed certain sexual acrobatics that had never been seen in any

Esther Williams movie. ". . . If you're dead set on this auction deal, I'll give you some input . . . just to make sure you nice people don't make any mistakes up front. But you're both going to have to guide *me*. I mean—I'm just an amateur at this game."

". . . You are the sweetest old thang!" sighed Joyce. "Do you have inny i-dea how brilliant you are?"

". . . Some," murmured G. Dudley, as they receded beneath the waves.

 ## Bridgeport, Connecticut

Acting on behalf of her heirs, under the instruction of her Executors, the lawyers for the Estate of Mrs. Laura Richards Fox had moved to petition the court for a minor change in one of the bequests in the will.

There was no intent on anyone's part to contravene the late Mrs. Fox's wishes, but various factors were now evident that made it difficult, nay, almost impossible, to comply with her directions as to the erecting of a mausoleum in which to house the remains of the late Mrs. Fox, together with her 1933 Plymouth.

To use Estate funds to build such a large mausoleum for Mrs. Fox's final resting place, to that there was no objection. But to design and have erected a building to serve as a combination last resting place *and* garage for a forty-five-year-old automobile presented problems that Mrs. Fox's heirs respectfully suggested to the court were difficult, nay, impossible, to carry out.

For a period stretching indefinitely into the future, they argued, such a mausoleum would require air conditioning, lighting, heating, an alarm system, burglar-proof devices, and full-time guardians and maintenance. In time, the Plymouth would certainly deteriorate physically. There then arose the question; was the car to be removed at stated intervals, (which were not so stated) now and into the twenty-first century, to be restored to its original condition, to be refurbished, and to have new paint, sparkplugs, oil, rubber tires, etc, etc, *if* available (which was impossible to promise). Assuming such a complex procedure were to be followed (and there was no existing definition that covered the question of Lifetime Care for said automobile), who, asked the lawyers, would undertake to carry it out?

The Executors were thus respectfully petitioning the court, with the complete agreement of all the stated heirs in Mrs. Fox's will, to amend this particular clause in her will. The mausoleum to house her remains would certainly be built, but said mausoleum should house only said remains. Whatever sum or sums that were saved by excluding the 1933 Plymouth from such mausoleum would be paid into a special fund and held in trust, the proceeds from said trust to be donated to a designated charity or to a school, as a donation in memory of Mrs. Fox.

As to the Plymouth itself, said car would be appraised for its value, and then, through reputable channels, it would be disposed of. Whatever sum was derived from its sale would also be donated to charity.

There ensued a series of closed hearings in Probate Court, and when the Judge of Probate had listened to all the arguments supporting the brief, he promised to rule forthwith on this peculiar problem raised by Mrs. Laura Richards Fox's whimsical bequest.

*   *   *

". . . Only people who'll get rich out of this are the goddamned lawyers," wheezed Gus Konecki, waving his newspaper. He was sitting in an old campchair in the backyard of Wayside Gardens, occasionally spitting into the nearby bed of wilted geraniums. "Where the hell you been, Benita? I missed you."

"On vacation," said Benita, handing him his Topstones. "Spent the time studying for my real-estate exams."

The old man snorted scornfully. "Real estate? That's for suckers. I was in real estate once—had land in Florida. Wetlands—under water!"

"People get rich from it today," said Benita. "You should've held on."

"I should've done a lot of things," said Gus. "You could be

rich without all that work if you listened to me, *muchacha,"* he said. With one hand he caressed her bottom. "I know how to make you a pile, believe me."

She removed his hand. "What is it now—some oil stock?"

"Forget oil," said Gus. "Those big oil companies 'll steal your eyeteeth." He laughed, and then the laughter became a cough. Since the winter, his cough had become more severe; there were several gasping paroxysms before he could catch his breath. He tapped the newspaper. ". . . Want me to tell you what's gonna happen right here? Those sharks will bust the old lady's will, you wait and see, and then they're gonna sell off her precious Plymouth." He beckoned her closer, and his voice dropped. ". . . And when they do, *muchacha,* you get your pretty little tush over there and buy it."

He lit a fresh cigar and puffed its acrid smoke greedily.

". . . I *have* a car," said Benita. . . . A 1976 Pinto, with still eleven payments to go on it, and the damn heap already needed new tires!

". . . Yeah, but that Plymouth ain't just a car," said Gus. "She's something special, believe you me."

"I believe you, I believe you," said Benita, and moved out of the range of his active fingers. "I've got work to do—"

"You don't want the rest of it?" asked Gus. "Hell, here I'm trying to do something for you that could change your whole life— and all you do is run like a rabbit!"

". . . Everybody is always looking to do something for me," said Benita. "The story of my life."

As she hurried out of the small yard back into the building, she heard his voice call out ". . . You'll be sorr—" and then the choking began, followed by another burst of coughing.

Stubborn old character . . . and fool Benita! No more of those cigars. They'd be the death of him . . . and *she* was helping him speed it up!

Several nights later, she came in to check on him. His chair was empty. "Gus?" she called.

He was lying on his bed, staring at the ceiling, with a blanket pulled up around himself. In the half light, the old man's face looked suddenly thin and gaunt, his sharp nose and the pink wattling beneath his neck covered with the white fuzz of a two-day beard giving him the look of an old bantam turkey cock. "You all right?" she asked, suddenly anxious.

"Nah, I'm lousy," he said. He seized her arm. "Don't tell anybody downstairs, you hear, they'll get me out of here and into some hospital, and I'm not looking to die in one of them butcher shops!"

". . . You're not going to die, not yet," she said, automatically reaching for his pulse. "You're too ornery to do that." His pulse seemed normal enough, but she did not like the waxen color of his face. She placed a hand to his forehead. Dry, but cold, perhaps too cold. And yet, perspiration here and there. ". . . You got a little fever, or something?"

"Nah," he said. "Had me a drink."

"Drink?" she asked. "Where'd you get it?"

He leered. "Under my pillow. Want a shot?"

She shook her head. "You know it's against the rules."

"Rules, the hell with the rules. All my life there's been rules, and the people that broke 'em always come out ahead of us idiots that didn't. Sit down and talk to me, Benita, you're the only person in this whole dump ever talks to me." He beckoned her closer.

She glanced at her watch. Nearly midnight. Everybody was sleeping; in a few minutes her night relief would come on. She'd go back to the apartment, make some coffee, and get to her textbooks. Next week was her exam; she needed to study—

". . . And don't give me that busy, busy," said Gus. He choked back a cough and glared at her. "This is important."

". . . Okay, five minutes," said Benita, and pulled his chair over to the side of his bed.

"Close the door," said Gus. "This place is full of busybodies who like to listen."

"Everybody's sleeping," she said.

"Can't be sure of that!" he said. "I don't want any snoopers, see?"

When she returned from closing the door, he had propped himself up into a sitting position and was trying to stuff his pillow behind him; she helped him and sat down. "Move over," he said.

"Why?" she asked.

". . . Because I like the feel of a live young broad against me," he said. "Is that so much to ask?"

She moved closer until she touched his shoulder; she could feel his bones. Now she was aware how thin Gus had become over the summer.

"Anybody comes in, you can tell 'em you was giving me mouth-to-mouth resuscitation," said Gus. "Now listen, Benita— you keep an eye on the papers and TV, see, and when you read about them lawyers busting the old lady's will, you go and buy that Plymouth—"

The car? *Again*—the old man was obsessed with that damn Plymouth—

". . . I don't care what they're asking for that little heap—it's worth a helluva lot more, believe you me," he insisted.

"Mind telling me why?" she asked.

. . . Might as well humor him.

". . . Sure, I'll tell you," said Gus. "But only you. Start blabbing about this and you'll blow the whole deal, *comprendre?*"

He told her the story of Mrs. Laura Richards Fox and her Plymouth.

. . . It was back in 1933, long before she'd even been born and brought to this country—

"I'm as native born as you are!" she scolded, stung.

"Okay, okay," he said. "You're a Yankee Doodle Dandy. So shut up."

. . . Gus had been working at the Richards Calibrated Valve Company, tool and die department. Those were rotten times—there had been a big bust down on Wall Street, all the stocks and bonds had gone into the toilet, the fat cats were jumping out of office buildings, banks foreclosing everywhere, lines of unemployed slobs waiting for soup and bread, veterans living in shanty towns, marching on Washington asking for bonuses—

"I know all about that, we studied it in school!" she said.

"Is this your story or mine?" he asked.

. . . Old Mrs. Fox was boss-lady at the plant, and when all those new rules and regulations started to come out of Washington, she'd gotten angrier and angrier at each one. Invasion of privacy, deprivation of her rights. In and out of the plant she'd stamp, raising hell with the foremen, arguing, tossing out federal inspectors, fighting off union organizers who were moving in on her business.

"Sounds like the original Women's libber," said Benita.

"Oh, she was a pistol, that one," grinned Gus. "One tough lady. Nobody could tell her what to do; least of all Mr. Roosevelt, down in Washington, D. C."

In 1933 there had been what they called the "Bank Holiday." In order to save the financial system, FDR had closed every bank and savings institution in the country.

"What'd people do for money?" asked Benita.

"They didn't," said Gus.

After the banks reopened, at least most of them had, old FDR placed an embargo on all gold shipments, in or out of the U.S. of A. "What he said was, all us citizens was forbidden to buy or sell gold, to sock it away, nobody could own it, see?" Gus snickered. "Of course, most of us didn't have any, so it didn't matter a hell of a lot."

. . . But said government order did not sit well with Mrs. Laura Richards Fox, no indeed. "Nobody was gonna tell *her* what to do with what was hers, nossir," said Gus. "Least of all her Uncle Sammy."

"Big deal. What could she do about it?" asked Benita.

"I'm *trying* to tell you!" said Gus.

He began to cough. When the paroxyms ended, he went right on puffing on his cigar . . . as if those heaters weren't killing him.

One day, Mrs. Fox had come to see Gus, down in the shop, he was one of the few still left on the company payroll, times were real rough now, damned few orders on her books.

She'd shut the door, sat down and talked to him, private. He'd been around for a long time, and she could trust him, right? Okay, so she'd promised him a bonus if he would do a small job for her, in complete secrecy. ". . . How could anybody turn down such an offer? I said sure."

. . . She'd led him outside to the parking lot, and showed him her new car, a Plymouth. "What she wanted, see, was for me to hide her gold in the car," said Gus.

Benita yawned. She was tired. Fairly soon now, she could go home. "In the trunk?" she asked.

"*No*, dummy!" said Gus, disgustedly. "She had some cock-eyed idea I could melt down the gold she had and cast it into wheels, get it?"

"No," said Benita. "She sounds like a kook."

"You bet—like a fox," said Gus. "You're so smart, why ain't you rich, like her, eh?"

". . . But gold wheels?" said Benita. "Anybody could rip off her wheels—"

"Not if they didn't know," said Gus. "And they didn't. Right up to now, they don't."

"Ah, Gus, come *on*—" she said. "You're telling me that old lady rode around forty years on wheels made of solid gold?"

"I never said that," he snapped. "I said that's what she *wanted*, right? I told her it wouldn't work—gold is too malleable, get it? Anything bangs it, it bends, heat melts it, if she went around a corner, it could split, all of that. Her idea was half-cocked. That's why she needed somebody like *me* to straighten her out . . ."

"Sure, sure," said Benita, and yawned again. "Listen, I better go—"

"You stay, sugar," instructed Gus. "I'm gonna make you rich whether you want to be or not. Now, *lissen*—"

. . . He'd taken the Plymouth into his shop, studied the problem. Made some drawings. Pulled the tires off, then removed the tubes—

"What are tubes?" asked Benita.

"Jee-sus, you can't be that young," said Gus. "Or me that old." He explained about tires with rubber inner tubes . . .

". . . So then, you poured her gold inside the tires?" she asked, trying to focus on his train of thought.

"No, no," he said. *"Inside* the wheels!"

". . . But you just told me you couldn't make her golden wheels!" she reminded him. My God, this old man was really going over the edge, wasn't he, rambling away—

"Not the way she wanted 'em," he said. "It took me a while, but I finally figured it out—and believe you me, it wasn't easy . . . I had to make special molds, copy the wheels front and back, die-cast 'em special, so's from the front or back nobody could ever catch on what was *inside,* see? Then I had to melt all her gold down, and pour it inside, lock it in, cover it with the steel rims—"

"Gus, I don't get any of this mechanical stuff," she said. "What do you want from me?"

"Think of a sandwich," said Gus. ". . . A big round bagel, hollowed out, see? Only instead of cream cheese inside, there's solid gold."

"Okay, but what's the point?" she demanded. "She rode around on four steel bagels stuffed with gold all these years—but gold isn't illegal any more. Anybody can buy it, right? So then why didn't she take off her wheels, and—"

"The hell with legal!" said Gus, disgustedly. "Don't you understand? She wanted to take it with her—stashed away in that crazy mausoleum! And she almost got away with it—only thing is, the damn lawyers got in there, they always do—and they'll beat that will, you'll see. The whole world belongs to the shysters—but for once, they're not as smart as they think they are—because *I* know, and they *don't!"*

. . . Who could believe any of this?

". . . Why didn't you ever tell anybody this before?" she asked.

"Ah, come on, supposing I'd said anything?" he replied, wearily. "Who'd pay any attention—my mouth against hers? Forget it. Besides, I'd made a deal—I took her money and I owed her. She kept me on, didn't she, working there when I could've been outside, pounding the bricks with plenty of other poor slobs."

He tugged at her arm. "But I don't owe her any more, do I? She's gone, and she won't get to take her Fort Knox on wheels with her, so now *you* got a shot, *muchacha.* All you have to do is to get your little hands on that Plymouth—get at the wheels—and then you won't have to spend the rest of your life rustling bedpans!"

. . . If this midnight fantasy he'd outlined for her was true . . . *If . . .*

He was grinning triumphantly at her, this old man who'd just shared his most precious secret with her.

Why not humor him?

". . . Okay," she said, finally. "How'm I supposed to do that?"

"You go get some money and you buy the damn heap!" said the old man, and began to cough again.

He clawed beneath his pillow and found a half-filled pint bottle, opened it, and took a long swig. "My favorite cough medicine," he grinned. "Now you know as much as I do, sweetie. Go get rich."

". . . Why don't *you* do something about the car?" she asked.

"You crazy?" said Gus. "Look at me. I'm so old and feeble I've got you a foot away from me in my bed and I can't even get it up. All the gold in the world isn't going to do me any good . . ."

"Ah, forget that kind of talk," she scolded. Crazy old man, smoking and drinking himself towards death. "You shouldn't feel sorry for yourself—"

"Who feels sorry?" he said. "I had a long life, I been places and I did plenty and seen even more, and I got nobody to worry about excepting me, see?" He finished his bottle, and belched. "Most people stink, but you're okay . . . so don't say I didn't tell you how to get rich . . ."

His eyes began to flicker shut.

It was well past twelve, and time for her to get out of this dark and gloomy way station, populated by the lonely . . .

She pulled the blanket over him to keep out the night chill. Half asleep now, he grinned up at her. ". . . How does it feel to be rich?" he asked.

As she drove home through the quiet, deserted streets, Benita tried to figure out how much of Gus's midnight rambling might have been true.

Wheels stuffed with solid gold—cast for a crackpot rich old lady?

. . . Who had driven around on them for forty, no almost fifty years?

No. Not possible. That was the kind of stuff you got out of some book, or on TV, dreamed up by some writers out in California, with James Garner, or Telly Savalas tracking down the car, winding up with a shoot-out, between commercials for dog food . . .

But right here, in Connecticut? In Bridgeport? Could it have happened—for real?

. . . Or was it simply another one of Gus's stories, the ramblings of that lonely old character who needed somebody, anybody, to listen to him, so that he could prove that he was still here, Gus Konecki, alive, with his juices still running. Not just another resident of Wayside Gardens, one of those zombies dozing in front of the TV, mouth half open, drooling a little, slipping quietly away, tranquilized inside and out.

But . . . suppose it was true, and that crazy rich dame had wheels of solid gold. And had driven around on them, with her mouth shut, all those years?

Maybe. Rich people did crazy things.

But one thing was for sure. A hell of a lot of good those wheels would do her now, wherever she'd gone.

Gold, or not.

She didn't return to Wayside Gardens until the following week.

Friday was test day, and she'd arranged to have Thursday off as well, she'd arranged with one of the other girls at Wayside Gardens to swap shifts with her so that she could do some last-minute cramming.

She stayed in her bedroom and studied, emerging only for coffee and something to eat, food forced on her at dinner time by her mother, who had scolded ". . . You can't take a test on an empty stomach, you'll make yourself sick!"

As she ate, there was the evening paper on the kitchen table, and her eye caught on one of the headlines.

SUPERIOR COURT APPROVES CHANGE IN WILL, it read.

Industrialist's Car Can Be Sold.

. . . Well, old Gus was right about one thing. The damn lawyers had certainly won out over that old lady. Next time she saw Gus, he'd sure be laughing . . .

. . . But right now, she had no time to worry about that Plymouth, wheels of gold or whatever. She had a test to take. She went back and stared at her textbooks, bedroom door closed to the throb of her brother's music, and the racket of cars in the street below.

Surprisingly, the actual test did not prove to be as difficult as she'd expected. When she finished and turned in her paper to Mrs. Gaffney, the middle-aged woman who taught the course, a toothy blonde who was rumored by some in the class to have lately made a bundle in a condominium deal outside Milford, Mrs. Gaffney actually smiled at her.

". . . I'll bet you did fine," she murmured.

"How'd you know?" asked Benita, startled.

". . . I've had my eye on you," said Mrs. Gaffney. "The one thing you've got going for you is drive. In the real-estate game, that's ninety percent of the secret, you know?"

She left the classroom feeling good for the first time in weeks. Saturday she took her mother and Pete out to dinner at Valle's, and then to a movie to celebrate. Sunday, blessedly, for the first time since she'd enrolled in the course, she slept late, nothing to study, and she loafed the whole rest of the day, slopping around the apartment in her robe.

Monday afternoon, she was back at the Wayside Gardens, bringing Gus a paper, but no cigars. She wasn't going to help him kill himself with those damn stinkers. She changed into her uniform up in the service room, and then went down the hall to look in on him. He had read the paper with the news of the change in the old lady's will? What did he have to say about it now—

Gus's room was empty. The bed was stripped bare.

There were no signs of his possessions on the bureau. His customary chair sat by the window . . . but no Gus.

. . . She felt an instant chill, a tightening of her stomach.

"Mabel?" she called, to the day-shift girl.

Mabel, a plump black, was changing into her street clothes in the service room. "Where's Mr. Konecki?" Benita demanded.

"Nobody tell you?" said Mabel. "He checked out."

"Left?" asked Benita.

"Yeah. The easy way," said Mabel. "Feet first. Satiday. They come in and found him lying there. Just like that."

"Nobody told me!" said Benita, stunned by the abruptness of the old man's death.

". . . Yeah, well, I guess we was all busy, cleaning up after the others," said Mabel. "It ain't like it was something new around here, now was it?"

She felt a sudden angry reaction to the matter-of-fact way in which Mabel responded to the death. Gus Konecki was not simply a statistic, was he, a two-line paragraph in the newspaper Death Notices—

—But then, it wasn't Mabel's fault. She lived and worked each day surrounded by old people, all of them waiting out their time. If she couldn't show any real emotion about Gus, it was probably because she'd long since trained herself not to become involved.

Mabel picked up her coat and purse. "Oh yeah, I almost forgot," she said. "He had an envelope under his pillow, had your name on it." She snickered. "Hey, girl, you gave him a little extra service, maybe?"

". . . So what if I had?" snapped Benita.

"Don't get riled up," said Mabel. "You dig old men—you sure in the right place!"

In the office, the girl at the switchboard handed her the envelope, a wrinkled manila envelope with her name printed in large letters on the front.

"When is Mr. Konecki's funeral supposed to take place?" she asked.

"Don't know," said the girl. "But I can get the name of the funeral home for you if you like."

"Do that," said Benita. Somebody had better go see the old man out of this world . . .

She ripped open the envelope.

Inside were three government checks. U.S. Treasury Social Security payments. $281.90, payable to Gustave Konecki, per month, for the past three months.

She turned them over. They were endorsed, in his handwriting, "Pay to Benita Lorenzo," and signed.

There was also a small scrap of paper, on which he'd printed a message.

"Use These," it said. "Buy that Car, Kid, and Make Sure You CHANGE THE TIRES, Get it? Love, Gus."

Upstairs, a bell was ringing.

No time to mourn Gus Konecki.

One of those fortunate to be here still, one who had enough strength left to press the button, needed some help from Benita Lorenzo.

. . . She didn't have time for a decent cry over Gus until late that night, when she sat alone with a cup of coffee, in the service room. Suddenly, nobody to talk to, and the only thing to read, the newspaper, that same paper she'd brought in, so long ago, this morning, for him.

Three times $281.90 made $845.70.

. . . To make a down payment on a set of wheels, courtesy of Gus Konecki?

Golden.   . . . or not?

*   *   *

1929 MODEL AA ONE-TON STAKE TRUCK
Serial # 87899-B

In first-class condition, well kept,
with new wooden stakes on the bed,
this is a prime example of its kind,
a reliable utility vehicle, with a
sturdy Ford four-cylinder engine. . . .

This vehicle was featured on the
cover of several record albums,
while it was the property of the
famous rock musician, Chuck Malone,
of the group known as *Pick Up Truck.*

New Jersey Suburbs

Fly a little higher every hour
Soarin' along so fine
Oh, look at us, baby, moving so proud.
People tell me yes yes yes
Never tell me no.
So much loot in my pockets
I'm bent over, leaning down.
Oh, this is such a sweet trip,
You an'me will last forever
Last forever
If we fly a little higher every hour!

That had been one of their big ones, only one of them, a gold disc, top of the charts, royalties pouring into their accounts like sugar out of a busted shaker, oil from a runaway gusher, sweet hot big bucks.

(Where in hell had it all gone?)

Everywhere they'd been, day or night, looking out windows at L.A., or London, or Central Park, Frisco—always a suite, best in the house, just call room service, Mr. Malone, your limo is waiting, gentlemen, your private jet is standing by, ooh, Mr. Malone, can I call you Chuck, I do dig your music, how about you and me balling together with my friend here, don't you worry, we can get the stuff we need for a real party, ooh, you're so wow, I mean, can I touch you, oh yeah, how your music turns me on.

(All gone?)

Double bed bigger than Kansas
Lock the door
Plenty of room for you and me
Tomorrow I'm goin' too.
But tonight it's so right,

Hold me, hold me   *tight*
We're makin' history in Kansas tonight!

. . . That had been another smash, it had blasted off, others
had picked it up and sung it, made records—even old Blue Eyes
himself had made it, backed up by one of those fat string sections,
had a good solid beat to it, almost a standard, churning out more
black ink.

(Look out the window now, what do you see, Chuck baby? New
Jersey, and this sure ain't no suite, it's somebody else's three-room
pad, Sally's, and you're lucky she's got the bread for the rent, oh
yes.)

(Where had it all gone?)

Four, five years ago, everything they'd touched had turned
golden, albums, singles, fans yelling, they were on T-shirts, next-
to-closing spot on the bill when they played concerts, Pick Up
Truck was hot—

—They'd chosen that name for themselves one wild night as
they drove down from some small town in California in the Model
AA he'd picked up from that crazy old coot who'd used it to haul
produce all these years, they'd even put its picture on their next
album—written the little darling Ford its own song.

People let you down
Not my pick-up truck.
Women leave you flat
Not my pickup truck.
People steal you blind, oh yeah, oh yeah,
But I can count on my
Sweet darling little pickup truck!

It hadn't made it, but he loved that song, loved to play it with his
guitar crashing crashing out the chords, good old Al Hunter on the
drums (where was Al now, somebody said he'd gone to Sweden?)
and little Billy Kress on that honking sax. (Oh God, Billy was gone
now, beaten up in some kind of a scrap down in Florida, hell, it
seemed only a few months back he'd gotten a collect call from Billy

begging him for the loan of some money. "Money, from *me,* baby?" he'd said. "Hell, I got about enough in my pocket to keep me together till tomorrow, if I'm careful—" "Man, you got to be putting me on," Billy'd protested. "Some heavies are breathing down my neck here, shee-it, where did it all *go?*")

(Who knew?)

Jack Adler had an explanation. Jack always did. Over the years he'd had lawyer-explanations, with plenty of yes, yes, yes in them. Now his explanations were one big No.

In his office in midtown Manhattan, with the flashy art on the walls and all the plants growing under lights, Jack was big on plants, wouldn't even smoke his cigars in the same room with them, didn't want to poison his precious green pals. "It is strictly the I. R. and S., cookie," he'd said. "They are after you with a big hook, and what they want from you is m-o-a-n-y, heavy green."

. . . So what about the accountants, and the managers, who'd gotten all those fat fees from arranging business for Pick Up Truck, setting up corporations here and in Europe, which controlled the copyrights and the recording contracts, and all the piles of big bucks?

"They were wrong," said Jack. "I've saved what I could for you, but those guys were writing down expenses that don't stand up under examination. '72, '73, '74—every year is under audit. We'll be lucky if they let you keep your shoes."

He'd showed Chuck reams of pages, figures, itemized, all up and down the pages.

Like some damn jigsaw puzzle, a cat's cradle of complicated deals, copyrights that were cross-collateralized (whatever the hell that meant!), corporations had used them as assets to borrow money to buy assets, some of them had gone sour, big bucks here one day, gone tomorrow. "Can you blame the I.R. and S. for challenging it?" asked Jack.

"Where were you when all this happened?" asked Chuck.

"I got here late, remember?" said Jack. "I'm your salvage crew."

"Have I got *any* money?" asked Chuck.

"It's all down there in black and white, cookie," sighed Jack.

". . . It's not all down there!" Chuck protested. "All I see here is Notes Due. Unrecouped Losses. Amounts Owed!"

"Correct," said Jack. He was plump, and wore long sideburns, now white, and when he grinned, he looked like a cheerful Santa Claus with a big cigar. "You got the big picture, cookie. You're the Mayor of Wipe City. But as long as you got your health, and your talent, and that nice broad in Jersey to take care of you, you have Potential. You'll come back. I'm counting on you, cookie."

Get off my back, Mr. Tax Man
Get your ass out of here, right now—
Get lost, you heard me! right now—
You got all the bread you're gonna get
You picked me cleaner
Than a goddamn Perdue bird
So get off my back
I sure can't carry us both!

He'd made that up, sung it one night at the Ace of Spades Lounge, he was crocked, sure, how else could you play such a rathole. (Lucky to get the booking, it had taken a while to convince the owner.) Packed with young kids who really weren't listening much to him as he played out there, solo, all they wanted was disco. (Who is that creep out there with the guitar plucking away? Don't you know him, that's ah, oh yeah, I remember, Pick Up Truck. No shit? Say, I think I heard about them. Geeze, he's a real old-timer, right? Why's he singing all that garbage about the tax man? It's nowhere.)

(The owner had said, "Lissen, pal, why don't you knock off that shit about the taxes? My crowd comes here to have a good time, y'know?")

"That guy's been calling again," Sally said, serving him his dinner.

Sally Hecht, a pleasant chick, placid, she was a dietician at the hospital in Newark, she had the day shift, when he worked, it was nights, that meant they got together maybe two hours or so at suppertime.

"What guy?"

"The one who's collecting on that bill for your sound equipment, remember?" she said. "He left a final notice under the door—he knows I won't let him in. I told him this was my place—he has no right setting foot in these premises."

"You tell him, lady" he said.

"But you're going to have to pay him something, Chuck," she said. "You don't want them repossessing your equipment, do you?"

"I'll think about it," he said.

"Think hard, before he comes around again," she warned.

You're not so flashy as other chicks
You've got a tongue that's sharp
You always know just what the score is
And you tell me,
And tell me, and tell me, oh how you tell me.
But I don't mind 'cause you're telling me truth
And I'm telling it to you right back.
You're not so flashy as other chicks
But right now I'm glad you're around,
So let me stick around—

(Hell, that didn't work, did it?)

. . . He hadn't been able to finish that one, and he wasn't sure he'd play it for her, anyway. She was a fan, right, and nobody should dump on a fan, not only that, this was her semidetached garden apartment he was living in (not permanently, but right now this was It), and long ago he'd learned—don't fight with the landlady unless you're planning to move out.

"Haven't you got any bread to pay the man, Sally," he told her.

"Sell something," she suggested.

"Got nothing to sell," he said. "Got to keep the equipment, how else can I work—when I work?"

"You can sell sometthing else," she said. "That truck."

People let you down
Not my pickup truck.

Women leave you flat
Not my pickup truck. . . .

"Not my truck!" he yelled, outraged.

"Why not? It's a classic," she said. "Sure, I know how it hurts, but when it's time for surgery, you bite the bullet and take out the knife."

"I'll think of something else!" he told her.

Something . . . anything, to hang on to his Model AA.

"They're always holding auctions," she said. "You could send it off to one of them, and you probably could get five, six thousand—that would keep you going until you hit it big again," she said, nagging away. "You don't really drive it, do you?"

(True. If he needed to get anywhere, he borrowed her van and the precious little Model AA sat safely in her garage, here in the Jersey suburbs. He had it carefully covered in a tarp, up on blocks, engine checked each week or so, locked up so nobody else could get his hands on it.)

. . . Borrow some money from Jack Adler?

He was already into him for more than he could keep track of . . . but maybe—

"Listen, I have to hang on to that truck!" he said.

". . . Oh, Chuck," she clucked. ". . . It's just a piece of machinery."

"Bullshit! It's more than that!" he said.

She came over to where he sat on her couch, she moved in beside him. She smelled vaguely of food—no matter how often she scrubbed and used toilet water, there was always that faint aura of meals, Eau de Cuisine . . .

"You're a big talent," she said. "Right now it's rough, but you're going to be back up there some day—"

"What is this?" he asked. "Group Therapy II? Ego massage, a speciality?"

"Look," she said, "if I had the money, you know I'd give it to you. But right now, what's the alternative? Those bastards won't give up, and if he gets a sheriff out there to take your equipment, you can't earn your living driving a truck!"

"What living?" he snarled.

"There's also the possibility that they could move into the garage and attach the truck itself," she warned.

". . . You sure think of all the nice things, don't you?" he said.

". . . *Think* about it," she urged. "Would you promise me that much?"

"If you promise not to nag me any more," he said.

You always know just what the score is
And you tell me, and tell me again
You figure when you let me slip it to you
You got the right to slip it back, right?
So knock it off, baby, knock it off!
Or . . .

(Or *what?*)

Another unfinished number. (Lately he had a lot of those.)

She went to bed early. He sat up, watching TV and pulling at the beer he'd brought in, trying to fiture out what to do. Of course she was right. The bastards would move in on him if he didn't pay soon.

There was one possibility.

. . . Transfer the title to Sally. Sure, that way, they couldn't get their dirty paws on his truck! . . .

(Oh, very shrewd, baby. Once they couldn't take the truck, they'd attach the equipment for sure, and where would that leave him, if not at the top of the creek, without even a guitar string to hang by?)

No, the answer was just what Sally had suggested. *Sell.*

Around midnight, whenever, he'd lost track of time now, he went outside, back to the garage, cool night, a couple of dogs barking in the distance, he let himself in through the side door. Snapped on the light.

Swathed in her tarp, she sat there, quietly, waiting for him.

Chuck pulled away at the heavy plastic until he had uncovered the cab. Opened the door and climbed into the front seat, the springs squeaked softly beneath his weight.

The key was on his keyring; he turned on the ignition.

. . . The tiny gas gauge (old Henry Ford had never been one for flash, had he?) indicated there was still a quarter of a tank.

Knock out the cement blocks, release her, turn on the ignition, start that reliable little four-cylinder engine, back her out the door, take her for a nice spin

Fly a little higher every hour
Soarin' along so fine

. . . Or there was another possibility.

Leave the back door shut tight, all he had to do was to sit there, behind the wheel, ten, fifteen minutes was all it would take, bye bye Chuck, you want a way to stop seeing New Jersey out the window every day? This one is the best. Cheap, efficient . . . fast.

Snap it on, inhale. You want to fly, this is the way. Final flight, you and baby here, and you'll have fucked 'em all, the bill collectors, the saloonkeepers who don't like your style, the asshole kids who used to love you but don't know who you are any more, the thieves who've stolen you blind, the connivers and the fawners and the bullshit throwers, the ones that don't *listen*—

They won't bother you any more, no way, baby.

Will that make them listen?

Oh yeah, sure, all the thieves who stole your record masters will hustle them out in new editions. (MEMORIAL TO PICK UP TRUCK: THEIR 20 GREATEST HITS!)

. . . But you won't be around to see it, Chuck, not you, nor Al, nor little Billy Kress, will you?   uh uh.

. . . No, it wasn't check-out time yet.

He yanked the key out of the ignition and put it back into his pocket.

Got out, gently closed the door. Replaced the tarp.

Patted the hood.

(What the hell, baby, no matter how much I love you, you have to face it, you are just a goddamned piece of River Rouge machinery. If it's time for one of us to go, it better be *you*, not me.)

Because *I*'m the one with the talent.

Bye, baby.

He snapped off the light and went back into the house.

 Tulsa

G. Dudley Lester's style may have seemed mighty relaxed and for-damn-sure casual to all those country-club Tulsa folks with whom he'd played cards, golfed, drank, and swapped Polish jokes. But once he'd settled the auction deal with Joyce and Old Ed, signed the paper that made him a partner in the joint venture they'd set up with the lawyers, there was nothing amateurish about his input, nos*sir.*

For starts, he'd gotten them in touch with a PR firm in Chicago, an outfit that could also handle graphics and lay out the advertising. After a couple of meetings with the two hot-shot kids who'd been assigned to service the account, the campaign evolved, with G. Dudley riding herd. ". . . We want to keep the feeling of a home-town affair," he instructed, "and at the same time, we appeal to the good old American impulses—preserve the past, safety of your investment *and* get-rich-quick."

The initial announcement and story heralding The First Southwestern Classic and Vintage Car Auction was planted in various trade magazines and papers all over the country, as well as in Europe. "That's where a lot of our customers will be coming from, those West Germans who are lying awake nights worrying about their Eastern pals taking them over, the Italians, the French—they all know about classic cars. They buy for two reasons—investment, and if they need it, a quick getaway."

"How do we get to the rich A-rabs? Advertise in A-rab papers?" asked Joyce.

"Hell no," said G. Dudley. "Them we get to through the *London Times* and the *Wall Street Journal.*"

"And the Japs?" she asked. "How do we get them to come?"

". . . They're already here," he said. "At home on your range."

He put Joyce to work on logistics. The rental of the Arena, the staffing, the negotiations for the catering and for other concessions, as well as the catalog.

"You're going to handle all of that while I'm away," he told her.

"Where you goin'?" she asked.

"I've got to go find us some salt for the old mine," he said.

Dismayed, she listened as he patiently explained. In order to attract a profitable herd of free-spending buyers and sellers to Tulsa, there would have to be offered a few items of seductive merchandise.

Such as what?

Oh . . . a rare Rolls. Possibly an old Duesenberg, a choice Pierce-Arrow, perhaps a car attributed to a celebrity, someone like a movie star, or a gangster from the '30s.

How did one go about assembling such wares?

It took some planning. One could purchase mailing lists from an outfit in Colorado; names of interested hobbyists and automobile owners. They would get a direct mailing, with a follow-up Mailgram, and then a phone call. Then, through some judicious maneuvering, G. Dudley had secured a list of live ones from a shadowy character in Paris, a certain party he knew who had access to auction records of a major house that had held several prior sales of such cars in the past year or so. "These people we call personally," he explained. "The way the market's going, some of them must be ready to take profits on what they've bought." Then there were private collectors, here in the Southwest, or up North and out in California and Nevada, the really fat cats here and abroad who for reasons known only to themselves and to their accountants wished to remain anonymous. They would need a visit by a representative of the auctioneers who would convince them to consign a car or two, a choice item, to Tulsa.

". . . Who's supposed to do that?" asked Joyce.

"I am," said G. Dudley.

". . . You're goin' to leave your Joyce, just like that?" she protested.

7 6

"It's strictly business," said G. Dudley. "You'll be minding the old store while I go drag us in a few star items."

". . . When will you be back?" she sighed.

"When I get the job done," he said.

"Oh, Lord, I'm goin' to *miss* you," she said, clutching him with fervor.

". . . I know, I know," he soothed. "This isn't going to be easy for me, either."

"You mean that?" asked Joyce.

". . . Oh, of course I do," murmured G. Dudley. "Don't you think I'd rather be here with you, instead of dragging my tail all over hell and gone, trying to persuade people to consign their cars?"

". . . I'm goin' with you!" vowed Joyce.

"Nothing would make me happier," he told her. "But this is something I have to do alone."

He spent several weeks away from Tulsa, and left her no forwarding address.

Nor did he call, or even send a postcard.

G. Dudley was enjoying his new-found solitude.

Truth was, he had never expected to extend his stay in Tulsa for such an extended length of time, and had it not been for the vintage car auction deal, which had popped up so unexpectedly, he would have departed Joyce's premises long before this.

G. Dudley's was not the sort of mind that can enjoy listening to a female prattle on endlessly about which color scheme would be right when she redid her living room. Or which of her friends she deemed suitable to invite over for drinks and barbecue. Nor could he whip up any sustained interest in the problems of Joyce's dearest friend, Ellie Sue Winters, whose third marriage was breaking up because her dentist husband was fooling around with his hygienist. The endless problems of what to wear, her hair-do, or her backhand may have been sufficient to keep Joyce occupied, but they certainly did not concern G. Dudley.

Once, long ago, G. Dudley had discovered a basic truth about sex. While it was happening, it was surely pleasant. When it was over, during the postcoital lull, what was there to talk about?

With Joyce, there was less and less sex, and more and more lull.

So, when G. Dudley, who did not necessarily relish travel, eagerly ducked out of Tulsa to disappear from her sight (and sound) it was a sign. And if Joyce Donaldson Wade had been a trifle more perceptive about this attractive, knowledgeable, well-dressed unmarried gent whom she had latched on to and so quickly learned to cherish, if she had been more of an educated G. Dudley Lesterwatcher, she would have picked up on his extended absence as the first indication that, where she was concerned, for G. Dudley, the bloom was beginning to rub off her apples.

But then, Joyce did not know that much about him, yet—to understand that she was far from the first, nor would she be the last person, male or female, to have been romanced, seduced . . . and then dumped, by G. Dudley Lester.

 ## London

Cyril Banks, for one.

The managing director of the MG, that oh-so-trendy private restaurant-disco-club on Davies Street, in Mayfair, some thousands of miles to the east of Tulsa, Oklahoma, he could certainly be called a survivor, not only of life, but of G. Dudley Lester.

. . . Dozing beneath the eiderdown, in his large double bed in the rear room of his small flat in Belsize Park, in a remodeled Victorian mansion off Haversock Hill. Through the velvet drapes the faint rays of the sun fought unsuccessfully to pierce the grey clouds. It seemed about to rain. Despite the double-glazing of those ancient windows, the damp seeped in. Cyril closed his eyes . . . a bit more sleep. He'd earned it, God knows.

He felt a gentle tugging, and then a warm tongue lapped at his earlobe, a warm body moved against his.

. . . Who? . . . ah, yes . . .

The Canadian. A tiny black girl. He'd picked her up at Cinema I on Oxford Street some days ago, chatted her up about Fellini and Ingmar Bergman, brought her home, they'd fallen into the double bed, then she'd gotten up and made him a marvelous supper. ". . . You're a great lay and a superb cook," he'd said. "What else do you do?"

". . . Nothing," she told him. She explained her job. She worked here in London as a cook, not in a home, but on some bloody big yacht that was anchored down off St. Catherine's Dock. It belonged to some corporation, which used it for entertaining, and she was on permanent galley duty. "A cook on yachts?" he'd mused. ". . . Sounds like some Russian officer." He'd dubbed her Cookanyats.

The ideal guest, she stayed over occasionally. Grateful for the size of his bed and his bath. Quiet, well read, she made him marvelous impromptu meals and spent the rest of the time listening to his collection of jazz records . . . perceptive girl, she'd learned to understand his moods. If he were busy and had no time for small chat, she would find something else to occupy herself. Never took it personally.

. . . Right now she was occupied. Her hands were moving across his back, her nails scratching gently. ". . . Time to get up, sir," she crooned. "You left a call." Her fingers were plucking away at the buttons of his pajamas. ". . . Just time enough for this before your breakfast."

". . . Thanks, no," sighed Cyril. "I need to sleep."

"Sleep is for the old," she scolded, and expertly tugged him about into a more accessible position. ". . . You asked me to wake you," she reminded him.

". . . I was only being polite," said Cyril. Eyes closed, he savored the fragrance of her insistent mouth.

It was not a question of age, he was tired. He had been up until almost three this morning at the MG, seeing to Ben Emir and his noisy party of friends and assorted hangers-on, waiting for them all to finish eating prime Scotch beef and swilling down Veuve Cliquot from the wine cellar. Anyone else he would have politely pitched out into the street long before that, but how did one eject Ben Emir?

He was the owner, from whom all of Cyril's current blessings flowed, and the MG was Ben Emir's private London playground. It was the young Arab's bottomless bank accounts here and in Switzerland that had financed the lease on that expensive building in Mayfair in which the MG had been established, a year or so ago. His flow of petrodollars that had endowed a pouf decorator, who'd done up the restaurant's premises in dark brown antique paneling and elegant yellow drapes. Ben Emir's capital had stocked the cellars, outfitted the kitchens, hired the staff, and installed the expensive sound system in that dark pit which was the basement disco club. (Members Only.) On the floor above the restaurant was a lavish suite of living quarters where Ben Emir stayed, and played, whenever he visited London. And it was Ben Emir's British bank manager who saw to it that whatever deficits accrued to the MG accounts each month were made up by fresh infusions of cash.

So when Ben Emir entertained, which was often, Cyril made certain that his young senior partner's every wish was gratified. Smiled at Ben Emir's quips, massaged his ego, and did a constant job of protecting this Arabian goose who laid, not only every young bird he could, but golden eggs as well.

If one had to have a partner, there were worse ones than Ben Emir. Far worse. Noisy, a bit rough around the edges, somewhat like a nervous puppy who constantly needed reassurance, Ben Emir presented few problems. He needed cajolery, a bit of flattery here and there, all designed to bolster his sense of security in a foreign country. Actually, in a peculiar sort of way, since they'd become involved in the MG, Cyril had become fond of the plumpish Arab. He felt a certain kinship with him. For no matter how hard he tried, nor how freely he spent and spent, Ben Emir would never push his way through into the upper-class world he so fancied here in England . . . and Cyril, the youngest son of a failed suburban shopkeeper whose name had originally been Berkowitz, understood that, knew the feeling.

For all their money, their Saville Row bespoke clothing and their expensive cars, their jewelry from Asprey's and their property investments, the private jets which whisked them to and fro across continents, these affluent Arab lads—of which Ben Emir was certainly one of the most—were somehow uncomfortable in London. No matter how rich they were, they would still remain wogs . . . just as a third or fourth generation British Jew, no matter how Anglicized, was and always would be a yid.

England in the '70s might have become the new Arab playground, but it wasn't an Arab colony, yet. It was an old British trick . . . to welcome the invader, sell him what he wants, and then ignore him, until he goes away.

Oh yes, in transactions that called for cash, the Arabs were adored. For them, Harrod's would stay open past closing hours, and frock-coated salesmen fawned on them. Women? No problem there. Any attractive bird was available to them. Everyone heard the stories; that milk-complexioned blonde salesgirl at Gucci who'd been propositioned by some oil-rich young twit who'd asked how much she'd take—not for the leather bag in the window, but for herself. He'd kept on raising the price, and then she'd finally said "Ten thousand pounds to *you*," he hadn't batted an eye, but slipped her his room number at Claridge's. The following morning, she'd left the hotel, carrying a shopping bag filled with banknotes, gone straight off to her bank and put it away, the next day to buy her old mum a cottage in Stanmore.

Whatever they could buy, they bought. But entree to polite society, to the private clubs in Whitehall, to the races at Epsom or Newmarket, or to the great country houses . . . in that particular league, the Arabs like Ben Emir were immigrants, still outside the windows, noses to the glass, peering in.

. . . Which was why Ben Emir, when he was here, felt more comfortable spending nights in his own private club, on Davies Street, with Cyril Banks, knowledgeable native Britisher, to wait on him and steer him about. And it was also how Cyril could go on taking home a sheaf of cash each week, marking it down on the books as "Expenses Out Of Pocket," for the accountants, nipping a steady bit here from this "Suppliers' Account," and a piece there of "Petty Cash"—never anything too much, mind you, Cyril had long since learned the arts of keeping a low profile . . . and Ben Emir was not a complete fool. But what he took was enough for Cyril to get by with, here in 1979 Great Britain. No one was expected to survive these days on salary, with the officious little farts from Inland Revenue peering over one's shoulder, grabbing it all back from you with those bloody ridiculous taxes each year. One used one's wits, remembering always that it was every Englishman's duty to pay as little tax as possible, and the devil take the hindmost.

. . . Little Cookanyats was pleasuring them both now, thrusting herself against him with increasing urgency, humming softly in his ear, practicing her own subtle rhythmic changes. Sailing happily upstream on her own private voyage. Her eyes closed, biting her lip as she concentrated on sexual exercises . . . she might have been doing Sixth Form Gymnastics.

Lord, what energy these young ones had.

. . . Ah, well why not? He was her host, wasn't he?

. . . He turned her backwards, became a participant, and still weary as he was from last night, he summoned up enough energy to bring her to a sighing, delighted climax.

And dozed off again.

Which should have been the end of it, except that minutes later, she was up, dressed, humming cheerfully as if such a satisfactory lay was the most usual thing in her mornings, the same as brushing her teeth, and now she was solicitously inquiring might she make him a bit of breakfast before she went off to her tiny galley on the yacht?

Amazing, she was.

. . . Not that he hadn't been as young and reckless, once.

Years back, when he'd just come up to London, a regular Dick Whittington from the suburbs, out to carve himself a niche. It was that time in the early '60s when the city came to be called Swinging London.

Rock stars everywhere, riding high, followed by their groupies and exotic models, the gambling casinos with their posh crowds flinging money about. Long-haired kids packing Carnaby Street to buy up kinky clothes, huge new buildings replacing old mansions and shops, the city was a vast playground, a Restoration scene brought up to date. Junkies queuing up at Boots, in Piccadilly Circus each night for their fix, expense-account company Rollses tieing up traffic, and everywhere, in between the sober-suited clerks and stockbrokers, the girls in their miniskirts. Oh yes, all those ample bums, jiggling up and down as they hurried down the block ahead of you, the short ones pertly twisting their hips, waving their goodies for all the world to see, and then the long-legged girls with their ample thighs encased in thin tights, flesh often turning slightly blue on cold London mornings.

. . . It was enough to drive any young heterosexual who'd come up from a decent sheltered lower-middle-class home stark raving mad.

Those were the days when he'd saved up his cash, and gone into his first commercial venture. Valuable Motors, Ltd., out in that drafty set of nondescript sheds near Lissom Grove, working with his partner, old Len Hopwood. A positive genius, oh, a rogue of the first water was Len. Len had explained that there was a thriving future in flogging old British cars to the tourists who were everywhere, and he offered to cut young Cyril in to the pie. "One day, you'll thank me for the education, lad," said Len, and Cyril had signed on, that's how they had teamed up.

Len was as good as his word. He would disappear for a foraging trip down to the country and return bringing with him ancient Rileys and broken-down Morris Minors. Exotic old wrecks which had been garaged since Dunkirk, a Lagonda, prewar Humbers, of even an Armstrong-Siddeley. They'd disappear into Len's workshop, and he would perform miracles back there; he could tune up the sourest old Humber engine with strange concoctions of oil, curse at it until it ticked away like some contented expensive clock, and be sold for a packet. Len knew ways to erase the worst rust patches, did magician's tricks to restore chrome, could fabricate spare parts out of odd bits until they functioned perfectly in motors they'd never been designed for.

They hadn't much capital, so it was Len who got the idea to run over to France and round up a flock of those ridiculous little 2-CV

83

Citroëns, ramshackle open cars that French farmers drove until they disintegrated. He'd shipped them all back here to Lissom Grove, cleaned them up, overhauled those ridiculous washing-machine engines that powered them, but it was Cyril's genius notion to sell spray-paint cans with each one, so that the purchaser could do his own paint job in psychedelic colors. That brought in all those young swingers who needed cheap transport. ". . . Economical, simple to operate . . . *and* you can express yourself, eh?" was Cyril's cheerful sales pitch.

With Len out back, seeing to the inventory, and Cyril in front, wearing an ancient Harris tweed jacket (Len had insisted he dress the part . . . ". . . You can't deal with our sort of customer if you look like some bloody spiv," he'd warned. ". . . You're an eccentric, now, get it?") they were well and truly launched.

The bait was that smashing old Bentley Open Tourer they casually kept parked out front, and it drew in the buyers like a magnet. After that, it was simple enough. Cyril would ever so casually wander over and go into his understated sales pitch, which involved the inherent values of the old British craftsmanship. ". . . We're selling out our heritage, you know," he'd mourn. "All of it gone, mind you, except what you see here. Every time we sell a car, I feel as if I'd lost a piece of my family."

And they bought. Everything, even the most dilapidated prewar Austin, or any other wreck Len could turn up. When Cyril finished his spiel, the customer couldn't wait to write out his check, to secure a piece of British history.

Wrapped in his robe, Cyril finished the last bite of the delicious omelet *fines herbes* Cookanyats had so effortlessly whipped up. Sat back and sipped coffee while she did the dishes.

Soon he'd have to dress and go downtown to the MG, to start another day attending to all the boring nonsense involved in running the place. Arguing with the suppliers, riding herd on the staff. The trick with running a restaurant was to stay on top of everything, to check the smallest detail. You couldn't rely on anyone else to do your job. Turn your back, and the bastards would steal your eye-teeth.

And while it certainly was one of the smartest spots in London, a place Cyril could be proud of, operating the MG well wasn't a patch on the fun they'd had, back in Lissom Grove . . .

". . . Must go now, love," said Cookanyats, and she began to assemble herself for her job on the water, bundling herself in that bulky naval pea jacket she fancied. When she had finished buttoning up, had stuffed her feet into gumboots and covered her head in a colorful woolen scarf, she looked exactly like a determined immigrant, headed across some Balkan border. "Now you take good care of yourself," she said, and patted him fondly on his head.

. . . As if he were her father. Which by God, such was the difference in their age, he might have been.

Although, had he bedded her mother, chances are Cookanyats might have turned out more of a light cocoa color . . .

". . . You too," he said. "Will I be seeing you again soon, my love?"

She shrugged. "There's talk of a cruise to the Mediterranean. Algiers. Morocco . . . the Casbah. All those exotic places. Not that I'd mind, I could use a bit of sun." She kissed him. ". . . So could you," she said. "How would you like me to smuggle you aboard the yacht?"

"As what?" he asked.

". . . As my own private stowaway," she said. "Then we could explore those places together. Have you ever been down there?"

He nodded.

". . . Will I like them?" she asked.

"Cover up your face with a sheet and don't go out alone," he warned. "I wouldn't want to lose you."

She giggled. "Who knows, perhaps I'll find some rich old merchant who'll fancy me, why not? What can I bring you as a souvenir?"

"Just this," he said, giving her behind a pat. "Un-contaminated, if you please."

". . . My, you do know how to flatter a girl, sir," she said, before she went out the door.

. . . Did he know those places?

Yes, and quite a few other sun-drenched resort cities. In Spain and on the Algarve, in Portugal, Tunisia, Majorca, and the Canaries. All of them thronged with affluent tourists, searching for low-cost winter alternatives to dark Britain.

That had been the bait which IOI, Ltd. dangled so seductively in front of the poor shivering pigeons, wasn't it?

IOI Ltd. His own particular Waterloo.

. . . where he'd met and been defeated by that outstanding tactician, Mr. George D. Lester.

Lester, the Vanished.

He was one of the waves of Americans who'd swarmed ashore into London, back in the '60s.

They were everywhere, it seemed, those rebels from the colonies who'd invaded England. Some of them assigned here by the large oil companies, others as junior bank executives staffing all those new American branches that were moving pell-mell into the City. Permanent types, not mere tourists, welcomed with six-months renewable Visitors' Permits by a British government that didn't worry about their presence unless they planned to replace worthy Britons in their British jobs. (At British salaries? Not bloody likely!)

They settled in at enormous rents in houses in the suburbs, or in Hampstead, others taking root in Fulham, or Chelsea. The more affluent ones roosted in Belgravia, clustered about Eaton Place and Chester Square. Those were usually Americans who'd come here to take advantage of the Eady Plan, by which films could be financed with generous British subsidies, or they were advertising men handling international-type accounts. You saw and heard them everywhere, oh-ing and ah-ing over the quaintness of the British countryside (which all of the natives were only too happy to evacuate, when given the chance), grumbling over the lack of decent central heating and whose idiotic idea had it been to put those silly pipes on the outside walls of buildings so that they constantly froze? (And were by the same token more readily available to the plumber . . . if and when he finally arrived.) They filled the good restaurants, where they complained audibly over the lack of any decent corned beef (the salt beef was far too fatty), they whined about British inefficiency and bureaucracy (as if they'd been the first to discover it) . . . but still they continued to move in.

And they bought. Like a plague of affluent locusts . . . Saturdays they pounded through Portobello Road or Islington, grabbing up antiques and silver and rugs. The shrewder ones soon learned to get over to Bermondsey at 5 A.M. of a miserable cold Friday morning, where the dealers came in to trade with each other, and to pursue the hunt by flashlight.

. . . Mr. George D. Lester was certainly one of the shrewdest, although in his unostentatious dark blue blazer, with his pleasant smile and somewhat naive manner, no one would ever have picked him out of a crowd as one of the most artful of dodgers.

He'd turned up at Valuable Motors, Ltd., just in time to encounter that '49 knife-edged Bentley four-door sedan, in top condition, a real prize that Len had literally stolen through the simple expedient of placing an advert in the *Times*. ("Dealer wishes to purchase antique Rolls or Bentley, '40s or '50s R-type. Highest prices paid promptly; satisfaction guaranteed. Box 788.")

For several weeks, there'd been no response, and then—jackpot! A strange little chap had turned up, meekish, with glasses and a toothbrush mustache, he called and then drove up, bringing up this immaculate Bentley, not a scratch or a nick on it, with a mere 9,000 miles on the odometer after fifteen years? He'd sold it to Len for a ridiculous 750 quid, they'd paid him on the spot, and then, when he'd signed the papers, Len, feeling a bit guilty, had asked ". . . pardon me sir, but now that you've got rid of this, would you mind telling me why you wanted to wished to sell such a fine specimen?"

". . . Well, actually," replied the little chap, "my mother had always insisted it was far too grand for me."

They'd put it out on the floor, and almost the first person who'd wandered in was this American, and when he'd asked the price, Cyril had tripled it. He hadn't blinked an eye, merely pulled out his checkbook and begun to write . . . so who'd been so bloody smart? Cyril knew he could have asked even more. Ah well, not to be greedy.

Following day, he'd returned to take the car away with him, but insisted that Cyril join him out at the local for a friendly pint or two.

". . . You know something?" he said, as they drank. ". . . You're one hell of a good salesman, Cyril. You've got the gift."

. . . Of course he had. Cyril had discovered that for himself months before, when the business had begun to flourish, and each successive sale had fortified his own self-confidence. Now that he was sailing along with old Len, taking down a nice profit on his original investment (borrowed from his mother) and living fairly well, (paying the old lady a bit of his weekly profits, why not?) he didn't need anyone, not even this rich American to flatter him. He knew damned well he was good.

But Mr. Lester wasn't about to stop there. ". . . I'll tell you something else, old friend," he continued, on the third round of drinks, ". . . I'd damned well rather have you working for me, rather than against me. Maybe someday, I will, eh?"

. . . That was how the seduction began, and he, Cyril Banks, so bloody sure of himself, eh? hadn't been bright enough to smell it. He'd never for one moment suspected what was going on.

Old Len had, though. Right off. Perhaps because it took one to know one, but whatever it was, he hadn't taken to their new customer, Mr. George Lester, of IOI, Ltd., not at all. ". . . It's nothing I can put my finger on, mind you," said Len, "but he's a proper rogue, that one."

"A successful one," he'd said.

". . . No matter," said Len. "I wouldn't want to walk down a dark street with him behind me, mind."

But when you were young and feckless, you didn't take advice, did you now, not from your father nor even from a wise old Len. No indeed, you were Cyril Banks, moving rapidly up in the world, England had changed, there were opportunities for lower-class youths that had never existed before, even cockneys were making it big, so were East End barrow boys, why not you? Here was a rich American magnate cooing sweet nothings in your ear and telling you about the exciting opportunities there were at IOI Ltd. in these exciting times—

IOI stood for International Overseas Investments, Ltd. There were other names engraved on the firm's demure letterhead, but they were strictly dummies, placed there to conform to the British investment regulations, window dressing. Were one to investigate past the letterhead, one would discover that the entire operation belonged to Mr. George D. Lester (U. S. A.), Managing Director, and it was a brilliant one, one that fulfilled a need, while appealing to greed. (Come to think of it, that might have been the proper motto. He'd suggested it one evening, after a busy day, but no one in the office could translate it into Latin!)

IOI, Ltd. furnished investors with a means by which they might squirrel away their capital into tax-sheltered resort homes, far from England. Such a simple plan; the firm offered them sunny flats in newly built blocks in Torremolinos, or villas in North Africa and Majorca. Once the investment had been made (easy financial terms were available through certain banks), the title would be transferred to the purchaser, and he would now have the best of both worlds. A place to travel to with his wife and family, to enjoy the sea and the warm rays of the sun . . . and when he returned to his dark grey home and hearth, he could sustain himself with the income derived from the rental of his vacation property to other, less fortunate tenants. Could one wish for more?

IOI, Ltd. was housed in a set of fancy offices in Hertford Street, with substantial antique furniture and tasteful hunting prints on the walls. The staff was mainly lovely young birds who answered the phones and discussed prospective purchases with the potential investors, most of whom had been drawn in by the seductive adverts which called to them from the Sunday travel sections. The emphasis was on underselling; the entire operation exuded affluence, with a warming sense of reassurance for the buyer, that poor shivering sod whose wife was nagging him to find them someplace where she could get a bit of sun. With the assistance of IOI, Ltd., those precious beams became tax-free, nay, profitable. No wonder they queued up to sign contracts.

. . . Cyril finished shaving himself, wiped his face, and patted on cologne. Then he stared at himself in the mirror. Pale white, no color at all. Lord . . . he could use a bit of that same sun right now, eh? In the old days, he'd have packed a bag, grabbed up whichever girl was available, driven out to Heathrow in a company limousine, and a few hours later he'd be lounging away on a white beach. And written off the entire jaunt to "Advertising and Promotion."

Certainly he had succumbed to George D. Lester's siren song. Who could have turned down such an offer? The American had made it all so unbelievably attractive. A nontaxed weekly drawing account with so many pounds involved that it was obscene. Commission on each flat or villa that he succeeded in selling to the prospects who crowded the offices, and the money to be banked to his account in a foreign bank, away from the Inland Revenue. A company car for his own personal use, an expense account which covered his rent, his travel, his entertaining. Far more than enough coming in each week for him to move to a decent Chelsea mews flat, to buy closets filled with the latest style in threads (no longer that stupid Harris tweed jacket), to spend his evenings with any bird he fancied, to buy her wine at whatever fashionable place he chose, to feed her, take her gambling, or dancing, before he bedded her.

. . . He'd never once asked himself *why me?* No reason to. In his own naiveté, he'd simply assumed—George D. Lester had selected him as his Sales Rep, he'd delivered, that was all there was to it.

. . . Of course, when he'd come to tell old Len that he'd made up his mind to join the IOI, Ltd. staff, that he was willing to sell out his minor interest in Valuable Motors Ltd. because he was on his way to become a property magnate, with the assistance of a perceptive American businessman who knew a young Dick Whittington with business genius when he spotted him, old Len had looked up from whatever engine he'd been rebuilding, and then he'd shaken his head. ". . . It's no good, my boy," he'd said, gloomily. "Old Newton knew what it was all about. The air is bound to come out of

90

that balloon, and it comes down, you'll be fortunate if you end up outside Wormwood Scrubs.''

Why did Len resent Lester so?

''. . . Because he's a proper thief,'' said Len.

"We've done our share of *that*," said Cyril.

'' 'Course,'' said Len. ''but we always give some value for money. You better watch yourself around that Yank.''

"I can take care of myself," he'd answered, annoyed at the old boy's negative stubbornness. ''. . . I wasn't born last Monday, was I?''

''. . . As the old maid said to the burglar,'' replied Len, and went back to his engine.

. . . And for quite a while there, several years it was, everything at IOI, Ltd. on Hertford Street went along swimmingly, didn't it, like a knife through soft cheese. Oh, those were the days, my friends, we thought they'd never end, with satisfied investors plunking down their pound notes, and a very healthy stream of black ink pouring into the firm's accounts.

Hanging on to George Lester's bespoke coattails, he'd had one smashing ride, always onwards and upwards. He was on his way; fairly soon now, he'd have assembled sufficient capital of his own to consider investing, not merely in a flat, but a block of flats, perhaps in those new developments down in the Algarve, a lovely site overlooking the ocean, near the golf club, perfect for retired British. And then, after that, he'd have enough credit to begin looking for a land property of his own, a piece or two which would put him into the same class as one of those major developers who were all coining such huge profits—

In the midst of all of that euphoria, without warning, Mr. George D. Lester, the glib and successful Managing Director of IOI Ltd. pulled the plug.

. . . let the air out of the balloon.

One dark and gloomy Monday, Cyril had returned from a trip to Portugal, to meet with Lester and to discuss the final plans for yet another development. This one would be the takeover of a hotel in Hammamet, in Tunisia, which IOI, Ltd. would proceed to syndicate to eager investors. ". . . Sorry," said the secretary. "He hasn't returned, and we haven't heard from him in several days."

Well, there was nothing out of the way about that, was there? Mr. Lester was given to dropping out of sight for periods of time . . . but he always turned up again, bright and cheerful, usually bringing with him the plans for some new and exciting financial venture tucked in his expensive attaché case.

Except that, by the end of that week, he'd still not returned, and when Cyril, still happy as a clam and unsuspecting, went down to the firm's bankers in the City, to see about the preparation of funds to cover IOI, Ltd's weekly payroll, he was abruptly informed by the bank manager in charge of the accounts that this day there weren't sufficient funds available to cover such a withdrawal.

. . . Why not?

Well, it seemed that a good deal of IOI, Ltd's capital was no longer here in London. Over the past few weeks, there had been a series of withdrawals from said accounts, the funds delivered to a bank account in Beirut, to a certain Bank of Asia, Ltd.

Ah well, that meant that Mr. Lester was obviously doing some sort of deal in Lebanon, eh?

. . . But there was still the matter of necessary cash, on an immediate basis. For the first week, the London bank arranged an overdraft, but a few days later, when Mr. Lester had still not returned, Cyril began to worry.

Far too late, as it turned out.

When he had finally gotten through to Lebanon—the Bank of Asia, Ltd. being difficult to locate, and even harder to reach by telephone, or by cable, some functionary there informed him that, ah yes, there were such accounts, but that their balance had been only recently depleted, alas.

. . . By whom?

By Mr. George Lester, in whose name they had been opened.

And where was the firm's money now? Ah, my dear sir, that was not the Bank of Asia's business, was it?

. . . And where was Mr. Lester? In Beirut?

"That is a question we are unable to answer," said the Lebanese gentleman. End of conversation.

In a matter of days, International Overseas Investments, Ltd. of Hertford Street, with its phalanx of satisfied customers who'd left their funds in the firm's treasury to cover "Running Expense and Overhead," etc, etc, had been abruptly transformed from a thriving respectable venture—

—into an empty shell.

Cyril scarcely had time to ponder this puzzle—the motives that would impel an otherwise shrewd businessman with the talent and ability of George D. Lester—to loot his firm and vanish with the proceeds—to tear down the structure he had devised, rip it apart, without warning—

—before he found himself dangling from the gibbet.

Beset by angry creditors, solicitors waving writs. Raging betrayed investors flocking into Hertford Street, jamming the firm's offices, drawn by some underground telegraph that had pounded out the disastrous rumors—

—all of them converted in a grim circle around the only visible executive left (the rest of the staff, unpaid, had jumped ship) a bewildered Cyril Banks.

The papers seized upon the story with ill-disguised glee.

PROPERTY MAGNATE RIDDLE!
SUN SEEKERS BILKED! . . .
. . . AMERICAN SCHEME
SWINDLES BRITONS!

Crash! went IOI, Ltd., and when the dust finally settled, Cyril had been able to rescue (only by grabbing them out of the closets of his now-padlocked flat, moments before the bailiffs had arrived there) two suitcases filled with his own clothing.

Everything else was gone with George D. Lester.

. . . And by that time, Cyril could no longer pass through the gates at Heathrow, or Gatwick, or even Stansted, and flee.

. . . There were Authorities who wished to ask some questions of him.

Dressed, Cyril put on his overcoat and locked up his small Belsize Park flat. Time to get downtown and to do an honest day's work at Ben Emir's MG. He went down the steps to the sidewalk, where his small car was parked. On the windshield was a parking citation, which he carefully removed and tucked into the glove compartment. There it would stay until this evening, when he'd return, park again for the night, and replace the citation in its customary spot, dangling from the wiper blade. Simple enough, it was an old trick that usually managed to appease whatever wandering metermaid might come down this quiet block . . .

He started the motor and steered his way out of the parking spot, into the street, and then towards Mayfair.

. . . It was some years now since l'affaire IOI, and he'd managed to put it out of his mind, but every so often, ugly memories of what transpired afterwards resurfaced.

Those court hearings, at which he had attempted to defend himself . . . His solicitors (whose fees had ultimately cleaned him out of whatever funds he had left) earnestly pleading that their client, Mr. Banks, had not been an accomplice, but merely the bewildered dupe of a master swindler. After all, they had argued, Mr. Banks could certainly not have been a party to Mr. Lester's vile machinations, else why would he have remained here in Great Britain, whilst the firm was being looted, and the hapless investors robbed? Was it ipso facto not evident that Mr. Banks had been easily as much of an innocent gull as the rest of those hapless Britons?

. . . The learned judges had taken the matter under advisement, and finally returned with findings that were astonishingly tempered with charity. Since Mr. Banks had been willing to testify so willingly, and to respond to all questions put to him, and since he had cooperated with the authorities in an effort to secure justice for the offended parties, there would be no charges brought to bear. He had obviously learned something of a lesson. Now he was free to seek other employment, hopefully (ahem, ahem) of a constructive nature.

. . . As to the absent Mr. Lester, the Court reserved judgment as to his behavior until he could be located. When he returned to Great Britain, he would then be dealt with.

It took a while before Cyril could reestablish himself as a man of commerce. There were not too many employers who wished to hire a young man whose recent brushes with the law had been so extensively covered by the press, and on the telly.

He'd gone back to Portobello Road again, but not to Valuable Motors, Ltd. which had long since gone out of business. He'd managed to get in with a very dykey antiques dealer, Mandy Pollock. She'd been one of those who'd sold furniture to decorate the IOI Ltd. offices in Hertford Street, but she was shrewd enough to have insisted that George D. Lester pay cash.

"I don't care a fig about your reputation," she'd said. "You're a good salesman. It's not your fault the bastard fingered you; you never knew what it was all about, eh?" That got him back on his feet . . . as the films put it, sadder but wiser.

Mandy eventually moved to grander quarters on Sloane Avenue, taking Cyril along with her. And that was when he'd finally run into old Len again.

Len had been off in the Far East, roaming through Hong Kong and Singapore and Malaysia, hunting down rare old prewar cars that had been stashed away by prosperous planters, and might still be there, long years later, under canvas in tea plantation sheds, waiting for a sharp bloke with the nose to track them down. And doing very well at it, thank you.

. . . They'd gone off to the local to have a few.

In all his extensive travels to Somerset Maugham country, had Len ever turned up any sign of a Mr. George D. Lester?

. . . Alas, he had not. And old Len was tactful enough not to remind Cyril of his original warning about that artful American bastard. For which Cyril was grateful.

". . . I can forgive him most of it," Cyril said, two drinks later.

9 5

"Fiddling the customers, hell, that was part of the game. But doing *me*—I was a part of it—like his own right arm. Inside. Why'd he fiddle *me*?"

"It wasn't anything personal," said old Len. "He can't help himself, the poor bleeder."

"Meaning what?" asked Cyril.

"Look here," said Len. ". . . There's some as can't stand failure. That's most of the world—all those sods who ride the Underground each day. But they've got no choice except to suffer with it, right? So they do. But then, there are some as can't stand success, see? They're a rarer bunch. So they call it quits, just when they're doing great. Sometimes you can see them at the roulette wheel, tossing the chips away because they feel so damn guilty about being successful, see? Your fella—he's one of 'em—only he's greedy. He took the chips with him . . ."

". . . Rotten bastard," murmured Cyril.

". . . By the way, whatever became of that lovely old knife-edge Bentley we flogged him?" asked old Len.

". . . The bailiffs took it," said Cyril, sadly. "Sold it to satisfy the creditors."

"Why didn't *you* buy it?" asked Len.

". . . With what?" he'd replied.

". . . Well, never fear, he's bound to surface again," said Len, paying for the drinks.

"Not here in England," said Cyril.

". . . Wherever," said Len. "And when he does, you can go ask him to his face why he fiddled you. And when he gets done telling you how bad he feels, he'll probably invite you in to be his partner again. And you'll say yes to him."

"Why'd you think that?" demanded Cyril.

". . . Because deep down inside," old Len had said, "you admire the swine."

"You may know all there is to know about cars," Cyril had said, "but you don't know about me. I can be fucked once—but not twice."

". . . As the old maid said to the burglar," grinned Len.

*   *   *

Fairfield, Connecticut

Benita Lorenzo followed the old man through the large rooms of Mrs. Laura Richards Fox's mansion. The place was like some warehouse, or a resort hotel out of season; the furniture sat swathed in dust cloths, the floors echoed with their footsteps in rooms where the carpets had been rolled up.

. . . It hadn't been easy to persuade him to take her on this tour. When she showed up at the gates below, old Mr. Hyde had come out and stared at the business card she'd handed him, the one she'd borrowed from Tom Poulos.

". . . Nobody told me anything about you," he'd muttered.

She'd explained that she'd been in the neighborhood, merely wanted to take a look if possible, that her office (which was stretching it considerably, she hadn't yet taken the state exam) specializing in listing larger properties, she'd hinted at a client who was looking for a house exactly like this one, with its beautiful landscaping, and a terrific view of the Sound.

". . . You don't look like a real-estate agent," he'd said, giving her the once-over.

"We come in all shapes and sizes," she'd replied, flashing her most persuasive smile.

"The place is pretty well closed up," said the old man. "Maybe you'd better call the lawyers first—"

"Of course I will," said Benita. "But I could save so much time if I took a quick look—then I'd know what I was talking about . . ."

She'd used all her talents. What the hell, she was good with the old ones, wasn't she, after all these months at Wayside Gardens?

Better than she thought. He'd finally agreed to let her in. She'd driven up to the main house in her Pinto, with him going along, then they'd gone inside, through room after room of the upstairs, and now down.

Soon, they'd get through with this tour, and then hopefully, to the garage located beneath the house, where Mrs. Fox's Plymouth must be stored away.

97

. . . Or was it?

In her purse was a small knitting needle. If the car were there, and she could get near enough to the car, perhaps even to the wheels, then she might possibly grab a moment in which to scratch at the paint . . . to find out if old Gus had been telling her the truth about old Mrs Fox's Fort-Knox-on-wheels?

But that would have to be done very carefully. If at all.

So she followed him around, nodding appreciatively as he pointed out the paneling in the living room, then took her across the wide hall into the dining room with its broad windows, the massive marble fireplace, the intricate parquet flooring. A long dining table, a set of chairs, all covered.

Had she eaten here every day?

Yep. All by herself.

". . . Nobody builds like this any more," she said.

"Nope, not even the rich," he said.

". . . You worked for her a long time?"

"Practically my whole life," he said.

"If they sell this place, what'll you do?" she asked.

Mr. Hyde snorted. "Go die somewhere," he said, briefly.

He led her through a swinging door into one of several pantries that led from the dining room into an enormous kitchen.

Dedicated to feeding only one person?

She glanced around the room, with its vast old stove, double-doored refrigerators (two?), and endless cupboards. Larger than the entire Lorenzo apartment.

"That's about it," said Mr. Hyde. "Downstairs below here is a full basement, the furnace, oil tanks, a lot of other rooms, and the garage—"

"Oh, could I see them?" she asked.

"Nothing much there," he said, dubiously.

". . . Just to get an idea," she urged.

He shrugged, then opened a heavy door and snapped on lights. Below was a flight of stairs going down. "This way," he said.

His feet clumped on the wooden stairs, and she followed him. Was it in the garage? Her pulse began to beat faster.

Downstairs, in various storerooms, she could see lawn mowers, rollers, and all sorts of equipment. Then through an open door, she could see the garage.

On the walls, tacked neatly, were license plates dating back to the 1930s. Three empty spaces; no cars. And then, there in the distance, at the far end, stood a small black four-door sedan.

Demure. Forlorn.

The 1933 Plymouth.

Her heart was pumping; she swallowed, then spoke, very calmly.

". . . That's Mrs. Fox's car?"

"Yep," said Mr. Hyde. "The one there was so much fuss about."

She came closer to peer at it. Immaculate, paint gleaming, there in the yellowing light, it waited meekly.

"Nice," she said.

"I take it out for a spin each day," said Mr. Hyde. "Needs to be run. Rotten for a car if she just sits there."

"Just like a human being," said Benita, her eyes on the wheels.

The hubcaps were small and demure. Around the rims, next to the whitewall tires, were chrome discs. On the wheels, the black paint shone. Not a speck of dust anywhere.

. . . How could she possibly get near enough to scratch at that damn paint?

"Seen enough?" asked Mr. Hyde.

". . . I'm wondering, what's going to happen to this car?" she asked.

He stared at her.

". . . You a car dealer, too?" he asked, finally.

"Oh no," said Benita. "But it's such a special little car—it ought to be kept by somebody who'd appreciate it—"

"Ahh! It's just a *thing!*" said Mr. Hyde, harshly. "No more—no less. People get crazy about things—they figure they'll last forever. She wanted to take this with her—wherever she was going—and they stopped her, the greedy SOBs—so what the hell difference does it make now? Where you and me're gonna end up, nobody needs a goddamned 1933 Plymouth, now do they?"

"But it ought to have a decent home," she said, startled by his outburst.

She edged closer to it.

He snorted. "*I*'m the one needs a decent home," he said. "Tell me—what's the good of all her money *now,* hey? Tight old bitch!"

". . . You didn't like her?" she asked.

"Listen," said Mr. Hyde, cryptically, "if it was up to me, I'd set fire to her whole damn place and run by the light of it."

She put a hand on the door handle, but he waved her away.

"Lookee, but no touchee," he warned. "Done enough sight-seeing?"

Damn him—she needed only a moment or two to get out her knitting needle and scratch the paint—

"Did you hear a phone ring?" she asked.

"Nope," he said.

". . . I'm sure I heard one, upstairs," she said.

He shook his head. "They're disconnected. Let's go."

". . . But what are they going to do with this old car?" she asked.

"Sell it, that's what," he snapped. "Same as everything else around here. All going up for grabs—dealers coming to clean out the house, they'll subdivide the property so's the money grubbers can put up one of them rotten condos, or maybe a bunch of crappy little shoebox houses. You ought to know." He grinned, knowingly. "You're a nice looker, but you're just another one of the mice, rushing in to nip away at the cheese . . ."

"I'm *not,*" she told him, irritated.

. . . And frustrated. Less than three feet away from her hand was the tire, the wheel, and how could she get at it with this sarcastic old bastard lecturing her?

But why should she be so annoyed by his accusation?

After all, he had her figured right, didn't he?

. . . no, he didn't. She was here only because that crazy Gus had instructed her to come, to rescue this stupid little heap before it fell into other hands.

So, did that make her more virtuous than the other mice?

"Okay, excuse me," conceded Mr. Hyde. "You're different."

He walked over to the foot of the stairs that led back up. "End of tour," he said. "After this, you'd better do your talking to the lawyers. I got other things to do around here."

It was no use. She wasn't going to get even thirty seconds alone with this car, and if she pulled anything else now, this character would immediately smell something fishy. A wasted trip.

Reluctantly, she moved after him.

Turned, to take one more look at the Plymouth.

". . It *is* a nice car," she said, and surprised herself, because she meant it.

"You buy it," said Mr. Hyde, waiting for her to pass. "Then maybe they'll let *you* bury it with you."

She went past him, and slowly began to climb the stairs.

Glanced back, to see him still standing below, his sharp eyes watching as she moved upwards.

. . . Why the horny bastard!

He was looking up her skirt.

"Are *you* coming?" she demanded, as she reached the top.

"That'll be the day," he said, sadly.

When she'd driven him back down the drive to the gatekeeper's cottage, he got out of her car. "Wait here a minute," he told her, and went inside.

Hiding her irritation, she waited.

He came out and thrust a business card at her.

HITCHCOCK, DUFFY AND PALMER, *Attorneys-at-Law,* it read. Beneath the names was a New Haven address and a telephone number. "You want to talk about buying that car, they're the ones," he said.

Startled, she managed to keep a straight face.

"What makes you think I'd want to buy that car?" she asked.

". . . You mean, you don't?" he asked her.

Grinned, and opened the gates.

She drove out.

. . . Horny *and* wily, wasn't he?

How had he figured it out?

What next?

She'd have to go phone up those New Haven lawyers, find out which of them to talk to . . . and then, go up and discuss buying a 1933 Plymouth—

—Without knowing a damn thing more about the car than she had before she'd actually seen it.

Gamble that Gus had been telling her the truth. That the car was worth buying, sight unseen, take a chance on the heap.

. . . Okay, Benita, how else do you buy a car? If you buy it.

She took another shot at it, this time through the front door. She called Hitchcock, Duffy and Palmer, Attorneys-at-Law, in New Haven.

Mr. Hitchcock? Out of town.

Mr. Duffy? He had been deceased for several years.

What about Mr. Palmer? He was in court.

. . . Okay then, who was left in the office she could talk to?

In reference to what, please?

. . . The Fox estate.

The which?

Mrs. Laura Richards Fox, the lady who died a few months ago and—

Oh yes, the *Fox* estate. If she would hold the line, the operator would put her through to someone who might be able to assist her. What was the name, please?

Lorenzo. Miss Benita Lorenzo.

Of which firm?

No firm. A personal call.

. . . Would she mind spelling the name, please?

L-o-r-e-n-z-o. Like in Lorenzo!

. . . Eventually a second voice came on, another cool and distant female. This was Mrs. Delehanty, secretary to Mr. French. Mr. French was in conference at the moment, but was there something Mrs. Delehanty might do?

Yes, there was. Miss Lorenzo would like to know about one of the items in the Fox estate—

Oh, yes, Well, that estate was in the process of being probated. Was Miss Lorenzo with a law firm?

No, she was a private party, and she wished to know if a certain item in the estate was possibly for sale.

And which item might that be?

The car which Mrs. Fox had left? That 1933 Plymouth she'd driven? Could someone tell Miss Lorenzo what price the estate would want for it?

Hmmm. This was a matter that would have to be taken up with Mr. French, who was in charge, acting for the executors, and he would have to get back to Miss—what was the name again?

Lorenzo. L-o-r-e-n-z-o!

Hmmm. Was Miss Lorenzo an automobile dealer?

No, she was a private party, who lived in Bridgeport, and if the price on that Plymouth was right, Miss Lorenzo would be willing to discuss a deal—

Yes, well then—could she perhaps write a letter, addressed to Mr. French's attention here, explaining exactly what this was all about, and stating her reasons, and then, after Mr. French had taken this matter under advisement, he would be in touch with Miss Lorenzo—

Couldn't she wait and talk to him on the phone? All she wanted to know was—

—Oh no, surely Miss Lorenzo must understand, such matters could not be discussed over the telephone, so if she would address her letter to Mr. French here, that was F-r-e-n-c-h . . .

"I think I know how to spell that, thanks!" said Benita.

. . . Thanks for what? For a godamn runaround!

. . . Okay, she'd write the letter.

What the hell, she had almost $2 invested so far in that phone call, for fifteen cents more postage she could afford to stay in the ball game.

"Dear Mr. French,"

she wrote.

"I am a private party who is interested in the 1933 Plymouth sedan which Mrs. Fox left in her estate. I am interested in the car because of sentimental reasons. One of my relatives once worked for the Chrysler company and in our family, Plymouths have always meant quality and good value. Who knows, maybe he worked on the assembly line when this particular car came through.

(Strictly bullshit, but maybe it would help to throw those hard-nosed lawyers off the track.)

I would appreciate you telling me what price you would take to sell said car. I realize you are a busy man, but I hope you will understand my interest. Please get back to me.
                    Very truly yours, (Miss) Benita Lorenzo."

"What are you writing there?" asked her mother.
"A letter to a lawyer," said Benita.
"You in some kind of trouble?" asked her mother, instantly.
"No, why?" asked Benita.
". . . Lawyers mean trouble," said her mother.
"Not this time," said Benita. "I'm writing to try and buy some-thing from one of his clients, that's all."
"What kind of a something?"
"A car," she said.
"You crazy?" demanded her mother. "You already got a car!"
". . . I know, I know," said Benita. ". . . But this one's spe-cial."
"What's so special about it?" insisted her mother.
And how could she answer that question?
She mailed it off.
The next few days were frantic ones; they needed her for over-time at the Wayside Gardens, and at the same time, she was trying to study hard for the state exam, which was coming up in Hartford.

When she came home late one night, there was a long envelope waiting for her on the kitchen table.

She ripped it open and read:

"My dear Miss Lorenzo.

Thank you for your inquiry of the 4th, regarding the property of the late Mrs. Laura Richards Fox.

Please understand that there have been other inquiries from several interested purchasers in re said 1933 Plymouth four-door sedan.

Therefore, in an effort to be fair to all parties concerned, both potential purchasers and the seller, the Estate of Mrs. Laura Richards Fox, whom we represent, a decision has been taken to put said 1933 Plymouth up at public auction. Arrangements have been made to have it consigned to Tulsa, Oklahoma, where The First Southwestern Classic and Vintage Car Auction (auspices of Donaldson Bros. Auctioneers,) will be held next month, on May 17th and 18th.

A catalogue containing particulars of the sale can be obtained from Donaldson Bros., in Tulsa. If you will forward $10 in cash or certified check to them, it will be sent to you by return mail.

Hoping that this information is of help, I remain,

Very truly yours, R. F. French, Att'y."

DF/RD

. . . An *auction?*

In Tulsa, goddamned *Oklahoma?*

. . . How much rougher can you make it, Mr. R. F. (for Royal Fucker-up, obviously) French, Att'y—for Miss Benita Lorenzo to get next to one of the wheels of that strictly pain-in-the-ass Plymouth?

". . . Well, they going to sell you the car?" asked her mother, the next day.

"No, they're not!" she said, wearily. These days she never seemed to get enough sleep. "They're giving me a hard time."

"So what are you upset about?" shrugged her mother. "You already got a car, right. We don't need two cars."

". . . I want to get my hands on *that* one," said Benita. "All I need is one lousy half hour with it—"

105

". . . Hey, Benita, you crazy or something?" said her mother. "You want to buy some car for a half an hour? Baby . . . I'm worried about you."

. . . Under the circumstances, her mother was probably right.

The whole thing was getting on her nerves. Forget it—Gus and his crazy story, that old lady and her fifty-year-old car—okay, not exactly fifty but close enough—and now these high-powered New Haven lawyers who wouldn't give her the sweat off their noses—

Screw it all! She had more important things to deal with. Benita Lorenzo did not have to spend the rest of her life chasing some imaginary pot of gold, on wheels.

Forget the Plymouth. They could hold the auction without her.

. . . But she still had the money Gus had left her.
Was that the act of a crazy man?

Two days later, she sent off a $10 postal money order to Donaldson Bros., in Tulsa, Oklahoma, to pay for one auction catalog.

*   *   *

1937 ROLLS ROYCE 40-50 HP PHANTOM III
FIVE PASSENGER SPORTS LIMOUSINE
Coachwork by Hooper, London.
Chassis No. 3AZ 114
Motor No. Q.74.J

Only 710 Phantom IIIs were made between
1936 and 1940. This is an early one,
the serial number indicating a chassis
completion date late in 1936. The
car carries four-door two-window sport-
formal coachwork with winding divider,
but no jump seats. It is in good
driving condition and only some 1,000
miles have been covered since a com-
prehensive overhaul of motor, transmission, and suspension. Some of the
original tools are still with the
vehicle. The car is painted in two-
tone beige and cream with cream
wheel discs and red coachline.
Upholstery in fawn leather thruout.

The car's complete service record
since its original purchase will be
supplied to the successful bidder.

To be sold by order of a private
collector in Santa Barbara, California.

 *Tulsa*

G. Dudley Lester returned from another of his frequent trips away from Tulsa and Joyce Donaldson Wade, bearing with him the first copies of the auction catalog.

Bound in glossy blue, it was an impressive piece of work, which heralded on its cover The First Southwestern Classic and Vintage Car Auction (DONALDSON BROS., YOUR RELIABLE AUCTIONEERS SINCE 1927). Carefully assembled by that Chicago P. R. firm, under G. Dudley's personal supervision, the inside pages proudly presented color photos and specifications of some of the more important cars that would be sold in Tulsa, on May 17 and 18.

"There you are, my sweet," he said, handing over the first copy to Joyce. "How do like it?"

". . . Mph! Classy!" she chortled, thumbing through it. She chortled at the display of classic and vintage merchandise. A 1927 Pierce-Arrow touring car, in original condition. A 1929 Marmon limousine. A 1940 Lincoln Zephyr 2-Dr. Business Coupe. A 1956 T-Bird (". . . Why, I had one of *those*," she remarked. "Used it for shopping." "You should have hung on to it," he replied. "It's a true classic." "Damn, I sold it to the gardener!" she sighed), a 1939 Cadillac convertible, ". . . once the property of Randolph Scott, the famous film star, and kept in storage ever since." ("Was that really *his* car?" she asked. "I was really crazy about him!")

". . . Oh, honey, I'm proud of you," she said, when she'd finished. "This is one sensational job! Sure beats selling farm equipment."

"Thank you," said G. Dudley, modestly. "Now that the mine is nicely salted, we go out and beat the bushes for the live ones. I've got mailing lists ready, and I want to set up a WATS line here in the office so we can do some personal calling—"

". . . Ah, don't you want to come home and relax a little, first?" she inquired, entwining herself.

". . . Business first," he said, when he'd emerged from her embrace.

". . . But you've been gone for weeks," she complained. "All that other stuff, I can turn it over to the girls here in the office.''

''. . . Now Joyce,'' he said, removing himself from her posses-sive embrace. ''If a job is worth doing at all, it's worth doing well. That's one of my mottos.''

''All work and no screwing makes Jack a dull boy,'' she said, pouting. ''That's one of *mine.*''

The next day, the first mailing went out to a specially-selected group of triple-A ''live ones.''

In sturdy cartons, the catalogs went by airmail to a list of inter-national names and addresses, a cross section of potential buyers and sellers (who were gently reminded in an attached letter from G. Dudley Lester that Donaldson Bros. would continue to accept prime-quality automobiles for consignment to the auction, right up till May 16th, the day before the first session) to newspaper and magazine writers here and abroad, (who were invited to cover the colorful event in Tulsa for their various publications), and finally to certain well-placed investment advisers and financial people (whose attention was directed to the interesting tax-shelter aspects and/or potential capital appreciation aspects involved in the acquisition of the classic motor car).

Late that afternoon, G. Dudley came back into Joyce's office.

''. . . That's all out of the way,'' he said. ''Why don't you and I run down a list of what's going on here. The arena lease?''

''Signed and sealed, we put down a deposit, and the balance due on the 14th of May,'' she said.

''The concessions?''

''. . . Every last one of 'em rented out,'' she said. ''Percentages agreed upon, and we got their cash deposits in the bank.''

''Extra staff?''

''They're bein' screened right now,'' she said. ''I also set up a deal with Cherokee Security for the guards we'll need, and I'm making a deal with a couple of the local motels to save us space for A-one customers, and the bank people are waiting to talk to us about whatever escrow accounts we'll be arrangin'.''

''Very good,'' said G. Dudley, impressed. ''. . . What else?''

Joyce stuffed the papers into the drawer of her desk, slammed it shut, and then rose, picking up her Gucci handbag. "Now that," she said, "is what I call one dumb question, G. Dudley. You been gone for almost a week. You ought to know damn well what else." She came across the office and seized him by the arm. ". . . And don't give me any more of that crap about business before pleasure!" she added.

 London

To penetrate Ben Emir's private living quarters above the MG restaurant, one first entered an anonymous door on the ground floor, leading from the side street. Once inside, one stood in a small airless corridor, facing a second door, while one's face was scanned by an invisible watcher through a small closed-circuit TV system. Through an intercom system, if the caller were acceptable, one announced oneself to the disembodied voice above. Then, and only then, would the second door (fortified with steel and triple electronic locks) be opened by whichever of Ben Emir's staff was on duty above; one could proceed to the small lift within that would take him—or more often, her—up three floors to the inner sanctum Ben Emir used during his visits to Great Britain.

". . . It's easier to get into the Tower of London, friend," Cyril had once complained.

"Oh, assured, a terrible nuisance, yes," Ben Emir cheerfully admitted. "But for people of my persuasion in these difficult times, an ounce of prevention, eh what?"

The lift door opened above, and Cyril stepped through the flat door, past the thick drapes, and into the brightness of Ben Emir's living room. It was after the lunchtime rush below, in the MG; it had been a trying day so far. The Italian chef had arrived late, one of the waiters was sick, and service had been spotty. Something of a shambles, in fact. Then he'd had a message from up here; could he please join Ben Emir for a matter of grave importance?

At the door, Cyril removed his shoes, and padded across the room, blinking in the light.

This space, which had formerly been the offices of a failed commercial firm, had been transformed at fearful expense, into a small oasis. Here in the heart of Mayfair, at one end of the vast room, there were large palm trees, basking beneath cunningly hidden recessed lighting. In the center, surrounded by rock formations, a shallow pool of water sparkled; on the floor, beneath one's feet, were deep carpets of the softest cashmere and mohair, and to one side, beneath a colorful canopy, were piles of cushions and hassocks. From stereo speakers, soft music echoed through the room; tame birds flew back and forth, twittering above. Where once there had been a bank of glass windows overlooking Green Park, the wall was now covered with a large photo mural of the Sahara desert, the sands stretching on into infinity. Whatever the weather outside, in here the temperature remained at a steady 80 or so.

Beginning to perspire, Cyril opened his coat, and loosened his tie. Three minutes here, you felt like a bloody Lawrence of Arabia . . .

"Ben Emir?" he called.

From a distance away, in the bedroom wing of the flat, there came the voice of his senior partner.

"Make yourself comfortable, dear friend. I shall be there shortly."

Cyril went to the bar, which was hidden beneath the canopy, behind a pile of hassocks, and poured himself a mild gin and tonic, just right for this climate. On a nearby low table was a stack of Ben Emir's current mail, opened and thrown into a careless pile.

Idly, he rummaged through it.

Ben Emir seemed to be on every list of affluent acquirers known to the modern commercial world. There was an engraved announcement from a firm of Swiss jewelers, inviting Ben Emir to a gala at Zurich at which the entertainment would include a fashion show and a display of their latest offerings. From Paris were cards to couturier openings; an announcement from Stuttgart of an auction of old masters and fine modern paintings. Here in London, Sotheby's and Christie's were holding various sales. There was a catalog from Previews, Inc., containing full-color photographs of estates, plantations, and castles available here in Europe, or in South America. Dealers in tax-sheltered principalities who specialized in precious-metal futures . . . a bill from Ben Emir's London tailors, the size of which Sum Outstanding would easily keep an average family of four for a year. An invitation to a charity dinner dance at the Savoy, the proceeds of which were to benefit the Fund For Aged and Disabled Jockeys, and a brochure offering selected investors the opportunity to invest in a syndicate being formed to build a new resort hotel in Mexico . . .

Cyril riffled on through the pile, wondering at the waste of it all. Lord, lord, as his grandmother had been fond of saying, *money goes to money* (and don't you forget it!).

It was a world he knew something about, didn't he? These graspers, the greedy, the international movers and shakers . . . once upon a time he'd been accepted into their affluent run-on-credit society. He'd had his own membership card (temporary, as it turned out) and he'd had a proper seat at the banquet table . . .

But that was before the roof caved in.

How quickly he discovered that he was no longer In. Moneyed people might be careless, on the surface, but when it came to trusting their valuables, they certainly weren't about to smile at Cyril Banks, who'd been so prominently featured in the press, in the IOI business, were they? Nor go in with him on any new venture. His calls went unanswered, his letters as well.

. . . And for quite some time, he hadn't moved in those circles.

Luckily, he'd finally latched on to Ben Emir.

In, of all places, the Motor Show, where Ben Emir, arm in arm with some busty little underage schoolgirl, had been enthusiastically trying to buy, off the floor, a newly designed German sports model, a flashy prototype brought in for the show. He'd eavesdropped, as Ben Emir offered the diffident young German sales rep a thousand pounds above the price of the car (which, *mein herr,* does not *have* a price yet!).

The young Arab simply couldn't understand why it was that his thick wallet was no open sesame here. "Everything is for sale!" he protested. "Otherwise, why indeed is it here?"

That was when Cyril had moved in and soothed Ben Emir's ruffled feathers. "Excuse me, but you don't really want this one, not at all," he'd said. And he'd proceeded to explain to Ben Emir that this expensive German toy, while an amusing whim of the moment, certainly, would, if he succeeded in buying it (which was unlikely) prove to be one enormous headache. Why so? Well, no mechanic in Great Britain would ever be available who could perform needed repairs to such a car, nor could he ever expect to find spare parts, could he? If Ben Emir were to toss his good money away on this complex piece of machinery, chances were excellent that it would end up sitting in his garage. And what about insurance cover? Which company would undertake to protect such a unique item? Not to mention the problems of parking the damned thing. ". . . no doubt it'll be banged into by some drunken" (he'd been about to say Pakistani, but thought better of it) "idiot the very first night," he'd told Ben Emir.

The young Arab had seemed impressed by Cyril's casual expertise, and his knowledgeable line of chatter. Leaving behind the arrogant Kraut salesman, they'd spent several hours wandering through the rest of the show, with Cyril giving Ben Emir and his bird inside information on the rest of the cars. By the time they'd left, Ben Emir considered him, if not a blood brother, at least a trusted adviser. "I think perhaps today you have saved me a considerable sum," he'd said. "How can I possibly repay you, dear sir?"

"With your friendship," said Cyril.

. . . He was aware that, after a long wait, he'd perhaps hooked himself a live one. Ben Emir certainly could not know anything about Cyril's prior commercial disaster; the trick would be to keep things on a good-chums social level.

The following week he rang up Ben Emir and invited him to a sports-car rally down in the country. Within a month or so, their friendship was firmly established. But Cyril played in his catch very slowly . . .

One night, over drinks at Ben Emir's suite at the Dorchester, while they waited for a pair of "escorts" that the Arab had ordered from a service, for the first time, the subject of religion arose.

"I understand none of the Jews come to this hotel any more

since the ownership has changed to the Arabs," remarked Ben Emir.

"I wouldn't know too much about that," said Cyril.

In fact, he had not been in the Dorchester since long before the change of ownership.

"Strange about the Jews," said Emir. "So clannish, wouldn't you agree?"

"Yes," said Cyril. "They have large hook noses, and they'll steal your eye teeth, as well."

"Nonsense," said Ben Emir. "You've never even tried to do that, now have you, eh?"

Cyril, startled, stared at his host.

". . . How'd you know about me?" he finally asked.

Ben Emir smiled cheerfully. "A wise man does not tell all he knows," he said. "And since I assume that you and I perhaps may go into some commercial venture together someday, was I not wise to learn something about you?"

". . . Bloody shrewd," said Cyril.

". . . So when *do* you plan to make your proposal?" asked Ben Emir.

Devious little chap, eh?

. . . And all this time, Cyril had fancied that it was he who'd been the angler!

It was only a matter of time after that before he'd come up with the plan for the MG.

. . . and a year or so before old Begin and Sadat had gotten together, *their* partnership had flowered.

There was a tinkling of temple bells, the birds fluttered away nervously to the other side of the room, and through the velvet drapes that hung at the entrance to Ben Emir's equally lavish sleeping quarters a young girl emerged. Dressed a bit younger than she actually was, she wore a school uniform. Her legs encased in knee-high white socks, on her blonde curls was a jaunty straw boater, with ribbons dangling down at the back. She was tucking a sheaf of bank notes into her school satchel.

". . . Oh, hel*lo*," she said, to Cyril. "Poopsie says to tell you he'll be right out. And now, I must *rush*."

Cyril's eyes ran across her ample bosom, which strained against the white cotton blouse, and those sturdy thighs that disappeared beneath the blue skirt. ". . . Don't be late for school," he cautioned.

"School?" giggled the tart. "I haven't been in one of those since Teacher did me."

She blew him a kiss and disappeared through the far end of the drapes.

. . . He'd asked Ben Emir once about his penchant for these nymphet-types. "What do you see in all those children?"

"Ah," explained Ben Emir. "I went to an all-male school. I suppose I am merely trying to make up for lost time."

Cyril glanced at his watch. Almost four. He had work to do downstairs. Up here, in this steaming bright oasis, nobody paid any attention to time, especially if one were a very rich young Arab who would never have to put in an honest hour's work as long as there were blank pages in his checkbook and ink in his Mont Blanc pen.

. . . But Cyril Banks did have work to do.

"Benny!" he called. "Who've you got in there, the rest of the Sixth Form class?"

"Shortly, shortly," came the reply.

. . . There was more mail on the table.

An invitation to fly to Norway for the gala launching party of a new-model turbine 78-foot yacht, at the shipyards in Trondheim . . . another bill, this one from Ben Emir's shirtmaker. The balance owed having remained outstanding for the past two years, they respectfully suggested his account might be considered Past Due.

. . . Well, that was a mark of the rich. They never paid their bills. And you did business with them at your own peril.

Ah, a catalog of an auction. The First Southwestern Classic and Vintage Car Auction. Glossy blue binder, pages bent back to reveal a full-color photo of a 1937 Rolls, with a nice Hooper body. To be auctioned off in May, in Tulsa, Oklahoma? . . . Wasn't that Indian country?

It seemed a lovely specimen. But who had time for this—he had to get back to work—

"Do excuse me, dear friend," said Ben Emir, emerging from his bedchambers, tying his speckled-silk tie into a knot, "I've been on the phone to my father. Dear old fellow loves to chat. Did I tell you he's going to be sixty next week? The plan is to have a large surprise party for him, in St. Moritz, and we're all flying in—incidentally, we're having the devil's own time with the hotel, seems they haven't got any decent caviar—do you think you could be helpful with that, eh?"

"I don't have any connections in Iran these days," said Cyril.

Ben Emir beamed. "I rely on you. Enough for a hundred or so guests."

"That will take a bit of doing," said Cyril.

"Yet how often does one's father become sixty?" asked Ben Emir. He glanced at the catalog in Cyril's hand. "Ah, I see you have spotted that Rolls. What do you think it should fetch?"

Cyril's mind was not on the Rolls, but on the problem of finding Ben Emir's guests their damned caviar. Enough for a hundred or so, all of them heavy feeders—where in hell did Ben Emir think he could conjure up so much Mallosol? He was a restaurateur, a host, a jack-of-all-trades—but not a damned genie!

". . . Give me your educated opinion," Ben Emir was urging.

"Ah, what do you want another Rolls for?" asked Cyril, carefully hiding his irritation. "Haven't you enough cars?"

"Of course," said Ben Emir. "But you can always use another, especially when it's such a good investment. Perhaps I should put in a bid, eh?"

". . . But at an auction in Oklahoma?" asked Cyril. "Those Indians will move in and destroy you."

"What I thought was that I might buy this Rolls and have it flown over to my dear father at the party—and I could present it to him as a birthday present." said Ben Emir.

"And suppose he doesn't like it?" asked Cyril.

". . . It's the thought that counts, eh?" said Ben Emir.

Cyril shrugged . . . what did he care if Ben Emir threw away a few thousand more than he should on a whim? "What do you want me to do?" he asked.

"There's a name there somewhere," said Ben Emir. "Would you be a good chap and ring up Tulsa, put in a bid?"

"Yes, fine," said Cyril. "Anything else? I do have a business to operate on *your* behalf, you know."

". . . I rely on your business judgment," said Ben Emir,

gently. "I hope you don't consider this an imposition, eh?"

"Of course not!" said Cyril, fervently.

Ben Emir bowed. "I leave it all in your capable hands," he said.

Cyril rose and bowed back.

Going down in the tiny lift, he scanned the letter that was clipped to the Tulsa auction catalog. On engraved stationery, it seemed to be a personal invitation to Ben Emir to avail himself of the excellent investment opportunities to be had by the astute buyer willing to make shrewd purchases of these valuable vintage automobiles.

And it was signed by the manager of the auction, one G. Dudley Lester.

. . . G. Dudley <u>Lester</u>?

<u>George</u> D. <u>Lester</u>?

<u>George</u> <u>Dudley</u> <u>Lester</u>?

. . . Was it possible?

Probable?

Some other George D. Lester, who signed himself G. Dudley— managing an auction in far-off Oklahoma, in the heart of the Indian country.

. . . Or *his* G. D. Lester?

Who'd dropped him overboard and sailed away, years ago?

And was now in Oklahoma (wasn't that where people waved their fists at you and sang about the wind sweeping 'cross the plain?).

What the devil would his G. D. Lester be doing there?

. . . Certainly not running an auction. That was not his style.

Holding it with fingers that trembled slightly, Cyril reread the letter.

Which offered no further clue to Mr. G. Dudley Lester's identity. But did offer a Tulsa telephone number.

. . . Allowing for a five-hour time change—or was it six?—it would be approximately 9:30 there on the Plains.

Ah yes, Ben Emir. This would be one telephone call Cyril would be delighted to make.

On behalf of both of them.

". . . Mistuh Lester?" cried the female voice, in far-off Tulsa. "Why, I do believe he's in a conference rat this minute—who can I say is callin'?"

". . . This is London," said Cyril. "It's in reference to that 1937 Rolls Royce with the Hooper coachwork in your auction catalog."

". . . And what did you say your name was?" asked the lady.

". . . Ben Emir," said Cyril. "I am a prospective purchaser. I wish to enter a bid."

"Oh, good!" said the lady. "This is Miz Joyce Donaldson Wade, and I'd be delighted to be of assistance—"

". . . If you do not mind," said Cyril, "I should prefer to speak directly to Mr. Lester."

". . . All right then," said Miz Joyce Donaldson Wade, obviously miffed. "I'll see if I can locate him. You hang on now, Mr. E-meer—"

"Oh yes, never fear," said Cyril, grimly.

There was a humming and singing on the international wires.

. . . And then there was a clicking as the phone was picked up. And a masculine voice, a very familiar voice, whose tones Cyril had not heard for some time, said "This is G. Dudley Lester, sir. Was there something you wished to know about that '37 Rolls we have in our catalog, Lot Number 72? Yes indeed, that's certainly a mighty fine specimen."

Now what?

Speak Cyril. Introduce yourself to your ex-employer, Mr. George D. Lester, the evil genius of IOI Ltd.

". . . Hello?" said George D. Lester. "Is this Mr. E-meer?"

. . . Cyril's throat was suddenly dry. He did not speak.

George D. Lester *was* in Tulsa, Oklahoma—running some sort of an auction of vintage cars. He, Cyril Banks, was in London, England, running a restaurant (plus various errands) for a spoiled young Arab twit.

He needed time to think.

". . . *Hello,* dammit?" said the voice from Tulsa. "Is this connection still working? Is there somebody on this line?"

. . . Somebody was on this line, but Somebody was not prepared to reveal himself.

Not yet.

". . . Get the damn operator back on, Joyce!" he heard in his ear. "We've been cut off!"

Carefully, Cyril replaced the receiver on its hook.

. . . *Not cut off,* G. Dudley Lester. No longer.

Cyril stared at the auction catalog.

It seemed a perfectly respectable commercial affair, an everyday offering of classic motor cars, designed to attract potential buyers. The '37 Rolls . . . a 1927 Pierce-Arrow touring car, a 1929 Marmon limousine, a 1940 2-DR. Lincoln and others. The terms of sale quite simple. Successful bidders would present cash or certified bank checks, to be deposited in an escrow account, the proceeds of which would then be remitted to sellers within a reasonable time by the firm of Donaldson Bros. (YOUR RELIABLE AUCTIONEERS SINCE 1927.)

. . . But if George Dudley Lester was involved—where was the bloody catch?

If George Dudley Lester was involved—there damned well had to be one.

Would it not be interesting to discover what his dear old ex-boss was up to?

No—to hell with that. What he wanted was to confront the bastard, to take him by the lapels of his expensive jacket, once and for all, to shake him until his teeth rattled—

—Pay him back for having dumped him, recoup some of the lost earnings—be paid for the humiliation and all the rest of it—

. . . Ah yes. A lovely prospect.

But before any such confrontation could take place, there was a small problem.

How to get himself to Tulsa, Oklahoma?

Simple.

He could go to Tulsa as Ben Emir's personal representative; mission, to acquire the Rolls. Ben Emir could easily underwrite such a trip—

That would put Cyril within arms' length of that wily bastard George, George the Artful, George The Dodger—George, who was obviously Up To Something in Oklahoma—but whose Time Had Come, had it not?

Ah, sweet retribution!

He jabbed at the intercom buzzer, to speak to Ben Emir, upstairs in his serene oasis.

. . . Down some dusty Oklahoma street, past the low store-fronts, in the bright sunlight, there would be just the two of them, moving towards each other, step by step, their hands dangling at their sides. ". . . Is that you, George D. Lester?" "Yeah, who wants me?" "I'll tell you who, George D. Lester. I've come a mighty long ways from England to settle up scores with you." "Lord Almighty, is that you, Cyril Banks?" "Yep, bet your ass it's me, The London Kid, and you and me is going to have ourselves a showdown—"

No answer from the oasis.

Damn. Ben Emir must have gone out. Just when he needed him.

By late that afternoon, he'd made half a dozen phone calls, and run the Mallosol to the ground. At a whopping price, he'd finally succeeded in locating enough of the precious stuff from various rogues down in Soho (no questions asked) to fill the gullets of not only Ben Emir's dear old dad, but all the other various overfed friends and relatives in St. Moritz. Tonight the rogues would assemble his shipment, tomorrow it would be delivered here to the MG. He would taste it to make sure it was edible (those same rogues were capable of anything) and then pay for it. It would be stored away safely in one of the refrigerators. (Under lock and key. Certainly no one could trust his staff!)

He tried the oasis again.

Ah. This time a female voice answered. A new one.

"Where's Ben Emir?" he asked.

"He is unavailable," she said.

120

"Tell him this is a crisis. I'll be right there."

". . . Whom do I say is calling?" asked the girl.

"Santa Claus," said Cyril.

There was a moment's pause, an then she came back on. "He says to tell you he does not believe in Santa Claus."

"Warn him to stand away from the chimney," said Cyril, cheerfully. "I'm on my way down."

He found his ticket to Tulsa prone in his cavernous sleeping quarters. Beneath the lavish rugs draped into a tentlike structure, Ben Emir lay relaxing on a gleaming steel table, a towel draped across his plump shape. Soft music played, the birds twittered, the air was redolent with musk, and Ben Emir was being pummeled by a blonde Scandinavian type in a leather-thonged bikini.

"Take off your clothes and have Ingrid do you," he offered, graciously.

"Not just now, thanks, I'm a bit busy," said Cyril.

". . . I'm exhausted," sighed Ben Emir, "but she has magic hands. When she has my tensions nicely reduced, she has other talents as well, eh, my sweet?"

"That's extra," said Ingrid.

"Good news," said Cyril. "I'm getting in enough caviar to feed all your guests."

"Of course," yawned Ben Emir, his head moving back and forth beneath Ingrid's firm grasp.

"It wasn't that easy," said Cyril. "I also called Tulsa. I think that Rolls is a very good buy. Your father should love it."

". . . What Rolls?" asked Ben Emir.

"The Rolls in the catalog!" said Cyril.

"Oh, that . . ." said Ben Emir. "Perhaps it is not such a good notion. I rather think he might like something else. I went out shopping this afternoon . . ."

"For what?" asked Cyril, dismayed.

". . . Perhaps a small yacht, eh?" murmured Ben Emir. "My father really is not such a good driver."

"Since when did he become a sailor?" asked Cyril. Damn—it was difficult to keep up with Ben Emir's whims. He must get him back on the track. "Listen, I've checked on that particular car. It's a most unique model, and it has great intrinsic value."

Ben Emir's eyes were closed. "I am so weary," he said.

". . . As a matter of fact," said Cyril, "I'll go there myself to make sure we get it at a good price."

"Go where?" asked Ben Emir.

"To Tulsa!" insisted Cyril.

". . . But you yourself told me they were all thieves there," said Ben Emir.

"I can handle them, believe me," said Cyril. "I'll take along enough of your money to buy it—anonymously—then I'll have it shipped back by air to St. Moritz—when it arrives it will be the talk of the party. What a splendid gesture, eh?"

Ben Emir's eyes flickered open, as Ingrid worked her way down his back with her expert fists.

". . . But . . . who . . . will . . . run . . . the restaurant . . . while you are . . . gone?" he inquired.

"I've thought of that," said Cyril. "We close down for a week—in honor of your dear old papa's birthday. See here, now, isn't it more important to provide him with such gratification? What does the old Koran say—a father is worth all the riches that a son can command?"

". . . That's not in *my* Koran," said Ben Emir. Ingrid rolled him over on his back. Primly, she rearranged his towel, and then bent down over Ben Emir's feet, kneading and caressing his toes, one by one. ". . . Ah, bliss," sighed Ben Emir. "After such a hard day, a man needs much relaxation."

". . . Of course he does," said Cyril. Bloody little sybarite, the closest he'd ever come to work was to tie his own shoelace . . .

". . . Perhaps," Ben Emir was musing, "I ought to buy my father three jet fighters. That might please him, eh?"

"I thought you said he was a man of peace," said Cyril. "Besides, how could you possibly present them to him at St. Moritz? The bloody Swiss would take it as a hostile gesture—why, you could be responsible for starting another war! On your father's own birthday? Shocking!"

". . . You make sense," said Ben Emir.

"Now see here," said Cyril, as he gently moved Ingrid away from Ben Emir's pudgy feet. "The Rolls is the absolute perfect gift. Opulent, yet correct. A very good investment, but in the best of taste. You fill the back seat with Dom Perignon, chilled, *and* the caviar, and then, at the climax of the party, you drive it right up and present it to him. He will be absolutely thrilled!"

". . . You do have a sense of the dramatic," conceded Ben Emir. ". . . Now, let Ingrid return to what she was doing, please?"

Resigned, Cyril moved away. What more could he say? He'd given it his best . . . never oversell.

Ingrid returned to the toes.

"Ahh," sighed Ben Emir. "Lovely. Now. Supposing I do give you all that money to go purchase the Rolls . . . how can I be certain you'll return?"

Cyril began to grin, and then thought better of it. He'd hooked him.

"Dear Ben Emir," he said, "are you suggesting you don't trust me?"

". . . That far away?" said Ben Emir. "Why, you might take all my money and invest it in an oil well."

"*That* would be carrying coals to Newcastle," said Cyril.

"Is there coal in Tulsa as well?" asked Ben Emir. ". . . Perhaps it would be amusing if I went with you. I might end up investing in a coal mine. Or something . . ."

"No, no," said Cyril, firmly. "You stay here. In any auction the trick is to keep a low profile. Leave it all to me. I will bring you back that car, and when you drive it up to him, you will be the pride and joy of your old Dad's life, believe me!"

Ben Emir was silent. Then a smile crossed his cherubic face. "Dear Cyril," he said. "I am impressed with your determination on my behalf . . . but I must stipulate two conditions. First, that you do not return empty-handed . . . and second, that you *do* return. Understood?"

Damned right it was understood.

And now, miraculously, Cyril Banks, the London Kid, the Mayfair Avenger, was on his way to Tulsa.

What a remarkable day's work.

". . . Absolutely," he said, and shook Ben Emir's limp hand.

". . . Should you fail," said Ben Emir, the smile still there, "I would be very dismayed. So dismayed, in fact, that I might be forced to forget that we two are gentlemen. I might even revert to my ancient hereditary blood lust. I do hope we would never come to *that*."

". . . Allah forbid," said Cyril.

"You handle the details," said Ben Emir. ". . . Now, Ingrid darling, do everything once again, but this time, surprise me, eh?"

"That's extra," said Ingrid.

*   *   *

1955 FORD THUNDERBIRD
TWO-PASSENGER HARDTOP COUPE
Serial No. 40A-TC25 BSU 47

Motor, eight-cylinder valve-in-head
V-type. Three speed Fordomatic
transmission, floor stick selector.

Henry Ford's famed "personal car" had
only a three-year run, despite promising
sales for a speciality automobile,
16,155 in 1955, 15,631 in 1956 and
21,830 in 1957. Thus it is today
one of the most collectable of native
Milestones. The car has covered some
38,000 miles since it was purchased,
has remained in one owner's hands
since that original sale, and is
currently in show condition.

Sold by the original owner's family.

 ## Liverpool, Indiana

Twenty-five years?

It was hard to believe they'd been married that long.

. . . Of course, when you said two and a half decades, the way they did on TV news, it didn't sound so . . . endless.

Twenty-five years since Dusty and she had stood up before the minister, Dr. Manning, in that church? She in her long white dress and veil and he in his sober cutaway and silk tie, it had been a marvelous sunny afternoon, all their relatives and friends there, both of them young, she crazy in love with him but filled with a certain hesitance. Then they'd had the big party her folks had given them at the country club, and she'd gone upstairs to change, they'd piled into Dusty's gleaming new T-Bird, there'd hardly been any room in that little trunk for their two bags, but what difference did that make? The apple of Dusty's eye, that lovely low-slung car, and he'd driven them both eighty-odd miles straight across the state until they'd finally come to that resort by the lake, the place that specialized in honeymooners, Deep Trees Lodge.

With the snug and comfortable log cabin which was set off in the woods, inside, the wide double bed waiting for them. Their own special playground for indoor sports, but first, they'd gone into the dining room in the main lodge for their special wedding-night dinner. She could remember the menu precisely. Shrimp cocktail, huge T-bone steaks and Caesar salad, baked potatoes with sour cream and chives dressing, strawberry shortcake, all of it served with a bottle of domestic champagne.

They'd finished and they'd gone for a stroll beneath the fragrant pine trees, it was twilight now, and she'd leaned against him, his arm holding her, she nuzzled his neck and she was feeling so (well, nowadays it was what the kids so easily said, *horny*) but back then, even if she had known what it meant, she hadn't been anywheres near so liberated as to use it, let alone acknowledge that's how she felt. Finally he'd kissed her and asked if she was feeling sleepy, and

126

she'd said yes, she was, and they'd both giggled a little at that, and headed for their cabin, for their first real night together.

. . . Sure, they'd had most of the preliminaries before, after all she wasn't exactly *that* naive . . .

All that wrestling around on the back seat of his father's Chrysler (before the T-Bird, in which any necking was impossible) throughout the time they'd been courting. In her own living room, where step by step she'd permitted him to go further, opening her clothes, touching her, using his hand, her doing the same for him (Lord how backward they had been compared to what was happening these days!), . . . how could he have known it was just as frustrating for her? Until one night when she had finally let him go all the way, suffered through the groping and the fumbling, the sudden sharp pain, and then almost as quickly as that it was finished.

There had to be more, even though she hadn't felt, well, much . . . to tell the truth, nothing. Tonight had to be different. If you loved a guy as much as she loved Dusty Bigelow, you wanted to be with him in a bed, feel him beside you, to have him awaken all sorts of wonderful new sensations . . . that was what marriage was all about, wasn't it?

. . . So she'd whispered to him that night, twenty-five years ago, that she'd go inside and get ready, and would he mind waiting for a few minutes while she did?

He'd kissed her and said he'd go for a little walk to get a breath of fresh air, because he was a kind and thoughtful guy, she knew that already . . . wasn't that one of the things about him that had caused her to fall in love with him?

Inside that cabin she'd taken off her traveling suit, hung it up, and gotten her nightgown out of her bag, that sheer dark blue job she'd gone shopping for weeks back. Slipped it on, dabbed a little of the perfume she knew he liked, Chanel Number Five, behind her ears and between her breasts, she'd even put a touch of it on the pillows, then she'd snapped on the little portable radio they'd gotten as a wedding present, and she'd gotten into that enormous bed and waited for him to join her, with the music playing very soft and sexy, something like Andre Kostelanetz . . . wasn't it?

127

Five minutes . . . ten minutes . . . and when he hadn't showed up, she'd gotten worried. Gotten up and gone to the cabin door in her robe and opened it. No sign of Dusty outside, just voices she could hear through the trees from other cabins, faraway laughter, the tree toads singing in the distance. A couple of people came down the path in the shadows, their voices murmuring . . . but where was her husband?

She'd gone back to her bed, feeling so confused. Nothing could have happened to him, that was ridiculous, not here at Deep Trees Lodge! . . . but what else could she do but lie there and wait?

. . . And then she heard men talking outside, footsteps on the porch; what was going on?

She'd gotten up, thrown on her robe and gone to listen at the door. One of the voices was Dusty's. He'd knocked. "Honey?" he called.

She'd peered out and there he was, with another man standing off in the shadows. *"There* you are, dear," he'd said, as if nothing whatsoever had happened and he hadn't been gone for almost half an hour! "I want you to meet Chuck Ross, he's from Illinois, he's just passing through here and you've got to see what he's driving, it's a 1941 Cadillac limo in the most beautiful condition you'd ever hope to see, come take a look!"

". . . Howdy there, Miz Bigelow," said Mr. Chuck Ross-from-Illinois. "A real pleasure to meet you, ma'am. Your husband knows how to pick 'em, both cars *and* women."

She'd even taken that as a compliment.

And in her robe and slippers, because she loved Dusty Bigelow so much, she'd actually gone out to that damned parking lot with the two of them and spent a good hour or so of her wedding night standing around, oh-ing and ah-ing with Dusty over that long low battleship of a 1941 Cadillac limo.

Oh sure, there'd been more. Finally Dusty and she had come back to the cabin, Dusty still babbling on about the car, even when they'd gotten into the huge bed. But pretty soon he stopped discus-

128

sing the Cadillac, they were together, feeling each other so close and there was no more talk, just that soft music playing and lord, she'd never had him so excited before he'd pulled her over to him, the two of them entwined, joined the way the minister had said it should be, he was moving against her . . . she had begun to respond to his urgency, and then she felt the first amazing sensations, far more exciting than any time before, more wild and unrestrained, it was what she'd always hoped making love (oh why not use the right word, fucking, lord knows she'd heard that enough from the kids!) would be, and she wanted it to last, oh lord he mustn't stop . . .

. . . he'd gasped. Peaked. Rolled away, spent.

Lying beside her, his eyes shut, with the music still in their ears, he'd whispered ". . . so beautiful."

She'd patted him. ". . . thank you."

"Mmm," he'd said. ". . . they just don't make Cadillacs like that any more . . ."   And fallen asleep.

At the time, she thought it was pretty funny. Not funny-peculiar, but funny ha-ha. They'd even giggled about it together.

She couldn't quite remember when it was that the Cadillac joke had ceased to amuse her.

Not too much did amuse her these days.

Twenty-five years? (Silver wedding anniversaries, weren't they for *older* people?)

It wasn't anything she could put her finger on. More a vague sense of . . . being depressed.

. . . It couldn't be that Dusty was a bad husband. A good provider, faithful (at least, she assumed he was), most often pleasant company. Good father to their two boys, Arthur, who'd moved to San Franciscico now, and young Walt, who was finishing college next year.

They'd all lived in this house, the large Bigelow place he'd eventually inherited from his folks, along with the family business downtown, Bigelow's Grain and Farm Implements. ". . . Plenty of space for you to rattle around in," her friend Alice Mowbray had said, enviously. "What are you going to *do* with it all?"

129

Well, Dusty had answered that question. There may have been plenty of space to begin with, but over the years, he'd sure filled it all up, hadn't he?

After a while, it was like living in a warehouse.

Down in the front parlor, the music boxes and the Victrola, and the old Edison phonograph, with all those round cylinder discs, on which you could listen to Sousa's band (if you ever wanted to) and those little coin banks he was so fond of. That big mechanical player piano with the flashing lights, that thumped out endless ragtime pieces . . . well, all of that was certainly fun, wasn't it? Sure it was, at the time.

And the library with those huge shelves stacked up to the ceiling with books, books, all kinds of stuff, Tom Swift and the Rover Boys, The Boy Allies, stuff he was so glad to pick up at flea markets so their sons could someday enjoy them. Movie magazines, and bound copies of old *Life,* and the *Saturday Evening Post,* well you just couldn't pass up wonderful stuff like that, could you?

Another one of the rooms he'd turned into a regular little movie theater, where he could show all those 16-mm movies, not the usual dumb family stuff all their friends might show, no indeed, these were the real good old classics, the westerns with Tom Mix and Hoot Gibson, those Laurel and Hardy comedies, and the Chaplin and all the rest, movies of early automobile races and Lord knows what else that he continued to send away for, and kept on swapping with people all over the country . . . well, it certainly beat the junk they were showing on TV, didn't it?

Upstairs he had an attic large enough for him to keep a complete set of old electric trains, on tables that ran the whole length of the house, those Lionels and American Flyers that were so valuable, and fun to operate, all the nights they'd spent upstairs operating the Bigelow Railroad Company, she and the kids running around taking orders from him . . . hadn't that been fun?

There were other rooms, one filled with old military stuff from World War II. Model tanks and toy soldiers, relics put into cases, the ceiling hung with all sorts of planes, models that had taken weeks to create. Everything you'd ever want—if you were interested in preserving the memory of this country's finest hour, when we'd licked the Axis and sent them reeling back. In another room, where he had a humidity control, were all his old 78-rpm records, behind glass, neatly filed and cross-indexed, those great old Glenn Millers and Benny Goodmans and Dorseys—they were all on tapes for safety, but here were the originals, preserved. Someday they'd go to the boys, and meanwhile, was there any music being played these days that could compare with good old Bob Crosby and his Bob Cats swinging through "South Rampart Street Parade?"

And all the while, he was collecting cars, too.

How many married women she knew could boast of going off in the front seat of Dusty's precious little Model A 1932 Ford roadster, and driving ninety or so miles of a Saturday across the state to some swap-meet, to join with other collectors? Well, how else could he show off that beautiful buggy, which he'd spent endless nights meticulously restoring in their garage, with their family cars parked outside because he needed that space? She'd camped out there in the hot afternoon, smiling and answering questions about the car, eating a sandwich and drinking coffee from a thermos while Dusty went off to spend hours wandering through the other exhibits, in search of somebody who might have a usable pair of headlights for a 1937 Buick—that was the one he'd bought from another collector in Arizona and had trucked back to their house. Because when you were married, that was what a wife did for her husband, wasn't it? What the magazine writers now called a Shared Experience . . .

Twenty-five years coming up, and now there really wasn't any more room left in their house. Dusty had long since moved his cars out of their garage, down to that new heated cement-block building he'd built on the property behind Bigelow's Grain and Farm Implements. The one that he and his accountant, Lew Davis, had carefully figured out so that it would make financial sense. At one end, there was storage space for the big trucks the firm used to make deliveries, and for the stock of farm implements they sold. Then, in the middle, partitioned off with heavy steel doors and a sprinkler system and a burglar alarm plugged into police headquarters, Dusty could keep all of his valuable cars, in a special sort of an exhibit garage, one he could spend as much time as he wished with that Pierce-Arrow touring car, the big air-cooled Franklin, his rare Kaiser-Darrin, the 1939 LaSalle, the Ford Model A, a couple of Packards—even that 1941 Cadillac limo—the same as the one they'd run into on their wedding night, twenty-five years back.

". . . Well, think about it this way," said Alice Mowbray, one day when she'd come up to the house for lunch. ". . . Things could have been worse. Dusty's never taken it into his head to collect airplanes—full size!"

That had been back in the days before Alice and Don had moved out of town to Arizona, to that new condo in Phoenix. Now it seemed as if most of the people they used to see in the early years of their marriage had all drifted away. More and more nights in which she was alone, up here in the house, while Dusty was down at the new shop, working on his cars. She might read a book, or watch TV, all alone in her bedroom most of the time, because it was sort of gloomy to wander through all the rooms, most of which were so full of his accumulated stuff . . . and now there were no sounds of kids racing through the halls, or music playing. The boys' rooms, packed with *their* own assembled possessions, athletic equipment, stolen road signs, and whatever . . . empty.

Oh sure, every once in a while somebody would call and ask them to come visit, but she'd long since given up trying to get Dusty to travel anywhere to a resort, or down to Florida. His time was so valuable, he'd only be interested if it were to see somebody's collection, or out to Reno to visit Harrah's, or up to some small town in Illinois to visit with some old character who'd been amassing stacks of spare Buick parts. You couldn't really say those were pleasure trips.

. . . Not any more, they weren't.

Perhaps once, but suddenly, not any more.

. . . She wasn't quite sure why, but when you looked back on twenty-five years of keeping a man's house, raising his sons, cooking meals and taking care of things, dusting books and polishing the old cabinets and keeping track of all that . . . *whatever*—

. . . You had to wonder, alone in your bed at night, not where all the time had gone, but *why*.

. . . And for what?

She didn't need to write a letter to Ann Landers to know that she needed Something. Something Else.

A job? Not necessarily. She wasn't fitted for anything much, and as far as volunteer work, well, hadn't she been doing that around the house all this time? Helping out at a blood bank, or running a rummage sale at the church (Lord knew, she didn't need to be around any *more* possessions, there were times when she wanted to run a giant garage sale of her own—except who could clear out the garage to find space for it!) or joining clubs—none of that appealed to her.

Traveling? Once they'd done their share, but these days Dusty seemed to have lost his taste for it. Oh, he was certainly willing enough for her to join some tour. But who needed to be dragged here and there in a bus, along with a guide and a pack of other women? Looking at old churches and Roman ruins, and running around hunting for souvenirs . . . who *needed* more souvenirs?

She knew other women her own age who'd found a way to fill the time. But to play Madame Bovary—that wasn't Louise Bigelow's style, thank you.

. . . Although there had been another man, once, a while back, about seven years ago, whom she certainly could have had. He'd made that very clear. One of those New Yorkers, full of wisecracks and easy chatter, he had grey hair and a mustache and was undeniably attractive. Murray Stone, and she'd met him down in Florida at one of those monster hotels where Dusty had taken her to some convention involving farm implements. (He didn't even go to those any more . . . claimed it took too much time away from more important matters.)

Murray Stone had been down on the beach where she'd gone in

the morning while Dusty was off at a sales conference. He seemed to be staying at the hotel for some other meeting, and she'd gotten into a casual conversation with him. It was all very casual and friendly, he helped pass the time, and he'd drawn her out, getting her to tell him all about the various stuff Dusty had collected, his cars, the old trains, all the rest of it.

"You know what, *bubie?*" he'd remarked. "If you don't mind me saying this, your husband sounds to me like a classic case of arrested development. Nothing dangerous, but he obviously stopped enjoying anything that happened to him after 1948 . . . maybe 1950. Right?"

"Does that include me?" she'd asked.

He'd shrugged. "You're part of the collection, sure."

What right did he have to tell her what he thought about a man he'd never even met? Someone she knew so intimately? "I really think you're being very unfair," she'd told him.

"Hell no, I'm *leveling* with you," said Murray Stone. "We're not kids any more, are we? I see a lovely young dame sitting in the sun and I figure she's well worth a shot, and if her husband is so inclined to take such a dish for granted, why the hell should I?"

"He does not take me for granted!" she'd snapped. He was beginning to get under her skin. "He certainly is entitled to his interests . . . and what makes you think I'd even give you a second look? Some . . . complete stranger I've just run into?"

Murray Stone lay back in the sun, his eyes closed, a faint smile on his face. "So okay, I could be wrong, *bubie.* You could be the happiest married lay in that whistle-stop you come from—"

"It's not a whistle-stop, it's Liverpool, Indiana, and people don't talk that way to each other there!" she'd told him.

"They do—you don't listen," said Murray Stone. "Anyway, if I'm wrong, sue me. If I'm right, my room number is 718. Twenty-four hour service, we aim to please."

. . . Naturally, she'd let it drop there. Who did this glib New Yorker think she was, some frustrated . . . *hustler*—available on a beach to any complete stranger?

. . . But in the years since that blunt proposition, there had been times when she'd thought about him. Sitting up alone in her bed, watching Johnny Carson, or some old B-picture, waiting for Dusty to come upstairs from whatever he was doing in one of the other rooms . . . she'd lapse into fantasies.

So she was still a lovely dame (perhaps not young any more) but with a good figure that certainly didn't need a girdle, thanks to her exercise class at the Y. And what would it have been like, the two of them alone in Room 718, his door securely locked and the blinds drawn, their clothes tossed aside on the bedside chair, and sunburned Murray Stone (she had trouble remembering his face, but the body remained distinct) grappling with her on the bed, forcing her into strange contortions, muttering obscenities in her ear, keeping the sound of the TV set turned up loud so as to drown out her cries of pleasure . . .

Why did she always return to that impersonal hotel room?

When she awoke, the early morning sun was filtering through the bedroom blinds. Beside her, the bed was empty; she could hear Dusty inside, showering.

. . . She must have gone to sleep with the TV still on, not even hearing him when he'd come upstairs to bed, nor knowing he was aleep beside her. Strange how often that had happened in the last year or so. More and more they seemed to move on paths of their own, meeting only over dinner . . . even on the weekends which had once been time they'd shared.

The water stopped. She heard the hum of his electric razor, and then he emerged. Quietly began to dress, getting himself ready for his day downtown.

Then he came over to nudge her gently. "You awake?" he asked.

". . . I am now," she said.

"You were sacked out when I came up," he said. "Had something to tell you."

She sat up. "I'll make you breakfast."

"No, I've got an early meeting with Lew Davis," he said, tuck-

135

ing his shirt in over the slight pot he'd developed. "We'll get coffee down at the office. When we're done, he needs to talk to you. You be around today?"

"What's he want to talk to me about?" she asked, reaching for her robe.

"Something very important," said Dusty, cryptically. "Two of us've been working it over for weeks now. He'll be coming over by eleven, then *he* can explain things." Whistling tonelessly, he put on his jacket. Threw back his shoulders and glanced at himself in the bedroom mirror. "Okay for an old man," he said.

"You look fine," she said, getting out of bed.

"You don't look so bad yourself," he said, kissing her lightly on the cheek. Patted her once on the shoulder. "I guess we're both holding up fine, right?"

Then he was gone, leaving behind the faint familiar scent of his aftershave, that same stuff he'd used all these years.

Moments later, she heard the throb of his engine as he backed the old Jeep Wagoneer out of the garage, and then he was off down the road, headed for his office. As he'd done most weekday mornings for the past twenty-four odd years.

. . . Twenty-five years *did* sound better if you said two-and-a-half decades.

But Lord, where had all that time gone?

Before eleven, she'd had enough time to go do her shopping, and stop by the cleaners to pick up what was there, and to pick up old Mrs. Hastings, who came in twice a week to clean up the house. (And who was beginning to complain that twice a week really wasn't enough to do the job right, especially since she was getting older, and Dusty's collections were getting larger.)

When Lew Davis arrived, she had a fresh pot of coffee ready. Not so much for him as for herself.

Lew Davis was a sober young man, a power in the Jaycees who was married and had three small sons; that gave him a proprietary interest in the local Little League. He had a small toothbrush mustache, wore jersey knits, and kept a bank of pens clipped to his jacket pocket in a plastic holder. As well as being a successful

C.P.A. he had also built up a very healthy business in the county for his more affluent clients in such exotic ventures as farm-equipment leasing and tax-sheltered cattle-feed lots.

His conversations with Dusty were filled with expressions such as "sale-and-lease-back," "depreciation factor," and "capital erosion controls," to most of which Louise paid little attention. Whenever the two of them had their conferences, which was often, she left them mostly to themselves.

But this morning, he wanted to talk to her. So she led him into the parlor, the one room left downstairs that was still left to her for social occasions, sat him down, and poured him coffee.

After he'd sipped it, and complimented her on it, he glanced at his watch, and cleared his throat. "I'll get right down to it, Mrs. B," he said. "Since it concerns you so basically, Dusty and I wanted you to be in on it from the first pitch, so to speak. He's asked me to run through it all for you, so here goes."

He opened his attaché case and withdrew a thick manila folder. "We'll get around to the signatures after a bit," he said, "but right here's the basic game plan. We start by recognizing that you and Dusty are very well endowed with, ah . . . property. The good things of life. Correct?" Without waiting for her reply, he continued. "Now in terms of future planning, I think we've done a substantial amount of practical thinking about that—the architecture we've devised here is legal, and at the same time," he tapped the folder significantly, "extremely beneficial to both your futures."

"Is this something to do with insurance?" she asked, mildly confused.

"No, and then again, you might call it that," he said. He held up the folder. "This is the blueprint. The establishment of the Bigelow Foundation of Our Past Heritage."

Louise nearly choked on a swallow of hot coffee. ". . . The *what?*" she finally asked.

He passed over one set of legal-sized pages. "You can read it all at your leisure, meanwhile I'll be needing your signature on these four other copies," he said.

"*Why?*" asked Louise.

Lew Davis cleared his throat. "What, in effect, is happening here is that your husband, very farsightedly, as owner of valuable properties, is setting up a foundation. In said foundation he is vesting all his vintage and classic cars, the building in which they're housed, his collection of related artifacts and literature, all pertaining to the automobiles, and he will also turn over sufficient funds to make sure that if anything happens to him in the future, there will be a guaranteed income generated by the Bigelow Foundation of Our Past Heritage to sustain the collection and keep it fully operative for generations to come.''

It was a very impressive speech . . . but what did it mean? Perplexed, she blinked at the documents. "Why in heavens' name do we need to do such a . . . thing?''

". . . Come on, now, Mrs. B,'' said Lew Davis. "The name of the whole game is t-a-x-e-s. If and when your dear husband . . . passed away, the corpus of his estate would contain all those valuable cars. Now, in come Uncle Sam's people, the IRS boys, and they want theirs, oh yes indeedy. Now what we're doing here is to make sure that Dusty's collection doesn't have to be sold to pay the bills for all that darned federal spending . . . which would work a terrific hardship on you, and your two fine sons.''

". . . But wouldn't we have enough money to pay the taxes?'' she asked.

"Oh, you're well provided for,'' said Lew Davis, serenely. "Thanks to some careful planning. You'd get this house, with your marital exemption, and you'd inherit his business, and there'd be insurance to keep you going, plus whatever other properties he's given you over the years. Your financial problems would be minimal, the boys would be provided for, but remember, there's *inflation*. Dusty paid peanuts for most of those cars—nowadays they're more valuable than gold!''

". . . I hadn't thought about that,'' she said.

"You'd have to,'' he warned, ominously. "If and when anything ever happened, and we *hadn't* set up this Bigelow Foundation. This is the way we're going to keep everything strictly status quo, aren't we?''

". . . Well, I guess if you two think it's right,'' said Louise, still dubious. ". . . If it makes Dusty feel more secure—''

"Does it ever!" said Lew. "See, we won't be questioned about intent, because in order to prove that we're completely open and aboveboard, what happens is that the building downtown becomes a museum—with a proper set of hours for opening and closing. It'll be staffed, of course, and available to the public whenever it's open. Then all the materials and books and stuff are there for students and scholars." He beamed. "Everything legitimate."

"Dusty's going into the *museum* business?" she asked.

"Oh no," said Lew. "You both are. After all, you're his wife and his partner in life. There should be a board to run it—besides the two of you, probably me, and his lawyer, that ought to do it . . ."

A *museum?*

Right here in Liverpool, Indiana?

One of those roadside places with coffeeshop and souvenir stand attached?

". . . No, no," said Lew. "Nothing like that. This will be very high class. Piped-in music, carpets, paintings, and pictures on the walls." He cleared his throat. *"Continuity,* that's what we're after. If anything ever happens to good old Dusty, why then you retain the major control of the board, you can be sure of that. And if . . ." he cleared his throat discreetly, "anything should happen to you, we've also made provision for the boys to take over." He beamed. "Don't you think it's a fine piece of planning? Preparing for the future—and at the same time, preserving the past."

It sounded like a motto on the wall of an insurance company office.

"Wait a minute, please," said Louise, her throat suddenly dry. How could he come in here and present her with this . . . *thing*— toss it in her lap, everything all planned and provided for, nicely typed up, for years and years to come! ". . . Why hasn't Dusty ever mentioned any of this to me before?"

Lew Davis nodded, very sympatico. "Oh, I know how you feel, believe me. But darn it, Mrs. B, it's been a very complex problem. We had to go through so many legal consultations, and check out every last little aspect. It took weeks, and your Dusty is one thoughtful guy, believe me. He figured he didn't want you worrying about any of this. I mean, until it all got itself straightened out, you'd be fretting your pretty little head unnecessarily."

". . . I might have been able to cope with that," she said, sarcastically.

Her sarcasm went unnoticed by Lew Davis. He held out his pen. "Okay, now that we're on the runway, ready for takeoff, you'll be consulted on every aspect of things, believe me. After all, you're primary."

"Put your pen away," she said. "I never sign anything without reading it first. I think you were the one who taught me that, weren't you?"

"Good point," said Lew Davis. He recapped the pen and tucked it away along with the rest of that arsenal peeping from his pocket. "I can always come by later. I was just trying to save us both a little time, but you give a holler when you're ready, right?"

". . . Now let me get this straight," said Louise. "This . . . foundation is set up to run this . . . museum . . . and I'm supposed to be the curator?"

He rose, holding up a placating hand. "Not quite yet," he said. "That's a contingency. Right now, old Dusty shouldn't have any problems running the place by himself, but of course *you*'ll be right there to help him whenever he needs you. As I've always said, you two are the best partners I've ever seen. Everybody should be so lucky."

". . . They're not?" she said.

He glanced at his watch. "Got to run—I'll be late for the Rotary lunch." He finished stuffing folders back into his attache case. "Oh . . . there's one other little thing I should tell you . . . but I guess I'll just leave that to Dusty to explain to you."

"There's more?" she asked.

He grinned. "Yep, but I think you'll really enjoy this one. I don't want to spoil it for you." He seized her hand and pumped it. "Between you and me and the lamp-post, Mrs. B, I think this is one darned fine thing Dusty's doing. Not only for you and the family— but think of what an asset it's going to be to Liverpool . . . for years to come, they'll always remember the both of you! Thank you, I'll let myself out."

140

Throughout her lunch, she sat and read through the nineteen page document that established good old Dusty's foundation, plowing determinedly through clause after clause, the whereases and the insofars and all the rest of the complicated, stiff impersonal language.

. . . She had a sudden vision of herself, years from now. She'd be in her sixties, or more, her hair done up in tight curls, wearing a sober grey outfit (by that time she'd probably wear glasses and have capped teeth—if they were still hers), and there she'd be, seated behind the desk in this . . . museum . . . smiling cheerfully at visitors and handing out little brochures that explained the Bigelow collection. Getting up at stated intervals to lead parties through, answering questions, perhaps telling little anecdotes about each of the exhibits, and how her late husband Mr. Bigelow had acquired it. ". . . Oh, Father and I were out driving one afternoon when suddenly he pulled the car over to the side of the road and stopped. You see, he had such a sharp eye—and he'd spotted this old touring-car sitting out back behind the farmer's house, all rusted, but it was definitely a classic . . ."

. . . *The late Mr. Bigelow.*

This pile of legal documents by her hand was a blueprint for the rest of her life.

Once she signed her name at the bottom, and had it properly notarized, that was going to be definitely that.

. . . A life sentence, here in Liverpool, Indiana.

". . . Mrs. Louise Bigelow, well-known throughout the county as the curator of her late husband's Bigelow Foundation of Our Past Heritage, in Liverpool, died today at her office in the main hall of the building, having devoted most of her later years to the care and preservation of the museum's extensive collection of American automobiles of the 20th century, as well as related artifacts of the period."

. . . What was it Murray Stone had said, that day on the beach? ". . . *you're part of the collection, sure.*"

. . . Damn him!

How had that shrewd New Yorker so quickly recognized what

141

she hadn't ever known before, about herself, and Dusty, and this marriage of theirs, which had gone on for almost twenty-five years . . .

. . . Until today?

Dusty's daily schedule rarely varied. By 5:45 he would be home from the day's business, have a single bourbon and ginger ale while he discussed the day's events and watched the 6 o'clock news, and by 6:30 he would be ready to sit down to dinner.

By 5:30 she had it ready, and she went upstairs and changed. Then she mixed herself a small vodka martini on the rocks and sat down in the parlor room to sort out the day's mail, taking out the few items addressed to her from the thick stack of the various bulletins, magazines, trade papers, and flyers from all over the country that clogged their mailbox daily. Dusty seemed to be on every active mailing list in America (and a few in Canada and Europe as well): he heard from firms which offered commemorative limited-edition plates, book-dealers with exotic lists of specialized books, he was a dedicated reader of catalogs, L. L. Bean and Norm Thompson, Gander Mountain Sports, Brookstone Tools, the Bike-cology Bike Shop in California, there were auction lists, today one from Tulsa, Oklahoma, announcing a sale of vintage and classic Cars, here was a new flyer from some stamp and coin dealer in Beverly Hills, California, announcing a Limited Edition Minting of 14-karat gold medallions commemorating Great Stars of the Silver Screen—

Dinner finished tonight, he would take all this into his study and spend an hour or so answering them, making notes, checking out each new opportunity to acquire, or to swap, or to sell, and then stacking it all neatly into the large piles on his already crowded desk. The rooms overflowed with bundles of literature he received over the months; he'd even taken to filling cardboard filing cabinets with all this out-of-date . . . junk!

. . . Once she'd asked, "Couldn't we go through it all and throw *some* of it away?"

"Lord no," he'd said. "I have it all indexed. You never know when you're going to need to refer to something, do you?"

Involuntarily, she chuckled. Such a clever planner, Mr. Lew Davis. In all those legal pages, he hadn't made any provision for a library, had he? Nor for a full-time librarian!

She was working on her second martini when she heard the sound of the engine as he pulled in, and then his footsteps coming slowly up from the cellar.

. . . Now he was beaming at her from the doorway. Holding something behind his back, hiding it from view, cheerful, grinning.

Something new he'd bought?

". . . Hi there, Mrs. Bigelow. How'd you like it—what Lew brought over? Pretty exciting, isn't it?"

"Exciting," she said.

"Isn't it a great feeling to know that everything's all nicely preserved for the future?" he asked.

"Oh yes. Including me," she said.

"You always did have a sense of humor," he said, and came over to kiss her forehead. "That's what really attracted you to me in the first place, y'know?" He glanced at her half-empty glass. ". . . Oh," he said, disappointed. "You started ahead of me."

"I was just sitting here toasting the future," she replied. "I mean, it's not every day that a girl gets herself cemented into a foundation, is it?"

"Nope, I guess not," said Dusty, proudly.

He thrust a wrapped package in silver foil at her. "Thought you'd like this—to celebrate the Bigelow Foundation properly."

She took the package. It was something round; beneath the silver it was hard. "What's this, a new muffler for my car?"

"Funny," he grinned. "Open it."

She ripped away the red plastic bow and tore off the paper.

Inside there was a bottle of champagne. Not New York state, but French . . . Moet & Chandon. "My, my," she said. "How lavish."

Dangling from its neck was a small envelope, on which was written *"To my favorite wife."*

"My heavens, what did I do to deserve this?" she asked.

"Look inside, you'll see," he urged.

Inside the envelope was a small silver ring on which dangled a car key, as well as a neat little silver tag on which was inscribed "25 Years Is Only the Beginning—Love, Dusty."

She stared at it. "My God—what's *this?*"

"Well, I'll tell you," he said, expansively. "That's the key to a car which you will find downstairs in our garage, Mrs. Bigelow."

". . . I'm getting a car?" she asked. ". . . But—I *have* a car."

"Not like this one, you don't," said Dusty. "This one is really something else. C'mon, don't you want to see her?"

Bewildered, she followed him down the cellar stairs. Through the several basement rooms which were piled high with various discarded automobile parts, the couple of old Locke power mowers he'd stored away ("The very best, you can't get them like that any more," he'd explained), and all the other stuff he'd insisted was worth keeping.

Parked inside the garage stood the car.

Low and lean, its finish gleaming, the trim canvas top immaculate, it sat on whitewalls, the 1955 T-Bird. The car in which they'd gone off on their honeymoon. Which he'd kept so carefully stored downtown these past years.

"There you are, Mrs. Bigelow," he said. "It's all yours."

. . . It was probably the vodka (for she never drank more than one) but she could not fathom what he was saying.

"Mine?" she asked.

"My anniversary present to you," said Dusty.

". . . But why give it to *me?*"

"Because you've always loved it as much as I do, right?" he suggested.

". . . Oh yes, I guess I did—but—*why*—" she stammered.

He beamed at her. "Because I know you'll always take good care of it," he said. "You are so . . . *reliable,* honey. No man could ask for anyone better."

He embraced her and kissed her, this time on the lips instead of his customary hello there on the forehead. ". . . Remember?" he asked, holding her close. ". . . We were so young and crazy back then, mmm?"

144

Yes . . . she thought, his arms around her. Young and crazy, and interested only in each other, not in rooms and closets and cabinets and cupboards packed with *things* . . . in stacks and piles and rows and all the rest of it, turning our lives into one great warehouse!

His hands were caressing her now, finding her body beneath her clothing. ". . . Hey," he suggested, "let's you and me drink this champagne and go to bed real early tonight, mm?"

. . . It had been such a while since he'd felt this way. ". . . All right," she murmured.

". . . Because I've got me a hell of a big day tomorrow," he said. "How about now?"

". . . Before dinner?" she asked, surprised.

"What's a better time?" he said, plucking at the buttons of her dress. "C'mon upstairs and we'll celebrate."

Up in their bedroom she pulled back the spread. Dusty was removing his clothes. She took off her dress and put it on a nearby chair, then her slip. As she peeled off her pantyhose, there was suddenly music, a lush string section that filled the room with some ballad she vaguely remembered . . . Dusty was grinning as he came towards her, bringing the glass into which he'd poured some of the champagne. "Remember?" he asked. "It's Hugo Winterhalter, and I've got it all on tape—I knew you'd like it." He handed her the champagne. "To us."

She sipped some of it (so champagne and vodka didn't mix, but what the hell, this was an Occasion) and then he put her glass on the bedside table, pulled her urgently to him.

. . . Then they were on the bed, this was a pleasant echo of the old Dusty and the old Louise, he was kissing her with all the passion she remembered from other times, other places . . . touching her in ways she'd shyly shown him she liked, carefully repeating it all . . .

He might have been taking inventory—

. . . But so what if he was? she was enjoying it, yes, yes, she needed this to make her feel part of him and his life again, not all those damned sheaves of legal pages with their clauses that foretold the future . . .

She lay beneath him, feeling the old responses flickering deep inside her, growing, ah so good, what did it matter now about the

145

time passed, and being middle-aged and all the rest of it, she was with Dusty again, whom she loved and so if he was difficult sometimes, ah so nice, better, better, he was hers, wasn't he? and other women weren't so lucky, oh, oh, beautiful, he mustn't stop now, please, here with her now soaring gently, velvet, velvet, soft deep darkness.

. . . Then he finally gasped. Peaked.

Subsided

—But generously kept moving within her until she cried out . . . in her own private explosion . . .

They both dozed, breathing deeply, the music playing on . . . and then she felt his hand on her. ". . . So nice," she said.

". . . Better than it's been for a long time," he agreed.

It was almost 8:30 when she awoke. Dusty snored gently, but she knew he would awaken soon, ravenous for his dinner.

She threw on her robe, found her slippers, and padded downstairs to the kitchen. Poor, tired Dusty, she'd bring him his dinner up to the bedroom on a tray. He'd certainly earned it.

Luckily, she'd left everything in a low-heat setting, and nothing had burnt. Amazing—while they'd been making love—*fucking!*— up there—the entire house could have caught fire, and then they'd really have gone up in smoke.

How would the papers have handled it? . . . LOCAL COUPLE FOUND MOUNTED ON FUNERAL PYRE?

She brought the tray with everything on it into the bedroom, put it down and nudged him awake.

". . . Oh, *hey* . ." he said, yawning. "Wow. That was something, wasn't it?" Totally relaxed, he stretched.

"Room service," she said, and handed him a napkin.

"Starved," he said.

". . . You always were . . . afterwards," she said.

"You didn't do so bad yourself, as I remember, Mrs. B."

They sipped the rest of the champagne and ate ravenously.

". . . You know something?" he asked, between bites. "That

Lew Davis is one real bright apple. If it hadn't've been for him, I'd never figured out the right way to give you that T-Bird.''

She blinked.

What had Lew Davis had to do with the gift?

''. . . Well, I don't have to tell you, that little buggy is a real classic, and it's worth a fat bundle now,'' said Dusty. ''So, for the past three years, he's fixed it so I transferred three thousand bucks equity in it, taxfree, each year, to you. Tonight, it's all yours. Shrewd?''

. . . So there'd been a tax angle to it. Of course. With Lew Davis, every breath you took was regulated financially. In his home, he'd probably regulated everyone—what to do with leftovers, taxwise, how to go to the toilet and get the most benefit out of it each April 15th, when to screw and get a deduction!

''Dusty,'' she said. ''Can I please talk to you about this foundation idea?''

''Why, certainly, honey, what?'' he asked.

She took a deep breath, and plunged. ''I don't want to be part of it,'' she told him.

Fork in midair, he stared at her. ''Why not?''

She hesitated, struggling to think of one reason that would make sense to him. Then she settled for the simplest.

''. . . . Because—it means we're talking about you being dead!'' she said.

Dusty went on eating. ''Oh, *that*,'' he said, cheerfully. ''So what else is going to happen to me? Not yet, of course, but some day . . .''

''. . . Don't you *see*,'' she insisted, working it out for herself as she spoke. ''. . . It's so final. It's because—that I'll have to live with that probability hanging over me, every day—getting ready for a life without you—''

''Ah, honey,'' he said, trying to placate her. ''You simply have to plan these things ahead of time. It's not like when we were kids— we have Obligations now.''

''That's the whole point!'' she cried. ''After you die—I do *not* want to become your Curator!''

He stared at her reproachfully. ''. . . Louise,'' he said, ''somebody's got to take care of it all. I mean isn't that why I gave you the T-Bird? Oh, I almost forgot—Lew's going to see about having a clause added to your new will, specifically stating that you bequeath the T-Bird to the foundation. You see, that way, it'll stay safe afterwards—and your estate gets the deduction for a charitable bequest. Isn't that a terrific piece of planning?''

. . . They had everything worked out, didn't they?

". . . Tonight," he said, and yawned, "I am really going to *sleep*. Ah . . . there's nothing better than knowing everything valuable in your life is nicely buttoned down . . . taken care of . . . mmm?''

He blew her a kiss, turned over, and burrowed into his pillows.

". . . Night," he muttered. "It was lovely . . .''

And began to snore, shortly afterwards.

She picked up the tray and carried it downstairs.

Tonight she *wasn't* really going to sleep.

She was wide awake. It wasn't the vodka, nor the champagne. Usually, after lovemaking, she went right to sleep as well, but tonight, she was filled with some sense of . . .

. . . Of what? Dread? Panic?

Suffocation.

She went through the hall, past the darkened rooms, the chambers of the Bigelow Foundation.

Upstairs, its founder, Dusty Bigelow, slept on, secure in the knowledge that everything valuable in his life was all nicely buttoned down . . .

Everything in his life, including her.

Mrs. Louise Bigelow. Curator.

. . . Cura*tess?* No, Curatrix? (Not CuratePerson, no way!)

. . . In the kitchen she finished rinsing out the dishes, stacked them, snapped off the lights, and went to the pantry. It was almost 11 P.M., and she never drank so late in the evening, but tonight was different. She made herself another drink.

Carried it back to the study. Sat down and snapped on the radio, to get some music. She needed to sit and think about this.

No she didn't. All she needed was a way of getting out of it.

On the floor were the piles of Dusty's mail, scattered where he'd left it, he hadn't yet taken them inside to stack them on his desk. Automatically, she reached down to pick them up, to put them somewhere out of the way.

On top of the pile was a glossy blue-backed brochure which announced The First Southwestern Classic and Vintage Car Auction, to be held in Tulsa, Oklahoma.

Another sale of automobiles?

Dusty would probably be drawn down there to buy something else for his collection, something *more*—

Which was wrong.

Get *rid* of things. *Simplify.*

. . . That was the whole trick.

But not with this man—this obsessed—

—Angrily, she started to toss the catalog away in the direction of the wastebasket—

Then, she stopped.

Stared at the catalog again.

. . . If things needed to be disposed of, oh yes, certainly—

Auctions were places where people bought—true—but——

Other people sold.

Now. If she did not wish to be Mrs. Bigelow, the late Dusty's faithful Curator/Cura*trix*—or whatever-the-hell-it-was . . .

Did that not put her into the category of *other people?*

Drink in hand, she sat and began to turn the glossy pages of the Tulsa catalog, her mind racing, grappling with this remarkable new possibility.

Turning over the amazing idea, relishing its effects.

. . . *Not* to sign these papers Lew Davis had dumped in her lap!

To sell—which meant to—

—Get out of all the walls Lew and Dusty were building around her—

—To become free of—*things*—

(Free for what, Louise?)

Never mind that now, the important thing was to follow this impulse, take Step A—

Downstairs was a T-Bird, but suppose you thought of it as a get-away car?

(Getaway cars need drivers, Louise.)

That meant putting the key into the ignition, Step B would be to start the engine in that pile of valuable steel and chrome and rubber and aluminum, back it out.

To where?

It had been so long since she'd made her own decisions.

Out the driveway, down to the main highway, away she'd go in her taxfree T-Bird—

To Tulsa, Oklahoma. To sell that precious piece of property—

(Take the money and do what, Louise? . . . *Leave* Dusty?)

"No way, *bubie,* not *you* . . ." said a voice that was unmistakably that bastard Murray Stone. "You go to hell." she said, aloud.

She went inside and found the vodka bottle, poured herself another little drink.

Then she went back to the library shelf to find a road atlas.

How many miles was it to Tulsa?

*   *   *

Part Two

TULSA, OKLAHOMA

Pop 349,000   Altitude 689 feet.

. . . Once known as the Oil Capital of the world, this cosmopolitan center is Oklahoma's second largest city.

Guided 1½ hour bus tours are available through the Sun Oil Refinery Mon.–Fri. at 10 and 2, and Sat. at 10. The Texaco Refinery conducts tours Mon.–Fri. at 9–3, by advance appointment only.

Among the city's parks is the Municipal Rose Garden, with approximately 1000 plants . . .

. . . The sun-drenched dusty street was deserted. Windows and doors closed, to keep out the glare of noon.

Far off in the distance, coming towards him, wearing a black frock coat, a black sombrero, smoking a thin cigar, his arms swinging ominously above the holsters at his waist, boots kicking up the Oklahoma dust, strode a man.

The man. The man he'd come to settle with, all these thousands of miles.

". . . All right then," he called out, stepping out into the street. "I been a-looking for you, friend. *Freeze!*"

The man in black wheeled, stared at him through narrowed eyes. Frowned. "Who wants me?" he asked, warily.

"Somebody out of your past, G. Dudley. George D. Or whatever the hell you call yourself these days!"

Silence. Then the man in black spoke. "Good heavens," he said. "Is that *you*, Cyril? What a pleasant surprise." He held out a cordial hand. "What brings you all this way to Tulsa, Oklahoma?"

". . . You and I have us a little unfinished business to attend to," he said.

"We certainly do!" said George D. Lester. "This is your lucky day, old friend. How'd you like to invest your hard-earned money in a nice piece of prime real estate? A fine spread of ranchland—not far from here, one that'll bring you security in your old age, and maybe even some nice capital appreciation, eh?"

His hand went for the holster at his hip, and with lightninglike speed, he withdrew, not a .44, but a tight roll of legal documents, which he thrust forward. "Here now, let me show you my brand," he said.

"I already know what your brand is, friend," he said, grimly. "It's IOI, right?"

"Why, Cyril, that's positively amazing," said George D. Lester. "How perceptive of you. Now, in order to save us both some time, why don't you just put your signature down here at the bottom of the page, and hand me over that sheaf of traveler's cheques you got in your pocket, and you and me can go have us a little whiskey to celebrate. I mean, it's not every day I come across a pigeon I can fleece the way I do you, Cyril, is it?"

153

. . . Furious, Cyril came awake.

It was past noon by his watch on the bedside table, he'd been sleeping here in his room at the Oil City Motel since . . . seven this morning? When he'd arrived in a cab from the airport—and luckily found a motel that had a vacancy . . .

This bed was wide, gargantuan by British standards. The decor in bright orange and dark brown was a bit confused. But the room was cool, the air-conditioning unit hummed softly, and the blinds were blessedly drawn shut to keep out that brilliant Oklahoma sunlight.

—Was it yesterday that he'd left old dark and grey London, to jet across the Atlantic to Atlanta, Georgia, then to change planes and to fly another long leg here to this bustling city, with its broad boulevards and obviously new business towers thrusting skywards from the Oklahoma plains. (Not a bit like the show he'd seen in London, years back, no meadows, no corn as high as an elephant's eye, merely traffic rushing through the streets.)

. . . The plump lady at the front desk had been cordial enough.

"Yes indeedy," she'd told him. "You can get yourself a taxi right out front and he'll take you over to the Arena pronto. You mean you come all this way to buy yourself some old car?"

"Possibly," said Cyril, as she studied his registration card.

". . . London, *England,* Mr. Banks?" she said. "You must want some car out there real bad, I bet."

Was everybody in this town so nosy? He wiped the perspiration from his forehead. "Possibly," he told her.

"Want to give me your credit card now, honey?" she suggested.

"I prefer to pay cash," he'd said.

"We don't get too much of that," said the lady, dubiously. "Course, we don't get too many of you people here, neither." She eyed the packet of traveler's cheques he'd proffered. "Are them dollars, or pounds? See, I know about your money—I been watching that 'Upstairs and Downstairs" ever since it first come on—"

"Pounds," he said.

". . . Well now, I guess they're good enough," she said "But

154

I'm not in the money-changing line, so why'nt you get down to the bank in the shopping center, 'cross the street, when it opens, you can change some of that for dollars, and when you come back, you and me can do a little horse-tradin', right?'' She handed him his key. "Now why'nt you go on up and wash off some of that London fog, mm?''

Along with the key she had handed him was a small printed card, which read:

WELCOME, STRANGER, TO THE OIL CITY MOTEL!
   HOPE YOU ENJOY YOUR STAY IN TULSA!
NOTE: THE MANAGEMENT IS NOT RESPONSIBLE
   FOR ANY ITEMS LEFT IN ROOMS.
     USE OUR SAFE: DON'T BE SORRY!

. . . Slightly ominous.

But then, a peculiarly apt warning, considering that George D. Lester was here in the same town.

Cyril got up and showered.

After one, now, but his body was still on British time, which meant it was sometime this evening, after dinner, perhaps, and how could he be hungry, surfeited as he was with airline food and drinks.

As he dressed (luckily, he'd brought along the one tropical worsted suit he still had, left over from the old days when he'd traveled to all the resorts for IOI, Ltd) he glanced at the literature placed on the bureau by the management.

WORSHIP AT THE CHURCH OF YOUR CHOICE.

DON'T LEAVE TULSA WITHOUT VISITING
   ORAL ROBERTS UNIVERSITY!
AN UPLIFTING EXPERIENCE FOR
   THOSE OF ALL FAITHS AND CREEDS.
2½ MI SOUTH OF I-44 AND US 66, AT
   7777 SOUTH LEWIS AVENUE.
FEATURES A 200-FOOT GLASS AND STEEL PRAYER TOWER,
   A SIX-STORY HEXAGONAL LIBRARY

There was also a magazine, *Tulsa This Week*. On its cover was a photograph of an elegantly kept 1955 Lincoln Continental, standing next to the car, a smiling blonde lady wearing an ornate buckskin outfit studded with jewelry, waving a sombrero and beckoning the cameraman to join her in the front seat. The caption read TULSA WELCOMES THE FIRST SOUTHWESTERN CLASSIC AND VINTAGE CAR AUCTION!

. . . But no sign of George D. Lester.

Specialist in the art of the low profile.

Right then, it was time to head for the Arena, to look over the Rolls he'd come all this way to buy, with Ben Emir's money.

. . . And time for a showdown on the dusty Tulsa street, with the man in black?

As he walked into the motel office, there seemed to be some sort of a crisis taking place between the manageress and a young lady who stood at the counter, obviously with the intention of becoming a resident.

". . . You're not with some firm?" the manageress asked, staring at the newly signed registration card.

"No, and I'm paying cash," said the young lady. "So what?" She was in her late twenties, with jet black hair that needed attention; her clothing was rumpled and she was obviously anxious to repair forthwith to a cool room and a hot tub.

". . . Well now, I don't ratly know, Miss Lo-Renzo," said the manageress, dubiously. "Y'see, we don't usually have much to do with the singles trade here—"

"Explain what that means?" demanded Miss Lo-Renzo.

". . . What it means is," said the manageress, clearing her throat, ". . . . . . ah, don't encourage unescorted females to register, do I make myself clear?"

". . . What's your name?" asked Miss Lo-Renzo, sweetly.

156

"Hereford," said the lady. "You could read it rat there on the desk card . . ."

"Mrs. Hereford, are you saying if I showed up here with some male clown, I could have a room?" asked Miss Lo-Renzo.

"Heavens, I never said *that!*" said Mrs. Hereford. "Lissen here—"

". . . *You* listen," said Miss Lo-Renzo. "Hard. I'm a nurse from Bridgeport, Connecticut, I've been six hours on a night coach flight from La Guardia that was delayed taking off, I'm down here in this sun-baked pits on business, I need a room for two nights, and if I have to do any more explaining why I'm entitled by the Bill of Rights to give you cash, right here, in *this* motel—"

"Now honey, you got a real short fuse—" said Mrs. Hereford

"—Instead of somewhere else, I'm going to go find me a good civil-rights lawyer and you'll end up showing your false teeth on 'Sixty Minutes!' "

Cyril cleared his throat.

Both ladies turned to stare.

". . . What do *you* want?" said Miss Lo-Renzo.

He held out his key. "Directions to the bank," he said. "Then you two ladies can return to your summit conference."

"Why sure," said Mrs. Hereford, and reached for a small map.

"Why don't you ask him what *he's* doing here, alone in your motel," said Miss Lo-Renzo, staring balefully at Cyril.

". . . Now honey, this fella is here all the way from England, and you don't want him gettin' the wrong i-dea about us Americans,—now do you?" said Mrs. Hereford.

"I couldn't care less about his ideas," said Miss Lo-Renzo. "Yours either." She held out her hand. "I want a room key."

"Oh, all *rat!*" conceded Mrs. Hereford, and handed one over.

"Congratulations," said Cyril.

Obviously in no mood for small talk, Miss Lo-Renzo snatched up her overnight bag and headed out of the office.

". . . Don't you want me to tell you where the room is?" called Mrs. Hereford.

The door slammed behind Miss Lo-Renzo.

Mrs. Hereford shrugged. "She sure sounds like one of them trouble-makin' Womens Lib people to me."

*   *   *

The Arena was a large shedlike building spread across a city block that loomed up at the end of a wide boulevard, a $6 ride from the motel. Years back, the original decor had been a sharp green, but long months in the Oklahoma sun and rain had given the exterior the look of watered pea soup. The sagging frame walls were bedecked with red white and blue plastic bunting that stirred lazily in the occasional breeze and hung like garish costume jewelry on the dowdy old structure.

From half a block away, the air was filled with the sound of public-address-system music, the Oklahoma afternoon echoing with the voice of some nasal tender who, to the accompaniment of steel guitars, chanted a hymn to the glories of his good old humble little prairie spread where he'd learned to ride and rope at the hands of his good old cow-punching paw. WELCOME VINTAGE CAR COLLECTORS! said a banner at the main gate.

Cyril went up to the ticket window, behind which perched a pretty blonde wearing a sombrero and a T-shirt that bore the same sentiment in large letters.

"Howdy, stranger," she told him. "Git yore catalog here and register for the auction? Tin dollars gits you in, starts you biddin' and may the best man win?"

"Yes indeed," said Cyril, handing over a bill, his eyes wandering across the splendid female display that strained, unfettered, beneath the thin cotton. He signed his name on the register, and she passed him over the catalog. She glanced at his signature. "Mmm-*hmm!*" she said. "All the ways from London, Englun?"

He nodded.

"I declare, you must want some wheels inside powerful bad," she sighed. " 'Course, we're gittin' 'em from all over. Big spenders and high-rollers, real excitin' y'know? Go rat in and find what you want and if you can't, just ask, heah?"

He tore himself away from the view and went inside.

The main area was brightly lit; in the glare were parked rows of gleaming automobiles on display, each with a large painted sign proclaiming its make and date, and with rope barriers set up to pro-

158

tect them from prying hands. Here and there uniformed security guards, revolvers at their waists, strolled casually past, eyeing visitors.

On went the music, and now the smell of cooking suffused the air. The odors set his stomach signalling; for the first time since he'd arrived from London, he was hungry. He made his way to one of the several stands by the wall; above it was a sign reading DOWN HOME COOKING.

Behind the counter was another spectacular Oklahoma female in the same uniform, sombrero, jeans and well-stuffed T-shirt. The menu offered CHILI DOGS, CHILI BURGERS, CHILI AND FRIES, CHILI TACOS, CHILI HOT! and CHILI HOTTER! COKE or BEER ON ICE.

. . . Hardly what one would select for breakfast, and yet, when in Rome . . .

He ordered a hamburger, sans chili. ''Nekkid?'' asked the girl.

''With tea, please, '' he added.

''*Tay?''* she exclaimed, puzzled. ''I don't ratly think we have inny of that.''

He settled for a cold beer. Since another sign cautioned PLEASE DON'T EAT FOOD AROUND THE CARS! he sat and chewed the moist sandwich of burnt ground beef and sipped at his beer, while turning over the pages of the sales catalog.

The Rolls Royce he had come for was Number 32, easily located on the map of the various items for sale that had been slipped between the pages.

When he had finished what passed for food, he began to stroll down the aisles, admiring the various automotive items due to be sold shortly.

An amazing feast for afficionados, for gawpers, for dreamers and tire-kickers.

. . . Here, an open Packard 1929 touring car, massive, chrome glittering in the bright light, resting placidly on its four huge balloon whitewalls, proud relic of the days when chauffeurs drove and ten-cents-a-gallon gasoline was available everywhere. There, a 1941 Buick Sedanet, with its odd-shaped slant-back silhouette. What was this peculiar little boxlike affair, known as the Willys Americar, some sort of automotive mistake, rescued from oblivion? . . . And here was something called a Henry J, over there a peculiar hybrid dubbed Tucker Torpedo. Next to it, a trim Morgan sports-two-plus-two, far from its British home. Then a rakish 1938 Chevrolet convertible, another strange item known as the Chrysler Airflow . . . on and on they went, a parade, a mechanical smorgasbord.

Then, at last, on a platform raised a foot or so above the floor, obviously one of the star items, there stood the 1937 Rolls.

Waiting patiently, with special spotlights outlining its classic lines, the car he had come thousands of miles to ransom, to snatch up and bring back to Ben Emir.

. . . Along with G. Dudley's scalp.

(This was Indian territory, was it not?)

He leaned against the railing to examine the Rolls more closely.

The paint work seemed fine, tires in good shape, excellent chrome. A trim little specimen, the Hooper coachwork was elegant, the beige and white color scheme restrained, this was a car that had obviously been pampered all its life, a rich man's toy. And yet . . . for the sort of money one might have to pay over for this item of automotive jewelry here in Tulsa, one should really inspect a bit more.

. . . A voice beside him said "Sorry, buddy, hands *off.*"

A security guard was standing beside him, glaring.

"How does one arrange to inspect the interior?" asked Cyril.

"I dunno, I only work here," said the guard. *"Off."*

"This is ridiculous," said Cyril. "I'm a *buyer.*"

"Good for you," said the guard. "I drive a pickup—"

"Howdy—any problems here?" asked a passing lady.

She was obviously someone In Authority, a trim, fortyish matron in jeans and a brightly patterned shirt, she wore sunglasses and her hair was piled amazingly high atop her head. There was a tentative smile on her nicely capped teeth.

"My name is Miz Joyce Donaldson Wade, and kin I help you at all?" she said. "I'm Management."

"Yes, indeed," said Cyril. "My name is Banks, I'm from London, and I'd like very much to have a closer look at this Rolls, *provided* I'm not suspected of trying to steal it."

"Oh my, you're a serious buyer," said Miz Wade. Her smile widened. "Why surely, it can be arranged. I'll handle this," she told the guard, and escorted Cyril past the rope barrier. Then she opened the rear door. "Now. Look at *that*."

The upholstery was of shiny fawn leather. Above the front seat was a sliding roof to permit the driver and his companion access to fresh air. Between the front seat and the small rear was a divider, operated by a hand crank, but the small Rolls, built during a period of obvious British austerity, had no jump seats. Rather, the car exuded a quiet sense of cautious opulence. One could imagine its owner saying, over a highball, ". . . Oh yes, things are a bit difficult these days, but one simply cannot do without the amenities, can one?"

"Very trim, indeed," said Cyril, impressed.

"Ain't she just?" said Miz Wade. "She comes with all her service records—in top shape. Part of an estate, see? Ought to bring a right nice price. We're estimatin' her at maybe seventy, in that ball park. Kinda hate to see her go, I really would like to have her in my own garage, y'know? Sure would get my neighbors starin' when I took her down to the supermarket."

"Oh, that it would," said Cyril. "Thank you so much—"

Above them, the p.a. system suddenly ceased its endless music and a disembodied voice called "Mrs. Wade. Mrs. Wade. Mister Lester is lookin' for you, please check with the office."

Mister Lester.

Ah. Mr. George D. Lester?

Mr. G. Dudley Lester?

The one and the same, once of Hertford Street, London?

. . . Miz Wade had pulled a small walkie-talkie device from her purse and was speaking into it. "I'm out here, by the Rolls," she said. "Tell Mr. Lester *he* can find *me*—I'm with a customer!" Then she turned back to Cyril. " 'Course, if the biddin' gets real high, and we get us some high-rollers in from Dallas, or them Arabs show up, who knows how high this little beauty might go? Eighty, ninety? You think you'd be ready to go that high?"

"Who knows?" said Cyril, casually. "One always tries not to get carried away, but during an auction . . ."

"That's what makes horse races, rat?" said Miz Wade.

"Exactly," he said. "Go for broke, as the man says."

"Oh, Mr. Banks, I like your style!" she said.

"Joyce!" called a voice.

A very familiar voice, this one.

"I've been looking all over hell and gone for you—" it said.

"Say hello to Mr. Banks from London," said Miz Wade.

Cyril turned to face Mr. G. Dudley Lester.

. . . Not on a dusty Oklahoma street, and not at high noon, but beside an opulent little 1937 Rolls Royce, with the p.a. system going on above, now it was some girl wailing about true love being worth more than solid gold, and when you found the man who'd stay with you, then you should stay with him for the rest of your natural days—

I found him alive, thought Cyril. And now—what next?

G. Dudley wore not a black suit but a trim blue blazer, with a silk handkerchief knotted around his neck. He carried a small attaché case, and his face showed no trace of surprise.

"Why hel*lo*, Mr. Banks," he said, offering his hand. "Welcome to Tulsa, Oklahoma."

"Thank you, Mr. Lester," said Cyril, shaking it. "How've you been?"

"Not bad, not bad," said G. Dudley. "And you?"

"You two know each other?" asked Miz Wade.

"We've met," commented G. Dudley.

"I've often wondered how you were," said Cyril. "Thought of you many times."

"I appreciate that," said G. Dudley.

"It's been quite some time, eh?" said Cyril. "And after all, you did leave rather . . . abruptly."

"Yes, true," said G. Dudley. "But then, he travels fastest who travels alone, correct?"

"So you taught me," said Cyril.

"And what brings you all this way to Tulsa?" asked G. Dudley.

"He's here sniffin' around this Rolls," said Miz Wade. "Ready to put down a nice fat bid, rat, Mr. Banks?"

"Hopefully, the winning one," said Cyril.

"Here on a buying trip, eh?" asked G. Dudley.

Not entirely, thought Cyril. I have one other fish to fry. . . . *You.*

162

He nodded.

". . . And that's all?" persisted G. Dudley.

You cheeky bastard, thought Cyril. After all this time, you're asking *me* questions—when I'm the one who's entitled to the answers!

He shrugged. "Isn't that sufficient?" he said. "After all, this Rolls should fetch a nice price.

". . . For yourself, then?"

"I'm taking it back to London," said Cyril.

"Ah, London. Still London?" asked G. Dudley.

"Oh yes. Still London," said Cyril. "Have you been there lately?"

"No, can't say that I have," said G. Dudley.

". . . You two know each other from *London?*" asked Miz Wade, her head moving back and forth as if she were watching a tennis match.

"Knew," said Cyril.

". . . Well, how come, if you're both such good buddies, you didn't come out straightway and tell me you knew G. Dudley here?" she demanded. "Hell, I mean, you come all this way—you act like a stranger—what're friends *fer?*"

"I often wonder," said Cyril.

". . . What sort of business are you in now?" asked G. Dudley.

"I've a restaurant," said Cyril. "Four-star."

"Must be, for you to be buying this Rolls here," said G. Dudley.

"Certainly," said Cyril.

. . . And that is all you're going to get out of me, chum, he thought. Until I get a few answers from *you*.

". . . Lissen, you two boys goin' to stand around here jawin' all day?" asked Miz Wade. "When we got us a lot of paper work to do? Tell you what, Mr. Banks, you stick around a while, then about five, when we're done, you come on out with us to the house and have yourself a little eighteen-karat Oklahoma hospitality, rat?"

". . . Perhaps Mr. Banks has other plans," suggested G. Dudley.

"None at all," said Cyril.

"You see?" demanded Miz Wade. "He's down here totin' around all that good English money he's itchin' to spend, the least we can do is to make him feel at home! Where's your manners, G. Dudley?"

"Thoughtless of me," said G. Dudley.

"Then that's settled!" said Miz Wade. She gave Cyril an enthusiastic handshake. "You come rat over to the office about five and let us take it from there!"

"Jolly good," said Cyril. "Thank you."

". . . she likes you," commented G. Dudley.

"She shows good taste," said Cyril.

"Damn right!" said Miz Wade. "C'mon, G. Dudley, let's get movin'!"

"Coming, my dear," he said.

They disappeared into the crowd.

Cyril glanced at his watch. Nearly four. He had another hour to wander through the exhibits, and then to spend an evening enjoying some eighteen-karat Oklahoma hospitality. To observe G. Dudley Lester in his new incarnation, respectable citizen.

Had the old leopard changed his spots?

. . . It did not seem likely.

*   *   *

The warehouse that dispensed Miz Wade's eighteen-karat Oklahoma hospitality was an opulent mansion in the suburbs, nestled behind a high wall (". . . Can't be too careful these days, if you know what I mean") there were water fountains on the tidy lawns, which glittered in the dusk through various colored lights (". . . ain't it a homey effect?"), and in the rear was the large heated pool ("Now you just help yourself to a suit and cool off, straighten out the kinks.")

At a small well-stocked bar, there were all sorts of drinks. (". . . I only take wan, but for you, bein' as how you're British, how about some of this 12-year-old straight malt Scotch?")

Food began to appear, hors d'oeuvres passed by a beaming black couple. On the patio, now changed into a diaphanous hostess gown, the hostess entertained her guests, another couple named

Hansen (". . . he's very big in tax shelters, honey, maybe you two could get together on a deal!") while nearby, on the patio—her *lanay,* a massive slab of beef sizzled in clouds of bluish fragrant smoke.

Cyril sipped the excellent whiskey, nibbled at huge shrimp, tiny baby pies (". . . them pizzas are just terrible for my waist, but I can't resist 'em!"), egg rolls, and spare ribs, nodded at the conversation, made small talk with the Hansens and with another couple who had just dropped by, the Axelrods (". . . nicest Joosh folks you'll ever want to meet, owns that new boutique downtown, I can't stay out of it!"), and eventually plowed his way through the barbecued beef with the baked potato and sour cream dressing, the salad, tasted the spicy chili, and cooled off his palate with the luscious watermelon that served as dessert.

Dinner finally over, he collapsed in a comfortable chair by the pool, away from the center of activity, and sipped a bit of the fine old brandy that was now being passed.

All evening G. Dudley had been immersed in conversation with the other guests, but now he pulled up a chair and sat down.

". . . Well now," he suggested, "Shall we have a talk?"

"About what?" asked Cyril. "Old times?"

"If you like," said G. Dudley.

"I do like," said Cyril. "Whatever became of all the capital?"

"Capital?" asked G. Dudley, inhaling his brandy. "What capital?"

"Oh, the IOI assets," said Cyril. "Surely you remember them, don't you? *I* do."

"Oh, those," said G. Dudley. "Mostly gone now."

"Gone?"

"Cost of living. Simply dreadful, these days," said G. Dudley. "Which is why I've had to go into this . . . little enterprise here."

". . . Just to make ends meet?" asked Cyril.

"Precisely," said G. Dudley.

. . . Lying bastard, thought Cyril. You really expect me to take you seriously? A second time? Not bloody likely.

"Now about you," G. Dudley said. "You're doing well, eh? Otherwise you might not have survived these last few years . . ."

"Can't complain," said Cyril. "I learned well at the feet of the master. That is, until the feet disappeared."

"Just so," said G. Dudley. "Well, life does go on. No need to waste valuable time looking back, is there?"

"Especially not in your case," said Cyril. "Who knows who might be following you?"

G. Dudley smiled.

"You?" he said.

Shrewd bugger. How quickly he'd come to the point.

". . . What could you do to me here?" asked G. Dudley. "Ruin my reputation by spreading it all over Tulsa that I was once the Demon of Hertford Street?" He shook his head. "Let me, as they say here, clue you in, pal. It wouldn't do you any good, and it certainly wouldn't hurt me. You see, down here is what they call frontier mentality. Goes back a long way. People admired the marshal who cleaned up the town, but they were also big fans of Jesse James. Nowadays, everybody talks a lot about law and order, but it's mainly to protect their own property, you see. Secretly, they still applaud crooks. The more successful the operator, the fonder they are of him. So . . . don't waste your time trying to bad-mouth me. I'm a solid citizen, and you'd end up sounding like some out-of-town sorehead. Nobody would listen to you. Down here, only money talks . . ."

"I've got money!" snapped Cyril.

". . . Not enough," said G. Dudley.

Cyril did not answer. For the first time since they'd met this afternoon, he was furious at himself. Why had he let his anger take over?

Obviously, the old wounds had very thin scar tissue.

"Ah, come now," said G. Dudley, as if to a recalcitrant child. "No hard feelings about the past. We've both survived, and who knows what we might accomplish, some day in the future?"

Cyril took another sip of the brandy, stared at his adversary through the wavering light reflected from Miz Wade's lan-ay.

"Together?" he said. "I don't know as I could afford that—not more than once. As a partner, you're very expensive, George."

G. Dudley chuckled. "I never did come cheap."

166

". . . *G. Dudley!*" called his hostess, her voice piercing the soft night. "Pick up the damn phone—it's Long Distance!"

"Coming!" said G. Dudley. "Sorry," he told Cyril, as he rose. "We get calls from all over."

He disappeared, headed for the house.

Long distance calls about what? mused Cyril. What is the fox up to now?

". . . How're you doin', English?" called Miz Wade. She had weaved through the darkness towards Cyril, and now she stood above him, a goblet of wine in hand. "You two catchin' up on old times?"

"You might say that," he told her.

". . . Know my ol' buddy real good, don't you?" she asked. It was obvious from her speech that his hostess had been attacking the grape all evening. ". . . And isn't he the shrewdest fella you ever did meet?" she chortled, plumping herself down in the vacant chair. "Lord, that man must lie awake nights just figgerin' out every last little way to get himself the edge!"

"Yes, indeed," said Cyril.

". . . I'm gonna tell you somethin' " she said, and nudged him. "I sure wish I had that man's brains is all. But if I can't have 'em, I'll sure settle for him havin' 'em, that's for damn sure. *Hooeeh,* if I was to tell you all the little gizmos he comes up with, I swear you wouldn't believe it!" She chortled happily.

". . . And what sort of little gizmos might they be?" asked Cyril.

The lady took a large gulp of her wine. "Now, now," she said, winking. "I might be a little pissed, but I learned one thing from my daddy—never tell everythin' you know—at least not till it's over, and mebbe not even then!" Again she nudged him. "Ain't that the truth, Nigel?"

"Cyril," he corrected her.

"Nigel, Cyril, all sound alike, English. Oh, hey! I got a treat for you!" she said, suddenly, and jumped up from the chair. "Sit rat there—you're my guest—I want you to hear somethin' special!"

She made her way into the nearby pool house, and then the stereo went off, leaving them all in blessed silence.

Not for long.

A moment or so later, there was a blare of music, and then an orchestra launched into a lush arrangement of what seemed to be an old song, one that he remembered from his youth.

"Hey, English, this one's fer *you!*" he heard her call, and then as the music continued, she could be heard, singing in a high, flattish soprano:

". . . There'll be bluebirds ovah
The wha-it cliffs of Dov-ah
T'morra, jist you wait 'n' see?"

It continued like that. Vera Lynn she wasn't.

When she finished, there were whoops from the other guests, and cries from the darkness for an encore.

. . . The alcohol and the food and the jet lag all combined to cause Cyril to drowse. As he slipped into sleep, he heard her soprano chanting something that sounded vaguely like a song dedicated to a mother who packed some sort of a pistol. . . . ?

. . . He felt himself being shaken gently.

"Time to go home," said G. Dudley. "Everyone's left. I called you a cab."

"Thanks," said Cyril. He was totally disassociated. What was he doing here, sleeping in this garden? He rose. ". . . Must say a proper goodnight to my hostess . . ."

"Don't bother," said G. Dudley. "She had quite a day—she's gone up. I'll say goodnight for you."

He escorted Cyril through the house to the front door, where the cab stood waiting outside.

"Drop you somewhere?" asked Cyril.

". . . Oh no, thanks," said G. Dudley, yawning. "I've made other arrangements."

. . . From upstairs, on the second floor, came a female voice, echoing down the stairwell. ". . . G. Dudley, you comin' up to bed or *not?*"

Cyril grinned, ". . . A very efficient arrangement," he said.

168

"Coming, love!" called G. Dudley.

"Strange," said Cyril. "I was sure that you traveled strictly solo."

"Man does not live by bread alone," said G. Dudley, and closed the front door.

* * *

By the time his cab had deposited Cyril back at the motel, his stomach was desperately churning.

Beside the motel, the neon lights of a small coffee shop were still lit. He retrieved his room key from the sleepy clerk, then went into the coffee shop, in search of a therapeutic cup of tea.

The place was deserted, save for one customer.

She appeared to be Miss Lo-Renzo, the nurse from Bridgeport, who sat moodily sipping coffee. Since the last time he'd seen her, she'd done her hair up, changed her clothes, and now she looked quite presentable.

He sat down beside her, and when the waitress emerged from the tiny kitchen to take his order, he requested tea.

"Don't drink it, it's foul," murmured Miss Lo-Renzo.

"But necessary," he said. "Foul tummy."

"You too?" she said. "Where'd you get poisoned, so I can avoid it?"

"It was a private orgy," said Cyril. "The native cuisine here is a bit rough."

"So are the natives," she said. "Stay out of Red's Rib Room, unless you're looking to be picked up by some hot-shot cowboy who's figuring if he buys you a beer he can have an anatomy lesson free. Do you know how damn tough it is to get yourself fed— alone?" She rummaged in her purse and produced a small tube, shook out two white pills. "Chew these," she instructed.

He dutifully munched them and washed them down. "I do appreciate that, Miss Lo-Renzo," he told her.

"Lorenzo," she said. "And don't feel obliged to continue the conversation. We can keep it all on a strict nurse-and-patient level, agreed?"

"As you like," he said. "Are you here on medical business?"

"No," she said. "If you really want to know, I came down here to buy a car at auction. Would you believe a relatively sane person could be capable of such dumbness?"

"How remarkable," said Cyril. "I'm here in Tulsa for the very same reason—"

"Sure, sure, Charley," said Miss Lorenzo. "Listen, when you're a nurse, you get every possible approach tossed at you, and I've learned to handle them all. I don't know why it is everybody figures because a girl is a nurse, she's automatically available. Take you. You're alone, you're far from home, you don't want to hit the sack alone, which is understandable, it's late, and you figure if anything goes wrong during the night, I'll be right there. But I won't be. Okay?"

He sipped his tea, which *was* foul.

". . . You may not believe this," he told her, "but at this very moment, I'm feeling equally as hostile as you. So I can't resent your paranoia."

"Oh, they have that in England too?" she said. Then she rose. She tossed him another white tablet. "This is in case your stomach doesn't improve. Now, I'm going to bed and try to forget where I am."

Then she left, and he watched her marching off towards her room.

Strange, he wondered . . . had old Florence Nightingale been such an angry lady?

*   *   *

1929 MODEL AA ONE-TON STAKE TRUCK

. . . Okay, so he had to sell his little darlin'.

As usual, Sally was right when she said if it had to be done, then it was like having a tooth pulled. Once you accepted it had to go, then the sooner you got it over with, the better.

. . . It was the damn waiting around for the dentist to reach in and yank that destroyed you.

So he'd agreed to it when Sally said she'd handle the arrangements, she and the secretary in Jack Adler's office. They'd located that big auction in Tulsa, Oklahoma. (Tulsa? He knew he'd played Tulsa, but somehow he couldn't remember much about the town, all those places blurred in his memory, seemed the same.)

He'd signed all the papers for consignment, then the title, and she'd even arranged it so that he wouldn't be around the house when the men were scheduled to come pick it up with the flatbed, to pick up the truck, load it carefully on the trailer, and haul it down to Tulsa.

". . . You go away, out of sight out of mind, it's better that way, believe me," she'd assured him.

. . . When he came back from Boston, after a weekend trip where he'd played a couple of nights in a Cambridge jazz club where the owner still remembered Pick Up Truck with fondness and was willing to pay cash, her garage was empty.

The Model AA was gone.

Just like' that.

After all these years . . . yanked from his life, like a pulled tooth.

Okay, that was that. He tried to concentrate on writing. Anything to forget it.

. . . But what Sally (who knew so goddamned much everything!) hadn't reminded him was that after you had the tooth pulled, and the anesthetic wore off, then the hurt began.

No matter what he used to deaden the pain, this hurt didn't seem to go away.

Booze didn't help much. He went out nights to a corner tavern a couple of blocks away, where the owner fancied polka music from

172

the jukebox, but kept the drinks coming without questioning if Chuck had had enough, and he came reeling home through the quiet streets, but the ache persisted.

He filched downers from Sally's bathroom cabinet and used them to try and get some sleep, but they didn't stop him from dreaming.

. . . Other nights he borrowed her van and went driving, aimless journeys to nowhere through highways, past empty shopping centers and gloomy factory buildings, a desolate landscape . . .

The ache persisted.
Would not go away.

. . . He would come back at four in the morning, to collapse on the couch in the living room, gulp down some vodka, and try to sleep.

Still aching.

. . . The dreams persisted. Always the little darling, chugging away down a street with him behind the wheel.

She was gone, but she wouldn't go away.

Damn you, he whispered, stay out of my dreams!
. . . Then he blinked, came awake.
Stay out of my dreams?
Across the room, on a chair, was his guitar.
He stumbled over and picked it up.
. . . Plucked a chord.
dum dum de dum dum   wait, no, it should be dum dum *dum—*
Hoarsely, he chanted "Stay out of my dreams . . .
My little darlin' "
Fumbled for another set of chords.

. . . From inside the bedroom, he heard Sally's protesting voice. "Dammit, Chuck, shut up, I'm *tired . . .*"
Furious at being interrupted, he got up and closed the bedroom door, then went back to the guitar.

173

". . . Stay out of my dreams, my little darlin'
. . . When you left, I was so sure it was the end," he chanted.
Hey, hey, not bad, he told himself. Let's see where it goes.
. . . And miraculously, it continued to go.
". . . But I was wrong, oh so wrong, little darlin'
Now you're gone but you keep coming back again!"

He kept on working at it.

Some time later, he had no sense of time any more, whenever he sat working on a song he was totally immersed, he now had most of it, except for the end line—

—Damn, they were always the toughest thing to come by . . . Write down what he had?

. . . Ah, the hell with that, in the morning he could remember it . . . whatever it was.

Besides, what the hell good was it without a last line?
Grey light was filtering through the living-room window.
You'll forget it if you don't write it down, pal.
. . . Okay, one more time.

On one of the bookcase shelves there was a small tape recorder, he was too tired to write it down, he'd sing it onto a cassette.

Blearily, he picked it up, snapped on the recording button.

". . . Stay out of my dreams, my little darlin'
. . . When you left I was sure it was the end.
But I was wrong, oh so wrong, little darlin'
Now you're gone but you keep coming back again!
Please stay out of my dreams,
My little darlin'
I can't handle seeing you the whole night through.
Please stay out of my dreams,
My little darlin' . . ."

174

And how to end it?

Da da da da da de da da da da!

Screw it!

He was too tired to finish anything now. Some other time.

He dropped the guitar to the floor, fell back on the couch and went to sleep, exhausted. Finally, for the first time in days, he slept.

Sleep, blessed dreamless sleep
. . . Something was pulling at his goddamned arm.
Not something, some*one*.
He blinked awake.
Sally.
". . . Goin' to work?" he asked.
"Coming home," she said.
. . . He'd slept the whole day?
She was holding the tape recorder in her hand.
"I played this," she said. "It's very good."
"What is?" he asked.
"The song you wrote."
"What song?"

"Listen," she said, and pressed the button. From the tape recorder came the sound of his voice, chanting hoarsely

"Stay out of my dreams, little darlin'
When you left I was so sure it was the end . . ."

Then he remembered. "Okay, *that* one," he said.
"It's very good," she said.
He rubbed his bleary eyes.
". . . But you haven't got a last line," she said.
"Story of my life, baby," he said.

He went to the refrigerator and found a container of orange juice. In a cupboard was a half-filled vodka bottle. He sloshed some vodka into the container, then drank thirstily.

". . . Before you proceed to get yourself bombed," said Sally, "why don't you try finishing this?"

"Why?" he asked.

"Because it's that good!" she insisted.

"Yeah," he said. "I need coffee."

"I'll make you the coffee," she said. "Go concentrate on the last line."

da da da da de da da da da . . .

"Get the last line and it could be a big one," she said. "You could take it and sell it."

"To whom?" he yelled. "Christ, leave me alone, I'm not even awake yet!"

". . . You could make some money with this," she persisted.

". . . Yeah, a natural for Dolly Parton, she's panting for me to bring it around . . ."

"She could be," said Sally. "When you finish it."

To get away from her, he went into the bathroom, took off his clothes, and got into the shower.

Last lines, last lines . . . where the hell did they come from? Sometimes you got lucky, other times you could wait forever and they never happened.

They sure didn't come from nagging women.

. . . But if it really was good, and Sally was right, and there was a buck in the damned song—

. . . Maybe even some big bread, enough to pay off the bill collectors—clear them off his back—

And get his Model AA back from that damn auction down in Tulsa, before she was sold to some bastard?

Damn, where was that last line?

He stood under the shower, water pouring down over his aching head, his mind struggling with it . . .

176

da da da da de da da da—
Nothing.
. . . Wait a minute.

Miraculously, it slid into his brain. Sharp. Lying perfectly on the chords.

He pushed aside the shower curtain, climbed out.

Dripping water all over the floor, he ran to the other room, snatched the tape recorder from the table where she'd left it— snapped it on, sang the song through, a rasping duet with his own voice—

". . . Please stay out of my dreams, my little darlin'
"I need my sleep as much as I need you!" he chanted.

Sally had come out of the kitchen. "Beautiful!" she said.

"I did it! I got the goddamn last line!" he croaked.

Grabbed her.

They collapsed on the sofa. ". . . It's terrific," she murmured, and then he kissed her, covering her mouth.

He felt her hand moving down to grasp him, her fingers stroking and fondling him, she moved against him, as excited as he was . . .

He strained. Thrust.

. . . But no use.

Nothing.

. . . Too tired? ". . . Sorry," he groaned. ". . . Must be getting old."

He was very tired.

Sally got up from the sofa. "Don't you ever say that," she told him. "You're in your prime."

". . . Yes, ma'am," he murmured.

"You just made something more important, believe me," she said.

. . . Depression was beginning to take over. "That song?" he said. ". . . Forget it."

He slept.

. . . Then she was shaking him. ". . . What?" he asked, his mouth dry.

177

"Jack wants to talk to you," she said, and thrust the telephone into his hand.

"What about?"

". . . I played him your tape over the phone," she said, "and he wants to talk to you about it."

". . . Busy little beaver, aren't you?" he complained, and cradled the phone next to his ear.

"Hey, there," said Jack. "Sally just played me your latest opus, and I have to tell you, right off the top, that is easily one of the greatest pieces of shit I ever heard!" He snickered. "What a great gag!"

"Hilarious," said Chuck. "Go fuck yourself, pal."

". . . It's so bad," continued Jack, "it *has* to be a hit!"

". . . *You* want to buy it?" he asked.

". . . Oh, I don't think it's *that* bad," said Jack, laughing again. ". . . But seriously, get me a lead sheet, do me a demo tape, and maybe I could unload it on somebody for you . . ."

"Sure, Jack, later," he said, and hung up.

"He wants to sell it," said Sally, happily.

". . . Oh sure," he said. ". . . He'll get it to Dolly Parton, she'll sit and listen to it, she'll flip for it, and then I get a five-figure advance . . . just like in the movies."

His eyelids were closing. Sleep . . . that's what he needed.

. . . But she was shaking him again. "Get up and do him a lead sheet," she insisted. "I'll make you some coffee . . . then you can maybe go to work . . ."

"What the hell for?" he demanded. "I give him the song, he'll go peddle it, maybe sell it off to some bastard who'll end up screwing me out of it? Who needs that?"

". . . Have you had a better offer today?" she asked. "Look, if you did get a few hundred cash in your hand, then maybe you could call up that place in Tulsa and save your little darling truck!"

. . . She was right.

As usual.

He sat up and rubbed his tired eyes.

"Make coffee," he told her. "Make a lot."

*   *   *

 **Tulsa**

When Cyril emerged into the white glare of the Oklahoma morning sunlight, on his way back from breakfast (harmless tomato juice, more foul tea, accompanied by something inedible called a Sooner State Sweet Roll, relatively innocent looking as it lay on one's plate, but totally lethal going down), he found Miss Lorenzo taking the sun on a chaise beside the tiny kidney-shaped motel pool.

She wore a two-piece iridescent bathing suit that revealed a startingly good shape. And quite a bit of it . . .

He tried not to stare as he said "Good morning."

"Stomach better?" she inquired.

"If I remember to remain on fluids, I may survive this local so-called cuisine," he said. "Thanks for your interest."

She glanced at her watch. Sat up and reached for her towel.

"You're leaving?" he asked.

"Going over to the Arena, it opens at 11," she said.

"Oh, good," he said. "Can I offer you a lift?"

". . . Persistent, aren't you, Mr. Banks?" she said.

"I merely thought we might cut down on expenses by sharing a taxi," he said. "I'm really not Jack the Ripper, you know."

She finally smiled. "Okay," she conceded.

He concentrated on the view from the rear as she walked off to her room.

. . . Very nice indeed.

As their taxi pulled up to the Arena entrance, it was forced to stop by a large truck, towing a flatbed trailer. Lashed on to the trailer was a smaller vehicle, another truck, but this one diminutive, a true antique, with a canvas top on the driver's seat, and a small stakebody to the rear.

Cyril paid the driver, and went over to take a closer look at the new arrival. ". . . Model AA, Ford 1931," he said. "Very rare example of a truck. In lovely shape."

"You really know your cars, don't you?" asked Miss Lorenzo.

"Hobby," he told her, cheerfully.

Inside the arena, the music was already blaring from the public-address system, and the aisles were already crowded with early visitors wandering through the rows of cars drawn up for inspection.

". . . Which one are you interested in?" he asked.

"Why do *you* want to know?" she replied.

". . . Oh come now, don't be so suspicious," he told her. "Unless it's the same one I'm here for, I'm no threat."

"Sure, sure," she said. "So what are you here for? That way I'm covered."

"A simple British-made limousine," he said. "Now. Does that absolve me of any intent to defraud you, my dear?"

"I don't know," she said. "How can I be sure you won't try to outbid me?"

"You don't," he said. "But by the same token, how do I know what you'll do when my car comes up? That's what makes auctions such dodgy affairs, Miss Lorenzo. One never knows how many sharks are sailing through, waiting to knock out the mugs."

"I wish I knew what you were talking about," she said.

"Then you'd better learn, and fast," he said. "Let me give you a bit of free education. The mugs—that's all these honest souls milling about—come in with their checkbooks, smiling cheerfully, ready to buy. The sharks—those are the pros, dealers, mostly, have already gotten together and decided what they want. They've done their homework, you see, they're at all the auctions. Now, when they've decided on what they want, they move in on it—"

"How?" she asked.

"Very simple," he said. "They come to an agreement among themselves, and they assign one bloke to do the actual bidding. All the others back off—that way they keep the price down, see? Their man tops the best bid, and takes the item away from the mugs, who never know what happened. Then the sharks all meet afterwards, and draw lots to see which one of them actually gets it. That's their game. Neat, eh?"

". . . That's a conspiracy!" said Miss Lorenzo.

"Is it really?" he said. "Well, it's a cold cruel world, in case you haven't heard."

". . . How do you know all this?" she asked, eying him.

180

He smiled. "Some of my compatriots invented the game, I'm afraid. Now that I've given you my nastiest trade secret, why don't you show me which car you're after?"

She hesitated. Then she shook her head. "I'll go alone."

". . . You can't be sure I won't follow you," he grinned.

"Tricky, aren't you?" she said. "I can follow you, too."

"Checkmate," he said. "I'll show you mine, if you show me yours."

Again she hesitated.

"This reminds me of a game I used to play when I was six," he said.

She laughed. "I'll bet you did," she said.

"You didn't?" he asked.

She walked down the aisles until finally they approached a small, compact black sedan. On its hood was a card reading: 1933 PLYMOUTH 4-DOOR SEDAN. DO NOT TOUCH! Ropes kept passersby several feet away from the vehicle.

Cyril eyed the demure little car. "Nice," he said. He consulted the catalog. "Estimated at approximately $3,500," he told her. ". . . Some sort of a whim on your part?"

"Whim?"

". . . Well, it's not really terribly choice," he commented. "In fine shape, but I shouldn't think it will appreciate too much as an investment. Is that why you're after it?"

"Stop cross-examining me!" she said.

"Right," said Cyril. "Still don't trust me, do you?"

"Nope," she said. "Now, show me yours."

"Round two," he said, and escorted her down the aisle to the Rolls. "There you go," he said.

Impressed, she stared at the car.

". . . Wow," she said, finally. "What do you think that's going to bring?"

"Ah," he said. "Now that is the vital question, isn't it?"

". . . Well, how much are you prepared to pay?" she insisted.

"Another imponderable," he said.

She thumbed through his catalog until she came to the page with the description of the gleaming Rolls. ". . . it's estimated at . . . *eighty* thousand?'' she said.

She stared at him. "I . . . don't figure you at all, Mr. Banks,'' she said. "You come all the way from England to go after this, at that price . . . and you're staying at some El Cheapo motel like poor folks?''

". . . It's known as maintaining a low profile,'' he said.

". . . And you're hanging around with me for the same reason?'' she said.

"I'm hanging around with you?'' he smiled. "Because we shared a taxi? My dear Miss Lorenzo, your paranoia is definitely showing. I never mix business with pleasure.''

. . . And I'm pleasure?'' she asked.

He shrugged. "Not so far,'' he said.

Before she could reply, a loud female voice cried "Hey, theah, Mistah *Banks!* you look mighty bright-eyed for a fella who had himself one late night!''

Mrs. Joyce Donaldson Wade, a Gucci portfolio under her arm, in gaily embroidered jeans and a pair of elaborate boots, was smiling at him. "Still hanging' around this little old beauty?'' she cried. "I have to tell ya, the flies are really zeroin' in on this honeypot. Why, I've been gettin' calls all mornin' about her. Big money folks, you know?'' She chortled cheerfully. "You just better get ready to dig down deep in your wallet, friend!''

"Yes, indeed,'' murmured Cyril. He wished she wouldn't announce his personal business to the entire world. Hoping to change the subject, he said, ". . . I'd like you to meet a friend of mine, Mrs. Wade—''

There was no one beside him. Miss Lorenzo had abruptly disappeared.

". . . Well, I'd love to stay and talk more with you and whoever your friend *is*, but I've got me a lunch date in town,'' said Mrs. Wade. "See you soon—when the fireworks start—''

"Miz Wade, Miz *Wade!*'' said a breathless girl, pushing through the crowd around them. "I've been trying to find you—before you left, you forgot to sign these papers—'' She held out a clipboard on which were a sheaf of documents. ". . . There's this power of attorney on the escrow account for Mr. Lester—and this second one, for the other one?"

"Shoot!" said Mrs Wade. "I plumb forgot. So much goin' *on*. Gimme the pen, honey . . ."

She took the clipboard.

"If you don't sign these," said the secretary, still breathing hard, ". . . Those banks won't honor Mr. Lester's signature . . ."

"I know, I know!" said Mrs. Wade. "There's just so many *details* . . ."

As she bent over the clipboard, Cyril, nearby, glanced over her shoulder. His eye caught the bold capitals on the second form. BANCO DE SAN RAFAEL, he read.

. . . Eh?

The second bank? A Mexican bank?

. . . Why transfer escrow funds to a *Mexican* bank?

Very interesting.

. . . What could Mr. George D. Lester be doing that for?

He leaned closer to get a closer look at the form . . . where was this Banco de San Rafael? . . . but before he could make out any address, she'd signed the paper.

"I'll get these right back to the office now," said the secretary. "I'm so glad I could catch you—"

"Oh, thank you, baby," said Mrs. Wade. "I just don't know what I'd do without you!"

She waved at Cyril, and disappeared into the crowd.

. . . Why would there be a second bank for the escrow account?

Still turning it over in his mind, he strolled off.

. . . From the next aisle, he heard raised voices, one of which sounded familiar.

Miss Lorenzo, who was protesting loudly "Lay *off!*"

He rounded the corner to discover her, near the 1933 Plymouth, flanked by two large uniformed guards. "Lookin' is okay, ma'am," said one of the men, "but you was *touchin'!*"

"I was checking the tire," said Miss Lorenzo. "Big deal!"

"Rules is rules," said the second guard, doggedly.

"I'm a *customer!*" she replied, as they backed her away.

"We saw you, ma'am," said the first. "Hands off the merchandise."

". . . This lady is a friend of mine," said Cyril. "I'm certain she meant no harm—"

"She could be anybody's friend, friend," said the first guard, "it don't make no never mind. We got orders."

Angrily, she turned and walked away.

He caught up with her. "Now really, Miss Lorenzo," he chided. "Tell the truth now, what could be so fascinating about the wheels of that little Plymouth?"

She stopped.

Turned to glare at him.

First with astonishment, and then obvious wariness. Her eyes flashed. ". . . *Why'd* you ask me that?" she demanded.

". . . No reason at all," he said. "Why are you so defensive, my dear? Certainly everyone is entitled to kick a tire or two . . ."

"Why don't you mind your own damn business?" she snapped, and walked away.

. . . Good advice, thought Cyril. Exactly what I shall do.

Business that involved a Mexican bank. In which there had been established an account on which Mr. George D. Lester seemed to have a power of attorney, enabling him to make withdrawals.

(If, in fact, there *was* such a bank.)

. . . That was definitely his business.

And as for Miss Benita Lorenzo, and her peculiar fixation with the wheels of that little 1933 Plymouth . . . well, that business might bear a bit of minding, as well.

*   *   *

Weary from her long drive into Tulsa, Mrs. Louise Bigelow carefully steered the 1955 T-Bird down the back street. Up ahead she spotted the rear entrance of the Arena.

"How about that!" she said. "I made it!"

Step A.
The big one.
Getting Out.

. . . Two days before she'd left Liverpool, Indiana, after breakfast. Packed a couple of small bags (nothing much else would fit
into that car) cashed a check from her own bank account, bought
traveler's checks, picked up road maps, and then, because he'd
never understood, never would understand . . . she'd written him a
note and left it on the dining-room table.

In it she explained that she was leaving for Tulsa, where she
planned to sell the T Bird—*her* T-Bird now—at auction. Whatever
she got for it, she could use to support herself while she figured out
what she wanted to do . . . but one thing she was *not* going to be,
and that was curator for his museum. ". . . Don't worry about me,
Dusty," she'd put at the end of the note. "You'd be surprised to
know that I'm perfectly capable of handling things for myself. And
so are you, so that makes it okay, right?"

. . . She *was* capable, dammit. She'd gotten safely all the way
from Liverpool here to Tulsa, hadn't she?

She parked, and got out. Locked the car, straightened her rumpled clothing, ran a comb through her hair, and walked over to the
small gatehouse.

"Help you, ma'am?" inquired the guard.

"My name is Mrs. Louise Bigelow," she told him. "I got in
touch with the management in there about putting my car into this
auction. I believe I spoke to a Mrs. Wade? It's that T-Bird over
there."

The guard nodded and consulted a sheaf of papers on his tiny
plywood table. ". . . Here it is," he said. "You're bringin' her in
from Liverpool, Indiana, right?"

"To be sold," said Louise.

"Okay, ma'am," he instructed, "you just drive 'er right on in
there, park over there to one side, and I'll call one of the men from
the office to come out and help you with the paperwork. Then you
can just relax and let all the folks with the money fight over your

car." He squinted at the parked T-Bird, which basked in the sun-light. ". . . Looks mighty clean for a car that come all that way . . ."

"I stopped off at a carwash," she said. "My husband always—I mean, road dust is bad for the finish."

"Mmm . . . that's one real beauty," said the guard. "I guess you got your reasons for sellin' something like that, but if it was me, I'd hang on to that buggy for dear life—"

"That's exactly why I'm letting it go," she said.

"Beg pardon?" he said.

". . . Dear life," she said. "Has there been anybody trying to locate me down here?"

He shook his head. "Not while I been on duty. Somebody special you was expectin'?"

". . . Not somebody special, possibly my husband," she said. "Mr. Bigelow. Mr. Dusty Bigelow?"

"Man who married a pretty lady like you, he'd be special," said the guard. ". . . How come he lets you run around loose?"

She winked. "He doesn't know what I'm up to."

"I'll just bet," said the guard. "You sayin' you're handling this whole auction deal yourself?"

"I certainly intend to," said Louise.

"Oh sure, I see," said the guard, who did not. "Well, good luck."

Louise started back to the T-Bird, unlocked it, and got in.

As she drove it through the gate, the guard peered out. "By the way," he said, "if your husband was to want to locate you, where *could* he locate you?"

"He's clever," said Louise. "If he wanted to find me, let him damn well find me."

She steered the T-Bird carefully into an open parking-space.

*   *   *

 *Tulsa*

If, in fact, there was a Banco de San Rafael, with an account on which Mr. George D. Lester had power of attorney, locating it through telephonic communication proved far from a simple task.

Cyril sat in his small motel room with telephone in hand while a three-way meeting at the summit developed between Mrs. Hereford on the motel switchboard, the long-distance operator in the Tulsa office, and finally a series of helpful but somewhat confused senoras who supposedly were in charge of Information below the border.

(Hello, mah party here is tryin' to get in touch with the Banco de San Rafael? buzzbuzzbuzz San what? Rafael. *Rafael.* R-a-f-a-e-l. Ah, si, si, San *Rafael!* Ah thought that's what ah said, ma'am. buzzbuzzbuzz Por favor, which San Rafael? Hold on just a minute there, ma'am, please sir, the lady's askin' which San Rafael you wanted, Are Code 905 or 903? Well, actually, I don't know which San Rafael it is. It is the San Rafael which has a Banco de San Rafael, I should imagine. Thank you, sir. buzzbuzzbuzz Ah, senora, mah party is lookin' for the San Rafael with the bank in it? buzzbuzzbuzz Por favor, which bank? Hold it a second, sir, they're askin' which bank? As I believe I said to begin with, the Banco de San Rafael! Okay now, don't get excited, sir, ah'm only trying to do my job here. Senora, mah party wants the Banco de San Rafael. R-a-f-a-e-l—si, si, one moment! buzzbuzzbuzz Por favor, we have here un, dos, tres San Rafael—Trace San Rafael? No, no, no, *tre* San Rafael! In your language, *three* San Rafael! Ah, hello there, sir, she says there's three, and which one did you want?)

Cyril groaned.

"Would it be possible," he suggested, desperately, "for her to try all three towns and find out from the local operator which one has this Banco de San Rafael?"

"Yessir," sighed the Tulsa operator. ". . . And when she locates this banco, exactly *who* is it you want to speak to at this banco when she gets through to the banco?"

"The manager," said Cyril.

". . . And his name is . . . ?" asked the operator.

"I truly wish I knew," said Cyril.

buzzbuzzbuzz.

"They're off the line, I'll have to call you back, sir," she said.

A glance at his watch told him he'd been at this international seesaw for more than an hour now. The room was chilly; the air conditioning was giving him a headache. Outside, the sun was beginning to go down, and the light was a bit softer. He called Mrs. Hereford at the switchboard and explained that he would be going out for a bit of fresh air, and if she needed to find him, would she mind calling him by the pool?

". . . You're expectin' another call?" she inquired.

"No, the same one," he told her.

He dozed in the chair outside, as the evening shadows began to move across the small motel pool.

. . . One thing about this endless inter-American telephonic confusion was heart-warming. It made Cyril feel that he was back home in England.

Beside him, the telephone on the table rang, awakening him.

"Mistah Banks!" said Mrs. Hereford triumphantly. "Your call is on the line!"

"Hello, hello?" he said.

buzzbuzzbuzz, and then a masculine voice came on, it was a rotten connection, he could hardly hear the man. "Banco de San Rafael, who is calling?" he said.

Ah. There *was* such a bank.

Good! "Ah, this is Mr. Lester, in Tulsa," said Cyril.

"Si si, Senor Lester," said the man in the Banco de San Rafael. "You wish to speak to the manager?" buzzbuzzbuzz ". . . Is there something wrong, senor?"

"No, nothing wrong," said Cyril. "I, ah, merely wanted to check on something regarding my account."

"Ah si, I am certain everything is in order," said the voice, fading in and out. "Most unfortunately there is no one here at this hour, we are closed. Will you call again mañana, Senor Lester?"

"Si, si," said Cyril. "Gracias!"

188

". . . Would you spell for me the name please, senor?" asked the man in the bank.

"Just the way it sounds, Lester," said Cyril, and hung up.

. . . So there was a Banco de San Rafael (damn—he hadn't asked for the location and number!) . . . if it were the proper Banco, it would also seem to contain the account on which Mr. George D. Lester had power of attorney. The *second* bank account, along with the local escrow account . . . on which he also had power of attorney.

That could signify some sort of a plan to transfer funds from the first account here into that second account there, correct?

. . . Or did it?

This little game involved Mr. George D. Lester. Cyril was a graduate of the Lester School for Sharpers. A specialist in sleight of hand was Dean Lester, a sharper who never did the obvious. His game was strictly three-card monte, in which the Dean was always the dealer. Watch the cards now, friends, very carefully, see me flip over this ace of spades here, now, flip, flip go these three cards, and now place your bet on which one is the ace of spades—Ah, you think it's there, do you? Well then, my friend, turn it over, and what have you found?

. . . Four of hearts?

Pity. Poor sod, you've lost.

So even if there were the account in the Banco de San Rafael, that did not necessarily mean that escrow money from here would ever end up in sunny San Rafael, did it?

The phone rang again. Now it was the Tulsa operator, inquiring whether he'd completed his call. Yes, he had.

". . . Oh good, Mistah Lester," she said. "I'll bill the call to your room there, Mistah Lester?"

"It's not Lester," he said. "I'm *Banks*. Cyril Banks."

Confused, the operator hesitated. "But *he* called you Lester," she accused.

"The man was obviously confused," he said, and hung up.

189

". . . Your name is Lester *and* Banks?" asked a voice. Miss Benita Lorenzo.

She was sitting a few feet away, beside the pool.

. . . How long had *she* been here?

Obviously long enough to overhear his phone conversation.

"Operator made a mistake," he said.

"Lester doesn't sound to me like Banks," she remarked.

"Bad connection," he said.

". . . You've got a little something going on the side, maybe?" asked Miss Lorenzo.

"Possibly," he said. "Don't we all? Listen, I'm truly sorry about today at the arena—if I said something that offended you—"

"I don't like people who ask so many questions," she said.

"Nor do I," he said.

She was silent.

"Why don't we make a pact?" he suggested. "From here on, neither of us will mind each other's business, and we can keep it all completely social, eh? What have you got planned for dinner?"

"Nothing," she said. "And—"

"In that case, why not join me?" he said. Before she could protest, in her inimitable hostile fashion, he added, "Strictly a protective measure. The two of us are strangers here, it would be much more pleasant than dining alone, and we can be poisoned by the locals together. Since you're a nurse, it will save on hospital expense. Come on, my treat," he urged her. "Mr. Rolls will host Miss Plymouth."

". . . Jesus," she said, "you are really a slick operator—and believe me, I've heard a lot of them . . . okay, I don't know what you're up to, but I'll say yes on one condition. Dinner—nothing else. Feeding me does not entitle you to ball me."

". . . Whatever that means, I accept," he said.

"You know damn well what that means," said Miss Lorenzo. "Every time I show up in this bathing suit your eyes practically fall out.

. . . Would old Florence Nightingale have ever used such language?

*   *   *

190

 *The Arena*

The guard at the main entrance to the arena waved G. Dudley through. "Workin' late," he commented, and yawned.

"Yes. All sorts of last-minute details," said G. Dudley.

"Miz Wade is waitin' for you in the office back there," said the guard. "She's been workin' late too. Big day tomorra."

"Hope so," said G. Dudley.

He walked through the darkened Arena, past all the rows of parked cars, which glimmered eerily in the vague light. Choice items of merchandise, in all shapes and sizes, tangible symbols of value. Once that sedan there had been merely the family Buick . . . tomorrow it would be a collector's item, to be fought over by greedy buyers. Two days hence, all these pieces of iron and steel and chrome, rubber and upholstery and glass would have changed hands, auctioned off to cash-rich customers . . . cash which would be accepted by the Donaldson Bros. attendants, all those lovely fat stacks of big bills and certified checks, which would promptly be deposited into the escrow account at the Oilmens National Bank (where he had this afternoon personally delivered the power-of-attorney forms that Joyce had signed).

And for the next thirty days, as per contract, all that loot would remain in the custody of the escrow account.

Ostensibly.

. . . There was light at the end of the tunnel now, lovely golden light, signifying mucho profits. (Translation: The G. Dudley Lester End Run.)

. . . The escape hatch, through which he could disappear, and return to a quiet, sunny existence, far far away from all these cheerful noisy Oklahomans, with their ostentatious ways and their loud laughter and backslapping.

Most especially, an escape hatch from one particularly noisy Oklahoman. A lady who was waiting for him in the office.

This too, shall pass, he told himself . . . and opened the office door.

Working late?

She was stretched out on the Barcalounger. Tonight she had out-done herself. She wore skintight black velvet jeans, her waist was held in by a broad golden belt, above it was a beige suede top that was decorated with elaborate cut-out beaded designs and many fringes. From her neck dangled a silver and turquoise chain, and on the desk, her feet were encased in crocodile-skin Tony Lama boots. On the head of his southwestern Madame Recamier was a broad white sombrero, and in her hand was a glass of champagne, taken from a bottle that sat on the desk. (The good Mumm's, reserved in the office refrigerator for the class A fat-cat buyers who dropped by.)

"My, my," he smiled. "You look sensational."

"Oh, honey," she said, petulantly, "you certainly know how to keep a lonely girl waitin'!"

He leaned over to kiss her briefly, not an easy feat when one dealt with that sombrero. ". . . I had all kinds of errands to attend to," he said. "Last minute details . . . for *us*."

"Poor baby, works himself so hard," she said. "Finish up around here and then we'll get over to the Tuttles, they're tossin' a bash for some Texan folks who just flew over, and we're ex-pected . . ." She poured more champagne into her glass.

". . . Not another bash," he said. "I thought perhaps tonight I might relax."

". . . When the auction's over, you can relax plenty," she said. "These Texas folks are *big* money—for you and me—" She waved a pocket calculator from the desk. "I been figgerin' what our take is gonna be—you think we're over a million yet?"

"It looks good," he said. "But—"

"Say a million five, right, 'cause all my daddy's boys know how to milk a crowd, you know that, so that means when it gets to Mexico, and we start earnin' twenty-two percent—" She began punching buttons.

"Joyce, *shush*," said G. Dudley. "That's nobody's business but ours—"

"Shoot, don't I know that?" she said. "Don't I know my man Dudley is the shrewdest little old cat, who knows how to get his

Joyce the edge?'' She went on punching buttons. "Three hundred and thirty thou, divided by twelve—oo*eeh!* Twenty-seven thousand five hundred in thirty days from Mexico—for Joyce! Lordy, ain't that na-ice?''

". . . You *got* to be quiet about that!'' he warned her. "If anybody catches on to that Mexican bank deal, they can raise a very big stink—''

"Don't I know that, lover?'' she complained. She got up from her chair and came over to him, her lips exuding the scent of good French grape. "Don't you think you can trust your Joyce?'' She moved closer. ". . . After all I done for you, what else do I have to do to prove myself?''

Tears were beginning to glisten in her eyes, threatening to cause a downpour of mascara . . . oh Christ, he hated it when she cried. There would soon be those great whooping gasps . . . usually brought on when she'd had too much wine.

All right, he'd soothe her ruffled feathers.

. . . After all, this charade wasn't going to last too much longer.

He put his arms around her shoulders.

". . . There, there, baby,'' he said, gently. ". . . It's not that G. Dudley doesn't trust his Joyce, you know he does . . .''

He ran a hand across her rear, beneath the expensive black velvet, stroking away.

A wrong move.

Instantly she had moved herself closer, entwining her arms around his neck, and her mouth was seeking his, finding it, her lips opened and her tongue began to dart at his . . . she held him tightly to her, and when she finally let him free, she was growling in his ear, ". . . *come on,* lover . . .''

". . . Not here in the office,'' he said.

"Damn right not here,'' she said. "It's so tacky . . . besides I can't get out of these jeans here . . .'' She held his arm and began to urge him outside.

To where?

"Let's you and me do it out *there,''* she suggested, like some coy teenager.

"Now just a minute,'' he protested. "We can't—''

193

". . . In the back seat of that baby Rolls," she said. "C'mon—I never did do it in a hundred thousand dollar car, and neither did you, lover—"

". . . There are guards out there!" he pointed out.

"They won't see us," she said, ". . .C'mon, I need a nice comfortable place where I can stretch out, so's I can skin out of these damn jeans—"

Before he could find another objection, blessedly, the telephone on the desk rang.

"Leave it!" she said. "The office is closed!"

". . . Could be a customer," he said, and broke free from her embrace.

"Let 'em call tomorra!" she groaned.

"I have a long distance call from New Jersey for Donaldson Bros.?" said the operator.

"Yes, I'm here," said G. Dudley. "Who is it?"

". . . This is Chuck Malone," said a hoarse voice. "You got my little darlin' down there, for that damn auction, and I'm calling to tell you she's not for sale. Send my little darlin' back!"

". . . Your little darling *what?*" asked G. Dudley, confused.

". . . 1929 Model AA Ford stake truck!" said Malone.

". . . Let me check," said G. Dudley, and reached into a drawer to pull out the latest inventory folder of sales items. Ran down the list. Yes, the vehicle was here, with the contract signed, ready to be auctioned off, with a $5,000 minimum value bid arranged. "We have it here, sir," he said.

"I know you do!" said Mr. Malone. "Now I'm giving you orders, it's withdrawn, see? I don't need the money any more—Jack Adler just made some kind of a deal for me, got me bread, see, up front, the song's a piece of shit but they think they can get some of the country and western prople to do it, so you see, I don't *need* to sell my little darlin', it was all Sally's doin, she's a hell of a chick—"

Joyce was standing behind him, her fingers plucking at his shirt buttons, her lips nibbling at his other ear. "I'm very pleased to hear that," said G. Dudley, ". . . but there's that small matter of a withdrawal fee. We figure that on a percentage of what you'd expected the merchandise to bring, so if we figure fifteen percent of $5,000, that's $750—"

"Wait a minute, we paid you to consign her!" protested Malone. "You *got* that money—"

"Ah, but you're withdrawing," said G. Dudley. "While we've had all the expense of advertising, and listing, and we have to charge a handling fee, that's another $100, but let's try to make it easy for you, sir—"

Joyce's fingers were inside his shirt now and she was going to work on his trouser buttons. ". . . Oh, hang *up,*" she was whispering in his ear.

"You guys are goddamn thieves!" said Malone, in New Jersey.

"Read your contract, it's all there," said G. Dudley. "This is a simple business transaction, sir, if you will have the cash, or a certified check for, let's see, $850, we'll allow you $250 credit for the consignment fee, say, that makes $600—"

". . . But the damn auction's tomorrow!" protested Malone. "How the hell do you expect me to get the money down to you—"

"A bank wire, perhaps?" suggested G. Dudley.

By now Joyce's agile hands had found what they were seeking and seized it.

"You're holdin' my little darlin' for ransom!" yelled Malone.

"My friend," said G. Dudley, "may I remind you that we are businessmen? We have to run this auction strictly by the book—"

"Oh shoot!" said Joyce, and plucked the phone from G. Dudley's hand, slammed it down. ". . . Come *on.*"

"You hung up on him," he said.

"We're busy!" she said. "The office is closed—and *I*'m open!"

She dragged him, unwillingly, through the darkened Arena, headed for the tiny Rolls. Good Lord, this was truly insane!

When they reached it, she lifted the rope that held off the prying hand of the public, and ducked beneath. Opened the rear door and promptly disappeared into the Rolls rear seat. Giggled from within. ". . . Oh, this is lovely," she said. ". . . Get your ass in here, G. Dudley."

He heard footsteps coming down the aisle. Quickly, he managed to restore his disarrayed clothing into some semblance of order, seconds before the flashlight shone in his face, and the guard's voice said ". . . Why, it's *you*, Mr. Lester. Anything wrong here?"

". . . Nothing at all," said G. Dudley. ". . . Fact is, Mrs. Wade and I were just—ah—inspecting this car."

"Mighty pretty thing, ain't she? asked the guard. Before G. Dudley could stop him, the guard had flashed his light across the trim lines of the 1937 Hooper custom body. Through the rear window, its beam picked up Joyce's startled face beneath the white sombrero.

". . . Why, howdy Miz Wade," said the guard. "Don't you look smart in there . . ."

". . . Thank you very kindly," said Joyce, forcing a smile, and pulling the rear door shut.

". . . Night now, folks," said the guard, and walked away.

His sentence reprieved, G. Dudley approached the Rolls. ". . . . Better come out now, honey," he said. "It's getting late and we really shouldn't keep the Tuttles waiting."

"Screw the Tuttles," said Joyce. ". . . But if you're too chicken to get in here with me, you'll just have to wait—because it's gonna take me at least five minutes to get these damn jeans back on!"

 ## Liverpool, Indiana

His first impulse, the day he came home and found her gone, leaving behind her letter, was to pack a bag and go after Louise.

. . . What the devil was wrong with her?

Perhaps it was physical. Sure, women behaved strangely, he'd read that, especially in their middle years, that was well known— the tantrums, the hot flashes, all the rest of it . . .

But Louise hadn't shown any such warning signs.

So what was behind this—this craziness? Suddenly, without

warning, to pack up and run out on him—in his—*hers* now—T-Bird?

He read and reread her letter so often that he could almost quote it from memory: I'm going to go to Tulsa and sell the T-Bird/ whatever I get for it I'll use to support myself while I figure out what I want to do/—

(Want to do? Was there anything she'd ever wanted to do that he hadn't gone along with?)

—Don't worry about me, Dusty/You'd be surprised to know that I'm perfectly capable of handling things for myself/and so are you, so that it makes it okay, right?/Love, Louise.

Selling the T-Bird—what was okay about that?

If it was money she wanted, why couldn't she have asked?

. . . But following her wasn't all that easy. He had a business to run, people who depended on him; things didn't just happen by themselves, did they? There were problems at his office. It was inventory time, they were shorthanded, besides which, a couple of freight cars full of All-Purpose Feed were missing, he had to get after the shippers and the railroad and track it down.

Going after her would simply have to wait until he was in the clear.

So he returned to their house, and his bourbon and ginger ale and then foraged for supper from the closet full of canned goods and the deep freeze. He really had no appetite, something simple was all he needed. Damn, what she'd done was really beginning to bug him.

He settled on chili and some frozen french fries.

. . . Hadn't he been a good husband to her, a decent father to their children, a steady provider? Their sex life hadn't been so terrible, had it? Lord knows he hadn't ever fooled around, and was there anything she'd ever asked for that he hadn't willingly agreed to?

He rinsed out the dishes and put them away. Inside the empty rooms echoed to his footsteps. There was mail piled up on the library table. Fresh stacks of catalogs and magazines, price lists, circulars from dealers . . .

And here was this envelope full of legal documents that Lew Davis had brought over for her signature.

. . . Which she hadn't signed.

Hell!

. . . How was he supposed to explain that to Lew, when he came to pick them up? (When he himself couldn't explain her ducking out in the T-Bird?) One couldn't fence around with Lew, he would have to confess that Louise hadn't merely forgotten to sign, nor would she be back here to do so . . . no, she'd gone, left Liverpool, taking with her his—*her*—T-Bird—and hadn't signed them on purpose.

(*More* crazy behavior. What was wrong with signing them?)

. . . Then Lew would start lecturing him, reminding him of things he already knew and knew well, that their house was in joint ownership, that there were securities in her name, insurance policies on his life which she owned, her equity in the business, all of which—if she had left him—would raise some delicate problems.

Right now he didn't want to think about any of that.

He went up to bed. The one he'd slept in the night before, it was still unmade.

Beside it was her bed, neatly made, exactly as she had left it.

In her dressing-room closets hung her clothes, neatly arranged, soft, silent. She hadn't taken much with her. (Of course not, how much could you stow away in his—*her*—T-Bird?) On the mirrored table were her perfumes. In the drawers beneath, her nightgowns, her lingerie, all redolent of that sachet she liked.

. . . He closed the drawers, but that scent lingered in their bedroom, and he couldn't escape it.

Finally he took himself down the hall to the guest room and slept there.

Badly.

. . . During the night he began to feel that same anxious sense he'd had before. That nagging feeling that something very valuable, part of his collections, was missing . . . he'd begin to think of a certain book, an early Tom Swift. Or maybe one of his model airplanes, a Fokker D-7 . . . or some old 78-rpm record, Ellington's

"Jack The Bear," or maybe an early Al Jolson, and he'd start to worry, he hadn't seen it in a while, had he? And he would try to remember where he'd seen it last, was it really missing? and then finally he'd wake up, and go prowling blearily downstairs, rummaging through his bookshelves, or into a cabinet, or through his albums, until he invariably came upon the exact book, or the model . . . or the record. There wasn't really any problem at all; there was his precious item, perfectly safe, right where it should be. And finally satisfied, he could pad back upstairs and go back to sleep next to Louise.

. . . Who certainly wasn't in her bed tonight, was she?

She wasn't a missing book, or a record.

Not on any shelf, or in an album.

. . . She was really gone.

For no damn reason he could figure out.

The next day down in his office was just as complicated, and having to attend to all the various items that piled up on him kept him from thinking too much about her.

. . . But on the way back to that empty house, at the end of the day, that same anxious feeling of loss took over.

But hold it—somebody *had* been here! He could tell that right away!

. . . Was she back?

. . . It took him some time to realize that it had been the cleaning lady (who had her own key and knew how to get in without setting off the burglar alarm) who'd come in to do her customary day's job, and had tidied up the place (in only those areas where she was allowed to function—she was under strict orders to stay far away from his various collections— *he* did the dusting and cleaning around them).

There was another stack of mail. But nothing from Mrs. Louise Rhodes.

. . . Not even one damn postal card!

He mixed himself his customary bourbon-and-ginger, and sipped it as he walked through the empty rooms. Strange, he couldn't remember having been alone here for such a long time without her.

No sound of her radio from the kitchen, and worse, no odors of food coming from the kitchen.

"Damn, you'd think she's have the courtesy to call and say she made it!" he complained, aloud.

And for an answer heard only the echoes of his own voice.

Eventually, he went into the kitchen and opened up a can of clam chowder, put it on the stove. Popped some frozen fish sticks into the oven. It wasn't Louise's idea of a meal, but it would have to do . . .

. . . Had she gotten to Tulsa yet?

He put in a long-distance call to Donaldson Bros., that was the outfit which was running the auction in Tulsa, they'd have to be the ones Louise would end up going to . . . but there was no answer. Closed for the night.

As he ate, he sat and watched the news.

A big automobile pile-up in a rainstorm near Akron. A fire in an Iowa motel. Somebody murdered in what appeared to be a gangland-style slaying, in an Ohio suburb, the body discovered in the locked trunk of a white '78 Lincoln Continental. (Someday that buggy would be a real classic.)

Depressed, he snapped it off.

Rinsed the dishes.

The food settled into his stomach like lead.

Later, he wandered into the front parlor. This place could use a little cheerful sound, music to keep him company. He snapped on the big player piano. Its machinery whirred and clanked, and on went the garish lights, rinkatinkatink, way she went, the keys gaily pounding out "Twelfth Street Rag," one of his favorite numbers.

. . . He suddenly remembered Louise, years back, at a party, when she'd gotten a little high and done the Charleston to this song, waving her arms and really stepping, her skirts flying, letting everybody in the place see what was beneath—

. . . Where the devil *was* she?

Finished, the player took its short breather, and then wheezed into the next selection, *rinkatinkatinka* went the keys, and then the chords went echoing through the rooms of the empty house.

200

"You've Got to See Momma Every Night, or You Can't See Momma at All!"

The words mocked him.

Angrily, he snapped it off. In midflight, the jazzy old tune sighed and died.

. . . Louise was somewhere in a small town, off the main road, she was having trouble with the T-Bird engine, so she'd pulled into a service station. Now the gleaming car was propped up on hydraulic jacks, and the mechanic, some kid with long hair tied up in back and a Zapata mustache, was stretched out under the car tinkering with it while the radio nearby put out raucous rock music. Damn fool kid, he didn't know anything about T-Birds, obviously, poor Louise stood there waiting for him to fix it, she was wearing a short dress covered with bugle beads? Now the kid was rolling out from beneath, wiping his hands, leering cheerfully at her, there was a part missing under the car, would she mind coming under there so he could show it to her?

Don't go under that car, Dusty warned her, he doesn't know anything about cars and neither do you, the damn thing could come down on your head!

But she wasn't listening, the mechanic had provided her with a wooden back rest, one of those little things on wheels, side by side with his own, Louise was lying down now, on her back, beside the mechanic, and they rolled backwards beneath the T-Bird, disappeared until all there was showing were his pair of grimy dungarees and her legs in shiny stockings, long stockings going up to her thighs, and as he watched, that sonofabitch mechanic rolled over, Louise's legs were spreading wide to accept him, and from beneath the T-Bird came soft giggles and then a happy crying sound.

Get off! he yelled, but neither of them paid any attention as he pounded on the hood and the T-Bird shook ominously.

Perspiring, he came awake.

. . . Lousy dream. And his stomach was seething.

He went to the bathroom and found some Titralac. Went downstairs and made himself some tea.

201

Sat at his desk and rummaged through catalogs, trying to distract himself, reading until light began to filter through the windows.

Shaved and showered and dressed, he went down to the office.

By mid-morning he'd gotten his call through to the Donaldson Bros. office in Tulsa. Some lady named Wade finally came on the line, asking was there anything she could do to help him?

There certainly was. He was inquiring about a 1955 T-Bird, a classic, which was possibly going to be auctioned off down there, a car coming from Indiana?

He waited while she checked.

Then she was back. "Oh yes, indeed, that particular car has been brought in, item 51, by the ownuh I do believe, she drove it down—"

. . . So she'd made it!

Safe and sound, all the way to Tulsa. Good. No need to worry about that any longer—

. . . But why the hell hadn't she bothered to let him know?

". . . She's a maty fa-in specimen," Mrs. Wade was saying.

(He needed *her* to tell him that? That T-Bird was one of the finest!)

. . . Was there any way of locating its owner?

". . . No, afraid not," said Mrs. Wade. "She's here in Tulsa somewheah, but she didn't give us a local ad-dress. I'm sure she's gonna show up for the auction, day after t'morra . . . now would you be interested in that particulah car?"

Interested? That was a hell of a word to use when you referred to an automobile he'd owned and loved and taken care of for the last twenty-five years, polishing it, keeping it tuned up like a violin—

". . . There's a lot of interest in its already," she was saying. "Big buyers all over the place, y'know, folks buyin' for investment, after all, cash ain't worth shucks these days, is it? Would you care to put in a bid, sir? We're estimatin' her at twelve thousand five—"

"That's not enough!" he protested. "It's worth much more!"

". . . I beg pardon?" asked Mrs. Wade, stunned.

Frustrated, he hung up.

Louise obviously didn't have a clue about what was going on down there. He'd have to get down there, pronto. Somehow, he'd have to stop his wife from making such a foolish mistake!

He had his secretary call the airlines to find out how to get to Tulsa. It turned out that he'd have to leave here at 4 A.M. or so, drive over to Indianapolis in time to pick up TWA 223 at 7, getting to St. Louis at 8, then picking up Ozark 961 at 10 A.M., to arrive at Tulsa by noon. Which should give him ample time to get to the arena there for the auction, day after tomorrow.

No . . . better yet, he'd leave here tonight, drive over to Indianapolis, leave his car at the airport, spend the night in a local motel.

As far as the business was concerned, it would have to get along without him for a couple of days. This auction was suddenly much more important. He had to keep some stranger from getting his hands on that T-Bird.

. . . Which meant he'd better bring along some money.

He called Lew Davis and explained his predicament over the phone. Not to argue, his mind was made up—Lew could keep an eye on the plant while he was gone, meanwhile, he was going down to the bank and arrange for traveler's checks—fifteen grand worth, at least.

"Whew," said Lew. "That's a nice price."

"It might go higher, I don't care," he told Lew. "I've got to get down there and rescue her!"

". . . Louise?" asked Lew.

"Her too!" he said.

His overnight bag packed, traveler's checks in his pocket, he made himself supper at the house, and then left, first making certain that the master control timer, which automatically switched lights on and off throughout the house, was working, that the telephone answering machine was on, and finally, that the burglar alarm system was properly triggered.

Then he stowed the bag in his car, got in, and steered down the driveway, headed out to I-78, which would get him to the motel in Indianapolis by midnight, an easy drive. Everything was in order, he had his tickets and a reservation at the motel. Tomorrow he'd be in Tulsa. Where he could put out the fire, straighten out this ridiculous situation, try to talk sense to Louise, settle things, once and for all—

Twenty-three miles out of Liverpool, his engine began to knock ominously. The car bucked, coughed . . .

. . . And a few hundred feet further down, on the broad stretch of an almost-deserted I-78, miles from the nearest service station, the car stopped. Dead.

What in the plu-perfect hell!

No amount of kicking over the starter got her going again. Not *here*.   *Not now!*

 ## Tulsa

The Old Chuck Wagon was a restaurant housed in a long, low wooden structure, flanked by the inevitable vast parking lot, already lined with cars by the time Cyril escorted Miss Lorenzo inside. Through the kind offices of Mrs. Hereford, at the motel, he'd made a booking for two (the place was her recommendation), and the headwaiter, in jeans and a flowered shirt, showed them to their table in the dining area.

The place was decorated in rustic style, redolent with Atmosphere, chosen to evoke the memories of the Old West. Artifacts were everywhere, brass lanterns hanging from beamed ceilings, the walls decorated with photographs of pioneers, oil paintings of cattle feeding, buffalo roaming, Indians attacking, wagon trains headed West, all from the great days when the range was wide and free. Diners sat in small booths fitted out with imitation wagon seats, with canvas hoods above; for floral decor there were clumps of what seemed to be cacti, but were actually plastic. Tinkling music burst forth sporadically from an upright piano player, and in front, there was a huge mahogany paneled bar, with a brass footrail. Behind it, beneath an elaborate painting of a reclining nude lady, bartenders, sporting handlebar mustaches and wearing shirtsleeves and red suspenders, toiled to serve the crowd of drinkers who were lined up, two and three deep.

It was noisy and confused, and hardly conducive to elegant dining, and Cyril found it difficult to adjust.

". . . You don't like this much, do you?" asked Miss Lorenzo. She'd changed into a simple evening dress, and done something nice to her black hair; in the dim light of their Conestoga wagon, she seemed very attractive.

"It's all a bit . . . overpowering," he observed. "And everybody here seems so aggressively . . . young."

"You're in frontier territory, friend," she said. "Get used to it."

The drinks they'd ordered were served in heavy glass mugs, along with a tray of hors d'oeuvres, some sort of crisp chips, and a pair of jars containing sauces. "Watch that stuff," she warned. "Liquid fire. For a man with a nervous stomach, lethal."

"I'm so glad I brought you along," he said. "Every man should have access to a good-looking nurse, full-time."

"I'm off duty," she said.

Conversation above the chatter and the player piano was not easy, and shortly afterwards their waitress appeared. She wore a vaguely Gay '90s outfit, complete with black Merry Widow, low-cut bosom, and a brief skirt that revealed almost all of her nether regions encased in sheer black hose.

Cradled in her arm was a large round silver tray, covered with some sort of translucent plastic, and in her other hand was a small flashlight. "This here's your menu," she announced, and snapped on the flash. By its light, Cyril could now see, spread out in an artistic display beneath the plastic, a circle composed of slabs of raw meat.

". . . Now this here's our KayCee Special," said the waitress, lecturing them like a museum curator, spotlighting each piece of bloody red in turn. ". . . Over here's our Stockmans' Sirloin, ain't that lovely? And this here's our Prime Chicago Strip, next to it is the Tulsa T-Bone, and down here is our Jumbo Single Pound Solid Sirloin Burger. Each one comes with choice of Fries or Baked Potato with Sour Cream and Chives Maison, meanwhile you go fill up at the Salad Bar. Call your shots, folks, so's I can get the chuckwagon chef to work on your order.''

As they passed down the salad bar display, splendid in its array of choices, Miss Lorenzo cautioned him once more. ''Stay away from those green and red peppers, and those spiced beans, and lay off the garlic croutons, and forget that chili—that's strictly for the locals, not you.''

''. . . Do all these people here come equipped with cast-iron intestines?'' Cyril asked her.

Their plates laden, they moved past the bar, towards their Conestoga wagon, threading their way through the growing crowd of boozers there. One particular young man, florid, resplendent in a checked cowboy shirt and designer jeans, grinned at Miss Lorenzo as she maneuvered her way through. ''Hiya there, baby,'' he commented. ''Your kind sure knows how to load up a plate! Damn, the management ain't gonna make any money on you tonight—''

''. . . Pardon me, you're blocking the way,'' said Cyril. ''And I believe we can dispense with your comments about my friend.''

''Say, we got us another furriner type,'' commented the young man to his friend, another wide-shouldered young drinker. ''Get all kinds down here, don't we, Buck?''

''Thought there was laws against illegal immigration, Tug,'' remarked his friend, who showed sharp terrier teeth as he grinned.

''There ought to be laws against clowns like you!'' said Miss Lorenzo, as she and Cyril found a free path through the crowd.

''. . . Just listen to that, will you?'' chortled Tug. ''A real spitfire.''

''Bastards,'' she said, as they sat down. ''Think they own the earth . . .''

''What exactly *was* that all about?'' asked Cyril.

''Just your common, ordinary day-to-day prejudice,'' she snapped.

''But . . . against whom?'' he asked.

''Against anybody who's different,'' she said. ''Don't you have it in England?''

. . . Ah yes, he thought, suddenly remembering *Jewboy, Jew-*

boy, rotten Jewboy being chanted in his face by a ring of nine-year-olds on a schoolyard, years ago. "Afraid so," he said.

". . . Ignorant creeps," she said, attacking her salad. "If we were home, I'd get a couple of my friends to clean up on them . . ."

". . . Does that mean you're ah . . . connected with the Mafia?" he inquired.

"Oh, Christ!" she said, irritated. "You're just as stupid as they are. Just because my name's Lorenzo, you figure I'm—"

"I didn't figure anything, I merely asked for the purpose of being educated," said Cyril . . . Lord, the lady did carry about a large chip on her shoulder. ". . . I'm a stranger here, remember?"

"And you've seen too many damn movies," she said. "I'm a nurse who earns a fair living swinging bedpans—do I look like anybody's Godmother to you?"

"Certainly not, you look positively smashing," said Cyril.

. . . But he could not help wondering—if this lady lived as mundane a life as she described, *why pursue an antique Plymouth?* Hard-working nurses saved up their money and dreamed of making a down payment on a Mercedes roadster, or something else equally sporty. Why would she come all the way down here, in pursuit of a four-door 1933 sedan?

". . . Now you're trying to get back into my good graces," she told him, "where you weren't."

"What shall I do to please you?" he asked.

"Change the subject," she told him.

"All right then, shall we order some vino to go with dinner?" he suggested.

"Fine," she told him, "—just don't assume because my name's Lorenzo I'll want Chianti!"

They ate their Prime Chicago Strips, which were not quite as succulent as their Lorelei waitress had led them to expect, and sipped the decent California red, which was the best the winelist offered. He tried to keep up the conversation, but the incident at the bar was clearly still bothering her.

And Cyril, as well, for it did not seem to have ended.

Through the half light he could see Tug and Buck and the others, standing there at the bar, drinking and talking loudly, guffawing at what were obviously hilarious remarks passed by their friends. Every so often, the crowd of locals would peer in their direction.

. . . It was far from a comfortable scene here.

As they sipped their coffee, Tug suddenly manifested himself at their table.

He made an elaborate bow. "Pardon me, ma'am," he said. "My friends and I been talkin' among ourselves, and we've got us a little wager goin'. Now I say, for fifty bucks, that you're some kind of Mex senorita, and Buck there, he's got fifty says you're a P. R. Would you oblige us by settlin' the argument? Whoever wins is gonna send you over a free drink for you and this character you're with, how's that?"

Cyril got up. "Piss off, chum," he said.

". . . Now that ain't a friendly way to talk, lover," said Tug, still smiling.

"It's the only sort you understand," said Cyril.

"Don't feel left out," said Tug, amiably. "We're gonna have us a bet on *you* and that funny fag accent of yours, next. It *is* a fag accent, right?"

"Don't bother with him, the asshole isn't worth it!" said Miss Lorenzo, but Cyril decided otherwise. With his hand, he reached out and shoved Tug backwards, causing the young man to stumble backwards.

"The hell I'm not!" said Tug, still smiling, and shoved Cyril in return. "Don't try any of them fag tricks on me, darlin'!"

His fists clenched, Cyril reached back, cocking his arm to swing at Tug's grinning face. Felt himself grabbed from behind by a strong pair of arms, which pinned him in a bear hug. "If you know what's good for you," rasped a voice in his ear, "you won't mix up with my buddy Tug. He'll wipe you away, sweetheart!"

Buck? He could not see who it was.

Tug's fist slammed into his stomach.

Suffused with pain, he struggled to free himself.

"Let him go!" yelled Miss Lorenzo.

"—When he learns to behave himself like a white man," promised Tug.

208

She was up now, the empty wine bottle in her hand, and she was swinging at Tug.

"Hey there, a real spitfire!" Tug cried, gleefully, fending over her blow.

Cyril elbowed the man behind him, hit what must have been a vital area, heard a wheezing grunt, and the arms holding him relaxed. He wheeled, found Buck looming up in the dark, fist cocked, but before they could exchange punches, others were moving between them, they were in the midst of others, a mustachioed bartender, and the headwaiter, who was asking, "What seems to be the trouble here, Mr. Sanborn?"

"No trouble at all," said Tug. "Just a couple furriners who don't know how to behave in a classy joint—"

"Asshole!" cried Miss Lorenzo. "You and your cheap shots—"

"Please pay your check and leave," said the headwaiter, glaring at Cyril. "This here's a family-type restaurant, and our customers don't relish such language!"

"The hell they don't," said Miss Lorenzo. "Here's some more for them. Your place sucks, so does the food, and the wine is piss!"

Eventually they were outside, the restaurant door firmly closed.

". . . How was *that* for your digestion?" she asked.

Cyril was massaging his stomach, which throbbed from the blow. "The natives are certainly unfriendly on your frontier," he remarked.

"Dummy," she said. "You took on too many!"

"I knew I could count on your help," he said.

"Foolish," she said. "I had to. The odds were so lousy . . . that loud-mouth slob, with his cracks." She eyed him sympathetically. "He got to you too, didn't he?"

"Shall we go somewhere else?" he suggested.

"No, wait," she murmured. "You and I have a little unfinished business here."

She strolled over to the waiting parking-lot attendant. "Padon me," she said to the youth. "We were just inside talking to old Tug Sanborn, you know him?"

"Why sure, ma'am," said the youth. "Tug there is one good old boy . . ."

". . . That's his blue Caddy over there, isn't it?" asked Miss Lorenzo, pointing into the rows of cars on the lot.

"Heck no, ma'am," said the attendant. "Why, Tug drives that there bright green Seville over yonder, that one with the silver bullhorns on the radiator?"

"Oh, sure, my mistake," said Miss Lorenzo. ". . . Would you mind calling us a cab?" she asked, handing the young man a bill.

"You bet, ma'am," said the boy, and disappeared into the restaurant hallway.

". . . Come on," hissed Miss Lorenzo. *"Cover me!"*

She hurried over to the green Seville.

As he came over to watch, she bent down by the front tire, fiddled with something on the wheel disc, and then there came a steady hisssing! from the darkness. The heavy whitewall tire began to bulge. The Seville, a beached whale, sagged forward.

". . . Hurry up!" she urged. *"Do the back!"*

Why not enjoy a little revenge?

Cyril bent to the task, flipping off the valve cap of the rear tire. *hissss!* and he was her willing accomplice, as the car began to sink on an even keel.

It was finished before the parking-lot attendant had returned. Sober and straight-faced, the two of them stood quietly at the restaurant entrance.

But once the cab had picked them up and they were moving, she exploded with laughter. ". . . That's how you fight on the frontier, amigo!" she said. *"Dirty!"*

"Marvelous!" he agreed. ". . . But I'm wondering whether Florence Nightingale would ever have stooped to such tactics . . ."

"I don't know about Florence, but *I* feel great!" she said, giggling.

Then, impulsively, she leaned over and embraced him. "Thanks—" she said. "You were terrific."

". . . Rose to the occasion," he said, modestly.

He kissed her. And she made no effort to fend him off.

When they broke free, she said ". . . Okay, partner, I guess you were entitled. But that's enough."

He paid off the cab driver at the motel.

Before she could say goodnight, he suggested a nightcap.

"Where?" she asked.

". . . My room," he said, casually.

She shook her head.

"A simple, sociable drink," he told her.

"Look," she said, softly, "it's not that you're not attractive, and I appreciate what you did in that joint tonight, that was very classy of you. But I really didn't come all the way to Tulsa for a one-night stand . . ."

She leaned over to kiss him. Without passion, but with sisterly affection. ". . . Tomorrow's a big day," she said. "We both need some sleep, right?"

"Ah, there speaks Florence again," he said, a bit ruefully.

"I can't help that," she said, softly. "That's the way I am. Too old to change now . . ."

"Age has nothing to do with it, Benita," he told her.

". . . Good night, Cyril," she said. "I really did enjoy it."

And that was irrefutably that.

"As did I," he told her.

She walked away. He shrugged. Now what? So early. Ah, well, there was always the telly to watch.

And then he could go to sleep. Alone.

But the evening was far from over.

. . . Half an hour later, there came an urgent rapping on his motel-room door, and when he opened it, there she was, her face contorted with rage. "Damn—*it's all gone!*" she wailed. "I've been robbed!"

"What?" he asked, confused.

"I've been ripped off!" she cried. "Right here in this damn motel—it must've been while we were out tonight, I had it before we left, I checked it and it was there—"

He managed to sit her down, then out came the particulars.

211

. . . She'd gone back to her room, and received a call from her mother, in Connecticut—there was a problem at home—her brother seemed to have been in some sort of an accident with the car—there was money needed and the lady wanted Benita to wire some cash home immediately, it was a crisis—she'd agreed, naturally, what else could she do? She'd gone to the closet where she'd put her bag, in which was her hidden store of money—

". . . How did you keep it?" he asked.

"In cash!" she cried, bitterly. ". . . And the bastards cleaned me out!"

"How did they know you had money?" he asked.

"How in hell do I know?" she answered, near tears. "All of it—everything except what I had in my purse—it's *gone*—"

". . . You didn't put it in the motel safe?" he chided her.

". . . I didn't trust them either!" she said.

. . . Quickly he went to his own closet, to check on his own thick store of traveler's checks, which he had tucked away in one of his shoes.

They were all there. He retrieved them, and put them into his hip pocket. From now on he would keep them on his person.

"How much did you have with you?" he asked.

"It was more than three thousand!" she wailed. "Enough to buy that car!"

". . . Have you reported this to the authorities?" he asked.

She shook her head.

"Then let's at least do that," he said.

The night clerk, a thin old man, was sympathetic, but of no assistance. "We got this sign here warning folks," he said, pointing at the card on the desk. "Right there, see?"

USE OUR SAFE: DON'T BE SORRY!

"Got a lot of problems with the criminal element lately," he sighed. "They take anythin' that ain't nailed down . . ."

"That's a big help!" commented Benita.

"We just can't be responsible, ma'am," he kept on repeating, before the police cruiser, its blue light flashing eerily in the night, arrived.

212

The two young police officers were polite, sympathetic but non-committal.

They went along with Benita and Cyril back to her room, waiting while she demonstrated the circumstances. Her open suitcase sitting on the closet floor. Her clothing undisturbed, but the suitcase itself, rifled.

"Bad news, ma'am," said one of the officers, making notes on a small pad, while the other checked the door lock and surveyed the bathroom window, which was still latched. "Must've used a master key—these guys are really professionals. Lots of 'em working motels around town, especially with this here auction tomorrow. Draws 'em like flies to sugar."

"Mind comin' down to the station so's we can get all the particulars?" asked the second officer.

"What good will that do?" complained Benita, distraught.

"Well, we can put it out to all our cars," he said. "Maybe we can turn somethin' up for you."

"Like what?" she asked. "The only thing I want to turn up is my cash—and I've got a big picture of that happening . . . *boy!*"

". . . This is what comes of listening to my mother," she said, on their way back from the frustrating hour or so in the dingy, noisy police station, where she'd impatiently answered all the same questions once more for the plainclothesman who'd typed it all out for the report.

"Your mother?" he asked.

"Yeah," said Benita, sardonically. "She always taught me to keep my money close by. Great advice, right?"

". . . Shh, calm down," said Cyril, and put his arm around her. "You're lucky they didn't come in while you were in the room . . ."

". . . I know," she said, and shivered. "Scary. Having somebody go through your stuff like that—it's such a—well, what right—"

"It's only money," he said.

"*Only?*" she said. "All the money I had, besides Gus's—every damn dollar I worked for, saved up—"

Gus?

". . . To buy Gus a car?" he asked.

She did not reply.

When they'd gotten back to the motel again, he suggested the nightcap. "Purely medicinal," he said. "To settle your nerves."

This time she did not refuse.

Up in the room, with the door securely locked, he sat her down and poured her a good drink of whiskey. "Drink that," he instructed. "You'll feel better."

"The hell I will," she said, and downed it. Neat.

Cyril sat down on the bed and said "See here, Benita . . . nobody brings that much cash to an auction to buy such a car without a good and sufficient reason. Wouldn't you feel better if you confided in me what yours is?"

She held out her empty glass.

He poured her another drink.

Which she gulped down.

Then she sighed. "Ah . . . what the hell," she said. "I can't win. Maybe I wasn't meant to win. I had it right in my hand—and now some sneaky bastard's blown the game for me . . ."

"*What* game, Benita?" he asked, softly.

She looked up at him. Her face was drawn and tired, and for the first time since he'd been with her, he saw her with her defenses sagging. "My brother is in big trouble up in Bridgeport," she said, "and I can't do one damn thing for him!" she said, in a small voice.

Touched by her sudden vulnerability, he heard himself saying "I can lend you some money."

She shook her head.

". . . Not enough," she said.

"Pay me back when you can," he suggested. "I'm certain I can trust you."

Again she shook her head. "Not *enough*," she repeated. "Don't you understand—I needed the whole stash—for tomorrow!"

"No, I don't understand," he said. "You won't tell me."

". . . Oh God," she said, wearily. "You're really a persistent bastard. So what the hell's the use? I can't get my hands on the damn car anyway . . . can I?''

"Then stop feeling sorry for yourself and tell me," he urged.

She held out her glass.

He poured another drink. This time, much less, because he did not want a drunken lady nurse on his hands . . .

. . . And then she began to tell him.

He listened to the story of a 1933 four-door Plymouth, and an old lady named Mrs. Fox in Connecticut, and a machinist named Gus Konecki, who seemed to have devised a set of hollow wheels which were then filled with melted-down gold . . . and which were supposedly still firmly attached to the car. Which would come up for sale tomorrow, here in Tulsa . . .

"That's why I wanted to buy the damn car," she said. "To do what Gus told me to—and go for the jackpot."

". . . You were willing to gamble all your money to find out if he told you the truth?" he asked.

"No, not all mine," she said. "Some of it was Gus's."

". . . Quite a gamble," commented Cyril, trying to digest this remarkable . . . legend? Fiction?   . . . what?

"Okay, a gamble," she conceded. "So what? Life is full of gambles. I figured I could take a ride and go for the brass ring—"

"The golden ring," he corrected.

". . . Whatever," she said. Her speech was a trifle slurred now, as the whiskey did its work. She lay back on the motel armchair and stared at the ceiling. No longer precise and definite Miss Benita Lorenzo, now she was a tired, defeated small girl. ". . . Well, we'll never know for sure, will we?" she murmured.

"Why not?" said Cyril.

. . . If she were telling the truth, and the old man's story was correct—and there was that one insane possibility that the four Plymouth wheels were actually mobile storage vaults—

". . . Look here," he said, "I don't mind taking a flyer ever so often. Why don't you and I make a deal? Your information and my cash . . . we could still have a go at it? Nobody else knows, do they?"

She shook her head.

". . . If they knew, would they put the car up for auction?" she asked.

"I've already thought of that," he said. "Let's go halves."

She blinked at him. "I . . . don't get you."

"Of course you do," he said. "I provide the cash for the Plymouth when it comes up for sale. We bid it in—and if the wheels are what you say—"

"Not what I say—what *Gus* said!"

He stood up, took out his wallet and removed some cash. "Here," he said. "Go wire this money up to your brother—get him out of trouble. Then tomorrow, when we go to the auction, I'll supply whatever else we need."

She eyed the bills he was holding out.

". . . We're talking about three grand tomorrow. Maybe more," she said.

"I know that," he said. "Now go send this off—"

Still she made no move towards the money.

". . . And what am I supposed to do after that?" she asked.

". . . Then you can go to bed," he said.

"Ah," she said. "That's the deal. Yours?"

He shook his head. "One thing has nothing to do with the other."

She stared, unbelieving, at him. ". . . You're trying to tell me no strings?"

He dropped the bills into her lap. ". . . Only if you provide them," he said. "Go. Rescue your brother."

She picked up the money, folded the bills, and got up. ". . . You bastard," she said. "You really know how to confuse a girl, don't you?"

He brushed her moist forehead with his lips. "It's a gift," he said. "Go."

After she'd left, to go find a Western Union office, he sat in the room, trying to sort out his own behavior.

. . . What sort of a demented fantasy had he accepted as fact? He'd promised to venture several thousands (of Ben Emir's funds) on the hearsay of a girl whom he'd met by chance here? Who'd spun him a wild story about some rich old lady, some female Silas

Marner . . . whose faithful machinist Gus had stored away her hoard of golden treasure in the metal wheels of an old Plymouth? Which she'd driven about for the next forty years, and wished to have buried with her?

How could any usually sober person believe such a bedtime story?

He hadn't come to Tulsa, Oklahoma for anything like this. No, his purpose had been strictly to try and pin down his old nemesis, George, of the vanishing Lesters!

So why had he chosen to rescue a damsel in distress—

(If in fact, she were one. It was over an hour now, and she hadn't returned, had she?)—to go along with her game? To buy a stack of chips and to enter this schoolboy find-the-hidden-gold-and-win-a-huge-prize-contest?

. . . The girl was attractive enough, true, but Cyril Banks was certainly not that desperate for a bed partner.

On the other hand, if she were telling the truth about the Plymouth, and there *was* gold—

. . . *If* she were telling the truth.

By midnight, he'd given up.

Miss L. had obviously vanished into the Oklahoma night, taking with him his money.

Time for bed. He snapped off the telly, got into his pajamas, and lay down, to sleep.

. . . Much, much later, there was a soft urgent knock on his door. Then he heard her voice calling his name.

When he opened the door, she asked, "Give up on me?"

He nodded.

"It took me a while to find an open Western Union, but I wired the money," she said. "Thank you."

He yawned. "You're welcome," he told her.

". . . And I agree to the deal on the Plymouth," she said, and held out her hand.

He shook it. "Fine," he said. "Goodnight."

She came into the room and closed his door behind him. Carefully latched it, turned, and put her arms around him.

217

"Listen," she said, "I'm not doing this because of the money, or the Plymouth . . . or the wheels—"

". . . I really couldn't care less why, Benita," he said.

"*I* could!" she said.

"Shhh!" he said, urging her towards the bed, his hands exploring her. "There's an old English saying, luv," he told her, as he began to undo her blouse. ". . . You can do anything you like inside, so long as you don't frighten the horses in the street . . ."

She kissed him, and pulled him close.

He winced.

"Mind the stomach," he warned. "Still sore . . ."

". . . Oh, this is going to be terrific," she said, sadly. ". . . You with your stomach, and me hung over . . ."

He tossed her clothing onto the chair. ". . . We can only do the best we can," he said.

*　　*　　*

. . . Benita's Uncle Dominick was holding her hand as they walked down the bright street, headed for the corner drugstore where Uncle Dom was going to buy her an ice cream. She wore a summer dress and held on tight; he was a small cheerful man who dressed very nicely, kept a mustache neatly trimmed, was fond of singing. As they walked, they sang a song together, one he'd taught her, some song about the Isle of Capri where he'd met her, she was singing the high part and he carried the bass.

She never quite knew what Uncle Dom did for a living, it was something to do with restaurants, he came to visit them often, always bringing her mother presents and candy for her, ever since her father had gone away, Uncle Dom had been very attentive to her mother, but was modest about it, why not, he always said, that's what a family is for, right?"

Now they were walking back from the drugstore, she was carefully holding her double-scoop cone, licking at it nicely, careful to catch the melting ice cream just right so it wouldn't leak down her hand, it was chocolate chip, her favorite flavor, and Uncle Dom wasn't singing now, he was lecturing her.

Benita honey, remember, in this world you need to protect yourself in the clinches, y'know what I'm saying?

218

. . . Sure, sure, Uncle Dom, she was busy with the ice cream and she'd rather they sang that song than have him lecture.

Without a sound, a car had come down the street, a little black sedan headed past them, there was a large puddle of water by the curb and the driver steered right through it, she couldn't see what he looked like, no it wasn't a he at all, it was an old lady.   *Splash!*

She was drenched with dirty water, her cone was covered with it, Uncle Dom thought it was funny, he was laughing, he hadn't been touched by the water at all, he'd jumped away—why did he think it was funny?

You saw it coming, she accused, near tears, *why didn't you say something?*

He kept on laughing, slapping his thighs with glee at the sight of her, she was cold from the water, wetness everywhere.

He was walking away now, still singing, how could he have done this to her? She trusted Uncle Dom, she felt like bawling.

And remarkably, she had no clothes on   standing there on this sunny street, bare-assed?

She'd better get home pronto before anybody saw her like this.

Desperately she began to run and one of her legs kicked out   to encounter another leg.   *Whose?*

And another arm holding hers, somebody from behind.

The street not so bright now, no, suddenly there were shadows everywhere and it seemed to be a hand from behind those shadows.

She shook off the grasp, she had to get away, on a street without her clothes.

Protectively she rolled over, so nobody could see Benita Lorenzo with not a stitch on, she pulled up her legs protectively huddled into a ball.

Lost on a strange street, no Uncle Dom, no ice cream
terrified, she opened her eyes and blinked
not a street at all.

. . . This was a bed, a strange bed, not her own, some sort of a room, air conditioning whirring, she wasn't alone in this bed, the arm next to hers, the leg she'd kicked belonged to a man.

JesuswhereamIandwhat
. . . Tulsa. Oklahoma. Motel
it all began to filter back.
. . . her wrist watch said 5:17
(she still had *that* on, anyway).

. . . And the rest started coming together, her suitcase rifled, the
dinner at that lousy restaurant   the two cops in the police cruiser,
her money gone   the medicinal whiskey he'd forced on
her   he handing her cash.

The midnight journey to Western Union   with
his money
her cheeks began to flush as she remembered the rest
how she'd thanked him.
her clothing, tossed all over that chair.

The first time it had been crazy, almost violent, a silent wrestling match on this bed, with no umpire to cry *break* as he went after
her. Unprotected in the clinches (are you there, Uncle Dom?). He
hadn't been gentle, not at all, despite all that nonsense about his
upset stomach.
    Then, had they slept?
    Was it hours later? When? She'd lost all sense of time, she'd felt
his hands reaching for her again, fingers moving insistently, touching, awakening her.   She'd wanted nothing but to sleep, but he
wouldn't let her, he'd pulled her gently over to him.
    then she was being aroused   feeling that remarkable widening
deep throbbing rings below, warmth   darkness with lovely all per-
vading heat that built and built.
    Explosions.
    Everything they told you in books   Grace Kelly and Cary
Grant and the fireworks, yes! and the songs   I'm in you, in you,
baby/hold me hold me hold me never let me go/love is better the
second time around   They were true!
    She'd made it. It had been fantastic
    Who could believe that here in Tulsa, in this tacky joint, in this
town full of loud-mouths with their cheap shots, thieves who ripped
you off, with this Englishman, thin, reedy character, who'd sur-

faced from nowhere, handed her money to save her brother's ass

She'd made it!

The same guy (she was remembering the rest of it, now) with whom she'd made a deal to go after the old lady's Plymouth—

—Fifty-fifty split?

Christ, had she told him all about the wheels, and Gus and everything else?

. . . Smart Benita. You really protected yourself in the clinches, didn't you?

(Okay, Uncle Dom. You were big with the advice, but where did it get *you?*)

She knew another rule, one that applied to *this* situation.

Fifty percent of something is worth more than a hundred per cent of nothing.

And if this stranger from London (who lay snoring quietly beside her   This same Cyril who'd taken her soaring up to the top of the mountain an hour or so ago   and over the edge.

(Lovely)

Was as good a businessman as he was a swordsman—went through with the deal he'd offered.

Then Benita Lorenzo would still have a fifty percent shot at those four wheels.

Two for him, two for *her*.

(Provided, of course, that there was gold.)

Otherwise?

She was back at square one. Benita The Broke.

But for the moment, at least, feeling marvelous.

She yawned, rolled over . . . to feel a series of sudden twinges, complaints from tired muscles in her waist, thighs

Okay, Tulsa may be the pits, but you sure didn't have nights like this in Bridgeport.

And tomorrow (not tomorrow, Benita *today!*)—the Plymouth . . .

*   *   *

(There seemed to be some sort of a large room, in front of him a group of be-wigged men . . . and he was standing in the dock, fac-

221

ing an inquisitor whose face he could not quite make out, who continued to press questions?)

rap rap rap   Mr. Banks—the name *is* Banks, is it not?

I believe so, m'lud.

Ah. Mmm. Now sir, explain what happened to you last night?

I beg your pardon, m'lud?

Come come, Mr. Banks, according to my best information, you are guilty of a patch of sloppy, sentimental behavior, totally foreign to anything we know of your previous character . . . such as it is. I see here that late last night, you attempted to seduce a young woman named—ah, mm—Lorenzo? by offering her money—

Not so, m'lud! The money I offered her was strictly a *loan*—

You would have us believe that you, Cyril Banks, who is well known for having behaved heretofore in a totally selfish and single-minded fashion, who made a trip to some city known as . . . Tulsa? for the express purpose of wreaking revenge upon someone known as George D. Lester? that you behaved toward this Miss Lorenzo, this stranger? in extremis—in a totally altruistic manner?

I believe that is so, m'lud.

buzz buzz buzz   rap rap rap!

Come, come, Mr. Banks—it *is* Banks, is it not?—you would have us believe that you subsequently did not proceed to extract your pound of flesh?

Extract is hardly the proper word, m'lud.

What, sir?

Inject, perhaps.

Eh?

The pound of flesh.

Do not flatter yourself, sir! We've inspected the member in question!

buzz buzz buzz

I will admit that it is a bit . . . withdrawn at the moment, sir, but earlier on, there were no complaints whatsoever.

Ah. Mmm. Ha. Yes, I see. To return to the matter at hand, I suggest you proceed to give us a clear explanation of your most uncharacteristic behavior of the past few hours.

I found the lady attractive, m'lud.

222

Come, come, Mr. Banks—

I *did,* m'lud.

—Get to the point! You maintain that there is no ulterior motive spurring on your actions? That you acted purely out of warmth? Pity? Care for your fellow woman?

It must be that deep down inside, I am at heart a sentimental person, m'lud.

Hogwash, Mr. Banks! Tommyrot and balderdash! We are here assembled to discover why you have accepted this young female's fantastic fairy tale concerning a 1933 Plymouth, owned by some mythical older lady, now deceased, who is purported to have stored away within the car's four wheels a hoard of highly valuable gold!

I will admit, m'lud, that Miss Lorenzo's story has its elements of fantasy—

But you believe it?

I am not at all certain, m'lud.

Ah, then, you told her that you would join forces with her at the auction merely in order to calm her? I submit sir, that when she appeared at your doorway last evening, obviously under stress, you began to think not with your head, but with your pound of flesh!

At the time, perhaps so, m'lud.

buzz buzz buzz

To the next question, sir. At this forthcoming auction, you will now be a man of your word? You are prepared to join forces with her, to bid for this 1933 Plymouth?

I believe so, m'lud.

To risk several thousands in cash (which strictly speaking, are not even yours, but are the property of a gentleman named Ben Emir?) . . . on this muddle-headed insane venture?

Excuse me, m'lud, but that several thousand of Ben Emir's cash are, in that rich young bastard's life, pocket money. And if he should complain that I wasted it on a 1933 Plymouth, which is assuming that he discovers what happened, then I can always resell that car and repay him—

Mmm. Yes, I see your reasoning. And if, by some insane series of circumstances, Miss Lorenzo's story should turn out to be true, and there are four wheels of gold attached to that 1933 Plymouth, you will abide by your word and divide the loot therein with her?

I seem to have agreed to that, m'lud.

And you will also provide Ben Emir with his fair share, for having risked his capital?

. . . .

Should I repeat my question, Mr. Banks?

. . . I would have to give the matter some thought.

I do not consider that a proper answer, Mr. Banks!

. . . It is the only answer I am prepared to give at this moment.

buzz buzz buzz   rap rap rap!

. . . .

Mr. Banks, please try to stay awake.

Yes, m'lud.

The lady, Miss Lorenzo, is still reposing beside you.

I believe so, m'lud.

She does not seem to be wearing any clothing.

Indeed not, m'lud.

She may have regaled you with a fantastic story, but later on, she behaved in a most pragmatic fashion. Sexually speaking, that is.

True, m'lud. True.

Mr. Banks . . . would that be one of her hands that has reached over and begun to fondle you?

. . . It would appear to be, m'lud.

And at this moment, are you prepared to take some action regarding this new situation, sir?

. . . I believe I could use a bit more sleep, m'lud.

Come, come, Mr. Banks. England expects every man to do his duty. I submit to you that she is now using *both* hands.

She is very deft, m'lud. It must be her training as a nurse.

No equivocations, Mr. Banks! It is obviously time for you to extract yet another pound of flesh!

Inject. m'lud.

Insert! Intrude! *Enter!* Let us not quibble, Mr. Banks. Repeat after me, sir, *once more into the breach, once more—*

. . . .

Yes, m'lud.

. . . . .

Yes, m'lady!

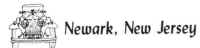

Newark, New Jersey

The boarding lounge at Gate 6, Newark Airport, was almost empty now. It was 6:51 A.M., and the passengers for TWA FL 421 (DEP 7 A.M. ST. LOUIS ARR 9:10 CONN FL TWA 73 ARR TULSA 10:15 A.M.) most of them businessmen, long-distance commuters bound for another day's labor halfway across the country, had filed quietly aboard the waiting jet. Overnight bags in hand, newspapers beneath their arms, stifling yawns, exchanging half-hearted gossip and lies about yesterday's triumphs and defeats, the last few passed through the doorway.

At the desk, in charge of the boarding process, Miss Leora Marden, an efficient young black lady with an efficient fixed smile, had completed her seat assignments and was now prepared to assign standbys. The reservation list for TWA 421 was full, but there seemed to be two no-shows. A Mr. Hathaway, a salesman who stood waiting, sample-case in hand, could shortly have one of those seats and then Miss Marden planned to go have her well-earned coffee.

". . . *Hold* it!" bellowed a hoarse voice.

Down the hallway, headed directly for her desk at a dead lope, came a strange apparition, a tall young man with dirty brown hair that flew loose from beneath his Sherlock Holmes tweed cap; he wore jeans and a T-shirt and sported a well-used dark blue British bobbie's cape that fastened at the neck. Over his shoulder hung a bright orange backpack, and it was obvious that with the high-heeled boots he wore, running was difficult. ". . . Hold the phone!" he cried. ". . . Don't leave without me!"

Panting, he arrived at her desk and thrust his ticket at Miss Marden. "Here, baby, get my body to Tulsa, pronto!"

"Do you have a reserved seat, sir?" she inquired, glancing at his ticket.

"No—they said downstairs I should stand by!" he gasped.

"Just one moment," she said, eyeing him. "Mr. Hathaway here has been waiting—"

Quickly, she punched out a boarding pass and handed it to Mr. Hathaway, who seized it and loped off through the doorway.

The clock said 6:53.

". . . Okay, baby, do *me,* I've got to get to Tulsa!" urged Chuck Malone. He seized her arm. "—If I don't get down there, I'm going to lose my little darlin'—"

"Your little darling?" asked Miss Marden, perplexed. "Are there two of you, sir? I'm afraid—"

"No, there's only me—I'm here, and she's there, and it's very heavy, see, I've got to get there and rescue her from those bastards in Tulsa!" said Chuck. "If you don't get me onto that plane, they'll steal her away from me!"

Miss Marden's smile never wavered, but her eyes narrowed.

"Excuse me, sir," she said, "but would you be intoxicated?"

"God no!" said Chuck. "I'm not smashed—I'm desperate!"

". . . We're not permitted to board passengers in a highly emotional state," said Miss Marden. "Perhaps, if you wished to wait for the next flight—"

The clock said 6:54.

"Too late!" he cried. "Look, lady—here's my ticket—give me wings! I'm not on anything, I'm Chuck Malone, I'm just a simple musician who's trying to get down to Tulsa to an auction today, where that creep Lester is planning to sell my lucky piece, my Model AA Pickup Truck—see? She's all I've got—we had her before we busted up, and now I've written a song about her and some clown bought it so I've got the bread I need to go rescue the truck—she's one of a kind, my Pick Up Truck—"

Miss Marden blinked. ". . . You're Pick Up Truck?" she asked. ". . . I believe I heard of them." She peered at him. ". . . But you don't *look* like Pick Up Truck . . ." she said.

From inside the boarding door, the second attendant peered into the lounge. "Closing up, Leora?" she inquired, waving a sheaf of tickets.

"What do you want me to do—*sing!*" yelled Chuck desperately. ". . . They're leaving without me—and it'll be your fault!"

Miss Marden hesitated. "O. . . Oh, what the hell," she said, finally. "I always was a sucker for musicians." She stamped out a standby card and thrust it at him. "Here," she said. "But if you make trouble on that plane, buddy, it's my ass—just remember that!"

"I'll remember you in my will, beautiful," said Chuck, and loped for the doorway.

"You were pretty good!" called Miss Marden. "What have you done lately?"

"I'll tell you when I get back!" he yelled over his shoulder, as the boarding door closed behind him.

 ## Tulsa

George Lester

(G. Dudley/George D. Lester) yawned. Opened his eyes, to glance at the tiny alarm clock beside his bed. 7:10.

. . . Nice. That gave him another twenty minutes or so in this blessedly empty bed, here in this small rented apartment he kept as his refuge, his oasis. His private retreat from Mrs. Joyce Donaldson Wade.

He'd finally ducked her last night, here the phone number was unlisted, she didn't have the address, he cherished the privacy available behind the venetian blinds; sleeping alone, in silence, in a furnished flat—any place where he could spend time away from her, was necessary therapy.

(". . . Why, I just cain't figger you out, here's this big old empty house of mine with me rattlin' around all alone, all by my lonesome, and you bunkin' downtown in some cheapo little place, tell the truth now, G. Dudley, you're keepin' a pad somewheres so's you can have somethin' on the side with one of them big-assed young girls you hired to dress up the auction, I been watchin' you, you can't keep your eyes offen 'em, shoot, I know you're ballin' somebody else down there, what the hell've they got between their legs that I ain't?")

. . . Thank Heaven he wouldn't be needing this little dump much longer.

Today was Der Tag. Forty-eight hours from now, it would all be accomplished.

. . . As he dozed, G. Dudley compulsively ran through a check-list.

It seemed that all the bases had been touched. Owners fees in hand; all the paperwork handled by the staff, and under control. Yesterday and today the staff would be registering potential bidders. (Their bank references checked, each one's face recorded on a Polaroid snap, to be kept on file, in case any of them should try to run out later on a purchase, and their $25 fees collected, steep, sure, but hell, this wasn't going to be any neighborhood tag-sale at the Arena!)

The merchandise all in, gleaming bait, waiting for the fishermen.

The hospitality suite for the high-rollers was tacked with good booze, snacks, and a cadre of tasty hostesses, who had instructions to pour with a heavy hand (Vegas style).

For the past two days, there'd been radio and TV spots, and feature articles in the local papers, that ought to bring in a good crowd, $3 at the gate, it should help cover the rent.

Old Ed was in complete charge of the auctioneering staff; he and his boys were specialists, respectable and well known. Come 11 A.M., they'd turn on the p.a. system, start the flash and class, and get things going.

On a brand new nylon carpet (dark red, of course), the cars would be driven through, one by one, and as each one arrived in front of the bleachers, Old Ed, or one of his glib assistants, would identify the piece, give its history, a brief sales pitch, and start the bidding.

"You got to get 'em steamed up good, both parties—the buyer *and* the seller," confided Old Ed. "That's why I got me a nice solid crew, good old boys I can trust, they can spot a live bidder half a mile away and they can work him up good. That's when I send in my secret weapons, Ham and Eggs, why, they can nervous up a bidder till he's wettin' his pants like some two year old!"

Ham and Eggs were to serve as pitmen; G. Dudley had witnessed them in action a week or so ago at another auction. Ham was a middle-aged red-haired clown with an open grin that induced instant confidence and a sense of he's-my-buddy. Eggs was a tall young rube-type with a bobbing Adam's apple who played the small towner to a fare-the-well. Both of them extroverts, they ran up and down the aisles, yelling, joking, insulting each other, coaxing, wheedling bids out of buyers, Ham confiding in total strangers that they mustn't let Eggs' man steal the item away, hot damn, *let's get it away from him, c'mon pal, open your wallet and top the bastard!*

A beautiful act, well rehearsed, cunning in its sleight-of-hand, Ham and Eggs were useful in the clinches. If an owner had an item on which he'd carefully set a reserve price, and the bidding went up but not quite to the reserve, one of the two boys could take the owner aside and steam him up too—persuade him to drop the reserve and go for broke—*hell, we're so close, don't let's let that live one get away!*

So The First Southwestern Classic and Vintage Car Auction was nicely oiled, poised and waiting, a smoothly assembled piece of machinery designed to suck up the big bucks.

By the end of this first day, G. Dudley calculated that there should be a nice fat take, almost a million, give or take, ready to be swiftly sent off to the escrow account. Why not? There were over a hundred cars already scheduled for sale (all prime pieces, no late-model iron, no junk, no gas-guzzlers being dumped by desperate dealers) nd tomorrow, when the really prime stuff was scheduled, the rest of the money would flow in, more checks and cash, another big day.

A really slick business (with no risk at all, not much work, and considering the fact that it was other peoples' merchandise you peddled)—one that turned a lovely fat legitimate profit.

. . . *If* you were interested in a legitimate profit.

Which G. Dudley was not.

Legitimate profits were strictly for ribbon-clerks. Insurance salesmen. Pension-plan managers, tool-and-die makers, bus-drivers, and all the rest of the yahoos and the clowns on the street, the folks who piled everybody in the car and went down to Burger King for a real blowout.

(What was it she'd said to him last night, in the office? "Don't I know my man Dudley is the shrewdest little old cat?")

. . . Damn right.

Shrewd little old cats didn't sit around making legitimate profits, taking single pieces of the pie, not when they could have the entire pie to themselves.

Once, years back, G. Dudley's father, who owned a thriving drugstore in Minnesota, and who worked long hours to keep the place going and to feed his family, had given him a brief lecture on how you ran such a business. "I operate on trust," he'd said. "I figure most people are honest, and they want to pay you what they owe, sooner or later."

"Suppose they don't?" asked G. Dudley.

". . . Well, you just have to count on their sense of fair play," said the old man.

"Yeah, but what if they end up screwing you?" persisted G. Dudley, unconvinced.

"I don't have the time to worry about all that," grinned the old man. "I figure they all have to live with themselves, see? You know that old saying—when you wake up in the morning, you have to face up to the guy in the mirror."

. . . When G. Dudley's father had died, a few years later, of a heart attack, and the family lawyer had come in to check his books in order to get the estate into probate, they'd discovered thousands of dollars owing in various charge accounts that his old man had never been able to collect over the years. So damned much debt, in fact, that the store had been sold in order to provide G. Dudley's mother with sufficient money to hang on to the family's house . . . the same place she'd converted into a TOURISTS WELCOME OVERNIGHT venture, in order to survive, and to live in (not well) for her remaining years.

. . . And what about all those four-flushers, those guys in the mirror?

They'd gone right on brushing their teeth and shaving. (Probably with the Gillette Foamy and the Dual-Trak razors they'd charged to his father's drugstore.)

So . . . *screw legitimate profits.*

It was all going to be his. Very soon, now.

G. Dudley threw back the covers.

Was amused to discover that he had an erection.

230

. . . Oh well, what the hell, money, large sums of it, had always gotten him almost as excited as any waiting female.

And if you were about to screw Tulsa, and Old Ed, and dear Mrs. Joyce Donaldson Wade, and all the rest of the ribbon-clerks who were staring in their mirrors this morning . . . why not be ready?

But there still remained one small untouched base. One which a careful operator should not ignore.

Cyril Banks.

So amiable, the other night at Joyce's. Smiling, letting-bygones-be-bygones. It didn't ring true. Somehow, G. Dudley could believe that Cyril had completely forgotten the IOI Ltd. affair (in which he'd had to leave the lad hanging there from the gallows, swinging in the breeze, unfortunate, yes, but under the circumstances, it couldn't be helped, could it? In these matters, it was strictly *sauve qui peut,* and the devil take the hindmost).

Cyril Banks claimed he'd come here to Tulsa to bid on that valuable little Rolls, but . . .

. . . Was that the real reason for his jaunt down here?

Even though there were plenty of big-rich marks, fat cats in London these days, was it likely that Cyril, who was bright enough, but strictly an affable smalltimer, had been able to promote some affluent buyer, conned him out of enough cash to swing such a deal? That Rolls would bring a fat price, certainly, six figures, hopefully . . .

Could Cyril, smiling Cyril Banks, truly be toting around that much ready cash?

Only money talked.

. . . If and when Cyril became the winning bidder, and topped all the rest of the greedy buyers who were collecting here today, then they'd soon find out whether he had the money—

. . . And if the Rolls had been his true motive for his little trip to Tulsa.

G. Dudley finished dressing. Donned his dark blue blazer, picked out a discreet tie and knotted it, and examined himself in the mirror.

Was satisfied with the image he now presented to the waiting world. Stable G. Dudley Lester. Fair-dealer. Reliable and trustworthy.

At the foot of his bed were his bags, packed for the most part, waiting to be closed.

His gear, ready, as always, for a quick exit. When the time came.

 **The Arena**

9 A.M., and the doors were opened.

Outside there was already a respectable crowd waiting, tickets in hand.

Into the vast, brightly lit space they moved. Eyers, buyers, lookers, feelers, gawpers. All shapes and ages, some with the money ready to go, others without, but just as eager, all drawn by an invisible force-field, a buy, a bargain, something really good.

A Saturday crowd on free time. Knots of young kids in jeans and leather jackets and boots, spreading out to eye the waiting classics with unmistakable lust (shee-it, how does that sexy little Model A grab you?). Grey-haired workmen, heavy-handed, in Sears work clothes, retired grease monkeys who wandered down the aisles peering into opened hoods, peeping beneath chassis, nodding sagely at the immaculate brass and copper, the valves, and finely machined, well-chromed long abandoned parts (hell, nobody does that work anymore, nowadays it's kiss it off and get it out for the fast buck), eyeing well-made power plants (look at that big mother there, old Walter Chrysler sure knew what he was doin, not like these jerks today). Young married couples, noisy kids in tow, out for a pleasant Saturday (because your Daddy wants to look at that old Chevvy, that's why, no we're not a-gonna buy it, but he's always wanted one and someday—no, durn it, you can't have but the one candy bar between the two of you!). Here and there middle-

232

aged businessmen, in their sporty weekend outfits (Damn, look here, Harry, that's a LaSalle convertible, I can remember the day when my Daddy came home with that same car, sure do wish they'd hung on to it). High-rollers here in town, carefully dressed in de-mure but nonetheless expensive clothes (I told you if you wore that mink everybody'd figger who we was, the whole trick is keeping a low pro-file!). Proud owners giving their precious vehicles one last flick of the dust cloth (Durn right, there's a whole lot of my sweat in that Packard, when I picked her up in Missouri, she was a total wreck, I had to put her back together from the ground up, hate to sell her, believe me, friend, but well, I've got me two others in the garage need restoring, I'm short of cash, see?). Dealers, cruising through, keeping an anonymous poker face as they checked out the merchandise, speaking to no one, answering no questions (Why in hell should I let on I want to grab that Buick there? Sure it's a hot piece but I know where I can turn it over fast, I mean to steal me a car while everybody's lookin' the other way, bet your ass I will, too).

Lining up at the refreshment stands to buy early morning coffee and an indigestible sweet roll, they quickly returned to the business at hand, to look but not touch (UNLESS YOU ARE NUDE, DON'T TOUCH THIS CAR! THANK YOU). To gossip (Yeah, I do believe I saw this same car a couple of weeks back over to Enid, at a Swap-Meet, guess he couldn't move it there), to calculate silently what each car should bring (bottom line, top line, what's the durn reserve?), to plan, to prepare, to re-assess each one's game plan.

. . . And to wait for the circus to start.

Overhead, the music played, country-and-western, patches of lively rock, the Arena was filling up, Mrs. Joyce Donaldson Wade, resplendent in an all-white jeans and a matching top, a glittering rhinestone bandanna around her neck, moved through the Hospital-ity Suite, greeting the big money, laughing and making everybody welcome.

The big electric clock showed 10:50. G. Dudley nodded to Old Ed. Who nodded back.

Time to get this damn show on the road.

On came the p.a. system, hummm, screech, and then a metallic voice said ". . . Testing, one-two-three. Okay, folks, hey there, would you mind turning down that music? Good. Thank you, it's time we got started here—take your seats up there on the ramp, folks, we're about to begin. Has anybody out there forgotten to register as a bidder? I just want to remind you folks there's some mighty attractive items for sale here today and tomorrow, you been a-lookin' at 'em and you know they're all pure cream, and now they're all gonna be auctioned off, you wouldn't want to miss out, would you? so if you haven't already done it, get yourself over to the office, it's right down there by the rear wall where all the purty gals hang out, sign in with them, pay up your $25, it entitles you to bid both days, you can't bid without the card, folks, then when you've made the winning bid, you get yourself over there to the desk within an hour and settle up for the little beauty you bought . . ."

". . . That's twenty-five bucks more I owe you," said Benita.
"I'm keeping count," said Cyril, reassuringly.
"I'm nervous," she said.
"Good sign," he told her.

". . . This is an official Donaldson Bros. auction, and we're prepared to handle all transactions fairly and speedily," said the voice. "We've been in business a long time, and we're known for fair treatment all over Oklahoma. We're just about off and running now, so hurry up, folks, settle down in your seats, open your wallets, and let's go!"

In his sharp grey gabardine suit with the red piping, wearing a broad sombrero, Old Ed Donaldson moved over to the dais. Popped a throat lozenge in his mouth, tapped the mike to make certain it was working, cleared his throat, glanced at his watch. Nodded to his crew of pit men, all of whom were wearing dark red jackets, the traditional Donaldson Bros. uniform. Old Ed winked at Ham and Eggs, who winked back, then he cleared his throat.

"Howdy folks, and welcome to The First Southwestern Classic and Vintage Car Auction, my name's Old Ed Donaldson, I guess we're ready to start now, we got ourselves a full card, and from the look of it, there's gonna be a lot of money changing hands here today. Now I don't need to tell you folks here what's been goin' on in the classic car market, do I? What with inflation and taxes, and the rising cost of living and nobody up in Washington doin' much about it, hell, does anybody here need to be reminded what a prime investment any one of these here lovely automobiles can be for your future?"

He grinned. ". . . So don't you be left out, this is a once-in-a-lifetime opportunity to grab yourself a piece of American history, something real you can hang onto! These ain't the kind of cars you can buy yourself down at the dealers, not one of those mass-produced low horsepower jobs that's gonna drop in value the minute you drive 'er out the door, nossir! These are strictly one-of-a-kind items you're gonna be proud to own, they're gonna be sittin' in your garage going up in value, making all the neighbors jealous 'cause you was smart enough to grab one off while they wasn't! Now here we go, you've got your catalogues, you know what it's all about, we make no representations about the merchandise, everything is sold strictly as is, you buy what you see, speak up loud and clear so's we can find you, and bid, bid, bid!"

He leaned over to one side and called out "Drivers, start your cars and let's get a-going!"

G. Dudley, seated discreetly to one side, behind the dais, where he could survey the crowd without being seen himself, glanced at Joyce, who hovered nearby.

"He's dynamite," he commented.

"Bet your sweet ass he is," said Joyce. "Oooeeeh! Here comes the money!"

rapraprap! went the gavel, and beneath the bright hot lights there appeared a gleaming 1939 Lincoln Zephyr V-12 convertible, its whitewall tires immaculate, not the barest trace of a scratch on its finish. ("We start 'em off with something prime," Old Ed had counseled. "Get 'em droolin' right away.")

Slowly the lovely car rolled to stop, dead center, in front of the crowd.

"In your catalogue, Lot Number One, 1939 Lincoln Zephyr V-12 convertible, a prizewinner last year at Hershey," said Old Ed. "Now ain't that a beautiful piece of craftsmanship, come right down if you want to take a closer look, they don't make 'em like that any more, you'd better believe it, we're gonna start the bidding now, I'm gonna start her off with a ten thousand." Old Ed's voice went up a notch or two and he began chanting, the high-pitched rolling auctioneer's intricately woven siren song. "I'm starting with ten, ten ten tiddley ten, do I have tententen I want tentententen, do I see nine? Do I see nineninenine a-diddleynine, where do I see nine, it's a beauty do your duty, where do I see nine? Do I see eight? Who's gonna start 'er at eight, eight eight-abeta eight?"

Up and down the aisles went the pit men, shouting and waving their arms, gesticulating like aroused madmen, coaxing, wheedling, reaching out to touch the silent crowd, plucking at bidders, as if pulling bids by physical force, and then one of them turned to wave and shout "I've got *six here!*"

"Sixsix, sixata six," called Old Ed, "six-five, five five six-five five five, I want six five a fiddly five five, I've asked for six-five, I got it, six-five, now I want seven, seven, seven diddley seven, seven, seven!"

Slowly the numbers rose, as Ham and Eggs and the rest of the pit men bent to their work, it was eight, eight two fifty, now it was eight thousand five, eight thousand seven-fifty, and now it was nine, nine thousand—

Old Ed paused to take a dramatic breather.

"Ladies and gentlemen," he said. "You're not looking here at *any* old car. You are looking smack dab at something unique, a very special elegant piece of machinery with a twelve-cylinder engine that old Henry Ford's factory turned out for very rich folks, at a time when a dollar could really buy you something, when gas was fifteen cents a gallon and who gave a damn?"

There was an answering titter from the crowd.

". . . And are you trying to tell me you're gonna sit there and let somebody steal away this beauty, this one-of-a-kind item, this precious buggy for the absolutely ridiculous price of nine thousand dollars? Nine thousand dollars that won't even buy you a medium-line Ford 1979 today?''

He eyed the crowd quizzically.

''. . . Nine, nine, ninety nine, I want nine-five, nine five, good, I have nine-five, nine-five, I want ten ten ten, tenten ten tenidy ten. . . .''

Two minutes later by the clock, the 1939 Lincoln Zephyr V-12 was knocked down to a buyer for fifteen thousand-five.

The price was high, a good omen, close to a record, much better than the estimate, several thousand above the reserve placed on his car by the owner, a retired insurance agent named Hub Knight, who'd brought the car in on a flatbed from Louisville, Kentucky.

''. . . Grabbed yourself a nice bundle there, friend!'' said the pit man, clapping Hub on the back, as the Zephyr moved out from beneath the spotlights. "Feeling good?''

Hub smiled weakly. ''. . . I guess I should be,'' he said. ''. . . But it's kinda like I sold off one of my family, y'know?''

. . . But the pit man wasn't listening, he was off and running as they all moved along on Lot Number Two, a creampuff 1948 Mercury four-door sedan, a lovely frame-up restoration.

By noon, Old Ed and his crew had disposed of seven more cars, all at fancy prices, and he was moving right along, sailing. This was a fat-cat crowd, Old Ed could feel it all the way down to the tips of his $350 Tony Lama boots and back up again, this bunch was here to buy, buy, buy, this wasn't your ordinary mob of Saturday lookers and hangers-on, no indeedy, and he worked away at them like a conductor leading the Tulsa Symphony, a cunning old psychologist who knew how to suck them along, goose them forward, to stroke their flanks, kid them, nudge them, tease them, raising the ante up and up, needling them into a tumescent frenzy, and then, like a really accomplished hundred-dollar hooker, letting 'em settle back there for a minute or two, all hot and bothered, while he paused (. . . Now just a minute there, my friends, are you seriously sitting there on your duffs and letting somebody steal this beautiful 1929 Oldsmobile? This is a piece of our American tradition, which really belongs in some museum like Mr. Bill Harrah's, instead of being parked in your private garage. Are you prepared to let some sharp out-of-town operator steal her for *nine* thousand dollars? I gotta tell you, I'm truly ashamed to watch it happen . . .).

That was Lot Number Seven, and when the excitement had died down, Old Ed had pushed the price of the 1929 Olds up to a lush fifteen two-fifty, according to the *Old Cars Price Guide* (which was being sold at the door by an enterprising dealer) a spectacular new record sales price.

". . . Just listen to him go!" said Joyce. "He's hot today!" She leaned forward to wave. "Go, daddy, sic 'em!"

"I'm doin' my best, honey," said Old Ed, happily.

Up came Lot Fourteen (1929 Model AA One-Ton Stake Truck.)

Its four cylinders chugging softly, the little truck rested beneath the lights.

". . . Now I ask you, ain't she a little sweetheart?" demanded Old Ed. "Let's hear it for her!"

There was a scattered round of applause. ". . . For all you music lovers," he said, "This is a real treat. This, my friends, is the exact same truck you've all seen on the cover of them albums, by the famous group known worldwide as Pick Up Truck!"

". . . Isn't that the same one the guy was callin' you about last night?" asked Joyce. "He wanted to withdraw it from the sale, right at the exact moment when—"

"I remember!" said G. Dudley.

"—Well, are you lettin' it go for sale?" she asked.

He shrugged. "Money's money," he said. "He hasn't showed up with the withdrawal fee, the reserve is on it to protect him—"

". . . Then we're off to the races, right?" she chortled.

Old Ed started the bidding at three-five. Got himself a bid, right off. And away he went.

. . . Buddy Lee Thompson, a thin, sharp-nosed young man with a lush handle-bar mustache drooping over his somewhat weak chin, stared down from the bleachers at the Model AA. His heart was racing, his throat was suddenly dry, but he was doing a John Wayne, showing no emotion, keeping his cool.

Okay, this was the one he'd come for, all the miles from Louisiana, toting the bundle of cash in his money belt. There she was, that beautiful little mother down there, and he wanted her. So bad he could taste her.

Nobody around him knew that Buddy Lee Thompson was not a simple onlooker. Hell no. He was a goddamn entrepreneur, a hustler, a sharp showman, a single-minded buyer. Once he got his hands on that Model AA, he knew fucking well it would be the jewel of his collection, the keystone of his fortunes, he'd take it back to Louisiana, handling it with love and care, and he had a place waiting for it, smack in the middle of the building he'd leased out on the main highway where he'd soon be opening ROCKARAMA MUSEUM! WORSHIP AT THE SHRINE OF AMERICA'S GREATEST MUSICIANS! *Refreshments And Souvenirs Available—Ample Parking* . . .

Buddy Lee sat listening to Old Ed's chant, impassive, but the palms of his hands were sweating, he was waiting for the price to level off, it was over five thousand now, let the rest of the bidders drop by the wayside so he could move in and pounce.   fivetwo fifty five five five five six   Buddy Lee wasn't quite ready yet, there were still a couple of buyers around, those two guys there who were obviously dealers by the look of 'em, over on the side, he wasn't going to show his hand yet, yell, one of these trucks could be worth easily eight, he'd have to wait a little until he was sure it was past the reserve, whatever it was, seven now, sevensevenseven five, Old Ed wasn't doing too well dragging bids out of the crowd, good, there weren't any other music-lovers here, only those dealers there, hesitating now, probably considering whether or not a damn truck was worth all that, which was exactly how Buddy Lee figured they'd behave, after all, how much of a market for antique trucks could there be? Excepting for Buddy Lee and his ROCKARAMA?   sevensix it was, sevensix, a long pause while Old Ed gave his throat a breath of air and a rest. ". . . Folks, am I gonna have to knock this beauty down for a mere seven thousand-six?" he scolded.

No answer.

Up and down ran the boys, Ham and Eggs doing their number.
"Who'll give me *seven?*" demanded Old Ed.

Now. Buddy Lee raised his hand.

"Well, hello there!" cried Old Ed. "Another state heard from! Seven, sevenseven, I want seven-five, five five—"

Two minutes later, Lot Fourteen was knocked down for eight thousand two hundred fifty—to Mr. Buddy Lee Thompson, here from Allen, Louisiana.

". . . Only seven fifty over the reserve," murmured the auction attendant who'd hurried up to record Buddy Lee's bidding number. ". . . You sure stole yourself that one, friend . . . going into the delivery business?"

For the first time today, Buddy Lee grinned.

"Yep, that's my motto—keep on trucking!" he said.

After 1 P.M., there was a changing of the guard on the dais. Old Ed needed a break. His throat, and his bladder, needed relief, and his assistant, another specialist equipped with a vulcanized larynx, took over. "Don't rush," muttered Old Ed, as he stepped down, ". . . with buyers like this, we're in no damn hurry to get home."

". . . Bleeding gold mine he's got here," said Cyril, admiringly. "These are very fat prices indeed."

"I wish I hadn't given up smoking," sighed Benita. "I could use a pack—what do you think my Plymouth will bring?"

". . . *Ours,*" he corrected.

"Whatever!" she said.

". . . It won't show up for a while, by the look of it," he said. "Come, let's go get a bit of nourishment."

As they went past the dais, Cyril encountered G. Dudley, who glanced up at him. ". . . Why hello, Cyril," he said. "Leaving so soon?"

"Oh, not yet," said Cyril. "D'you know you're beginning to resemble a cat?"

". . . Am I?" said G. Dudley.

". . . The Cheshire, who's swallowing all the cream," said Cyril. "How's the food in your hospitality suite over there—to which I seem not to have been invited?"

240

"No? Must've been an oversight," said G. Dudley. "Perhaps nobody recognized you . . . as a high-roller."

"You knew I was," said Cyril. "I remember telling you so."

"Did you?" asked G. Dudley. "Sorry . . . there've been so many people around, all of them claiming they were here to get big-ticket items . . ." He glanced at Benita. ". . . The lady's a high-roller, too?"

". . . Miss Lorenzo is a friend," said Cyril.

"Of course," said G. Dudley. "Anyone with half an eye could see that." One of the auction attendants had appeared, to whisper urgently in his ear. "Excuse me, I've got to get over to the office," said G. Dudley. "See you." He left them.

". . . And screw you too, chum," said Cyril, sweetly.

He escorted Benita across to the entrance of the hospitality suite. "Friends of Mr. Lester" he told the guard at the door, and moved Benita on inside to the waiting buffet and bar.

". . . What did he mean with that crack about me?" she demanded. *"Is he a friend of yours?"*

"Was," said Cyril. "Once." He browsed through the food.

"Care to explain that?" she asked.

"No," said Cyril. "I'm hungry. If I talk about him, while I eat, I shall have indigestion."

". . . But you don't seem to understand me," the girl in the office was saying to the young man in the cape and Sherlock Holmes cap who was counting out money on the counter. "I cain't accept this money—it's us folks owe *you*—"

"Take it from the top, honey," said Chuck Malone. "I'm a little late because of the damn weather in St. Louis, but this is the withdrawal fee, $600—here, you count it—and now all you do is gimme back my title and the keys, and me and my truck'll be on our way—"

"Put that money away, they's pickpockets out there for damn sure," said the girl, patiently. "Now, your truck's all nice and sold, and for a durn good price, too—" She had picked up a clipboard, to consult the tally-sheets, "—and as soon as everything goes through escrow, you're gonna be getting—"

". . . What do you mean, *sold?*" he demanded.

"Now what do you think I mean, sold? *Sold*—for cash money— man was in here and paid up—look here, Lot Fourteen, eight thousand two hundred fifty—"

"Who in hell told you to sell my truck!" yelled Chuck.

"—Why—you did, Mr. Malone," said the girl. "Here's all the papers you signed—"

"*I'm gonna sue you!*" bellowed Chuck, as G. Dudley appeared in the doorway, followed close behind by a heavyset security guard. "No! The hell with that!" Chuck raged. "That's my truck out there and I'm going to take it! You keep the money—you had no damn right to sell it out from under me like that, I called you and said to hold it—you said okay—I should bring you in this money and here it is—"

"You never spoke to *me*, sir," said the girl.

"No, indeed, it was I," said G. Dudley, genially. "But you did not arrive here to withdraw your lot in time, sir, did you?"

Breathing hard, Chuck turned to glare at him. "I'm in charge of the goddamn weather over St. Louis?" he said. "Just gimme back those truck keys, *now!*"

"Oh, we can't do that, sir," said G. Dudley. "There are laws here, you see. The title is now in transfer, the new owner's money is in escrow, we've accepted it in good faith, he made the winning bid in good faith, the price went over your protective reserve, and we are now obliged to sell the vehicle to him—as are you."

"Don't hand me any of that legal shit!" said Chuck. "I got a lawyer up in New York who can handle it—speak to him!"

He lunged toward the office door.

To find that the security guard was firmly in his way.

"What the hell is *this?*" he demanded. "You think you can keep me away from my own damn property by force?"

"Not at all, sir," said G. Dudley. "Now—if you'll merely calm down for a bit, I'm sure we can sort all this out . . . why don't you come over and have a drink—"

"I don't want your booze—I want my little darlin'!" said Chuck, near tears. "You tricky bastards—"

"*Shh!*" urged G. Dudley. "Please. Let's approach this problem in a rational fashion. The new owner—'' he glanced at the girl, questioningly.

"Mr. Buddy Lee Thompson," she said, consulting the paper.

"—Mr. Thompson is, I'm sure, a reasonable man. Perhaps we can sit down with him and talk things out. There is more than one way to skin a cat, you know—'' he said, smiling.

"Who's doing the skinning?'' asked Chuck, balefully.

"Perhaps we can persuade him to come to some sort of a compromise," suggested G. Dudley, ignoring the sarcasm. "Is Mr. Thompson around?'' he asked the girl.

"Nossir,'' she said. "Mr. Buddy Lee Thompson paid up, all in cash, I gave him a receipt, and he left. Said he'd be back later on . . .''

"Great!'' said Chuck, bitterly.

"When he comes back,'' said G. Dudley, "I'm certain he can be talked to. Why don't we wait?''

He nodded to the guard. Took Chuck Malone by the arm, and led him out of the office. "Come over and enjoy some of our hospitality, sir,'' he suggested.

They walked past the rows of cars which had already been sold. Halfway down the line, they came to the Model AA Pickup. Chuck moved away from G. Dudley, walked over to his precious vehicle, opened the car door and tossed his backpack inside. Then he climbed into the front seat and firmly closed the door.

"I'll wait right here,'' he said, through the open window.

". . . Suit yourself,'' said G. Dudley.

He walked away, leaving the security guard behind.

Cyril and Benita emerged from the hospitality suite. "See you soon,'' he told the guard, and the guard tipped his hat.

They walked through the rows of cars still waiting to be sold, headed back to the bleachers. ". . . It's going to be a good while before ours turn up . . .'' he remarked.

But she was no longer beside him.

When he found her, she was beside Lot Seventy-One, a 1933 Plymouth, once the property of Mrs. Fox.

She was peering, mesmerized, at the wheels. Then she began to crouch down, to slip behind the barrier, her hand outstretched to touch—

He yanked her arm back.

Startled, she looked up. ". . . D'you want the entire world to know what you've come for?" he scolded.

"Nobody's looking!" she protested.

". . . One can never be certain of that," he warned her, and led her firmly down the aisle.

". . . You're a little paranoid, you know that, don't you?" she said.

"I come by it honestly, believe me," he said.

It was well after 3 now, and the proceedings had brought the auction slowly but successfully to Lot Forty-Two.

(1954 Hudson Hornet, 4-Door Sedan, 6 cyl, 330 cu inch sedan, totally restored, Serial 125565-A-91.)

Its owner, drove the large car onto the carpet, and parked it beneath the bright lights.

There was little response from the crowd.

". . . Look at this one!" said Old Ed. "Don't get to see too many of these beauties any more, do you, folks? The owner here, Mr. Hagerty, wants to tell you a little bit about his car here, so pay him some attention now . . ."

Mr. Hagerty, blinking in the glare, stepped out of his car and took the proffered hand mike. Cleared his throat. Smiled.

". . . Just wanted to tell you this is a car I personally spent a lot of hours on," he said. "She's restored from the frame up, she runs like a top . . ." One of the pit men had raised the hood, to permit any interested onlookers to peer at the power plant within, giving the Hudson the appearance of a crocodile awaiting examination of its teeth. ". . . she's a fine piece of transporation, reliable, clean and ready to roll . . . and I sure wouldn't be selling her here today excepting we don't have the room to store her properly, you know how it is when you're married, and there's a kid on the way?" He grinned.

". . . Okay then, Lot Forty-Two," said Old Ed. "Who's gonna

start this beauty off with five? Five, five, I want five? Five? Five? Four-five then. Fourfivefourfive fiddly five?"

The crowd did not respond, not even to the urgent cries of the pit men, who showed no signs of fatigue yet. "Four?" asked Old Ed. "Fourfourfour? Start 'er at threefive, then? Threefive, threefive?" Silence. *"Three?"* he asked.

A few feet away, in the shadows, stood Lot Forty-Three, a Ford T-Bird, property of Mrs. Louise Bigelow, of Waterloo, Indiana . . .

Who stood beside the car, her ears ringing with the echoes of Old Ed's voice on the p.a. system (". . . why, folks, you heard the man here, he's sellin' an honest piece of transportation, maybe it aint a Mercedes or a Caddy, but I'm lookin' for two-five now, why you couldn't buy yourself a used Volks for that today, could you? Shame on you, folks—"). Louise Bigelow's hands were trembling now, she'd never before faced such a large crowd, all of them strangers, a nice middle-class Indiana lady who'd spent this whole day wandering up and down the aisles of the Arena, staring, not at the other cars that were for sale, but at the people, glancing this way and that, as she searched for one very familiar face . . .

. . . Which was conspicuous by its absence.

In a very few minutes now the T-Bird, this low-slung beauty would be going out there, on the carpet, to be sold, to cut the cord. The chips (her one chip) would be down, and if he didn't care enough to have followed her down here to Tulsa, then the hell with Mr. Dusty Bigelow—

Then, incredibly, she saw him elbowing his way through the onlookers, headed towards her.

Dusty?

Yes! Dusty, disheveled, needing a shave, his clothing wrinkled, weary-eyed, not a mirage, it was him, all right, a small overnight bag in one hand—

Well now, if he'd been planning to come here, he'd certainly taken his own sweet time getting here, charging in like the U.S. Cavalry in the ninth reel—

". . . You sure don't make it easy on a guy, do you?" he asked. "Getting here from Indiana was a bitch, believe you me. Everything went wrong—"

"I didn't have any trouble getting here," she said, controlling herself; she wasn't sure she was glad to see him or how she felt, confronting him, right here down at the wire.

He stood beside her. "You really wanted out so badly?" he asked.

She nodded.

"You never told me," he accused.

"I guess I could never find the right time," she said.

". . . Oh c'mon," he chided. "Was it so terrible?"

". . . Not terrible," she conceded. "But . . . I couldn't handle it any more."

His eyes flickered across the T-Bird. Perplexed, he shook his head. "But why do you have to sell this?" he asked her. "Doesn't it mean anything to you at *all?*"

She shook her head. "No!" she said. "It's only a . . . *thing!*"

". . . I'm at two-seven, two seven, two seven . . ." Old Ed was chanting, up on the dais.

". . . But, I gave it to you because I thought you felt the same way I did!" Dusty protested, confused.

"Wrong!" said Louise. "Be honest—you gave it to me because it was a tax deduction!"

"That wasn't it at all!" Dusty said, angrily. "It was—" He stopped. Sighed, and shook his head. "Okay, dammit," he told her. "If you don't want it, neither do I!"

Oblivious to the passersby, they stood glaring at each other.

Old Ed mopped his forehead. Damn—selling the cheap ones was somehow a lot tougher than the big ticket jobs! ". . . Do I hear two eight?" he pleaded.

He glanced to the rear of the dais, where one of his pit men had young Mr. Hagerty, the owner, by the arm now and was muttering urgently in his ear. (I know you got a reserve of three on 'er, but why don't you play it smart, drop the reserve, take the two-seven, you come all this way, you don't want to waste the trip, do you? Grab it while you can!)

246

. . . Mr. Hagerty broke away from the pit man's grasp, shook his head. *"No!"* he said. "I got more 'n' that in her—she cost me plenty!"

The pit man turned to signal Old Ed. No deal.

"Shucks," said Old Ed, to the crowd, "this ain't no Goodwill Industries sale, we can't give 'em away." He waved the Hudson—125565-A-91—off.

And as the Hudson disappeared, he said "We needed three to sell 'er, folks, you missed the boat. *Next*—Lot Number Forty-Three, sold by owner's orders!"

The owner, Mrs. Louise Bigelow, got behind the wheel of her 1956 T-Bird (Serial #40A-TC25 BSU 47), and steered it carefully out to center stage.

There was a sigh of recognition from the audience, people craning forward to get a better look at the lovely little car, and then a spontaneous rattle of applause.

"Darn right she deserves a hand," said Old Ed. "What do I have to tell you about this beauty? You're all shrewd buyers—mebbe even a mite too shrewd." There were a few catcalls. "This is a true American classic . . . you know and I know it, and when I tell you this is her *original* condition, un-restored, you'll know why I'm asking for eight to start 'er! Eight, eight diddleydiddley *eight?"*

Louise stepped to one side, as various members of the crowd came down to eye the car closely, to peer into the front seat . . .

(The same bucket seats in which she and Dusty had driven away on their honeymoon, all those years back.)

He had seven five, seven five, seven five, *eight*—

. . . Someone was peering into the tiny open trunk.

(They'd had to make so many trips to bring the wedding presents in that silly trunk over to their first apartment, those three rooms downtown where they'd settled.)

—eightfive, eightfive fivefivefive, eight seventwofifty!

Someone else was examining the whitewall tires . . .

(On the wheels that had carried them off to the hospital, that winter night she'd had labor pains, Dusty excited but soothing her, telling her not to worry, the car would get them there in plenty of time.)

She glanced at Dusty. Who stood nearby, stony-faced, his mouth tight, as he listened to the bidding, nine, nine two fifty, nine five, the bids were still coming fast, Old Ed was dragging the crowd up past ten, ten two fifty, oh, these buyers knew perfectly well what a piece of jewelry that T-Bird was, they'd gone past the reserve now, moving up to a dizzy eleven thousand . . . the money that was going to be hers, which was her passport out of Liverpool, away from Dusty—

. . . Who still said not a word.

Stood there, having come here all this way, stubbornly watching his beauty roll away, out of his life. (His beauty, she thought, which one are you referring to, Louise, yourself or the car out there? And what difference did it make, he wasn't going to do a damn thing about either, was he?)

. . . Eleven-five now, eleven seven-fifty . . . twelve. The crowd was chasing the T-Bird like a pack of salivating hounds going cross-country after a fox. Twelve five, thirteen—

Some spectator was crawling inside the car now, examining the chrome hardware latches that released the hard-top, left the car open to the breeze—

(Afternoons in summer they'd taken the baby and gone for a drive, it was a tight squeeze, dangerous, even, what if they'd had an accident? but who thought of that? The baby gurgling with glee as the breeze tickled his face, all of them happy, she hadn't thought about such days in so long.)

Thirteen-two-fifty,   Five, five five. Thirteenfive

Dusty said nothing.

Was he really going to let it go?

. . . Their whole life was out here, stripped down to that car that would be sold to some greedy jerk who'd never appreciate it—

And once it was gone, that was going to be that.

(Well, isn't that what you wanted, Louise? *He* must have figured that out by now)

. . . Thirteensevenfifty, fourteen, fourteen twofifty, fifteen

She glanced at him. There was perspiration on his forehead, the muscles in his jaw were working. Well, at least he wasn't enjoying this, she'd seen that miserable expression on his face a few times, when he was really upset—

The poor bastard—this was tearing him up—

So he *did* care—

Whether it was about the car or about herself, what difference? The idiot was being noble about it!

She moved over and grabbed his arm.

". . . *You* keep it!" she told him. *"Bid!"*

He gaped at her.

". . . But—*you* want to sell—"

"Forget what *I* want!" she told him. "You always have, anyway, so stop being such a saint—"

". . . You mean you want me to—"

"We both know what it's worth—" she said. "I'm the owner— I'm telling you to *buy!"*

As if on a spring, Dusty's arm shot up, he waved.

"Fifteenfive, five five—"

Old Ed hadn't spotted Dusty's hand.

Louise gave him a shove, out to where one of the pit men could see him, and his bid. One of them did, it was Ham, who grinned and transmitted the bid to Old Ed—why not? He had himself another live one who'd take it up to sixteen, now it was a whole new ball game!

When it was finally ended, the T-Bird had been sold, sold— SOLD! to this gentleman down here in the front for a final bid of (Old Ed loved to repeat numbers, caressing them with his tongue and false teeth) nineteen thousand two hundred and fifty dollars!

"Satisfied?" he asked her.

"Are you?" she replied.

He shrugged.

". . . Well now it's yours again, isn't it?" asked Louise.

". . . This whole damn thing was ridiculous!" he cried. "First I give you the damn car—now I have to pay you all that money to get it back! . . . What are you going to *do* with all that—" He turned away, furious.

"I could buy you dinner," she suggested.

He didn't answer.

Okay, what the hell. She went over, climbed into the front seat of the T-Bird and drove it out, away from the lights and the crowd, and parked it over to one side, beneath the sign which read SOLD. I *tried,* she told herself.

. . . Clip-board in hand, another attendant came up to Dusty. "Well sir," he said, "that was damn nice, plenty of action, now if you'll just give me your bidding number, we can go settle up—"

". . . afraid I don't have a bidding number," said Dusty.

"Hold it," said the pit man. ". . . You mean to say you just wandered in here and bid—we don't have any credit references on you—nothing?"

Dusty nodded.

"Oh boy," said the pit man. ". . . And you're into that lady for nineteen thousand two fifty—?"

"I'm not exactly a stranger," said Dusty. "Go ask her, she'll identify me!"

The pit man drew him over to Louise.

"Ma'am," he said, "we might have us a little problem here with this fella who bought your T-Bird . . ."

"The two of us have had problems before," she said. "What is it now?"

". . . Seems I'm not qualified to bid," said Dusty.

". . . The bid-fee's $25," said the pit man, "and if he ain't registered with us, he wasn't eligible to *buy*—"

Louise opened her purse, pulled out her wallet. "Here," she said, producing bills. "I'll put up the $25 for him."

"Thank you very much," said Dusty.

". . . My pleasure," she said.

The pit man shook his head. ". . . That's fine," he said, ". . . but there's also that nineteen thousand two hundred fifty he owes."

"I'm sure he's good for it," said Louise. "Aren't you, Mr. Rhodes?"

". . . You two know each other?" asked the pit man.

"You tell him," said Louise.

"The lady is my wife!" said Dusty.

". . . I'm afraid I don't get it," said the pit man. ". . . You had to buy your *own* car?"

"You get the picture," said Dusty.

". . . And you're prepared to settle up?"

". . . Why not?" he said.

". . . It's kind of irregular," said the pit man, "but let's us go over to the office, okay?" He glanced at Louise. "Maybe you better come along, ma'am?"

"Glad to," said Louise.

. . . As they walked down the aisle, away from the bleachers, he said ". . . Did you mean that about dinner?"

She nodded.

". . .Well, I might take you up on it," he said, gloomily.

"You don't want to eat alone," she said. "You never did."

He snorted. "Never mind food," he said. "When these guys get through with me, I may not even have carfare home to Liverpool."

". . . Don't worry," she told him. "Happens I still have a little mad money left."

". . . Mad money?" he repeated. "Mad money! Jesus—I haven't heard you mention that since . . . before we were married!"

". . . That's right," said Louise.

She thought of saying *Think of it this way, Dusty, you're not losing a wife, you're gaining a car . . .*

But didn't.

 **5:10 P.M.**

Standing outside the auction office, eying the crowd as people began to leave, G. Dudley smiled genially at the paying guests.

. . . *Idiots,* he thought to himself. *You really do deserve to be taken.*

The first day's session was done, Old Ed had valiantly gotten through sixty-eight separate lots, and according to the tabulations, sixty-two of the cars had been sold up to now. An amazingly high percentage of success. But this was a buying crowd here, you could tell that for sure. Even the owners of those cars which hadn't met their reserves (like that nervous kid Hagerty and his Hudson parked over there) were ready to try again; they'd agreed to let Old Ed run their merchandise through tomorrow for a second shot.

So far, a total of $602,700 had been dragged out of them.

All of which, in cash money, travelers' checks, and certified bank checks, had left here moments ago, in a well-guarded truck, to be delivered downtown to the Oilmens National. All that lovely money which buyers had cheerfully paid over in such hefty sums . . . that the buyers would count over in their heads tonight as they lay awake in their temporary beds.

. . . And outside of a few small hitches (ridiculous snags like Malone, that long-haired fool who was still sitting guard out there in his little Ford pickup truck, waiting for some yahoo from Louisiana to return) . . . so far, it had all gone like a knife through butter, with damned few complaints.

Nobody had refused to accept the thirty-day escrow clause in the sale's contracts. Oh, certainly there'd been questions about it, but the girls were all primed to explain how complex was the intricacy of clearing motor vehicle titles here in Oklahoma, as well as in all the various other states from which the cars had been brought. Buyers could take delivery with temporary papers; sellers would have to wait, a mere thirty days. And so the buyers—most of them still riding the high which had parted them from those dizzy prices—and the sellers, delighted to have reaped rewards for their foresight, hard work, and shrewd investment, were now all going home, euphoric.

Amazing, he thought. Isn't it wonderful how all you people need an astute somebody to lead you around by the nose?

. . . And isn't it fortuitous for you that I was dropped down here in Tulsa, to do exactly that?

He continued to beam at the passing throng of class-A, certifiable pigeons.

. . . And spied Cyril Banks coming towards him in the crowd, beside him that dark-haired young girl . . . what was her name? Lorenzo? Cyril had always had a knack for latching on to available females—but truly, this one did not seem up to his previous conquests, did she? Rather plain . . . good ass, however. G. Dudley had noticed it earlier, as she wandered about that rather dull little 1933 Plymouth which had been consigned from up in Connecticut . . . Miss Lorenzo had been bending down, crouched over . . .

. . . Eying the wheels of the boxlike little black automobile.

Now why would she be so interested in *that* sober antique?

He'd watched as Cyril came back, found Miss Lorenzo, and quickly pulled her away, leading her down the aisle, obviously scolding her.

. . . Cyril Banks was here in Tulsa ostensibly to bid on a Rolls (or so he said.)

People who were prepared to bid on six-figure (from the looks of this crowd, it ought to bring that) Rolls-Royce limos, did not associate with young ladies who fancied 1933 Plymouths, did they?

It was a situation which bore some attention.

". . . Ah then, we'll be seeing you tomorrow?" he said, as Cyril approached. "You and your lovely lady here?"

"Oh, we'll be here," said Cyril.

". . . May fortune smile upon you," said G. Dudley. ". . . Both of you."

"Thanks for the hospitality," said Cyril, and then they were both gone.

". . . *G. Dudley!*" cried a most familiar female voice. "I've been lookin' all over for you, you old fox!"

"I've been here all along," he told Joyce.

Smiled and put his arm around her.

. . . *Another* idiot, he thought . . . the one who will be taken most of all, eh? But then, who deserves it the most.

". . . I want to tell you somethin' rat now," she said, fiercely. ". . . After a big day like today, Old Ed's gonna go home and gargle with some bourbon, but you 'n me's gonna celebrate tonight . . . and it's gonna be at *my* house, hear?"

"Why not?" said G. Dudley. "We're entitled."

Forced himself to give her bony shoulders an affectionate squeeze.

As they stood outside the Arena, inhaling the fresh evening air amid the crowd and waiting for a taxi, Cyril said softly ". . . I do believe he's on to you."

"Who is?" asked Benita.

"G. Dudley," he said.

"—On to me *what?*"

"That you're here to grab off something," he said. "And I shouldn't be surprised if he's figured out what it is, too."

"How do you know?" she demanded.

"I know him," said Cyril. ". . . I warned you to keep a low profile in there."

"Hell!" she said, angrily. "I'm nervous enough without you needling me! Now I've got to wait until tomorrow—unless I take a Valium, I don't know how I'll get any sleep tonight—"

Cyril grinned. "Ah, I'm certain you won't need a Valium tonight, sweet . . ."

She glared at him.

". . . Is that all you can think about?"

"Of course," he said. ". . . Believe me, I'm as nervous as you are." He pinched her cheek gently. "It's an excellent cure for the nerves. Think of it as therapy . . ."

". . . For you," she said. "I *thought* this was a business arrangement."

"With a few side benefits," he said. "Shall we go home and enjoy them?"

*　　*　　*

 **12:16 A.M.**

Louise Bigelow dozed in her bed.

. . . Luckily it was the large king-sized type, with plenty of room for two. (The nights she'd spent here in Tulsa alone this same bed had seemed so strange and vast, so cold . . .)

Now she had a man beside her. Snoring softly.

. . . Having spent the hours after dinner, right here in this bed, making it. Somehow strange bedrooms had always filled sex with more excitement . . . and tonight it had been very good.

It wasn't anything she'd planned on.

. . . When they'd gone to the Donaldson Bros. office at the Arena, to settle up the deal on the T-Bird, and Dusty had produced that sheaf of traveler's checks, begun to sign them and count them out, she'd gaped at them, surprised . . .

Fifteen thousand he'd brought with him?

(The rest he owed he'd have to pay by personal check, one that could be verified by telephone to his bank in the morning, was that acceptable? Well, it wasn't exactly regular business procedure, but in this particular case, provided it was okay with Mrs. Bigelow, the owner of the car? . . . the office girl was amused by the situation, of course she was.)

. . . Yes, the owner, Mrs. Bigelow, was prepared to go along with Mr. Bigelow's offer.

And at that point, she'd become aware that he'd come here to Tulsa *ready to bid.*

. . . And he hadn't.

Why not?

When they went out to get some dinner, afterwards, she finally asked him. Right out flat.

". . . After I got here," he said, "I realized I could get the car back . . . but it wouldn't mean I'd get *you* with it."

". . . And which one did you want?" she asked.

He hesitated.

". . . Both," he told her.

. . . How could you resist that?

". . . Well, you got the car," she said. "Are you happy? You're batting .500."

". . . No," he'd said, finally. "I'm not. Are you?"

". . . Happy?" she'd answered.

. . . No, she wasn't happy, and it wasn't because he hadn't been a good husband, or that their life together had been rotten, that wasn't the case—

Then what was it?

By now she'd had her second scotch old-fashioned, and she'd been able to tell him, straight out, some of what she'd kept bottled up inside, that she'd been thinking about while she was alone, down here in Tulsa.

That while he had plenty going on, to keep him busy, it was fine for him, but not for her. She didn't want a job, or a hobby of her own, it was because she didn't like *what* she was in Liverpool. That surrounded by all those things that he loved so much, made her feel like a prisoner—

—And that she'd had to break out.

Dusty had listened to her ramble on, sober-faced.

When she'd finished, trailing off, he'd told her he understood, it was okay . . .

But she wasn't sure he did.

Because she wasn't even sure *she* understood.

And then they'd stood outside the restaurant. No T-Bird to go home in. Besides, where was home?

He told her he'd get a cab and drop her off at her motel.

On the way, she asked where he planned to stay tonight?

He hadn't thought much about that, yet.

. . . Well, he might as well stay at the same place she was.

So damn silly, he said, when they got there. Then he turned to grin at her. Me coming in to the desk with you, Mrs. Bigelow, and you standing there with your key while I'm registering Mr. Bigelow, and asking for a room, and they want to know what's going on with these two?

Besides, he'd said, now that I bought your T-Bird, I haven't got the price of a room. Lady, you cleaned me out!

It *was* funny. The two of them had laughed.

. . . He'd laughed himself right into this bed, hadn't he?

It had been much later, when they were together, here beneath him, him moving urgently against her, that she'd thought *what about tomorrow?*

What Dusty was doing then certainly caused her to forget the question.

. . . For a while, at least.

But now it was back again.

. . . What about tomorrow?

Louise slept.

She was awakened by a faint light across her eyes.

. . . Morning? So soon?

She blinked. No, it wasn't coming through the venetian blinds, it was here in the room, the lamp beside the armchair was on, her clothes had been moved (she'd thrown them onto the chair last night like some anxious teenager), there was Dusty, sitting in the chair.

. . . Reading?

She squinted at him.

Yes. He was immersed in that large catalog, the one Donaldson Bros. had given her at the Arena when she'd come in with the T-Bird, full of color pictures of all the cars that were due to be sold here.

Four in the morning by the bedside clock, he was turning the pages, his lips pursed, his eyes fascinated with the sight of the antique beauties being offered here in Tulsa. He was totally involved—even now that he had his T-Bird back—

God. No matter how much he had, it would never be enough, would it?

Which was the answer to her question about tomorrow, wasn't it?

Tomorrow (today) he'd be over at the Arena—

—Probably bidding on some other car.

She burrowed beneath the covers, closing her eyes, turning her back to the light. Tried to go back to sleep.

Your move, Mrs. Bigelow, she thought.

. . . While Mr. Bigelow happily read on.

*   *   *

 **9:30 A.M.**

Passing Mr. Sami Kallil on the street, as he emerged from the taxi which had brought him here from the airport to the Arena, the second day of the Donaldson Bros, auction, one would barely give him a second glance.

A smallish, bespectacled gentleman, in a cheap dark blue suit, wearing his open sports shirt, the modest briefcase in his hand, Mr. Kallil might well have been taken for a novelty salesman. An accountant, or perhaps a schoolteacher.

Such anonymity was an integral part of Mr. Kallil's life-style. For many years since his youth, in the countries he had passed through, he had maintained this modest appearance, smiling and giving soft answers to any and all questions. Only a very few of his trusted friends and relatives knew (and they only what Mr. Kallil wished them to know) that S. Kallil Esq. was well endowed with sufficient tangible assets to make him, even by Dun & Bradstreet standards, a rich man.

A man with a mission here in Tulsa, today.

Who had arrived, tourist-class, from California.

He was part-owner of a large block of very prime real estate on Roxbury Drive, in Beverly Hills, on which sat a five-story office building, with its own parking garage. Several oil tankers (chartered under Panamanian registry), which regularly made the profitable run from the Persian Gulf to Eastern American ports. A small apartment house in Paris, on the Avenue Foch, and another one in Torremolinos, in Spain (where he kept one flat for vacations). Ranchland in the Ruby Valley, in Montana (which he'd visited only once), irrigated, producing crops and money.

Besides the several numbered Swiss accounts where he kept an ample supply of gold, Deutsche marks, and stable Swiss francs, Mr. Kallil had other stashes of funds in carefully chosen banks and financial institutions elsewhere. He carried a Greek passport, slept some nights in his small co-op apartment on East 69th Street, in Manhattan, and others in the house on North Elm Drive in Beverly Hills where his good wife supervised the raising of their family. If

258

one were to find any single pattern of existence to govern Mr. Kallil's life-style, it would be the one based on this rule, i.e., be well hedged against whatever financial reverses, political uprisings, or terrorist attacks that the future of this troubled planet may bring. And always keep a bag packed.

Mr. Kallil enjoyed his assets, but they were inanimate. Utilitarian. His supreme pride and joy came, not from any of his astute investments, but from his son and future heir, Dann. Oh yes, his two daughters would be married, and they would bear him grandchildren . . . but Dann, ah . . . truly a jewel.

Within a week or so Dann Kallil would be graduating from that large Eastern university where he had been assiduously studying Business Administration (at his father's behest). Then Mr. Kallil would be assured an honest partner for his later years.

What should a proud father present to his son, on such a heartwarming occasion?

In between all of his conferences and meetings, Mr. Kallil had pondered the problem.

In time to come, certainly, Dann would achieve possession of a good deal of the Kallil wealth. And he would manage it well, of that Mr. Kallil was certain. But a son who was so pleasant, so hard working and loyal to his father's wishes . . . he should be rewarded with something tangible, something splendid for his labors . . . *now.*

It would be the sort of gesture that could express his gratitude.

. . . A Vacherin & Constantin watch, perhaps? A small yacht, some sporty racing model. A thoroughbred horse . . . or a tax-sheltered piece of real estate . . .

None of them seemed appropriate. It should be something the boy truly fancied.

The last time he and Dann had met, over lunch in a Boston restaurant, he'd made discreet inquiries.

. . . But the dear boy had seemed totally disinterested in any of the subjects Mr. Kallil had raised. The only thing that Dann seemed to look upon with any interest these days was a certain old car which one of his classmates had lately acquired. Some British vehicle, an ancient Jaguar?

Mr. Kallil, who drove himself around Beverly Hills in a leased Ford sedan, had no feeling for automobiles whatsoever. In his world a car was strictly a means by which one got oneself from one business meeting to another. Or, in a crisis, across a border.

He'd listened as the boy discussed that car. Remarked on its lines, its vagaries, laughed with him as he related its mechanical problems. Mr. Kallil was a good listener; he allowed his son to explain the intrinsic beauty of old cars, especially those known as "classics" . . . such exotic vehicles as Packards, TR-2's, Nash-Healys, Bentleys . . . some strange machine known as an Auburn Boat Tail.

Later, he had accompanied Dann on a trip out to some small Massachusetts town, where there seemed to be something called a "swap-meet." There, owners of such cars came together to spend the day exchanging old pieces of machinery, rubber tires, license plates, even literature—from the backs of wagons and in stands. Amazing . . . the entire affair had reminded Mr. Kallil of his own youth, when his father had taken him to the nearby town, to market, where peddlers and merchants, calling out and arguing, beckoned buyers to their wares, spread out on the dusty street.

And here was his own son Dann, excited, involved, responding to such a marketplace. Could it be what the scientists here referred to as heredity?

Whatever it was, that long warm afternoon he'd spent there, watching Dann proceed through the field, examining the old cars, inspecting them closely, had finally provided Mr. Kallil with the answer to his problem.

As a gift to Dann, he would buy the boy such a car.

Yes, indeed, but not simply *any* such old car.

He must buy this son one of the very best.

He had made inquiries through some of his California business associates, and become knowledgeable on the subject. The best way to acquire such a vehicle (which, he was pleased to discover, was a superb investment for the future, as well) was not through dealers, but at an open auction. There, only money spoke.

Mr. Kallil understood that at the first session here in Tulsa, yesterday, there had been many cars bought and sold. But he had bided his time, for he knew that today, at the second session, the really choice items would be auctioned.

Peculiar things listed in the catalogue, but they were valuable. A Marmon (whatever that might be). A Tucker Torpedo. An open Packard touring car from 1929. (The stock-market crash in New York, he knew that date well.) Something called a Chrysler Air-flow. A 1937 Rolls Royce sedan. (That one he could understand, Beverly Hills was full of such expensive automobiles, the parking lot on Roxbury was jammed with them. But those California film people and his doctor tenants fancied the later models, yes? Not the vintage ones Dann discussed.)

In Mr. Kallil's briefcase was his toiletkit, a clean pair of socks, and a change of underwear (the shirt he wore could be washed and dried overnight), as well as a substantial sum of Swiss-franc traveler's checks he had withdrawn yesterday from one of his safe-deposit boxes in Los Angeles.

Tomorrow evening he had a business meeting in New York, where he would discuss the purchase of a loft building on West 19th Street that could be easily converted into boxlike apartments that would spin off a fine return on the investment.

But here in Tulsa, today, he would spend the next few hours shopping.

Mr. Kallil hurried inside, to spend his money on a splendid present, for his splendid son.

 **9:32 A.M.**

. . . His head ached, throbbed like a bass. Sour waves churned rhythmically in his gut.

His back was stiff and his left shoulder was sore, one of his legs was numb, this was the hardest bed he could ever remember, every which way he tossed or rolled something sharp reached out to jab him—

Bed, hell, he was lying in the back of his little darlin'—his truck . . .

Over the years he'd slept in some crazy places, but this was Desperation City.

. . . She was a beautiful little truck but she was no substitute for a Sealy mattress.

But his head. Must've been poisoned, no, it wasn't food, it was the booze.

—That pint he'd brought with him from Jersey, he'd drunk it last night to wash down that soggy hamburger he'd eaten from the Arena stand before the place closed up for the night.

(He'd called Jack Adler long-distance, laid it all out for him, asked what to do? Jack had told him to sit tight, he couldn't get down there, he couldn't practice in Oklahoma, so he'd try to locate a lawyer locally, meanwhile *stay with the truck* . . . so nobody could move it, hang in there, kid, he'd be in touch.)

—He'd sneaked back down the aisles here to the truck, ducking the security guards, climbed up inside the bed, wrapped himself in his cape, put the backpack beneath his head, tried to sleep.

It had been so damn chilly in here he'd finished the booze for warmth. Finally dropped off to sleep . . .

Desperately needing to pee now, Chuck sat up, discovering new aches. Clambered down from the back, in the course of so doing skinned his shin against something, damn!

Made his way through the darkened aisles, miles down drafty corridors, keeping silent so as to attract no attention.

Relieved, he sloshed cold water on his face, drank thirstily from the mens' room sink tap.

. . . Then made his way back to the truck, climbed back in, tried to find a comfortable position, dozed off again.

When would that bastard Thompson show?

Sudden light flashed across his eyelids, a white glare.

Then brassy music began to blare from the goddamn p.a. system, causing his head to ache even more fiercely.

Damn—could it be morning already? They'd be opening up!

. . . Thompson would have to show up today.

Meanwhile, he needed more sleep.

. . . He burrowed, molelike, beneath his cape.

". . . There she is," said Buddy Lee Thompson. "Ain't that a perfect doll?"

"Durn right," said the trailerman, a brisk businessman in a shiny green suit, a clipboard in hand. ". . . Won't have yourself no trouble with this. We get her up on the trailer, lash her down tight, nylon cord, then we cover her up with a special tarp so she's protected, and away she goes. I better figger out what it's gonna cost you . . ." He pulled out a pen from the array he carried in his plastic-pocket case. "Mileage," he said. "Gimme your destination."

"She goes to Buddy Lee Thompson, that's me, and you make out the bill to Rockarama Enterprises, Box 9, Allen, Louisiana."

". . . Mind my asking what the hell's that?" asked the trailer man.

". . . That's my museum," said Buddy Lee, proudly. "She's gonna go on display there, the original Pick Up Truck from that famous group, of the same name . . . and folks're gonna come from everywhere to Allen, just to get a look at Chuck Malone's personal Pick Up—"

". . . *She's not going anygoddamnwhere!*" said a hoarse voice from the back of the truck.

His hair flying, eyes bleary, clothes rumpled, Chuck rose, a figure of biblical wrath, to glare down below.

Buddy Lee gaped up at him.

". . . What're you doin' in my truck?" he asked.

"*My* truck!" said Chuck.

". . . I bought her!" insisted Buddy Lee. ". . . Now you *git*—"

"Up yours, Charlie!" said Chuck. "I been waiting here since yesterday to settle up with you."

He clambered down from the truck-bed. Stood firmly on the floor, hands on his hips. "Legally, you have no sale, and this vehicle isn't going to any damn museum—"

"Who says so?" demanded Buddy Lee.

". . . Me," said Chuck. "The owner."

". . . The hell you are," said Buddy Lee. "The owner was Chuck Malone!"

"You better believe it," said Chuck. "Chuck Malone. Of Pick Up Truck. Take a good look."

Buddy Lee stared.

". . . Je-sus H. Christ," he said, at last. ". . . I thought sure you was dead or somethin'."

"Not yet," said Chuck. Put a hand to his head. ". . . Although I could be."

". . . You're going to need insurance, portal-to-portal," said the trailerman, figuring away at his clipboard.

"He's gonna need more than that!" said Chuck. "Try to haul this out of here and I'll have my lawyer sue your ass off—they had no legal right to sell you this yesterday, get it?"

"I paid cash money!" protested Buddy Lee.

"Go get it back," said Chuck. "Then you can buy yourself somebody else's truck, not mine. *This* baby you're not getting—"

Buddy Lee moved closer to peer at him. ". . . You *really* Chuck Malone?" he asked.

". . . What do you want me to do, play you a concert?" said Chuck.

". . . Hey now," said Buddy Lee, impressed. "How about that! Chuck Malone, in person. You know, you was pretty good back there . . ."

". . . And I'm going to need a deposit," said the trailerman, still working away.

"I'm *still* pretty good," said Chuck.

He belched.

"I'll just bet you are," said Buddy Lee. "The fans never do forget . . ."

". . . They have lately," said Chuck.

"Shoot, all you need is a little publicity," suggested Buddy Lee.

". . . Not by having my truck parked in some fleabag museum in the sticks," said Chuck balefully. "Thanks for nothing . . . when my lawyer gets here, he'll lay it all out for you."

264

"I paid my money, I got a receipt, and a contract," said Buddy Lee. "I can get me a lawyer too."

". . . Where I'm at so far, is $690 for towing and delivery," said the trailerman. "That's *without* insurance—"

Buddy Lee attempted a grin. ". . . Now listen here, Mr. Malone," he said. "No sense the two of us getting riled up over this, is there? Why don't we go somewheres and get us some coffee—"

"I'm staying right here," said Chuck. Wincing, he sat down on the running-board.

". . . Hell, I ain't about to steal her," protested Buddy Lee, aggrieved. "Man, I'm one of your *fans*. Why do you think I laid out all that cash money here?"

". . . With fans like you, I could be dead," said Chuck. He gently caressed his forehead. ". . . which I feel like."

". . . I got all your records," said Buddy Lee, and sat down beside Chuck on the running board.

"Collector's items," said Chuck.

Buddy Lee sighed.

". . . I know one thing for sure," he said. "Once the damn lawyers get to arguin', we'll both be shafted, ain't that the truth?"

"I'll take my chances," Chuck told him.

". . . But you and me ought to be able to work something out here," Buddy Lee suggested. ". . . So's we'll both end up happy?"

Chuck shook his head. "Cool it," he said. "I got here too late to stop the bastards from selling my truck to you—but they had verbal instructions not to let it go. So I know where *I* stand here. And I'm not moving . . ."

". . . Adding in the insurance, and the charge for dead-heading back from Louisiana, I'm at $914," said the trailerman. He began to fill in a series of printed forms.

Buddy Lee eyed the truck. ". . . Sure does cost, don't it?" he asked.

"You want to own a truck like this, it sure as hell does," said the trailerman. "You got an investment to protect."

". . . She's a museum piece if ever I saw one," mused Buddy Lee.

". . . Not for your museum, buddy," said Chuck. "No way."

From the pocket of his jean jacket, Buddy Lee took out a pack of cigarettes. Shook one out, lit it. Offered the pack to Chuck. Chuck took one with fingers that shook slightly.

They smoked in silence.

". . . Listen here," said Buddy Lee. "Sposin'—just for the sake of talkin' matters out here—supposin' you was to hang on to her—and I got my money back . . ." He rubbed his chin. ". . . If what you're sayin' about the sale yesterday is true that is . . ."

"It's true," said Chuck.

". . . well now, why couldn't you and me make a deal?" asked Buddy Lee.

"Deal?" said Chuck.

"Yeah," said Buddy Lee. ". . . For you to show up in Allen, every once in a while."

Puzzled, Chuck blinked.

"Why would I ever do that?" he asked.

". . . Personal appearances is what I'm suggestin'," said Buddy Lee. ". . . You *and* the truck."

Chuck blinked again.

". . . In *Louisiana?*" he asked.

"Why sure," said Buddy Lee. "You got a lot of fans down there!"

". . . No shit," said Chuck.

"You bet!" said Buddy Lee. "Folks that don't forget . . . folks that appreciate real talent. Hell, the woods're full of 'em!"

". . . So that's where they've been," remarked Chuck. ". . . In the woods."

"If they knew you was comin' down, they'd get all excited," promised Buddy Lee. "They'd all come around . . . see, I'd take ads on the radio, put up billboards, get 'em all in—'Coming Next Week—To The One and Only Rockarama! In Person—Your All-Time Favo-rite—Chuck Malone—and Pick Up Truck!' "

". . . The one you think you bought here," said Chuck.

"Oh, it'd be wild," said Buddy Lee, warming to his vision. ". . . See, I got this big old field out back, we'd fill it with 'em, charge 'em for parkin', sell 'em booze and food—then you come out and do your songs—you could probably even get a record out of it, we'd get the TV to cover it—''

"NBC, sure—'' said Chuck. "Or Don Kirshner? Mm? . . .''

"You ain't takin' this seriously,'' said Buddy Lee, "but I'm willin' to talk contract with you. You'd get you a big fat fee, we'd put you up in the best place in town . . .'' He winked. "Get you plenty of nice young poon-tang, too, before *and* after. Why hell, you'd end up rich *and* exhausted!''

Chuck nodded.

"Let me clue you to something, friend,'' he said. "Chuck Malone doesn't work for a damn fee, I'd take a percentage. Of the *gross.''*

"Uh huh,'' said Buddy Lee. "I guess that figures . . .''

The trailerman held out his clipboard and the pen.

". . . Who's signing this?'' he asked. "I'm gonna want me cash—no checks.''

"Hold it there for a minute,'' said Buddy Lee. "Mr. Malone and me's *talking* here. You don't interrupt him—he's a *star,* y'know . . .''

Chuck shook his head. "You know something?'' he remarked. "You look like a shit-kicker, but you got your brain from IBM.''

"Like my old daddy says, it takes one to know one,'' said Buddy Lee, jovially. He rose, stamped out his cigarette. ". . . Why don't you'n'me both go get us some hot coffee and talk it all out? Old truck here won't be goin' anywheres while we're gone, will she?''

Chuck nodded. Painfully rose to his feet.

". . . I'm buyin','' said Buddy Lee. ". . . So far it's been me doin' most of that here, anyways, right?''

". . . Okay, shit-kicker, let's go,'' said Chuck.

The two men started down the aisle.

". . . Hold it!'' called the trailerman, confused. ". . . What am I gonna do with all these forms?''

". . . You really want me to tell you?'' called Chuck.

*   *   *

 **II:2I A.M.**

Old Ed, his vocal chords restored to full volume by a night's rest and liberal applications of his secret elixir (sour-mash bourbon, honey, and hot tea) was up to Lot Eighty-Seven now. Very shortly he'd be calling for the 1933 Plymouth to be pushed forward.

In the middle of the crowd, smoke from a nearby cigar causing her eyes to smart, Benita sat, by herself.

Lot Eighty-Eight. The winning number, the jackpot . . . the car she'd come all this way for, following Gus's instructions, on this lunatic journey.

So far, she'd been insulted, pushed around, robbed, and screwed. (That part of it she couldn't really complain about, could she?)

Beside her sat a tight-faced young man in a business suit, tapping his teeth with a pencil. Behind her was a trio of noisy middle-aged ranchers in jeans, muttering jokes back and forth, on the aisle across from her was a willowy boy in a Cardin suit, escorting a busty woman whose shoulders were draped in a fur cape, her face frozen by some expensive plastic surgeon into a permanent smiling mask.

. . . Maybe one of them was after the Plymouth.

(How high should I go? she'd asked him, over breakfast.

As high as it takes to buy the bloody thing, he'd said.

. . . But we don't know if there's a reserve on it, do we? If it doesn't go high enough, they could pass, right?

You *are* learning, aren't you? he'd said. Stop fretting. Remember, if the price is too low, some dealer will try to steal it—so bid. And for God's sake, don't freeze up on us. Then I'll come settle up with you, *you* can pay them.)

. . . She sure as hell wished he'd stayed with her, but this morning he'd been insistent that they split up. (Not together, pet, makes it a trifle less obvious, you can be sure he's watching the two of us closely.)

He?

. . . That Lester. The one who was moving around, by the dais, in his blazer, dapper, smiling, the one who'd made the smarmy cracks about her yesterday. What went on between him and Cyril? The way they smiled pleasantly at each other, they should be friends . . . where did they know each other from? What was the story? Every time she'd asked Cyril since, he'd clammed up on her.

. . . So maybe they weren't friends?

For that matter, what did she really know about this slender English character, whose bed she'd shared for the past two nights? (Not so willingly the first night, much more so the second.) Who was prepared to bankroll her into buying the Plymouth?

Not a whole hell of a lot.

He ran some restaurant in London, he was here to buy that fancy little Rolls, and he was her partner.

But Benita was past the age where she believed in Santa Claus and tooth fairies.

Was it really a half interest in the gold he was after?

(It better be what your old friend Gus told you it was, sweet, he'd said, last night. Otherwise we shall be royally stuck with a nice little 1933 Plymouth, won't we?)

. . . You've come a long way from Bridgeport, Benita, she told herself.

If worst comes to worst, you can always drive home in a 1933 Plymouth.

. . . Of which you will own half.

If yours is the winning bid.

". . . Lot Number Eighty-Eight!" announced Old Ed.

Into the lights chugged the reliable little four-door sedan in which Mrs. Laura Richards Fox had conveyed herself back and forth from home to factory, each day for almost forty-five years.

Melvin Decker, the owner of Import Cars, Inc., Aurora, Illinois, peered down at it.

". . . *That* one?" he muttered.

"Yep, that's her," said his son, a thinnish boy in his early twenties. "A beauty."

". . . I don't figure you, Larry," said his father, softly. "A '33 Plymouth? Strictly iron."

"A sleeper," whispered his son. "Got to go up."

"They haven't so far," murmured his father.

"That doesn't mean they won't," said Larry Decker.

". . . Worth two thou maybe," said his father. "Tops two-five."

"You could be wrong," said Larry.

"Not on Plymouths," said his father.

". . . Now ain't that a sweet little thing?" asked Old Ed. "A real little darling. Take her home, start her up, she'll drive you anywheres you want to go, one of Mr. Walter P. Chrysler's finest, and real low mileage, gaswise, folks. Let's get her started, folks, do I hear fifteen hundred?"

Silence.

"Ah come on now," wheedled Old Ed. "Who's gonna start 'er off?"

Nervously, Benita raised her hand.

From below, Ham smiled and relayed her bid.

". . . fifteen, fifteen, thank you kindly, I want seventeenfive, seventeenfive, I've got seventeenfive, now I want two, I want two, twotwotwotoodledeetwo—"

She raised her hand again.

"Good, now I've got twotwotwo, two twofifty? I've got it, where's two five? Twofivefivefive—"

She felt a slight trickle of sweat beneath her arms, her blood was beginning to pump faster, again she raised her hand—

Now it was twofive, but somebody here was topping her bid, who could it be? she couldn't spot anybody around her, she raised it to two seven fifty—

Ham and Eggs and the other pit men were trotting up and down the stairs, whooping and hollering, bright-eyed and bushy-tailed here today, they'd had a good night's sleep with some local talent they'd picked up, today their batteries were recharged and they were rarin' to go, go go! They sensed money here and like a team of expert bird dogs they were in hot pursuit of the live ones . . . three! came from somewhere, over to the right. Three two fifty back from Benita Lorenzo—

". . . Somebody else wants it," muttered Melvin Decker. "Lay off."

"Why?" demanded his son. "They *know.*"

"They know what?" asked his father. "Who told you to bid?"

"I'm having fun," said his son, defiantly.

And raised his hand.

Three five it was, then three seven two-fifty, Old Ed was happy, the bidding was good and strong, he was looking for four, and he got it—

Four thousand? How had it gotten to that number so soon?

One of the pit men was staring at her, beckoning, waiting for her to top it. Once again Benita raised her hand.

"I've got fourtwofifty!" said Old Ed, "I want fourfive—oh, don't let her get away, folks, she's a lovely little joy wagon, an investment—who'll say four five?"

"Four five for that little pig?" hissed Melvin Decker. "You got to be crazy!"

"Hell I am!" said his son, jubilantly. "I'm gonna get it!"

"Four five, I want foursevenfifty!" called Old Ed. Oh, this little mother was a real sleeper, here was some action, he was going to ride it out like a surfer coming into shore, they'd passed the reserve of $4,500 and from now on he could be sure it was a sale—"Give me foursevenfifty!" he urged.

Benita was frustrated, confused, she was getting a headache, somebody else around here wanted the car, somebody consistently topping her, no way to see who it was—

"Go to it, honey!" suddenly said the woman across the aisle. "Don't let the bastards steal it away from you!"

On reflex, Benita raised her hand.

"Four sevenfifty!" cried Old Ed. "And worth every damn dollar, believe you me, folks, do I hear five, I want five, five—"

". . . You're out of your goddamned bird," said Melvin Decker. "Five g's for that heap?"

"For damn sure," grinned Larry, and bid.

Old Ed had the five, he wanted fivetwofifty, who would give it to him?

. . . Benita stared, hypnotized by the car in the lights below—

Benita's hand went up.

". . . Six thousand!" acknowledged Old Ed. *"Now* we're gettin' there, do I hear sixtwofiftyfiftyfifty—?"

Silence.

. . . Oh, stay the hell out of this, whoever you are, give up, don't drag any more money out of me, prayed Benita . . .

". . . *Back* me!" pleaded Larry Decker. ". . . They're stealing her away—"

"—come on, kid, wise up!" said his father, "—for six thou, it's no theft!"

The two Deckers glared at each other.

Melvin reached out to seize his son's arm. "Listen to me," he said, softly, urgently. ". . . it happens to a lot of people, this wouldn't be the first time somebody went bananas at an auction, got a hard on for something, get all wrapped up in the bidding, and go off the deep end, see? You're gonna thank me later, you'll be—"

". . . Six then?" boomed Old Ed's voice on the p.a. system above. ". . . *Sold!*"

Melvin released his son's arm.

Larry Decker drew a deep breath. Exhaled.

"Okay, you talked me out of it," he said. "Just remember, you could be real wrong . . ."

"Shit, wouldn't be the first time," said his father, relieved.

". . . Got yourself one helluva buy, honey," said Ham, giving Benita's shoulder a friendly pat. "Go pay for it now," he said, and trotted off, back to the fray.

. . . Mrs. Fox's 1933 Plymouth, which, as soon as six thousand dollars, plus sales tax and title fees, etc., were paid over, would belong to Benita Lorenzo and Cyril Banks, moved off the spotlit stage. Benita stared at it as it rolled off on four wheels . . . made of what?

For six thousand dollars, she'd—*six* thousand *dollars?*

"Nice bidding, honey," said the lady across the aisle, tilting her frozen smile in Benita's direction. ". . . What do you plan to do with it?"

Without thinking, she answered "Change the tires."

"They looked okay to me," said the lady. "Why waste good money on radials?"

. . . *Or* on a 1933 Plymouth? Benita asked herself, and left the bleachers.

To go in search of Cyril, the man with the money. Her British Daddy Warbucks.

. . . Finally she found him, coming towards her, moving stony-faced through the crowd that hung around the edges of the action.

"Did I do all right?" she asked.

He grimaced, touched a finger to his lips.

". . . Sorry," she told him. "I got carried away."

"You certainly did," he said. "Six thousand was rather a bit more than I'd ever counted on paying out for that . . . thing."

The Plymouth was slowly chugging by, headed for the far reaches of the arena where the SOLD items were neatly parked.

. . . Okay, so she'd paid a lot—why was he suddenly so pissed off? He stood to make plenty—if—

—*If.*

"Sorry," she told him. "You told me not to freeze up—"

"Let's not discuss it further," he said. He drew her into the shadows, behind a pillar. Proceeded to count out traveler's checks, sign them, and handed them over. "Go pay up, I'll find you outside the office when you're done."

"Listen," she said, "you're not going to be disappointed—"

"I've got no time for that now," he said. "What's done is done!"

Inside the office, she waited until one of the busy staff was ready to take care of her. She counted out the checks, began signing the sheaf of legal documents that were involved in the transfer from the Estate of Laura Richards Fox.

When could she take delivery?

". . . As soon as we clear all these documents, ma'am," said the harried girl. "We're working as fast as we can . . ."

She kept on signing.

". . . Strange," said a familiar voice. "I had no idea our friend Mr. Banks had come all this way from London, merely to buy that black Plymouth . . ."

"*He* didn't buy, *I* did," said Benita.

"Really, now?" said G. Dudley Lester. ". . . With *his* traveler's checks? A very interesting arrangement you've got going there, my dear."

"We like it," said Benita.

"I should think you would," said G. Dudley, cheerfully. ". . . Well, enjoy your new acquisition. You can both take turns at the wheel, eh?"

Half an hour later, most of the paperwork was done. But there was still no specific time set when she could take delivery . . . perhaps sometime tomorrow?

Finally she emerged from the busy office, a folder of papers in hand.

The Plymouth, parked over there now, drew her like a hypnotist's thimble.

She started towards it.

Before she could get there, however, she felt Cyril's hand firmly on her arm, and he was steering her away from it.

". . . Stay away from the car!" he said. "Especially now. Keep walking and tell me what he said inside."

274

She repeated the conversation. "Sonofabitch has some mouth on him," she remarked.

Cyril nodded. "How'd you register the car?" he asked.

"In my name," she said. "Oh, and there's—"

"—very interesting, considering I put up the money," he said.

"Je-sus, honey," she said, "I'm sorry. I just thought—you didn't want anyone to know—"

"Bugger that," he said. "The car is half mine. Why did you leave my name off?"

"I'm *sorry,* Cyril," she said.

". . . I'm beginning to think I am, too!" he said.

"What the hell does that mean?" she asked.

He stared at her. "Hard to say," he said. ". . . Perhaps I'm not cut out for the role of the good samaritan . . . and you're not precisely Our Little Nell, eh?"

"I'll go back and have them rewrite the damn title!" she said, angrily, "—and all the other papers—you're welcome to come along and make sure I'm not out to screw you—"

"I'm sorry," he told her. "I'm a bit tense is all, the Rolls is due to be sold any moment now—"

"Oh sure," she said. "It's nice to know how your partner trusts you—"

"I *do* trust you!" he said.

But she'd already walked away.

Making his way back to the bleachers, he wondered . . . why had he attacked her? The girl hadn't really done anything so dreadful, she'd put down six thousand, he still had enough to buy the Rolls certainly, he'd find a way to repay Ben Emir—and if there was anything like the gold she'd promised in the wheels, it certainly was a good investment—

—And the important thing here was neither the 1933 Plymouth, or the Rolls—

It was G. Dudley Lester.

Who was so busy watching Benita Lorenzo and Cyril.

And perhaps so busy that he wasn't aware that Cyril was watching him, eh?

. . . This had been a very brisk day, the sales figures were even healthier than yesterday, the take was mounting like a helicopter, it was almost down to the wire, Old Ed planned to do a job on this Rolls that was coming up now, get a nice fat price, push her over the $30,000 reserve placed on the car by the owner, and then go home and spend the rest of the week whispering and drinking. His voice was raspy now, but by God, it had been worth it!

"Lot Ninety, ladies and gentlemen," he said, as the trim 1937 Rolls purred forward and stopped beneath the lights. The driver moved to open the doors so its lush interior would be seen by all. "Take off your hats, this one is a real piece of royalty. A 1937 five-passenger sports sedan, Phantom III, coachwork by Hooper, she's rare and gettin' rarer every hour, I don't have to tell you what good investments these beauties are . . . now, who's gonna give me fifteen to start her?"

He got the fifteen from a slender young man in a carefully studied expensive Western outfit, over on the left. His name was Lew Tolkin, he'd been born in Belmont, Massachusetts, thirty-seven years ago, the son of a surgeon who'd forgone medicine to become the designer and owner of a line of high-fashion menswear known as Corral, who'd dropped by the auction here today on his way over to do some selling at Nieman-Marcus, he fancied that Rolls because he had an idea that he could use it as the trademark of a new line he had on the drawing board, sportswear, sooner or later this Western fad would peak and Lew would be prepared, and besides, he'd always wanted a Rolls—

Seventeen, eighteen, nineteen, up climbed the price. "Do I hear twenty for this lovely piece?" asked Old Ed.

. . . He got his twenty from a pot-bellied Texan named Junior Brennan, in an Eddie Bauer goosedown vest, a Resistol stetson, and $750 boots, who was figuring that the Rolls would make a jazzy little present for his wife Dorene, back in Waco, what the hell, she'd been a good old girl this year, for their anniversary he might give it to her and she'd get a lot of attention when she took it to the supermarket . . .

Twenty-four now, twenty-five, twenty-six . . .

. . . The twenty-six came from Cyril Banks, who'd decided it was about time to make his move, he'd calculated his funds, he now had (minus that six thousand he'd just paid over to Benita) forty-four thousand in American dollars, more than enough to snare the Rolls handily for Ben Emir, certainly?

But now it was twenty-eight, twenty-nine. Thirty.

. . . No wonder Old Ed up there was beaming, his voice was failing but not the action, they'd gone to the reserve and now it was up, up and away—". . . Who'll say thirty-one?"

. . . Mr. Sami Kallil, far over to one side, in his cheap suit and his wash-and-wear shirt, his briefcase in his lap, said it. And when the price moved on past that figure, continued to bid. For Mr. Kallil had made up his mind, and anyone who'd ever done business with him knew that was that. Quiet little Mr. Kallil was going to get what he had come here for, so he rode upwards with the price, which wasn't rising quite so quickly now, was it? Thirty-two. Thirty-three. Thirty-four—

". . . Screw it," murmured Lew Tolkin. "This is no bargain basement they're running here. I can do better *leasing* one . . ."

Thirty-five.

". . . Shee-it," said Junior Brennan, disgustedly. ". . . Dorene can go on doing her shopping in the Caddy!"

Cyril raised it to thirty-six.

. . . Piss *off!* he thought. *Enough,* whoever you are!

Thirty-seven came back.

He waited a moment or so, to see what would happen elsewhere, but the Arena was silent. The crowd hushed in mass reverence, in the presence of a fat price.

Cyril tried thirty-eight.

Back it came, thirty-nine.

Buggered! he told himself. If this keeps up, where do I find the extra money? . . . that bastard G. Dudley wasn't about to allow him credit, that was certain.

. . . Ham was hovering over him now, waiting for his next move. "Squeeze it, chum!" he urged. "Don't let 'er get away!"

Cyril raised a finger.

. . . Into the Valley of Death rode the brave forty thousand dollars, he told himself.

"Over on my right!" announced Old Ed. "Forty-one!"

. . . Who was the bleeder responsible for this? Where was the Artful Dodger who was pushing him up? He looked, but couldn't see his opponent.

Raised his hand again. Forty-two, you bastard!

. . . Back came forty-three.

Hell—he was almost out of capital—

—and the ball was definitely in his court.

"Go, go *go!*" urged Ham, in an excess of joy.

Cyril gave it another try, to forty-four—

For Ben Emir's father, this was *it.*

. . . Silence.

Then Old Ed grinned. "Fortyfive, I've got fortyfive, now we're really going, folks, somebody knows what he's doin' here—"

Hands folded placidly in his lap, Mr. Sami Kallil twiddled his thumbs and awaited future developments.

From somewhere in the crowd, forty-six.

Ah. Mr. Kallil shrugged. Old Ed was staring in his direction. With a fine sense of the dramatic, Mr. Kallil waited. Why not? He had sufficient money to go much higher, and he would. Ever so casually, he raised his hand. Forty-seven.

. . . And now Old Ed was after Cyril Banks.

The only other bidder left, now quite definitely in over his head, but when one climbed a bleeding Mt. Everest, one didn't quit a few feet away from the summit, did one?

Desperately, Cyril raised his hand.

Forty-eight!

. . . back went the seesaw, now the tension was thick enough to cut with a knife.

". . . Whooeeh!" murmured Joyce, rocking back and forth beside G. Dudley. ". . . Isn't this really amazing?"

G. Dudley's eyes were on Cyril, up in the bleachers. ". . . I'm not sure yet," he said.

From the opposite side of the crowd came another brief signal from Mr. Kallil.

Forty-*nine!*

"I want fifty, fiftyfifty!" cried Old Ed, eying Cyril.

. . . who had reached a dizzy plateau, one where he was sans equipment, but where was the bloody summit?

He raised his hand.

"Fifty!" cried Old Ed. "Now I'm looking for fiftytwofiftytwo, twotwotwo—"

. . . enough, thought Mr. Kallil. I am tired of the game, we could go on like this all afternoon, it is time for the knife to the throat. He glanced up at Old Ed.

Then Mr. Kallil held up a hand with four fingers extended.

"Fifty *four!*" chortled Old Ed.

. . . You, chum, have had it, Cyril told himself. This isn't Mt. Everest, it's definitely the Valley of Death—

Old Ed was looking at him.

Sweet fuck all, there were other Rolls Royces about, weren't there? When he got back to London, he would pay Ben Emir back, yes, explain to him that this one had gone too high, that acting in his best interests he'd decided to pass—that he'd find him another Rolls, his father wouldn't be disappointed—by the time he got home he'd have his patter all rehearsed—

—or should he bid?

"At fifty-four thousand dollars, then," said Old Ed, with the reverence of a revival minister, ". . . *Sold.*"

With whoops of joy, Ham and Eggs ran to congratulate the winning bidder. Old Ed peered down at him. "Name sir?"

Kallil beamed. Mumbled it.

"A very shrewd buyer, sir," said Old Ed. "You certainly know quality when you see it."

Along with the rest of the crowd, Cyril watched as Kallil rose to go. Since mankind reveres a winner, even a short fattish balding one in a rumpled suit, he was accorded a brief spray of applause.

. . . Stubborn little wog! thought Cyril. I've seen your type all over, up from the souks and now you're out grabbing off the white man's treasures. Good thing he hadn't gone after him—the little bastard could have broken him—*and* Ben Emir.

One more try, though.

He caught up with Mr. Kallil as he made his way to the office.

"Excuse me, Mr. Correal—"

"Kallil," corrected the wog, still walking.

". . . Bloody good show back there, with that Rolls," said Cyril.

"Thank you," said Mr. Kallil, never faltering.

"I'm in the trade you see, Mr. Kallil," said Cyril. "Should you ever decide to trade her in for something . . . a bit more expensive, as befits a man of your style, I might be able to find you a buyer for that car . . ."

"No thank you," said Mr. Kallil. "Please do not bother me further."

He hurried on towards the office.

". . . Don't count on that, chum," murmured Cyril.

He followed along. Stood standing outside the office doorway, to peer in at Mr. Kallil being congratulated and fawned over by the office staff, G. Dudley doing the honors, personally seating him in a chair, offering him a drink—

Benita found him there. "Did you get it?" she asked.

He shook his head.

"What *happened?*"

He nudged her over to see Mr. Kallil, inside the office, as he opened his briefcase and pulled out a wad of traveler's checks, preparing to sign with a cheap ball-point all those thousands of dollars he'd amassed in what, the rug trade? or speculating in banana futures?

"He happened," he told her.

". . . Look at all that money," she murmured, impressed.

G. Dudley looked up, saw them, then came to the office door. "She was a bit too rich for your wallet, eh?" he remarked. "Ah well, Cyril, that's always been your problem, hasn't it—champagne taste—on a beer budget."

"Bugger off," said Cyril.

"The feeling is mutual," said G. Dudley, and closed the office door.

". . . Well, cheer up," said Benita, as they walked towards that entrance, past the Plymouth. "You own fifty percent of *that*."

". . . Ah yes," he said. "Our own little 1933 Plymouth Eldorado . . . hopefully."

"It's there," she said. "It's got to be there!"

"I admire your enthusiasm," he said. ". . . But we're not King and Queen Midas yet . . . are we?"

 **8:02 A.M.**

She couldn't sleep any longer.

. . . Not that Benita had slept much.

Dinner last night hadn't been pleasant, neither of them had spoken much, after the last two days they were both still nervous, he obviously let-down by losing the Rolls to that fat man, when they'd returned here to the motel he hadn't even seemed very interested in whether or not she would bunk in here with him. She'd felt sorry for him, but she didn't let on, joined him in the bed while he lay there watching some mindless TV sitcom. Their love-making was brief; he'd finally rolled over, taken her almost savagely, impersonally, it was as if she were merely some available body. When it was ended, neither of them had enjoyed it.

. . . He'd pulled up the covers, muttered something about picking up their Plymouth tomorrow, and gone instantly to sleep.

No sleep for her.

Spinning wheels turned endlessly through her wide-awake mind, all night long, wheels without tires that gleamed and spun, always just out of touch, dangling tantalizing, mocking her.

Now there was daylight seeping through the venetian blinds.

Leaving him snoring away, she got out of the bed.

Went to the bathroom, came out dressed, running a comb

281

through her hair. Tried to repair her face. Picked up her purse, and the folder with all the documents they'd given her at the Arena office yesterday.

She took a piece of kleenex and scribbled on it . . . *back soon.*

She wasn't going to wait any longer. Let him stay here and sleep—she'd go over to the Arena and somehow she'd collect the car, bring it to some garage—

—with gold bringing prices that rose every day, she had to know. *Now.*

. . . Quietly, she let herself out of his room.

Over at the Arena, the party was definitely over. Workmen were removing the gaudy decorations, others were packing away folding seats, taking down the lights and sound equipment.

Rows of cars stood quietly in the gloom, a few unsold, sequestered to one side, near the office, but the majority beneath the SOLD banner.

Benita came up to the drowsy security guard at the rear door, waved her buyer's identification at him, and went inside.

He waved back.

She went down the aisle, eying the cars until she came to the Plymouth.

Opened the front door.

Became aware of another security guard who'd strolled over.

"It's mine," she said, and waved the documents.

He blinked, then nodded. Satisfied, he moved on.

. . . Always act like you own the place, and they believed you.

Act like it—hell, she *did* own it!

Inside the car everything was immaculate . . . but—

There was no key in the ignition.

Damn! She hadn't figured on this.

. . . But of course, they'd keep them all stored safely in the office, wouldn't they?

Now what?

The lone woman in the office was busy working over a table full of papers, adding up figures on a small computer, sipping coffee

282

from a container, obviously annoyed at having to be in here so early.

How to get the key out of her?

Improvise, Benita.

"Excuse me," she said. "I have a problem here. The, ah, serial number on this title here doesn't seem to match up with the ah . . . official number—the one that usually on the car key, right?"

Confused, the lady blinked.

". . . Which car?" she asked, finally.

Benita patiently explained about the 1933 Plymouth. Produced all the papers, the ones with the name on them, *Benita Lorenzo, Owner.* The woman surveyed them. ". . . You've got all the keys here, haven't you?" asked Benita.

Yes, she had them, but they were all on that rack over there, taged and filed, she wasn't authorized to pass any of them out—

Improvising away, Benita continued. She needed to place an insurance binder on the car, the agent she'd called had spotted the error in the numbers, she'd merely need to borrow the key for a while, to go over and check the body number on the frame, a nuisance, a technicality, but that's how it was these days, wasn't it? She smiled her most winning smile. ". . . Help a girl out, would you?"

The woman sighed. Moved over to the wall where all the keys hung on rows of hooks. ". . . Hell, we never have these problems at regular auctions," she complained. "You said a 1933 Plymouth?"

Keys in hand, exultant at her own cunning, Benita came out of the office.

Quietly made her way back to the Plymouth.

Now, to get it out of here.

Inside the car, on the front seat, the door closed softly, she turned on the ignition.

Nothing.

Why not?

. . . Of course not, dummy! These old cars all had their starters on the floor!

She found the pedal, stepped on it.

The engine caught, churned into life.

The shift was on the floor, over here was the clutch—she'd never driven one like this, had she? She'd have to continue improvising, mustn't go forward, she'd hit another car . . . where was reverse?

She found it.

. . . Backed very slowly out into the broad aisle behind her.

Braked, turned the wheel, and steering with great care, she headed down the aisle to that wide open doorway where there was still that one security guard she had to get past, and then she was safely out—

Drove on out, into the sunlight, past him.

Waving briefly with one hand as she steered out.

The guard rose from his campchair, blinked at the unexpected sight of the demure little black sedan driving past, headed for the street, away from the Arena, the girl at the wheel—what the hell?

Ah, sure, it had to be an owner, someone who hadn't sold his car yesterday and was going home with it . . .

He waved back, dropped into his chair, picked up the morning paper and went back to studying the baseball scores.

Where to now, Benita?

She had no street map, she didn't know Tulsa, did she—this was a section of town with broad boulevards flanked by factories and nondescript vacant lots and a lot of traffic, she had to find herself a garage, somewhere to get this car hoisted up so that someone could pull off the tires—

She paused at a stop light.

On the sidewalk were a couple of local citizens. One of them whistled. "A real beauty!" he said, an acned youth in dungarees. His sidekick, an older man, moved over to survey the car.

"Listen, where's the nearest service station where I can check my tires?" she asked.

"Two blocks down, two blocks over, Tony's Gulf," he said,

shaking his head. ". . . Say, you know, I had one of these myself once?"

"I'm sure you did, thanks," she said, and kept on going.

Keeping an eye out for the signs.

. . . Finally, down the next block, she saw the one she wanted. Made towards it.

Her engine coughed once, twice, then stopped.

Dead.

Je-sus!

. . . Behind her, the sound of brakes screeching as the car stopped, then an angry voice bawling at her to watch what the hell she was doing—

Horns behind it beeped and blared.

Stopped here in the midst of traffic, she tried to get the car started again, but it wouldn't.

From the curb she heard a voice yell, "Get a horse!"

Then another face peered in the window, an unshaven thin man who eyed her. "What's wrong, lady?"

"What's wrong is that I bought a clunker!" she told him.

". . . Well, this is what happens when you buy 'em used," he grinned, relishing his own wit. "Lemme take a look under your hood . . ."

She watched while he unlatched the hood, raised it to peer at one side of the engine. Cocked his ear after he'd instructed her to try the starter again. "Sounds okay," he said, fiddling with something. Then he looked up. "Say, did you check to see if there was gas when you left home?"

Gas?

Of course she hadn't checked that!

He replaced the hood. "Looks stone dry to me." he said, sagely.

. . . For what she'd paid for this heap, they might have at least put in five gallons!

She smiled her sweetest. ". . . Could you give me a push down to that garage?" she inquired. "I'd be so grateful."

". . . How grateful?" he asked, leering.

285

. . . Here on this street, in the middle of morning traffic, and he was horny?

". . . I'm meeting my husband," she lied.

"Shoot," he said. "Oh, what the hell, I'm a sport—I'll get you down there. Just hope I don't end up with a hernia . . ."

"You're a prince," she lied.

Slowly, the car rolled towards the sign which read Tony's Gulf.

 10:46 A.M.

Cyril was awakened by the sound of urgent rapping.

. . . It seemed to come from his motel-room door.

"Get that, would you?" he murmured.

The rapping continued.

He blinked his eyes open.

. . . No Benita?

Ah. She'd probably gone out and forgotten the room key . . .

He got up and opened the door.

It was not Benita, it was G. Dudley Lester who strode inside the room. Immacculately dressed, fragrant with cologne, attaché case in hand.

Cyril blinked. ". . . To what do I owe the pleasure?"

"It's no pleasure, believe me," said G. Dudley, advancing on him.

"What's up?" asked Cyril.

"I could ask you the same question," said G. Dudley. "Your little ah . . . lady friend seems to have taken off with one 1933 Plymouth whose title has not yet been cleared—and the money is in escrow, ergo she has illegally helped herself to someone else's property—where'd she take it?"

". . . Gone?" asked Cyril, confused. ". . . Why, I haven't a clue—"

. . . What in hell was all this about?

286

"No games, laddie," said G. Dudley. "You two have been up to something—I saw you buy that car yesterday—"

"She bought it!" protested Cyril.

"—*You* paid for it," said G. Dudley. "Not out of love, I'm sure. What's the little ploy?"

. . . Perhaps she was gone, who could tell? but he'd be damned if G. Dudley would find out any more than that.

"Mind if I dress?" he asked.

And proceeded to assemble his clothing.

. . . On the dresser was a piece of Kleenex with *back soon* scrawled on it, printed in lipstick. Quickly he crumpled it up and tossed it away, then proceeded to climb into his trousers.

. . . Well, if she were up to something, at least she'd let him know about it . . . whatever it was—

"I'll wait," said G. Dudley, evenly.

He sat down.

The room door was pushed open, and the ruddy face of a uniformed security guard, a holster heavy on his large hip, stared in, eyes masked in aviators' glasses. "No sign of any damn Plymouth down there, sir," he reported.

"All right," said G. Dudley. "They obviously haven't brought it here."

"Want me to work this one over?" asked the guard, hopefully.

"Thanks, no," said G. Dudley. "I'll handle it from here."

"You sure you can handle him?" asked the guard.

"I can handle him," assured G. Dudley.

The guard nodded. "You want me to go with you to the bank?"

"I can handle that too," said G. Dudley. "See you back at the Arena."

Obviously miffed, the guard left, closing the door.

"Now, I might see my way clear to avoid pressing charges," said G. Dudley, "provided you let me in on your little fiddle. Why'd you want that car in the first place?"

Cyril buttoned his shirt. "Cue me in on *your* little fiddle first," he said.

"I beg your pardon?" said G. Dudley, and lit a cigarette.

"Oh, knock it off," said Cyril. "This is *me*, George. I learned at the foot of the master, didn't I?"

"Learned what?" asked G. Dudley.

"A short course in you," said Cyril. "You're the sort who spends his time building up some marvelous big smashing legitimate deal—like IOI—or this fat-cat auction here—"

"That's me," said G. Dudley, agreeably.

"—and when it's done, and all running smoothly, you can't stand all that perfection, so you simply have to wreck the whole show, don't you?" said Cyril. "You stick your hand in the cash drawer, empty it out, and let the whole thing go to pieces while you run . . ."

He went into the bathroom, relieved himself, and then began to shave. He needed time—whatever Benita was up to, he'd cover for her—

"Quite the parlor psychiatrist, aren't you?" commented G. Dudley. "Since you're so damned clever, why don't you tell me what I'm supposed to be up to?"

". . . Something to do with that escrow account," said Cyril. "In the Banco de San Rafael. Where all that money is supposed to go, eh?"

He peered into the mirror, where he could watch G. Dudley's reaction, but his old mentor merely shrugged.

"Why shouldn't it?" asked G. Dudley. "At a very decent twenty-two percent interest, it should help us counter inflationary pressures, eh? And while all the titles clear, there's no law says we can't pick up a nice piece of extra change, is there? That's merely shrewd planning, my boy."

Cyril washed his face free of soap. Dried himself, combed his hair.

Then he came back into the room.

". . . Now," said G. Dudley. "My half of the truth game is over. Let's hear yours."

Cyril shook his head. "Everybody here may believe you, but I don't. I know you too damned well, my boy."

"You really ought not say such things around here," said

288

G. Dudley. "There are laws against slander, you know." His smile was gone now. "You're frustrated because you lost that Rolls to that fat little Iranian . . . and because your little pussycat's run out on you, but in Tulsa, Oklahoma, folks do not take kindly to being called crooks, especially by cheap barrow-boys from the East End. You know, a restaurant is just about right for you, Cyril, you never were cut out to play in the big leagues."

He snuffed out his cigarette and flicked the butt carelessly across the room. It landed on Cyril's jacket, which was on the bed. "Oh, I am sorry," he said, casually.

Arrogant bastard.

He stood up. "We'll be watching for that tart of yours," he promised. "And the car she pinched—if, in fact, she pinched it from you . . . which would only go to show how careless you are about whom you screw, eh?"

He picked up his attaché case, and started for the door.

"Watch away, fiddler," said Cyril, removing the cigarette butt.

G. Dudley went out.

. . . And I'll be watching too, Cyril told himself. Grabbed up his coat, brushed off the dead cigarette butt (bastard!) grabbed the crumpled kleenex, spread it out so that *back soon* was visible again, tossed it on the bureau—

Went out the door.

Down below, in the parking lot, he could see G. Dudley, attaché case in hand, striding over to his car. Not a care in the world, the very model of an affluent sober businessman. King of the hill.

. . . Off to the bank, was he?

Why? The money from the auction was already in the escrow account, it had to be, nobody left that much cash lying around—

—so his next move would be to transfer it to the Banco de San Rafael.

Or was it?

(Watch closely, my friends, I have nothing up my sleeves, now I have here three shells, and this tiny red ball, one two three, under which one of these shells is the ball? Here? Here? Ah sir, you think it's this one? Would you care to make a small wager?)

Right then, my fine East End barrow-boy. If you're ever going to nail that arrogant bastard, run the old fox to the ground . . . *get cracking*.

Cyril went down the steps.
To follow the fox.

 **11:17 A.M.**

Louise came out of the bathroom, her face made up, and began to pack her second bag with her toilet articles.

Dusty was still on the phone with Lew Davis, in Liverpool, one of those endless involved conversations he enjoyed, checking out each and every detail. She couldn't really fault him for that; he'd stayed away from business all day yesterday, hadn't he? Of course they'd gone back to watch the second session of the auction at the Arena, but it had been pleasant enough.

. . . If you enjoyed watching a crowd of people bid up old cars.
And he'd restrained himself. He hadn't bought anything.
He hung up the phone.

". . . Hey, you sure did make us a problem selling me that T-Bird," he said.

"Didn't I though?" she replied.

". . . I don't mean it that way," he said, and grinned. "I'm talking tax-wise now."

"Must we?" she murmured.

"Listen," he told her, consulting figures on his small memo pad. "You owned her at a cost of nine thou, that's the value of her according to my gift. Now I come down here and I go a little crazy, and I buy her back, for nineteen thousand two fifty, right?"

". . . Because you wanted to," she said.

"Oh, no argument," said Dusty. "I didn't want to lose her to some stranger, did I? So what happens now is—give or take a few hundred, for expenses, and cost of sale, etcetera, you end up with a clear profit of about nine thousand five. Which is ordinary income, *not* capital gain, because you haven't owned it long enough, see?''

"Too bad," she said, zipping up her bag. "But as you always say, that's the cost of doing business, isn't it?"

"Agreed," said Dusty. "But don't you worry about it, because it goes into our joint return—so it'll come to a lot less tax for Uncle than if you were filing single, see, and—oh, wait a minute—"

She was packing the other bag now, as he scribbled more figures. "I got it!" he said. "What we do is, we give the car to the foundation, and then we take a deduction for it as a gift, and maybe knock off the whole nineteen—oh wow! It looks like you did us a real favor, honey!"

"Congratulate me," she said. But he was already on the phone, placing a call to Lew Davis.

By the time it came through, she'd finished the other bag and had them both by the door. "Hey, Lew," he was saying, "I've got a little gimmick here we ought to check out—I'm amazed you didn't think about it, boy—"

He looked up, as she picked up her coat.

". . . Where you going?" he asked.

". . . down to the Arena," she said.

"Wait a minute, now," he said. "What for?"

". . . To collect the money you paid in that they owe me for the T-Bird," she said.

"Well, hold on, honey, I've got to go pick up my car, don't I? Just a second, Lew," he said, into the phone.

"I'll be down there," she said. "You finish up here."

"Okay, sure," he said. "Then we can leave together, fine—"

He returned to Lew.

She placed her two bags outside the door, then closed it. From the outside.

She wasn't waiting for him.

Not any longer.

*　　*　　*

 **11:31 A.M.**

". . . I told you it would take time," said Tony, a middle-aged garageman with a belly that reflected years of high-caloric fast foods washed down with beer. ". . . damn Mex kid never showed up, I'm short-handed here today . . ."

Forty minutes now she'd been waiting—

—While he filled her car's tank, then moved it into the garage bay—

Kept on running out to service gas customers, then returning to her car, to check and see if he had the proper-sized tires for her, then to find a jack, to raise the Plymouth's front end—

Finally to pull off one wheel. Bring it over to this machine here, one of those large devices which removed the tire. Where it still sat while he went out to fill some idiot's tank!

Now he was back again.

"Okay," he said. "Off she goes."

He pressed a button. The large knifelike arm that he'd inserted beneath the tire's edge spun around, flipping off the limp tire, leaving it lying there like some bloated dead serpent.

Beneath it peeped a faded red rubber casing.

". . . Tube," he said. "Don't see many of those. . ."

He released the clamp, pulled off the tire, then the tube—tossed them onto the floor—

dingdingding Another car outside.

". . . Be back," he told her.

The wheel sat on the machine, its black paint gleaming.

. . . she couldn't wait any longer.

Beneath the paint?

She grabbed a screwdriver from his toolbox nearby, bent down and scraped the black paint.

Which flaked away.

. . . Beneath it was bright metal.

Grey.

Gold is not grey.

. . . This had to be steel.

Wheels were made of steel.

Any idiot knew that. Even these wheels.

Despite the babblings of old Gus Konecki, who'd promised her that he'd personally cast old Mrs. Fox's gold hoard into these—

—furiously, she scratched at another section of paint.

To find more greyish metal beneath.

. . . Shit! Ridiculous old fool, with his wild fantasies, who'd lured her all the way down the yellow brick road to Tulsa—

"Hey, lady?" asked Tony, returning. "What're you scratching the paint for?"

"What do you care?" she snapped. "It's a hobby!"

. . . She'd been had.

He'd merely been playing games with her, leading her on.

She'd bought herself absolutely nothing here except one well-kept 1933 Plymouth which she needed like an extra arm—

. . . Wait a minute.

What had Gus said . . .

. . . all those months ago?

Something about a bagel.

. . . *Big round bagel, hollowed out*

Sure, that's what he'd told her, and she'd forgotten—all that technical stuff about gold being too malleable, that he'd had to make the wheels over, cast them like a hollowed out bagel *with the gold inside*

"Okay, gonna mount this tire here," said Tony. He hefted the new radial, raised it, carried it over to slide it over the steel wheel—

"Hold it!" said Benita.

He stopped to stare at her.

"Lady, what do you want from me—I'm busy—you want this tire or not?"

"I want to look at that wheel first," she told him. Before he could protest, there was another blessed *dingdingding* from outside, at the pumps. Tony muttered a curse. Dropped the tire, went out to see his customer. She knelt down, peered at the inside of the rim.

. . . Covered with a thin film of grime and dust.

How to open it?

What did you do *here*, Gus?

She turned it slowly, searching for some sign.

The light here was rotten and she couldn't see anything, no visible evidence of his work that would reveal—

. . . Wait a minute!

Beneath the grime. *Yes!* Here . . . a tiny screw-head, fitted snugly into its beveled hole, flush with the surface.

With hands that shook, she seized the screwdriver, tried to fit it into the head of the screw.

Too big!

. . . She went searching for a smaller screwdriver.

Dredged one out of Tony's toolbox.

This one fit. The screw began to turn.

"Hey lady," said Tony, who'd returned. "Mind telling me what the hell you're doing there?"

". . . I was . . . checking the wheel," she told him.

"Am I doing this or are you?" he complained. "Lemme get there, will you?"

"No!" she said.

"Whatcha mean, no?" he asked, perplexed.

"I mean—not yet!" she said.

He stared at her. "Hey, you're some kind of a fruitcake," he sighed. "I've got a lot to *do* around here—"

dingdingding! Another reprieve from out front.

He shambled out again.

. . . She bent down over the wheel again, worked at the screw. It came away from its snug hiding place. She tugged at the top of the rim.

Nothing moved.

Of course not, dummy. A good tool-and-die maker would secure such a mold with *two* screws.

Where was the second one?

She spun the wheel around, searching—

—until she finally found another one, buried beneath the coating of grime.

Unscrewed it. Now . . .

She tugged at the top of the rim again.

It moved. Lifted. Came off.

To reveal, beneath, a second round inner wheel—

And this one wasn't grey, it was yellow, not burnished or gleaming brightly, it had been inside the casing stored away hadn't seen the light of day since 1934? covered with a dull patina

But definitely yellow.

She stared at it. Sudden perspiration on her forehead.

Forgive me, Gus, she thought, I apologize for everything I thought about you, for doubting you, God bless you, stingy Mrs. Fox, wherever you both are, I love you, I'm rich, if this is one, then there are three more, four wheels full, I own four—

No, *two*—Cyril Banks gets *two*—

Okay, two—I'll settle for *two,* I'm not greedy, two's plenty!

She put the wheel back together.

Close up the vault. She replaced the first screw.

She'd gotten to the second one and was turning it back in when Tony returned.

She stood up.

When she spoke, finding her voice, it was hoarse. "I've changed my mind," she said. "Would you put back the old tire and tube, please?"

He gaped at her. ". . . You don't want the tire?"

"No, thank you," she said.

". . . None of them?" he asked.

"None of them," she said.

"Lady!" he said, and he was obviously pissed off, and who could blame the poor bastard? Would he believe that she'd opened up a mobile Fort Knox here?

". . . I'll pay you for your time," she said.

"Swell," he said, disgusted.

Reluctantly bent down to replace the tube and the tire onto the precious wheel.

"Gas, and labor, two hours easy," he muttered. "Forty bucks—plus the cost of a new valve."

"Fair enough," she told him.

She reached into her purse.

Then she remembered.

Rich as she'd become—

—after paying for the cab that had brought her here, she had four lone dollar bills tucked in her purse.

Crazy!

She snickered.

". . . What's funny?" he asked.

"I've only got four bucks," she told him. "No credit cards . . . so I guess you're going to have to trust me."

He shook his head.

"All right," she said. "I'll call my friend to come down here with some cash. He's got plenty."

He pointed to the pay phone on the wall.

. . . There was no answer in Mr. Banks' room. No, they didn't know where he was, he was out, would she like to leave a message?

Damn!

She hung up. Tony had finished replacing the tire.

"Listen, I'll drive back to my motel and get you the money—" she said.

He shook his head.

How ridiculous could it get? "Don't you trust me?"

Now he nodded. "The car stays right here till you come back with the forty."

"You expect me to leave my *car?*" she protested.

". . . I'll admit it ain't much," he said, eying the Plymouth, "but it'll have to do for security."

Oh will it ever! she thought.

*　　*　　*

 12:40 P.M.

Cyril opened the motel room door.

The bed still unmade. No sign of Benita Lorenzo.

. . . Which left him doubly frustrated.

Downtown, outside the Oilmens National, he'd sat in the taxi, watching and waiting, while G. Dudley had gone inside.

He hadn't been able to see exactly what had happened in the

bank, it wasn't business that took place out front by one of the tellers' windows, but when G. Dudley finally reappeared, he was escorted to the door by some type who was obviously In Authority, who shook hands with G. Dudley at the doorway.

. . . What did that signify, beyond the fact that G. Dudley was an A customer?

Alone on the street, he'd seen the fox reach into his inside pocket, pull out a long envelope, pat it briefly, then tuck it back into his pocket.

What was in that envelope? A deposit slip?

. . . A withdrawal. A check?

Spending money for the next few days?

(Not likely, that he could get at the office, out of Petty Cash.)

Or was it the proceeds of the escrow account.

Off to Mexico?

Why not, that's where G. Dudley had freely admitted it was going, hadn't he?

Watch closely, my friends, nothing up my sleeve.

To the Banco de San Rafael, to earn a hefty twenty-two percent interest.

. . . But if you wanted to send money to an account in Mexico, certainly this bank in Tulsa could wire the funds down there for you, would it not?

(From somewhere, Cyril remembered a story one of his aged uncles was fond of telling, of the two Jews who met on a train in Poland. Where are you going? asked the first. To Cracow, said the second. Now hold on, what a liar you are! said the first. When you tell me you're going to Cracow, you really want me to believe that you're traveling to Lemburg. But I'm sure you're really traveling to Cracow—so why *lie* about it?)

So where the devil was the fox off to now—with a check (if it was a check) in his inside pocket?

. . . In his cab he'd followed G. Dudley—

To the Arena.

. . . Where he'd gone inside.

Now what?

. . . *Here's the little red ball, friends, here are the three shells.*

You're back to Square One, Cyril, he told himself.

The cab had brought him back (a lot of cash spent on this little jaunt). He had one possible ploy. He could make a long-distance call to Mexico to that Banco, and find out whether or not they'd received a deposit, it was a long shot, but worth trying, while waiting for Miss Benita Lorenzo to return—

If she returned.

He finished placing the call to Mexico, was told it would take time, they'd call back, when there was an urgent knocking on the door.

He opened it.

Benita.

A wide triumphant smile on her face, she threw her arms around him, hugged him exultantly and yelled "I need forty dollars, partner, congratulations—"

"Where in hell have you been?" he asked, "And *where* is our Plymouth?"

"I know where it is, and we're rich!" she cried, and kissed him. "Forty bucks—a down payment on your fortune—congratulations!" She slammed the motel room door shut and danced him around what space there was. "We made it! It's *there!*" They stumbled against the bed, he tripped and fell backwards, with her on top of him. The girl was demented with joy. "It's *all there!*" she said. "We pulled off one wheel, I got it open, if there's one wheel full, so are the others, right? A mother lode—I didn't weigh it yet, but it's got to be *pounds* of it—how do you figure it out by ounces, call somebody, find out what gold is worth today?" She kissed him again, fiercely. ". . . How's that for a good day's work, Mr. Banks?" she chortled. And covered his mouth with hers.

While her tongue sought his.

. . . Hard to believe, eh, Mr. Banks?

Once, when he was still a kid, he'd heard some old relative saying that in America the streets were paved with gold. But no one had ever said anything about four golden wheels which ran *on* those streets!

". . . Bloody marvelous, love," he told her, when she finally let him up for air.

"Worth waiting for?" she said, her eyes glittering with pleasure. She got up. "Come on, let's go ransom the car—I didn't have forty to pay him, would you believe, I had to come back here—me, I'm filthy rich—and I'm flat-assed broke!" She rearranged her clothing. "Come *on*—this'll be the best forty bucks you ever spent, friend—"

". . . Certainly is," he told her, and asked, involuntarily, "Tell me, would you have come back here if you'd had the forty?"

She stared at him.

". . . What the hell kind of a question is that?" she asked.

"A fair one," he smiled. "*I* might not."

"You really are a prick, aren't you?" she said, finally.

Poor idealistic creature. How could he explain to her that in the world he'd grown up in, dogeatdog, deviltakethehindmost, upyoursmate, *I've got mine,* that it had been almost a reflex for him to suspect that even Benita Lorenzo could fiddle him.

. . . And now he felt bloody ridiculous for having thought so.

"Damn you!" she said, furious. "How could you think—"

"Shhh!" he told her. "I *didn't* think. Forgive me, *please*—I'm a bastard, but you're a smashing character, Florence Nightingale to the end, and it's a positive pleasure to be your partner."

He seized her unwilling body, pulled her close.

Caressed her until finally he felt her respond, her tenseness subsiding. ". . . You're still a prick," she warned him, but now her hands were beginning to explore him, ". . . but I'm stuck with you."

He stopped her then. "No, no," he said. "First the forty dollars for the car, remember?"

". . . Ah, let it wait," she said. "It's been there since 1934, another hour won't matter. Afterwards we'll drive it out of here, get out of this town—"

"The hell we will," he said. "We don't have a clear title to that Plymouth, we couldn't get a mile down the road before we could be stopped, and the way it looks, we may not get a clear title, ever—"

"What does that mean?" she asked.

The phone rang.

It was the long-distance operator, reporting that all the lines were tied up, she hadn't yet been able to get through to the Banco de San Rafael, did he wish her to keep trying?

No. Under this new set of circumstances, he did not. He'd place the call later. He had other business to settle, didn't he?

". . . Let's go collect our wheels," he said. Took her by the arm and left the room.

". . . What did you mean with that stuff about titles?" she asked, in the taxi. ". . . And what were you calling Mexico about?"

"Friend G. D. Lester," he said.

"Him," she said. "What *is* it with you and him?"

"It's a long and nasty story," he said.

"Tell me!" she insisted.

"He screwed me once in London," he said, "and now I suspect he's about to repeat the same procedure."

"Explain that," she said. "Now."

". . . It's a bit complicated," he said. "From what I can gather, friend Lester has drawn all the proceeds of the auction out of the escrow account, a very substantial sum, to switch it to a Mexican account where he and Mrs. Donaldson will collect twenty-two percent interest on it while the various titles clear."

"I'm a simple girl, I don't get it," she said.

". . . the question before the house is—will G. Dudley actually switch that money to Mexico, *or,* will he stick it in his pocket and disappear with it. All of it. And leave everyone holding the bag."

"Jee-sus," she said ". . . a *swindle!"*

"Indeed," he said. "Of us all."

"He could do that?"

"He could," he told her. "I know his habits. Which is why it behooves us to dump that little Plymouth, pick up those four wheels, and get them somewhere out of Tulsa, on the double."

". . . And what happens to everyone else?" asked Benita.

Cyril shrugged. "If he behaves as I expect him to, they're fiddled."

". . . But, don't you want to *stop* him?" she asked.

"I did," he said. "But that was before you made us rich. Now it's strictly *sauve qui peut."*

"What does that mean?"

"It means," he said, "We're home and dry with the wheels, and let the rest of them sue."

"That's rotten!" she said.

"Happens all the time, it's a cruel world," he said.

". . . *No,*" she said. "You can't let him get away with this." She shook her head firmly. "Show him up. Call the police—*do* something!"

"I have no evidence," he said.

"You can't just walk away!" she insisted.

"Ah, listen to me, love," he said. "There's no way to change the world. People get fiddled by people like G. Dudley every day in the week."

She sat silently beside him as they drove towards Tony's Gulf.

". . . You learn to live with it," he said. ". . . As the old maid said to the burglar."

Their cab pulled up outside Tony's Gulf. The Plymouth was still inside, behind the garage door.

Cyril got out. "Wait here," he told the driver.

". . . Why should he wait?" she asked.

"So he can take us and the four wheels back to the motel," he said.

Benita shook her head. "Go pay the forty bucks, *I'll* drive the Plymouth back to the arena."

"What the hell for?" he demanded.

"Somebody's got to blow the whistle on your friend, don't they?" she told him.

"Let it be somebody else!" he said, angrily.

She held out her hand. "Advance me the money for the bill," she said, "That's all I want. I can handle it alone."

"No you cannot!" he said. "Neither can I. Let it *be!*"

". . . I'll figure out something," she said, her hand still outstretched.

"Crikey!" he exploded. "Ninety million American women and I have to get mixed up with a bloody idealist! *Why are you doing this?*"

"Because *you're not going to!*" she cried.

301

"I don't need your damned psychology, nurse!" he told her.

. . . But she was right, wasn't she? He'd come all this way, he had all the chips suddenly piled in front of him now—why should he let that bastard G. Dudley off the hook—

(If, in fact, he was on one.)

. . . When it would only cost forty dollars cash to find out? A fair bet.

All right, Cyril. Once more into the breach.

(Or close the wall up with our English dead.)

He paid the cab driver.

Dismissed him. Then turned back to her.

"I'll go with you," he said.

". . . Conscience bothering you?" she asked.

"No indeed," he said. "Half that Plymouth is mine. I'm merely protecting my investment."

"I don't care what your reason is," she said. "We're going to show up that bastard."

". . . God only knows how," he said, moodily. "Nor how we're going to get that car to the Arena without being picked up by the police."

"We'll drive very carefully," she said, cheerfully.

*   *   *

Side by side in the front of the Plymouth, with Benita at the wheel, they drove through the streets, Cyril giving her directions from the street map Tony had provided (none too cheerfully) of downtown Tulsa.

He kept her off the main boulevards, to avoid any possible detection.

". . . I'm not even certain the bastard'll still be there," he grumbled.

"Why would he leave?" she asked. "Wouldn't it look better if he stayed around there—and didn't make a break for it until nobody was looking?"

". . . You're beginning to think like a real swindler," he said.

"Thank you," she said.

302

". . . Chances are, with all that loot in his pocket, he'll take off. Anybody would," he said.

". . . *I* didn't," she said.

"Touché, madame," he said.

". . . Besides, you said you weren't sure he had it on him . . ." she commented.

"Right now, I'm not sure of anything," said Cyril. "Expecting that I do not believe G. Dudley Lester is a leopard who can change his spots, nor will he—"

Behind them came the raucous sound of *tahootahootahoo-tahoo—*

—Which had to be that police car with its lights flashing as it raced down the block and whipped past them, and then screeched to a stop, blocking their path.

Benita braked, and the Plymouth rolled slowly to a demure stop.

As the Tulsa policemen, in helmet and goggles, their hands at the ready above their revolvers, were peering into the car. ". . . Okay, lady," said the one on Benita's side. " '33 Plymouth?"

"Yes, officer," she said. "Something I can do for you?"

". . . Ma'am, this particular vehicle is being looked for all over town," he said, evenly.

"Don't I know that?" Benita replied. "That's why we're taking it back to the Arena, where it belongs."

"Yeah," said the cop. "Why don't we just make sure of that? I'll follow you, and don't try gettin' away from us, my partner here's got a very nervous finger."

"We certainly appreciate your thoughtfulness," said Benita. "Considering that the car belongs to us."

"Yes indeed," added Cyril. "We shall recommend you to all our friends."

Under escort, they continued on to their meeting? confrontation? Summit conference? or whatever.

*   *   *

 **1:10 P.M.**

Old Ed was home, resting his vocal chords. He'd earned the day off.

As the girls in the office coped with the paperwork, quite a few cars had been removed from the Arena now, leaving gaps in the rows. The prizes, the jewelry, the big-ticket items were leaving, carried off by their new owners.

Down at the end, a small collection of losers huddled together beneath the UNSOLD sign. Tail-enders who hadn't found someone new to love them, at any price. Waiting, forlorn, to be retrieved by their masters. (What the hell, they's another sale next month over to Missouri, Joplin, I'll drive 'er up, stick 'er in, somebody'll want this '52 DeSoto, I'm tellin' you, she's a sleeper!)

G. Dudley sat at his desk in the inner office, a calculator at hand, checking figures from a tally-sheet, sipping coffee, and occasionally scribbling his initials on various documents.

Giving a remarkable performance. One that would certainly have won him, at the least, an Academy Award nomination. (. . . In the role of successful, sober and resourceful promoter, the shrewd businessman who was lately pulled off one of the most remarkable two-day sles ever held in this area, Mr. Lester exuded quiet power, a sense of inner strength.)

. . . He would not have to play the part much longer.

By five o'clock, the office would be closed. After which, G. Dudley would end his run here in Tulsa.

He would return to his little hideaway apartment, pick up his bags and his passport, take a taxi to the airport, and board the international flight on which a seat was booked.

Destination, Mexico City. And after that, there was another ticket booked, with another destination, thousands of miles away from Tulsa. Away from all these assorted clowns he'd had to deal with, these tiresome backslappers and noisy high-rollers, the shit-kickers . . . sufficient miles from Tulsa to guarantee that he would never again have to hear the sound of Mrs. Joyce Donaldson Wade's strident voice—which was audible outside the door, she was calling his name.

She pushed open the office door, came in and closed it behind her. Today she was wearing a vivid lavender pants suit topped off with a kelly green scarf that was flecked with gold appliqué. ". . . now listen *here*, G. Dudley," she said, "I got to tell you, me and the girls've been doin' an awful lot of fast talkin' out there, but they're buyin' it!" She winked.

". . . Of course, they are," he said. "Because you are very good at it, aren't you?"

". . . Shoot, now quit the bullshit, this is *me*, lover," she said, fondly. "You're the best, you gotta come out now and do your dog-and-pony act. There's a lady out there won't buy that thirty-day thing no way—"

"Read her the fine print," he said.

"Didn't I already do that?" she protested. "Her name's Bigelow, and she's an absolute pain in the ass about her money—" She grinned. ". . . The money that's on its way to old Mehico. Or do you want me to tell her that's where it's at?"

"I think not," said G. Dudley.

"Then get your bony ass out here and talk to her!" ordered Joyce, caressing him as if he were her pet Yorkshire terrier.

"I love your way with the language," said G. Dudley.

He sighed, rose from the desk, and followed Joyce outside.

. . . Four more hours of this nonsense, and he'd be over the wall, and out.

The office was crowded, the air was blue with smoke, the office staff busy filing and checking papers. Tomorrow this temporary setup would be dismantled and everyone would return to the Donaldson Bros. headquarters.

(Everyone minus one.)

Mrs. Bigelow was a nice-enough lady, neatly turned out, going a bit to middle-aged plumpness; she had a sheaf of papers in hand and she was waiting impatiently at the counter when Joyce brought him over.

"I believe there's some confusion about your payment?" he asked.

"No confusion," said Mrs. Bigelow. "I merely want to be paid for my T-Bird, that is all."

"And you certainly will be," said G. Dudley. "But as clearly stated in the contract you signed with us, we allow thirty days for clearance, et cetera . . ."

"I don't get this at *all*," she said. "You mean, you have to clear a check my husband gave you, to buy my car from *me*—before you can pay me? Why? His check is good—"

"Of course it is," he said. "But this is standard business practice, now I won't say it will necessarily take thirty days to clear his check, but we must protect ourselves—"

"I want the money *now!*" she insisted.

Stubborn bitch. Before he could think of his next ploy, someone's hand was plucking urgently at his sleeve. "You the head honcho around here?" drawled a scruffy young man who waved a portfolio of papers at him. "I'm Buddy Lee Thompson—"

"He's the one," said his companion, whom G. Dudley recognized vaguely—oh yes, that damned hairy musician from New Jersey—the one with the truck—

"See, we got us this problem here," said Buddy Lee. "Chuck here wants his truck back and I'm ready to sell it to him for what he paid for it, see?"

"Sounds marvelous," said G. Dudley. "Congratulations to you both, now if you'll pardon me—"

"*Bread,* friend," said Buddy Lee. "The loot. Folding stuff—all those dead presidents I laid on you when I paid for the little darlin'—"

They were crowding in on him, and G. Dudley who never enjoyed crowds, despised the crush of bodies against his, loathed subways or buses, always traveled first cabin to avoid such mob scenes, backed away—

tahootatahootahoota   faint sound of a police car?

. . . Seemed to be coming directly this way.

Police? *why?*

Yes, indeed, the sound was coming closer.

He went to the office door, to peer out—

. . . Saw the 1933 Plymouth driving into the Arena, headed this way, followed by a police car, its lights flashing.

The very last thing G. Dudley desired at this point was any intimate contact with the forces of law and order.

"Who sent for the police?" he demanded.

"I did," said Joyce. "That car ain't legal, the girl pinched it, I sent out an alarm to pick it up. And now they got her!"

The Plymouth door opened and Benita Lorenzo stepped out.

On the opposite side, Cyril Banks emerged.

The Tulsa policeman ushered them across the Arena floor.

"These here the folks you been lookin' for?" he asked. "Picked 'em up with that there ve-hicle—it is the correct one—'33 Plymouth—Connecticut registration—"

"For damn sure it is!" said Joyce. "Good work, officer!"

". . . And this lady here is the per-pe-tratah?" asked the officer.

"Per-petrator my ass!" cried Benita. "We're the owners—we *bought* this heap—so let's stop this crap, or you're all going to end up with one hell of a suit for false arrest!"

"That's a good one!" said Joyce. "You come in here and help yoreself to a car, without a proper title, then go runnin' off with it, you and your accomplice here—"

"Accomplice, am I?" said Cyril. "What an amusing way to put it, eh, G. Dudley?"

G. Dudley was silent, his mind turning this latest unexpected problem over, searching for the escape hatch—

Joyce swiveled around to him. "What's he mean by that?" she demanded. "Put 'em both in the can, right? Prefer charges—make an example of 'em—nobody screws around with us—"

. . . Christ, how could he shut her up!

No frontier justice. He did not wish to go to a police station anywhere. Not today. Not *ever*.

People were peering out of the office door, eying them curiously, drawn by the raised voices.

He pulled Joyce aside.

". . . Now listen to me," he said, urgently. "The girl is the owner, remember? *Drop it*—it's rotten public relations—"

"The hell I will!" insisted Joyce.

". . . Don't blow our whole deal with this sort of grandstand play," he pleaded. "Get rid of the police—we're playing for much larger stakes, *remember?*" He winked.

". . . Oh," said Joyce, slowly. "Oh. *Oh.*"

"Exactly," said G. Dudley.

And gave her a slight push.

"We'll handle it from here on, officer," she said. "It's really not a legal matter at all, y'know what I mean? Just a little friendly misunderstandin' is all . . .

"You sure, ma'am?" asked the policeman, puzzled.

". . . Why, *absolutely,*" said Joyce. "We're all goin' into the office and straighten everything out pronto. And thanks for doin' a hell of a job—I'll see you get mentioned to the right folks downtown . . ."

Mollified, the Tulsa gendarme returned to his partner in the waiting cruiser.

Cyril turned to G. Dudley. "Couldn't face the heat, eh?" he remarked.

"What heat?" asked G. Dudley.

"The heat we're about to turn on you," said Cyril.

"One brief word to you, friend," said G. Dudley. "I shouldn't try anything here. You're an English citizen, you have no rights, even though you may be shacked up with your lady here. You're really very much out of your element, yid."

He patted Joyce. "You handle things in the office, dear," he said. "I'll be with you in a moment or two."

There was a telephone booth at the far wall.

He headed for it.

Through G. Dudley's frontal lobes flashed the signal he'd learned to live by, all these years. The one essential rule for survival.

Leave the party early.

The operator at the radio-cab service assured him that a taxi would be waiting outside the Arena for him within exactly four minutes.

He hung up, and strolled, ever so casually, towards that open door at the other side of the cavernous hall, the one that led to the street.

Farewell, Tulsa.

Farewell to you all, you suckers, you marks, you idiot pullets who'd been well and truly plucked, the certified checks were tucked in his pocket, and as the sun sets over Oklahoma we say farewell to the Sooner State, to barbeque and chili and bourbon, to noisy over-dressed loud-mouthed ladies and their yahoo friends, G. Dudley Lester is murmuring farewell, *auf wiedersehn,* see you all anon, and don't call me, I'll call you—

. . . And good riddance to you all.

"All right," Joyce was saying. "Once we get to the office, we can get this little matter settled once and for all."

Purposefully, she led the way.

Cyril glanced back.

Spotted G. Dudley strolling in the opposite direction. Walking, ever so casually, towards a far-away door.

And through Cyril's frontal lobes there also flashed a warning signal.

The artful bastard was doing his exit number.

Encore!

Just as he had, years back, in London.

But this time, he was not about to get away with it.

Softly, Cyril turned, plucked at Benita's arm, pulled her in the opposite direction. ". . . Come!" he murmured.

"Where?" she asked.

"With *me!*" he instructed.

. . . By now the shadowy figure had vanished from sight.

Pulling Benita with him, Cyril walked purposefully in that direction.

A few feet away, he broke into a run.

Headed for the open doorway, made it just in time to spy G.

Dudley's shadow, far down there on the sidewalk, in the bright sunlight, as the shape rounded the far corner which led to the main street.

Grimly, Cyril put on speed.

Dashing along behind him, heard Benita call ". . . Can't run . . . in these shoes!"

He made the corner, rounded it.

No sign of G. Dudley.

"Blast!" he gasped. "Lost him!"

Peered through the sunlight.

Then, spotted something moving behind a pillar, a few yards down. Something dark blue.

Standing in a protective shadow, G. Dudley.

With his back to him.

Ah, you bastard! he thought. I've got you!

Panting slightly from the exertion, his heart beginning to pound, a jogger with a mission, he moved forward.

Ran, leaped forward.

Knocked G. Dudley to the pavement.

Who fell flat, hitting the hard unyielding surface with a sickening (but satisfying) thud—

And lay prone, limp, unstruggling, beneath him.

"What did you do?" gasped Benita. "Why'd you?—he's *hurt!*"

Pulses still pounding in his ear, Cyril got up.

Benita bent down, turned G. Dudley over.

The man's eyes were closed. His breath was irregular. The color had faded from his cheeks.

He lay there.

She spread his arms wide and then straddled him.

". . . He's faking," said Cyril.

She put her ear to G. Dudley's chest. "Don't be too sure," she said. "He's hurt."

She undid his jacket, loosened his tie.

"Mouth-to-mouth resuscitation?" asked Cyril. "Careful—he'll steal your teeth."

"Go away!" warned Benita.

"In a moment," said Cyril. His hand snaked down, seized the contents of G. Dudley's inner pocket. Wallet. Passport. Airline ticket.

And two long envelopes.

G. Dudley's eyes had opened and his hand reached up to slap away Cyril's—but not soon enough.

He struggled, but Benita sat firmly on his chest.

Cyril opened the envelopes, removed the checks inside. Waved them beneath her eyes.

"Made out to him," he said. "And cashable, to him."

"They're mine!" protested G. Dudley, struggling to rise.

"Not any longer," said Cyril. "Now, after Miss Lorenzo lets you up, you're going inside and return these to Mrs. Wade—"

"Piss off!" said G. Dudley.

". . . And she'll probably accept your devious explanation," said Cyril, "since you have some ugly physical hold over the lady. However, she will never allow you out of her sight again, I can assure you—"

"Piss off!" snarled G. Dudley. "Bastard!"

"—And so, you will live out the rest of your days, affluent, well-cared for, as a willing stud for Mrs. Wade—here in Tulsa," promised Cyril.

He glared down at the prone nemesis he'd been pursuing for all these years.

. . . This arrogant prick, amoral glib artful dodger, who'd dumped him so readily, left him dangling in the breeze.

". . . Show mercy," said G. Dudley, at last.

It was a strange sort of a face-off, was it not? Not quite the same showdown one had expected, on this dusty southwestern street.

". . . Say *please—Mr. Yid,*'" said Cyril.

". . . Please . . . Mister . . . Yid," replied G. Dudley, a repentant schoolboy.

Cyril produced a pen.

"Now autograph the backs of these checks," he instructed.

"Bastard," said G. Dudley.

"I learned at the feet of the master," said Cyril. "Sign—or it's Mrs. Wade."

G. Dudley had finished the signatures, as the radio taxi pulled up.

"Hey, somebody call a cab?" asked the driver, a Tulsan accustomed to street theater.

"This somebody," said Cyril. "Let him up, Benita."

G. Dudley rose. Brushed off his blazer.

Cyril handed him back his wallet, his passport, and his airline tickets.

G. Dudley glanced into his wallet.

"Where's the rest of my money?" he demanded.

Cyril shrugged. "Took it to cover an old debt," he said. "But you've plenty more at home, haven't you?"

"It's *my* money!" protested G. Dudley. "I earned it—you bastard!"

"Running out of conversation, aren't you?" said Cyril. He passed over a twenty. "Here," he said. "Buy yourself a drink on the plane—on me."

With G. Dudley slumped in the back seat, the radio cab pulled away.

Disappeared.

Benita stared at Cyril. "You were real hard-ass there for a while," she said, finally. "Then you went soft—let him *go?*"

He nodded.

". . . Did you know he had the checks right in his pocket?"

"No," he confessed.

". . . You were *guessing?*"

"An educated guess," he told her. "Based on prior experience with the gentleman . . ."

Benita shook her head, impressed. ". . . But supposing the checks *hadn't* been there—"

Before he could answer, Joyce Donaldson Wade bore down on them. ". . . Now where in the hell did you two get to?" she demanded. "Here I am tryin' to be decent, and meet you half ways—and all you do is give me a hard time, shoot! You make it awful tough—"

She stared at the two checks which Cyril had thrust into her hand.

Studied them both.

Her lower jaw hung open.

". . . And made out to *him?*" she croaked, at last.

"Now cashable by you," said Cyril, turning them over to reveal the endorsements.

". . . How'd you get these?" she demanded.

"From G. Dudley Lester," said Cyril. "He left them behind. Had a change of plan, you see . . ." He smiled. "He expects you to take this money and pay everyone the money that's due them. It's a completely different social attitude, you see. You might say, our mutual friend has undergone a miraculous—"

"Where in the hell is he?" screeched Joyce Donaldson Wade.

Cyril hesitated.

The ultimate revenge was available.

With one brief paragraph, with one sentence, actually—he could button up G. Dudley Lester's future.

Seal the old bastard's destiny. Jail? No. Bad P.R. She would be businesswoman first—his jailer second.

". . . Where'd he *go?*" she demanded, insistently.

Say the magic words, Cyril. Airport—Flight Number—

Ah no.

Let the old dodger run free.

Face it, Cyril. He's yours—not hers.

Your world would be a much duller place without G. Dudley.

"He's taken a car," he told Joyce Donaldson Wade. "Some sort of a rented car, and I believe he means to head over to New Orleans—"

"Thanks!" she said, and dashed inside the Arena.

*   *   *

Within an hour, there were signs, hastily printed, tacked up behind the office counter. WE WILL TRY TO COMPLETE ALL PAPER-WORK TODAY, they announced, YOUR CHECKS WILL BE PAID TO OWNERS LATER THIS AFTERNOON, OR IF YOU CANNOT WAIT, MAILED TO YOUR HOME ADDRESS TOMORROW. THANKS FOR YOUR PATIENCE. SEE YOU AT OUR NEXT AUCTION. MRS. J. D. WADE.

"There you go, folks," said the harassed girl behind the counter, handing over a folder which contained the documents legally conveying title to the 1933 Plymouth from the Estate of Mrs. Laura Richards Fox to its new owners. "You now own the car. Bet that little number saves you plenty, gas-wise . . ."

". . . That's why we bought her," said Benita. "Up in Connecticut we're really energy-conscious . . . oh Lord!" she said. "Got to call home—could I borrow your phone please? I have to tell my mother what I've been up to here for the past couple days—"

". . . *All* of it?" asked Cyril.

While Benita spoke to her mother inside the office, he strolled outside.

What next?

Drive the Plymouth back to their motel—make arrangements to pull off the wheels—divide the loot—

Then he would be off to London.

(. . . And Benita? Well, she could return to Bridgeport, Connecticut, a very rich lady. With her new capital, she'd have no problem finding some man to make her a good husband . . .)

While he returned to the restaurant business? No, no need for that—as well endowed as he would be now, now he had Capital, did he not? Cyril Banks, financier.

Returning to London, sans the Rolls.

That lovely little 1937 beauty, parked a few feet away there, its chrome gleaming in the half light.

The car he'd promised Ben Emir.

Pity to lose it, but . . .

What was the old saying—*you can't win them all.*

He strolled over to bid it farewell. Eyed the SOLD sign on the windscreen.

Put out a hand to stroke the well-lacquered hood.

". . . Please, do not touch!" said Mr. Sami Kallil. Its new owner.

Ah yes, that ridiculous rumpled character with his briefcase and his tatty suit and shirt, he was standing at the other side, with him a man wearing a badge which red Prestige Car Delivery Ltd.

Arrogant Mr. Kallil. A wog for all seasons.

Why the devil should *he* have it? Merely because he had the money? He did not deserve it.

Cyril strolled over, his mind ticking.

". . . Lovely piece of automotive work you bought here, sir," he said. "A prime example of British craftsmanship at its very peak of perfection, eh?"

"A good investment," said Mr. Kallil. "Excuse us, I'm busy."

He turned back to the man from Prestige Cars Delivery Ltd. They seemed to be haggling over the price of delivering this car to Beverly Hills, California, to Mr. Kallil's son.

A minor bolt of lightning struck Cyril. *Ah.* You *can* win them all!

". . . I'm so glad to see you're arranging to have this chap here transport the car *for* you," said Cyril. "It'd be quite a problem for you to ride in the car yourself, eh?"

"It is not for me, it is for my *son,*" said Mr. Kallil.

"Oh? How's he planning to drive it, then?" asked Cyril.

"My son knows how to drive a car!" said Mr. Kallil.

". . . Religious lad, is he?" asked Cyril.

Kallil stared at him.

". . . Why should you ask that, please?"

". . . Well," said Cyril. "I know how your religion strictly forbids your people from coming into contact with anything unclean. Such as what comes from the pig."

He turned and opened the front door of the Rolls. ". . . And since this upholstery here is the finest pigskin available . . . isn't it lovely, though?" He fondled it. "Touch?"

When he turned back, Mr. Kallil's face was ash-colored.

His hands had gone up, and he was instinctively backing away from his new/old Rolls.

"Ay!" he moaned. *"Pig*skin!"

"Front seat *and* back," cooed Cyril. "Touch it."

Mr. Kallil began to sway softly from side to side.

". . . Oh, not to worry," said Cyril, cheerfully. "Luckily for you, I'm prepared to help you out of this most embarrassing situation. Let's say, for the sake of discussion, that I bought the car back from you, Mr. Kallil—at a bit less than you paid for it, true . . . but after all, we're both realists, aren't we?"

Dusty Bigelow sat beside Louise, twirling the keys to the T-Bird impatiently in his hand while she waited at the counter. ". . . Listen, honey, you don't really need the check, why don't we have the lady here mail it up to Liverpool?"

". . . No," said Louise. "If you don't mind, I'm going to wait here."

". . . But if we don't get started driving back home," he said, "I'm going to lose another couple of days back at the office—"

"Tell you what," said Louise. "You go out and get in the T-Bird and go on ahead without me."

"Alone?" he asked.

"You could find your way there, couldn't you?" she asked.

". . . It's a long ways," he protested.

"I did it," she told him. "All by myself."

". . . You want me to drive home alone, and wait for you?" he asked.

"Why sure," she said. "Leave a light burning in the window of the museum . . ."

He grinned.

"You know something?" he said. "If it was anybody but you, I wouldn't dare trust them. But why don't I leave you these keys—and *I*'ll fly home—and *you* can drive the T-Bird back, nice and safe —how's that?"

". . . You're not worried I'd sell it again?" she asked.

". . . Now why would you want to do that?" asked Dusty.

You'll never know, will you? she thought. You'll just never damned well know.

He dropped the keys into her hand.

"Well now," he said, rising. *"That's* settled, isn't it?"

They stood beside the Rolls Royce.

Benita shook her head. ". . . He sold you *this?*" she asked. "Just like that, while I was in there?"

Cyril nodded.

"Why?" Benita asked.

". . . Oh, a small matter of the pigskin upholstery," he told her. "Seems it runs counter to Mr. Kallil's religion, alas."

She peered inside.

". . . How could you tell it was pigskin?" she asked.

"Oh," said Cyril. "*Is* it pigskin?"

It was a moment or so before she'd digested what he'd said.

"Oh, Christ—" she said, "you *are* incredible!"

"On my good days," he said. "Seems this was one of them."

A small trim Model AA Ford Pickup truck came towards them, chugging its way towards the Arena exit. As it passed, it slowed, and the driver hooted his horn at them. Then leaned down and grinned. "Hey, baby, want a ride to New Jersey?" asked Chuck Malone. "I could sure use a beautiful co-pilot."

". . . No thanks," said Benita. "I've got wheels of my own."

". . . I'd sing to you all the way," he wheedled.

She shook her head. He shrugged, accelerated, and drove off. "Your loss!" he called.

They approached the Plymouth.

". . . Now we have *two* cars," she said.

"No, we don't, love," he told her. "*We* have *one*. I will take that Rolls back to London. After all, it's what I came for, isn't it?"

Her hand on the door handle, she turned.

". . . Wait a minute," she said. ". . . You're dumping me?"

"Beg pardon?" he said.

". . . Where's *our* Plymouth going?" she asked.

"Mm," said Cyril. "What a very good question. Tell you what . . . let's go back to the motel, go to bed and talk about it."

"In bed?" she said.

He nodded. "I find I get my best ideas in bed," he said.

She shook her head. "There won't be room for you and me *and* this Plymouth, buddy."

"In the bed?" he asked.

". . . We're sure as hell not going to leave it out on the street, are we?" said Benita.